$\mathcal{A}$n impressive and
dmirable debut . . . If FRANK LLOYD WRIGHT
the reason people will pick up this book,
AMAH BORTHWICK is the reason they
ill keep reading it. . . . *Loving Frank* [is] a
eautifully designed, innovative and noteworthy
vork of art." —**CHICAGO TRIBUNE**

"It takes great courage to write a novel about historical people, and in particular to give voice to someone as mythic as Frank Lloyd Wright. This beautifully written novel about Mamah Cheney and Frank Lloyd Wright's love affair is vivid and intelligent, unsentimental and compassionate."

—JANE HAMILTON, author of *When Madeline Was Young*

"Horan's nuanced evocation of these flawed human beings plays beautifully against the lurid facts of their situation. As in the best historical fiction, she finds both the truth and the heart of her story." —*Los Angeles Times*

"[Nancy Horan] does well to avoid serving up a bodice-ripper for the smart set. . . . She succeeds in conveying the emotional center of her protagonist, whom she paints as a protofeminist, an educated woman fettered by the role of bourgeois matriarch." —*The New Yorker*

"*Loving Frank* is one of those novels that take over your life. It's mesmerizing and fascinating—filled with complex characters, deep passions, tactile descriptions of astonishing architecture, and the colorful immediacy of daily life a hundred years ago—all gathered into a story that unfolds with riveting urgency."

—LAUREN BELFER, author of *City of Light*

"This novel is so great, it's hard to believe it's the author's first." —*Jane*

"Fascinating . . . what we expect to get from great fiction: timeless truths about ourselves." —New York *Daily News*

"Masterful." —*People*

"This gripping historical novel offers new insight into the mind of an American icon through the woman he loved." —*Parade*

LOVING FRANK

LOVING
FRANK

a novel

NANCY HORAN

BALLANTINE BOOKS

NEW YORK

Loving Frank is a work of historical fiction. Apart from the well-known actual people, events, and locales that figure in the narrative, all names, characters, places, and incidents are the products of the author's imagination or are used fictitiously. Any resemblance to current events or locales, or to living persons, is entirely coincidental.

2008 Ballantine Books Trade Paperback Edition

Published in the United States by Ballantine Books, an imprint of The Random House Publishing Group, a division of Random House, Inc., New York.

BALLANTINE and colophon are registered trademarks of Random House, Inc. RANDOM HOUSE READER'S CIRCLE and colophon are trademarks of Random House, Inc.

Originally published in hardcover in the United States by Ballantine Books, an imprint of The Random House Publishing Group, a division of Random House, Inc., 2007.

Grateful acknowledgment is made to the following for permission to reprint previously published materials:

Holy Cow! Press: "Farewell" by Else-Lasker Schüler, translated by Janine Canan from *Star on My Forehead*, translation copyright © 2000 by Janine Canan. Reprinted with permission of Holy Cow! Press, Duluth, MN.

Sony BMG Music Entertainment: excerpt from *Mefistofele* translated into English by Barrymore Laurence Scherer, copyright © 1990 by Barrymore Laurence Scherer & Sony BMG Music Entertainment. Reprinted from the Sony Classical compact disc *Boito: Mefistofele* (S2K 44983), courtesy of Barrymore Laurence Scherer & Sony BMG Music Entertainment.

The 1914 letter from Frank Lloyd Wright to the *Weekly Home News* and the lecture entitled "The Ethics of Ornament" delivered by Frank Lloyd Wright in 1909 are reprinted courtesy of the Frank Lloyd Wright Foundation, Taliesin West, Scottsdale, AZ.

LIBRARY OF CONGRESS CATALOGING-IN-PUBLICATION DATA
Horan, Nancy.
Loving Frank / by Nancy Horan.
p. cm.
ISBN 978-0-345-49500-6 (acid-free paper)
1. Wright, Frank Lloyd, 1867–1959—Fiction. 2. Cheney, Martha Borthwick, 1869–1914—Fiction. 3. Architects—Fiction. I. Title.
PS3608.O725L68 2007
813'.6—dc22   2007014810

Printed in the United States of America

www.randomhousereaderscircle.com

2 4 6 8 9 7 5 3 1

Book design by Barbara M. Bachman

FOR KEVIN

ONE LIVES BUT ONCE IN THE WORLD.

—*Johann Wolfgang von Goethe*

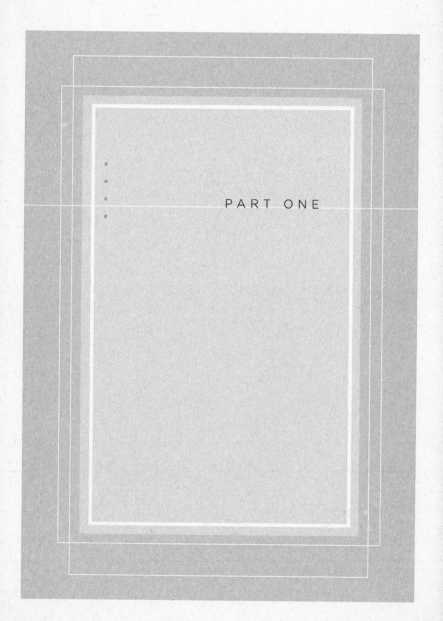

PART ONE

t was Edwin who wanted to build a new house. I didn't mind the old Queen Anne on Oak Park Avenue. It was full of the things of my childhood, and I found it comforting after so many years away. But Ed was possessed by the idea of having something modern. I wonder if he reflects on those days now—on the fact that it was he who craved a place entirely his own.

When we returned from our honeymoon in the fall of 1899, we moved into the house I grew up in for the sake of my widowed father, who had never adjusted to living alone. At thirty, after years of study and solitude and independence, I found myself sharing dinners not only with a new husband but also with my father and my sisters, Jessie and Lizzie, who often came by to visit. Papa still went off to work to run the Chicago & North Western's repair shops.

It was not long after Edwin and I settled in that my father returned home from his job one day, curled up in his bed, and passed to the other side. At seventy-two, he wasn't a young man, but he had always seemed invulnerable to my sisters and me. His sudden loss left all of us reeling. What I didn't know then was that the worst was yet to come. A year later, Jessie died giving birth to a baby girl.

How can I tell the grief of that year? I only remember parts of 1901, so numbly did I move through it. When it became clear that Jessie's husband would be hard-pressed to properly care for the infant he had named Jessica after my sister, Ed and Lizzie and I took in our niece. I was the only one not working, so it fell to me to care for her. In the midst of our mourning, the baby brought unexpected joy into that old house.

The place was laden with memories that should have haunted me, I suppose. But my hands were too full. In a year's time Ed and I had our own child, John, who was an early walker. We had no nurse in those days, and only a part-time housekeeper. At night I was too spent to lift a book.

Still, in the three years I had been married, it hadn't been so hard to be Mrs. Edwin Cheney. Ed was kind and rarely complained—a badge of pride with him. At the beginning, he came home nearly every day to a parlor crowded with Borthwick women, and he seemed genuinely pleased to see us all. He is not an unsophisticated man. But he draws his contentment from simple things—Cuban cigars, the morning streetcar ride with the other men, tinkering with his automobile.

The one thing Edwin has never been able to abide is disorder, though, and he must have been tried sorely in those years on Oak Park Avenue. His touchstones are the surfaces of furniture: his papers neatly waiting on his desk at work in the morning; his personal cabinet where he puts his briefcase and keys when he comes home; the dinner table where his fondest wish is to find a roast and the people he loves gathered around it, waiting for him.

I suppose it was order, or the lack of it, that finally pushed him to do something beyond talk about a new house. I tried to keep things neat, but what can anyone do about a dark old place with windows painted shut and fretwork curlicues cluttering the corners of every doorframe? What can you do about horsehair-stuffed furniture with two decades of dust that simply can't be pounded out?

What Edwin did was quietly begin his campaign. First he took me to the home of Arthur Huertley and his wife. He and Arthur rode the streetcar together in the morning. Just about everyone in Oak Park had made it a point to stroll past the Huertleys' new house on Forest Avenue. It was either an outrageous aberration or a stroke of brilliance, depending upon how you felt about its architect, Frank Lloyd Wright. A "prairie house," some called it, for the way courses of long, narrow bricks ran horizontally across it, like the lines of the Illinois flatlands.

When I first saw it, the Huertleys' house looked like a heavy rectangular box to me. Once inside, though, I felt my lungs expand. It was all open space, with one room flowing into the next. Unpainted beams and woodwork the color of tree trunks gleamed softly, and the most glorious light poured through the green and red stained-glass windows. It felt sacred inside, like a woodland chapel.

Edwin, engineer that he is, sensed something else inside those walls. He was basking in the harmony induced by rational systems. Built-in drawers. Clean-lined chairs and tables made specifically for those very rooms—furniture with a purpose. There wasn't a superfluous object in sight. Edwin walked out whistling.

"How can we ever afford a house like that?" I asked when we were out of earshot.

"Ours doesn't have to be that big," he said. "And we're doing better than you think."

Edwin was the president of Wagner Electric by then. While I had been changing diapers, trying to find a little time for a walk outside, Edwin had been methodically making his way up to the top of the company.

"I know Frank Wright's wife," I confessed. I had been ambivalent about encouraging Edwin, so I hadn't mentioned it. "She's on the Home and Arts Committee with me at the club."

That was when his campaign picked up steam. It isn't Edwin's way to demand, but he nudged very forcefully after that, in much the way he had courted me. Persistence. Persistence. Persistence. If he had been alive during the Crusades, that's what his banner would have read as he galloped off to battle.

It was his doggedness that wore me down to marry him in the first place.

We had known each other at school in Ann Arbor, but I hadn't thought about him in several years. Suddenly, he appeared one day at the boardinghouse where I lived in Port Huron. He had a gift for small talk and an infectious laugh. It didn't take long for him to win over the inhabitants of Mrs. Sanborn's boardinghouse on Seventh Street. When, to my dismay, he began to show up on Friday evenings, the landlady and her little family of renters—including my college roommate Mattie Chadbourne—cleared out of the parlor so the relationship could blossom.

I was running the public library back then and was usually pretty tired on Friday evening when Edwin called on me. One night, merely to fill the awkward air between us, I told him about an employee who seemed always to be moping, despite my efforts to encourage her.

"Tell her happiness is just practice," he said. "If only she acted happy, she would be happy." There was something profoundly appealing at that moment in those words. Edwin wasn't literary or particularly reflective; his strengths were different from my own. He was a good man. And he got things done.

All those years in Port Huron, while I was teaching at the high school and, later, running the library, I romanticized what I did by day—handmaiden to knowledge, doctor of the soul, dispensing books like pills to my students and patrons. At night though, I lived uneasily among stacks of papers in my room: a long, unfinished essay on individualism in the Woman Movement, an unpublished translation of some eighteenth-century French essayist who had possessed me for a while, books upon books with pages marked by newspaper clippings, envelopes, pencils, postcards, hair combs. Despite great bursts of energy, I couldn't seem to put together a proper magazine article, let alone the book I imagined I would eventually write.

I had been in Port Huron for six years. My friends were marrying around me. Looking across the parlor that day at Ed Cheney, I thought, Maybe our traits will rub off on each other.

I suppose I said yes to a new house the way I said yes to the balding young man who kept traveling from Chicago to Port Huron to ask me to marry him. After a point, I just plunged in.

In those early days of our marriage, it wasn't only order Edwin pined for. He wanted a home where we could entertain. Perhaps it was too many years spent in his own parents' humorless household, or maybe it was the sadness still floating through the rooms of my folks' home, but he wanted a place full of youngsters and friends and good times. I suspect he pictured his college glee club sitting around the living room, singing "I Love You Truly." In any case, things moved rapidly once Catherine Wright arranged a meeting for us at Frank's studio.

Who wouldn't be charmed by Frank Lloyd Wright? Edwin was. I was. There we were in the light-filled octagonal room attached to their house, with the enfant terrible of Oak Park architecture, the "Tyrant of Taste," someone at the club had called him, and he was listening to us. Did we entertain? What kind of music did we enjoy? Was I a gardener?

He looked to be around thirty-five or so, close to my age, and he was very handsome—wavy brown hair, a high forehead, intelligent eyes. People said he was eccentric, and I suppose he was, given that a big tree was growing straight up through the middle of his house. But he was also wildly funny and intensely serious in turns. I remember two of his children were up on the balcony above us, sailing paper airplanes down at the drafting tables. There were several young men bent over drawings, but the main architect who worked for him was a woman—a woman!—Marion Mahony. Frank sat there calmly sketching in the midst of it all, seemingly oblivious to the chaos above him.

By the end of the afternoon, we had a thumbnail sketch to take home with us: a house with two levels, similar to the Huertleys', only on a smaller scale. We would live on the upper floor, with a dining room, living room, and library that all flowed into one another; a great fireplace would stand at the heart of the house; and window seats all around would accommodate a crowd. A wall of stained-glass doors across the front of the house would open onto a large terrace surrounded by a brick wall that kept it private. If you stood out on the front sidewalk, you wouldn't be able to see into the house because of the wall. But from inside, up high, you'd have a fine prospect for viewing the world outside; in fact, you'd feel part of nature, because Frank Wright had designed the house around existing trees on the lot. Small bedrooms were tucked at the back of the house. And there was a lower floor where my sister Lizzie would eventually have an apartment.

After that visit, Edwin didn't have to prod anymore. I took on the job of working with Frank, who seemed delighted by my tentative suggestions. Standing at the work site on East Avenue with John on my hip, I started to comprehend cantilevered roofs and the rhythmic beauty of bands of leaded windows he called "light screens." Pretty soon I was part of the team. I spent hours dreaming up a garden plan with a landscape architect, Walter Griffin, at the studio. By the time we moved into "the good times house," as Frank had called it from the beginning, we counted the Wrights among our friends.

I still think about my parents' old house on Oak Park Avenue. I remember so vividly the night Ed and I got married there. My sisters had filled the parlor with yellow and blue flowers, the University of Michigan's colors. A mandolin orchestra played the wedding march from Lohengrin. Mattie, my closest friend, was my maid of honor, and I recall thinking she looked prettier than I that night. I was far too nervous, perspiring through the silk. But Edwin was his steady self. He pulled me into a corner when it was all over and promised to be my anchor. "Take my love for granted," he said, "and I shall do the same for you."

Why didn't I write down those words then? When I look at them now, they seem a recipe for disaster.

It has always been on the written page that the world has come into focus for me. If I can piece all these bits of memory together with the diaries and letters and the scribbled thoughts that clutter my mind and bookshelves, then maybe I can explain what happened. Maybe the worlds I have inhabited for the past seven years will assume order and logic and wholeness on paper. Maybe I can tell my story in a way that is useful to someone else.

Mamah Bouton Borthwick
August 1914

CHAPTER 1

Mamah Cheney sidled up to the Studebaker and put her hand sideways on the crank. She had started the thing a hundred times before, but she still heard Edwin's words whenever she grabbed on to the handle. *Leave your thumb out. If you don't, the crank can fly back and take your thumb right off.* She churned with a fury now, but no sputter came from beneath the car's hood. Crunching across old snow to the driver's side, she checked the throttle and ignition, then returned to the handle and cranked again. Still nothing. A few teasing snowflakes floated under her hat rim and onto her face. She studied the sky, then set out from her house on foot toward the library.

It was a bitterly cold end-of-March day, and Chicago Avenue was a river of frozen slush. Mamah navigated her way through steaming horse droppings, the hem of her black coat lifted high. Three blocks west, at Oak Park Avenue, she leaped onto the wooden sidewalk and hurried south as the wet snow grew dense.

By the time she reached the library, her toes were frozen stumps, and her coat was nearly white. She raced up the steps, then stopped at the door of the lecture hall to catch her breath. Inside, a crowd of women listened intently as the president of the Nineteenth Century Woman's Club read her introduction.

"Is there a woman among us who is not confronted—almost daily—by some choice regarding how to ornament her home?" The president looked over her spectacles at the audience. "Or, dare I say, herself?" Still panting, Mamah slipped into a seat in the last row and flung off her coat. All around her, the faint smell of camphor fumes wafted from wet furs slung across chair backs. "Our guest speaker today needs no introduction . . ."

Mamah was aware, then, of a hush spreading from the back rows forward as a figure, his black cape whipping like a sail, dashed up the middle aisle. She saw him toss the cape first, then his wide-brimmed hat, onto a chair beside the lectern.

"Modern ornamentation is a burlesque of the beautiful, as pitiful as it is costly." Frank Lloyd Wright's voice echoed through the cavernous hall. Mamah craned her neck, trying to see around and above the hats in front of her that bobbed like cakes on platters. Impulsively, she stuffed her coat beneath her bottom to get a better view.

"The measure of a man's culture is the measure of his appreciation," he said. "We are ourselves what we appreciate and no more."

She could see that there was something different about him. His hair was shorter. Had he lost weight? She studied the narrow belted waist of his Norfolk jacket. No, he looked healthy, as always. His eyes were merry in his grave, boyish face.

"We are living today encrusted with dead things," he was saying, "forms from which the soul is gone. And we are devoted to them, trying to get joy out of them, trying to believe them still potent."

Frank stepped down from the platform and stood close to the front row. His hands were open and moving now, his voice so gentle he might have been speaking to a crowd of children. She knew the message so well. He had spoken nearly the same words to her when she first met him at his studio. Ornament is not about prettifying the outside of something, he was saying. It should possess "fitness, proportion, harmony, the result of all of which is repose."

The word "repose" floated in the air as Frank looked around at the women. He seemed to be taking measure of them, as a preacher might.

"Birds and flowers on hats . . ." he continued. Mamah felt a kind of guilty pleasure when she realized that he was pressing on with the point. He was going to punish them for their bad taste before he saved them.

Her eyes darted around at the plumes and bows bobbing in front of her, then rested on one ersatz bluebird clinging to a hatband. She leaned sideways, trying to see the faces of the women in front of her.

She heard Frank say "imitation" and "counterfeit" before silence fell once again.

A radiator rattled. Someone coughed. Then a pair of hands began clapping, and in a moment a hundred others joined in until applause thundered against the walls.

Mamah choked back a laugh. Frank Lloyd Wright was converting them—

almost to the woman—before her very eyes. For all she knew five minutes ago, they could just as well have booed. Now the room had the feeling of a revival tent. They were getting his religion, throwing away their crutches. Every one of them thought his disparaging remarks were aimed at someone else. She imagined the women racing home to strip their overstuffed armchairs of antimacassars and to fill vases with whatever dead weeds they could find still poking up through the snow.

Mamah stood. She moved slowly as she bundled up in her coat, slid on the tight kid gloves, tucked strands of wavy dark hair under her damp felt hat. She had a clear view of Frank beaming at the audience. She lingered there in the last row, blood pulsing in her neck, all the while watching his eyes, watching to see if they would meet hers. She smiled broadly and thought she saw a glimmer of recognition, a softening around his mouth, but the next moment doubted she had seen it at all.

Frank was gesturing to the front row, and the familiar red hair of Catherine Wright emerged from the audience. Catherine walked to the front and stood beside her husband, her freckled face glowing. His arm was around her back.

Mamah sank down in her chair. Heat filled up the inside of her coat.

On her other side, an old woman rose from her seat. "Claptrap," she muttered, pushing past Mamah's knees. "Just another little man in a big hat."

Minutes later, out in the hallway, a cluster of women surrounded Frank. Mamah moved slowly with the crowd as people shuffled toward the staircase.

"*May-mah!*" he called when he spotted her. He pushed his way over to where she stood. "How are you, my friend?" He grasped her right hand, gently pulled her out of the crowd into a corner.

"We've meant to call you," she said. "Edwin keeps asking when we're going to start that garage."

His eyes passed over her face. "Will you be home tomorrow? Say eleven?"

"I will. Unfortunately, Ed's not going to be there. But you and I can talk about it."

A smile broke across his face. She felt his hands squeeze down on hers. "I've missed our talks," he said softly.

She lowered her eyes. "So have I."

ON HER WALK HOME, the snow stopped. She paused on the sidewalk to look at her house. Tiny iridescent squares in the stained-glass windows glinted back the late-afternoon sun. She remembered standing in this very spot three years ago, during an open house she and Ed had given after they'd moved in. Women had been sitting along the terrace wall, gazing out toward the street, calling to their children, their faces lit like a row of moons. It had struck Mamah then that her low-slung house looked as small as a raft beside the steamerlike Victorian next door. But what a spectacular raft, with the "Maple Leaf Rag" drifting out of its front doors, and people draped along its edges.

Edwin had noticed her standing on the sidewalk and come to put his arm around her. "We got ourselves a good times house, didn't we?" he'd said. His face was beaming that day, so full of pride and the excitement of a new beginning. For Mamah, though, the housewarming had felt like the end of something extraordinary.

"OUT WALKING IN a snowstorm, were you?" Their nanny's voice stirred Mamah, who lay on the living room sofa, her feet propped on the rolled arm.

"I know, Louise, I know," she mumbled.

"Do you want a toddy for the cold you're about to get?"

"I'll take it. Where is John?"

"Next door with Ellis. I'll get him home."

"Send him in to me when he's back. And turn on the lights, will you, please?"

Louise was heavy and slow, though she wasn't much older than Mamah. She had been with them since John was a year old—a childless Irish nurse born to mother children. She switched on the stained-glass sconces and lumbered out.

When she closed her eyes again, Mamah winced at the image of herself a few hours earlier. She had behaved like a madwoman, cranking the car until her arm ached, then racing on foot through snow and ice to get a glimpse of Frank, as if she had no choice.

Once, when Edwin was teaching her how to start the car, he had told her about a fellow who leaned in too close. The man was smashed in the jaw by the crank and died later from infection.

Mamah sat up abruptly and shook her head as if she had water in an ear. *In the morning I'll call Frank to cancel.*

Within moments, though, she was laughing at herself. *Good Lord. It's only a garage.*

CHAPTER 2

Mamah woke to the sound of Edwin moving through his daily ablutions. Clink of his shaving brush against the porcelain cup, soft thud of a collar on the dresser. Snap of cuff links. It was Saturday morning, but he had a day trip planned to Milwaukee. In a few minutes he would be out the door with his derby and attaché.

The next sound she heard was John's bare feet pounding down the hallway.

"Mamaaaa," he shouted, leaping into the bed and flopping his skinny little body on top of hers.

She feigned sleep, then flipped the elfin boy suddenly onto his back, tickling until he was helpless. "What's the magic word?"

John squealed deliriously.

"What's the magic word?"

"I don't remember!"

"Hint," she said. "It's a vegetable."

He moaned. "Can we have a new word?"

Mamah pondered for a moment. "All right, then. Pirate."

John registered surprise. "I like that."

"Everyone likes pirates," Edwin chimed in, "no matter how bad they are." He kissed the tops of their heads. "See you around eight tonight, if all goes well."

She got out of bed, put on a robe, and went to get the baby out of her crib. Martha was standing at the rail, bobbing and babbling. Mamah changed her diaper, then set her feet on the floor. The girl grabbed hold of her mother's thumbs and walked haltingly down the hall toward the living room. This time of year, the west windows and the heavy woodwork conspired to make the living room dark. Mamah aimed her daughter toward the adjoining library, where sun streamed through a south-facing window. There she paused to stand in the light. The warmth felt like joy itself to Mamah. It seemed that sometimes, when the sun hit her face in just this way, her skin had its own memory. She could be five years old again, looking out at the summer fields from the window of the Iowa farmhouse where she'd been born.

Dear God, how she loved the sun; this past winter had been the darkest, most paralyzing one she could remember. It was nearly April, but no spring was in sight. The usual soggy sadness would have to run its course for another month. All she really needed, she thought, was just one ray coming in. She could sit in this place and think about the day ahead, make a plan. Maybe she could accomplish something for a change.

Lizzie was in the dining room, still wearing her nightgown and studying the morning paper, her hair loose around her shoulders. "Huge sale at Field's today," she called to her sister.

"Nobody died?" Mamah picked Martha up and carried her to her high chair.

"Well, actually, the Cat Woman? Over on Elmwood? She died."

Mamah settled Martha, then nuzzled her niece, Jessica, who was eating cereal next to John. She enjoyed the sense of reprieve that Saturdays brought, with the children in their slippers and nightclothes all morning, the help gone, and Lizzie at home, reading the obituaries out loud over breakfast.

"How was the Cape's speech yesterday?" Lizzie asked.

"Oh, you know Frank. He charmed everyone to death." Mamah laughed. Her sister had private nicknames for people whose foibles she found amusing. Lizzie was pretty in the same way Jessie had been, with delicate features and fawn-colored hair. While Jessie had been the den leader and cockeyed optimist, though, Lizzie was the dry wisecracker. "You are wicked, you know. Who would guess the sweet second-grade teacher from Irving School has a stripe of meanness as wide as a skunk's?"

Lizzie lowered the newspaper and flicked her limpid eyes in John's direction. "I think your mother just called me a skunk." The dark-haired boy bent over in giggles. "Do you need anything from Field's?" Lizzie asked Mamah.

"We could use some new sheets for John and Jessica's beds," Mamah said, tucking a napkin around Martha's neck. "But I can't go. I have something—"

Louise came out of the kitchen, drying her hands on a towel. "I could take the children," she offered.

"You're not even supposed to be working today," Mamah chided.

"And what was I going to do?" Louise planted her fists on her hips. "Go swimmin'?"

"You can't push the pram in this mess."

The older children looked up from their cereal. They sniffed an adventure.

"I'll go along, and we'll take turns carrying Martha," Lizzie said.

"You should take the car if it will start, Liz. Let me see if I can get it going."

"All right, then. I'll be dressed in ten minutes. What about the rest of you?"

In a heartbeat, John and Jessica were on their feet, scampering down the hallway.

CHAPTER 3

When the house was empty, Mamah went to the bathroom to fill the tub. Sitting on its edge, she stared at the ceiling, furious with herself. *Why on earth did I invite Frank Wright to come over here?*

It was perhaps six months since she and Ed had gone to the theater with Frank and Catherine. For a period after they'd built the house, they had socialized with the Wrights fairly often, perhaps once a month. Now a friendly distance had developed. Frank's reputation had grown considerably since those early days when they'd consulted on the house. Not since then had she and Frank shared a private conversation.

During construction, with some building detail as a starting point, they had lost themselves time and again in deep discussion. Those six months of collaboration seemed enchanted to her now. Frank Lloyd Wright had ignited her mind like no other person she'd ever met. At first their conversations were about ideas. They talked about Ruskin, Thoreau, Emerson, Nietzsche. Mamah told him of her passion for Goethe. He spoke reverently of his years working for Louis Sullivan, the great architect he called "Lieber Meister," dear master.

They began to see each other as fellow outsiders, making jokes about "Saints' Rest," the name Oak Park had earned for its church spires and absence of taverns. In the village, there was no question that people perceived Frank as an artist on the fringe. What fascinated him was that she saw herself as an outsider, too.

"I'm like the trunk of a cactus, I suppose," she told him. "I take in a dose of culture and time with friends, then I retreat and go live on it for a while until I get thirsty again. It's not good to live so much inside oneself. It's a self-imposed exile, really. It makes you different."

Their deep discussions were a stark contrast to her discourse with Edwin. It was when Mamah found herself saving up insights to tell Frank—thoughts she never would have shared with her husband—that she knew they'd grown too close.

By that time the two couples were good friends. When she understood how near to the edge she was walking, the house was nearly built. She had turned then toward Catherine to cultivate a closeness with her.

It was at the housewarming party that Mamah had invited Catherine to give a joint presentation on Goethe to the Nineteenth Century Woman's Club. She understood now what she'd been doing. She had been using Catherine, quite unawares, as a buffer between herself and Frank.

Sinking into the bathwater, Mamah recalled one of her last meetings with him. The memory of it had been a private place she'd gone to again and again during the past couple of years. It was 1904; the house was nearly finished. She and Edwin and John were living in it by then. Frank was in the middle of building Unity Temple, far too busy to come by to settle the last few details of the house. Nevertheless, he had appeared one morning, plopped down some plans on the table, and said, "Let's settle a few things."

She had looked back at him innocently, though she'd been terrified that he might come forward with some declaration of his feelings.

"First of all, where on earth did you get a name like Mamah?"

She'd burst out laughing. "Strange, isn't it? Well, my real name is Martha, but my grandmother started calling me Mamah when I was quite small. I think she made it up because it sounded French. She was French, you see, and descended from Philippe de Valois, Marquis de Villette—a decorated officer of the Royal Military Order of Saint Someone or Other."

"Is that where your gift for languages comes from?"

"That's where it started. She insisted we speak French in the house when she was visiting." Mamah had leaped up then. "Would you like to see her in a ball gown? I just came across a photo in one of the boxes." She went into the bedroom, where the movers had put their things, and carried a box out to the dining room table.

Frank had laughed out loud when he saw the portrait. A delicate Marie Villette Lameraux sat in front of a painted backdrop of Mount Olympus in some long-ago photographer's studio, her girlish personage festooned with garlands from the swirling braids over her ears to the loopy ribbons draped between rosettes on her gown. She stared grimly at the camera.

Frank was grinning when he stood up to peer into the box. "What else is in there?"

"Just some of my old things. Papers . . ."

He sat down again and looked at her. "Tell me everything," he said.

Tell me everything. He might as well have said, "Take off your dress." She had pulled one thing after another out of the box. She'd shown him her master's-degree thesis and her graduation photograph. She'd talked of her years in Port Huron, teaching English and French at the high school with her college friend Mattie. She'd shown him photos of her family in front of their house on Oak Park Avenue.

"This must be you."

"Uh-huh. This is my sister Jessie. She was the oldest." Mamah pointed to the smiling sixteen-year-old and felt the familiar sad squeeze in her chest. "And Lizzie. Well, she looks just the same, doesn't she? She's the middle girl."

Frank went back to the black-haired girl who struck such a confident pose, one hand holding a croquet mallet, a leg crossed jauntily in front of the other. "How old are you here?"

"Twelve."

"Such pluck for a girl so young."

"Oh, I was at just the right age then, I think. Smarter than I ever was before or since. There were no grays. I worshipped my father. I loved my dog. I adored reading."

Mamah stared at the family picture. The sight of her and her sisters wearing middy blouses jogged another memory. "We were wild children, really. You see, my father was as an amateur naturalist. That was his great love, even more than the railroad. In summer he would take us down to a dry stream near Kankakee to hunt for fossils. It was an area where there had been a shallow sea in prehistoric times. He taught us to look very closely, and my eyes—at least my near eyesight—became quite acute. Nothing made me happier than crawling around the streambed for hours on end, looking for tiny patterns of shells in the rocks. My father always brought along a hammer. And when I cracked open a rock that looked promising—when I actually found imprints left by creatures that lived there five hundred million years ago—well, it was like opening up a whole world and falling right into it." Mamah laughed. "It worried my mother to death."

Frank looked surprised. "Why?"

"Because she preferred finding God in the second pew of Grace Episcopal Church. It unnerved her to see her daughters smashing rocks with hammers. She was wary of trilobites and Darwin and my father's talk of the 'human animal.' And she thought I was far too . . . dreamy, I guess, or suggestible. I remember when my father brought home a telescope around this time. It was a good one, and he was excited to show us how it worked. That night we all went outside, and Jessie and Lizzie got to look through it first. They were awestruck by how many stars they could see with it. But after my mother had a good long look through it, I heard her say to my father, 'Don't show Mamah. It will be overwhelming for her.' "

Frank stared at her thoughtfully.

"It wasn't too long after that that my mother took me in hand. My rock-smashing days ended, and dance lessons began. But by that point I was a bit of an odd one, not really interested in what most other girls cared about. I became something of an introvert, a bookworm, I guess you'd say."

Mamah felt giddy at Frank's attention, and a little embarrassed for revealing so much about herself. Yet she continued pulling things out of the box. "Another of my mother's edification projects," she explained, showing him the little German readers she had started with when she first learned the language. And then she showed Frank her birth certificate.

He held it up to the light. "June nineteenth, 1869," he read. "Interesting. I was born June eighth of the same year."

At any other moment, the remark might not have seemed unusual, but that afternoon, as they sat at the dining room table in the new house they had planned together, the coincidence struck Mamah as preordained. She wasn't a superstitious person or particularly religious, but it seemed a kind of proof that they were meant to know each other, that fate had spat them out into the world at the same time, in nearly the same place, by design.

He looked at her graduation photo and spoke with sadness in his voice. "I wonder what my life would have been like if I had run into this young woman twenty years ago. To find someone so . . ." He paused. "I was a boy when I married Catherine—just twenty-one. She was only eighteen. The marriage never should have been permitted, really. Now . . ." He looked away, sighed heavily.

When he turned his face back, it was etched with tenderness. He took her hand. "You are the loveliest woman I have ever known," he said, leaning forward to kiss her cheek.

She let his mouth stay on her skin for a heartbeat before pulling away.

HE CAME BY FOR three consecutive days after that. To show Mamah other garages he'd built—that was the flimsy pretext. Neither Lizzie nor Edwin seemed suspicious.

The first morning, a brilliantly clear day, he drove her out to the far north prairie. They climbed out of the car and waded into the high grasses. Frank snapped the wheatlike head off a stem. "I wasn't a rock smasher," he told her.

"What were you, then?"

"Oh, something close. When I was a boy, I worked summers on my uncle's farm in Wisconsin. At the end of the day, if I wasn't exhausted—because he worked me hard—I went out into the hills and explored. I'd pull things apart to see how they were put together—flowers, plants like this . . ."

"And you fell into them?"

He smiled. "I did. Flower blossoms first, of course, because they're so seductive. But then I saw how the stalk inevitably led to the leaf and bloom. It didn't matter what plant I looked at. The structure was always sound, and the design essentials were all there: proportion, scale, unity of idea. Mind you, I was just a boy pulling things apart at that point."

"Did you always know you wanted to be an architect?"

"Absolutely. For as long as I can remember. The idea of building shelters that let you feel you are living out in the open—that came later. But the instinct—the feeling for it—was seeded in me out there on the hillside. So, when I went to the university to study, I was excited because I had all these ideas about organic architecture based on how nature works out its building projects. But nobody wanted to talk about architecture that way. It was all about Palladian windows or Corinthian columns. So I left school."

"That's when you came to Chicago."

"Yup. Apprenticed myself to Silsbee at nineteen, and moved on to Sullivan's office a year later."

A strong wind was blowing, pushing the grasses and wildflowers eastward.

"You landed in good hands."

"Didn't I tell you some of this when we worked on the house?"

"Yes, but not all of it."

"Well, Sullivan was a marvelous teacher, and I was the pencil in his hand. He was continually talking about making *American* buildings. By the time I left him to start my own practice, I was bent on doing something new—making houses that speak of this prairie land rather than some French duke's notion of what a house should look like."

Mamah pulled wind-whipped strands of hair away from her mouth. "Was it always houses with you?"

"I couldn't think of anything more noble than making a beautiful home. Still can't."

He gestured out toward the horizon, where a clear sky bordered prairie grasses as far as the eye could see. "Eventually, I fell under the spell of that line out there. It was so simple: a huge block of blue on top of a block of gold prairie, and the quiet line between heaven and earth stretching endlessly. It felt like freedom itself to look at the horizon. I had been drunk on forms since I was a boy, and here was this simple line that expressed so much about this land."

Mamah watched his hands. Whenever he talked about architecture, his hands spoke their own language, moving gracefully as he formed right angles with thumb and forefinger, or mimicked planes with the flat of his palm.

"Of course, the horizon isn't a perfectly straight line, but I wasn't out to imitate it, anyway. I wanted to abstract it in a way that expressed the essence of it. When I began stacking one horizontal plane on top of another—parallel to the prairie, as I did in your house—the homes I designed began to look and feel grounded, like they belonged in this place." Frank glanced quickly at her. "Am I boring you?"

"Not at all. In fact, you reminded me just then of when I was a small child. We were living in Iowa, and there was still prairie all around in those days," Mamah said. "My father would put me on his shoulders so I could get the big view, and he'd talk about the wildflowers and grasses and clouds. He had a name for the bottom of the sky—'the hem of heaven.' "

Frank smiled. "I like that." He fell silent for a while.

"You were talking about organic architecture," she said.

"It's the only kind of architecture that makes sense to me. It's all I want to do now."

"Then you *must* do it. In fact, I think it's your destiny."

He let out a laugh and embraced her. "Do you know what's wonderful about you, Mamah? You understand things others can't begin to grasp. People think I'm being sentimental, eulogizing the prairie because it's nearly gone. But that's not what I'm after."

She felt awkward and extricated herself from his arms. *What am I after,* she wondered, *that I court disaster standing here in this field with you?*

They moved apart. The wind seemed to have calmed some.

"I'm sorry," he said finally. "It's just such a relief to talk. It's so easy with you. The truth is, I live a pretty stultifying existence at home. I love my children, but . . ." He shrugged. "My life is not in them the way Catherine's is. Her whole being is invested in them. I've done the same thing with my work, I know—taken refuge in it. But she and I have reached an impasse. And we are too far gone to fix it."

Mamah thought, *Take me home.* They had left the safe territory of architecture. "People change over time," she said. "I think it happens in a lot of marriages."

Frank waited.

"That's not what happened in my case, though," she said. "I was mature enough—too mature. My head trumped my heart." She looked at the ground, ashamed to betray Edwin in this way. "Ed is a good, decent man," she said. "We're just mismatched." She did not confide what she'd been feeling these days. That lately, when her husband came into the same room, she felt as if the air had been sucked right out of it.

By the third day, there was no use pretending. There were furtive caresses, followed by long silences.

On the fourth morning, Mamah awoke nauseated and knew almost immediately. She called Frank's office and left a message with his secretary: Mrs. Cheney is unable to meet today.

When he appeared unannounced the following Tuesday, she kept the screen door closed when she told him she would not see him again. Standing on the stoop, he looked stricken.

She put her palm on the wire mesh between them. "Frank," she said, tipping her head back so the tears wouldn't breach. "I just found out." She forced cheer into her voice. "Ed and I are expecting a baby."

MAMAH SNAPPED FROM her reverie, climbed out of the tub, and returned to the bedroom, where she stared blankly into the closet.

I miss our talks. Had he said that to other women? In the two years since the day she'd told him she was pregnant, she'd seen Frank driving his Stoddard-Dayton around town with one woman after another next to him. People called his car the "Yellow Devil" not only for its color and speed but also, she suspected, for his devil-may-care attitude about gossip. It was humiliating to think that he might regard her as he did those other clients or prospective clients or whoever they were.

When Mamah glanced at the clock, she realized she had only half an hour before Frank was scheduled to appear. She put on a white waist and black skirt, dug into her jewel box for the thin gold chain with one fat pearl. Brushing her hair into a twist at the back of her head, she leaned in close to the mirror to examine her face. She knew she'd done too much of that lately, looking for more evidence, as if she needed it, that she was nearly thirty-nine years old.

As a thin child, she had thought her features were freakish—a pole neck, a square jaw out of proportion to the rest of her, wide high cheekbones that earned her the nickname "bone face" in the schoolyard. Her horn spectacles had hidden the green eyes her father said were pretty. Only the arching brows might have been acceptable had they not behaved so infuriatingly. They gave away everything. "You're angry," her mother would say, studying the roiling black line across her forehead.

Around the age of eighteen, she had grown into her face. Her clumsy limbs became supple, and she found herself moving through the world with a new ease. The boys who had taunted her suddenly came calling.

With her hair swept up now, the long neck looked pretty with the pearl resting in the shell-like dip between her collarbones. She touched cologne on her wrist, took off her glasses, and closed the bedroom door.

CHAPTER 4

"Where is everyone?" Frank asked when he stepped into the foyer. He handed her the rolled-up drawings he carried under his arm and removed his long silk scarf.

"Lizzie and Louise took the children down to Marshall Field's." She felt awkward as she waited to take his coat, standing so close to him that she could smell the fragrance of the shaving cream he'd used. He was no taller than she, and his eyes—always so direct—were level with her own and impossible to avoid. He looked to be glowing; his face was ruddy from the cold.

"Ah, Field's," he said, inhaling with mock serenity, "the pinnacle of civilization."

"It's always matters of taste with you, isn't it?" Mamah teased, showing him into the dining room.

"Well . . ." He rolled his eyes toward some syrupy pink carnations on the sideboard. She'd bought them at a greenhouse.

"I know. You'd rather see some old dead branch. But I like them."

"That's good."

"Don't patronize me, Frank Wright," she said, half serious. "I'm not some client's wife who lets you dress her." The words came out wrong, but he knew what she meant. She wasn't one of those women who permitted him—paid him—to design her china, her linens, even her dresses so she looked *right* in a Wright house. She wasn't going to let him tell her she couldn't put pink flowers on her mantel.

"I've never thought of you as some client's wife. Not for a minute."

Already, she thought. She sat down at the table, smoothed the drawings flat. "Where were we when we left off on this project? It's been a while."

He took a chair across from her. "We were talking about true things." His voice took on an edge. "Things that kept me sane for a time. Or don't you remember?"

"I do."

"Do you recall when you first came to see me at the studio? You had just been through Arthur Huertley's house. You quoted Goethe. You called it 'frozen music.' "

"It's true. I wanted to dance right through that house."

Frank shook his head. "I can't begin to tell you the impression you made. Here was this beautiful woman, so articulate and gifted, who *comprehended . . .* Tell me something, Mamah. In all those hours we spent together, was I the only one feeling that wonder?"

She stared at her hands in her lap. "No."

"So it wasn't my imagination?"

Mamah looked up at him. *So quickly,* she thought. *I am putty in your hands so quickly.* She hesitated, pressed her lips together. "Do you remember my third visit to the studio?"

"Third?"

"Well, I do," she said, "vividly. Your secretary let me in. I was early for an early appointment, so it must have been about eight-thirty in the morning. A big fire was already going in the fireplace. You were up on the balcony chatting with that artist—"

"Dickie Bock."

"Yes." Mamah drew in a breath. "He was up there sculpting away. I remember that you didn't see me because I was off in a corner. Then Marion Mahony came in, and she didn't see me, either. I must have been in shadow." Mamah smiled, remembering the pleasure of watching the morning unfold at the studio.

"Marion looked so stylish," she said. "She had on a heavy coat and a paisley turban. I can see it now. You looked down at her and said, 'What is that thing on your head?' I wanted to giggle out loud, but I kept quiet because she seemed wounded at first. She said, 'Don't you like it?' "

"You came over to the railing then and teased her. You said, 'On a magician, I like it.' And without missing a beat, she shot back at you, 'I *am* a magician.' "

Frank let out a belly laugh.

"Do you remember what you did then?" Mamah asked.

He shrugged.

"You put up your hands in surrender."

Frank was grinning now. "She thinks she performs miracles for me."

"Does she?"

"She keeps me sharp. She's quick with the repartee."

"Well, let me tell you something. I wanted to *be* Marion Mahony that day, more than you can imagine. I wanted to begin every morning by making you laugh out loud." *Here I go again*, she thought, feeling her eyes growing moist. "To sit next to you, to look up and see someone sculpting. . . . To feel the creative energy swirling in that room. . . . That day in the studio, I longed to be someone you absolutely counted on. The truth is, I still do."

Frank reached out his hand and ran it over her brow, then down one side of her face. His forefinger touched the pearl at her throat.

Mamah felt her heart racing. "Do you always fall in love with your clients?"

"Only once," he said. "Only one."

He stood up, took her hand, and led her to the sofa in the living room, where he gently eased her down. They lay together for some time, her head on his chest, before his hands began to move. His wrist bones cracked as he unbuttoned her shirtwaist and put his mouth to her breast. A rill of electricity shot down her body, yanked up her hips. Her hands were seeking him, struggling frantically against fabric. In a moment his whole length was next to her, the naked landscape of his body gliding over hers, as they wordlessly found a common rhythm.

t was a summer of breathtaking risks.

For every careful plan, there was a careless visit. She would hear a knock on the door and find Frank standing there with his shirtsleeves rolled up and the blueprint for the garage under his arm, as if he had just popped over to settle a small detail.

Most of the time Louise and the children were at home. On those days he would get down on his knees and play with them, hauling John and Martha and their playmates around on his back while Mamah sat on the window seat in the library, fiddling with her skirt, balling up the linen, then smoothing it out again. She wondered if her jitteriness was apparent to Louise, if the sparks flicking like fireflies under her skin showed on the outside.

"You look radiant," Mamah said one afternoon when Frank came through the door. He had a lilt in his step and his eyes were twinkling. His face and forearms were burnished from hours outside at work sites. Standing in the library, he glanced around the other rooms.

"They're in Forest Park," she said. "They all went over to the amusement park. About an hour ago."

Frank tossed the drawings onto the window seat, put his hand behind her waist, and swirled her around the tiny library as if they were in a ballroom.

"Frank," she protested, laughing. She felt exposed next to the open, uncurtained windows. Once, at the end of a dinner party, she had sat on the window seat with another woman, both of them drinking wine and smoking cigarettes. She'd looked up to see the Belknap girls gazing down on her from their bedroom window next door, and she'd had a distinct sense of being spied on. Was anybody up there now? It was impossible to tell. She tried to lead him to a back room, but he was pulling her down to the floor, and then it was too late. Their loving was muffled and furious.

Afterward, briefly, she lay with her head in the hollow of his shoulder, listening for footfalls on the pavement. Sunlight slanted over the roof next door and fell hot on her legs.

"It's going to be the best damned garage in Oak Park," Frank said, stroking her hair, "but it could take years to finish."

IT FRIGHTENED HER TO FEEL so out of control. But any thoughts of ending the affair floated away the minute he set foot in the same room. Frank Lloyd Wright was a life force. He seemed to fill whatever space he occupied with a pulsing energy that was spiritual, sexual, and intellectual all at once.

And the wonder of it was, he wanted *her*.

When she looked in the mirror, she saw a woman pink-faced from desire. And from *being* desired. My Lord, what a narcotic! She hadn't felt such a sense of power since she was a twenty-year-old college girl with a clutch of suitors.

"Ring me once and hang up, then I'll call you back," Frank instructed her. She did that only a couple of times. Isabelle, his assistant, would pick up, and Mamah would quickly lose her nerve. Instead she waited for him to contact her, and the waiting nearly killed her.

LATER THAT SUMMER, when Frank took office space downtown in the Fine Arts Building, their trysts became easier. Mamah used the excuse of a Wednesday-afternoon class to get out of the house. She took the train into Chicago, walked to Michigan Avenue, and went up in the elevator to the tenth floor. Once, as she hurried down the hallway hoping not to meet anyone, the door across from Frank's opened, and she caught a glimpse of Lorado Taft chiseling in his studio. Mamah knew the famous sculptor was a longtime friend of Frank and Catherine. He had looked up from his work that day, caught her eye, and smiled in a disturbing, knowing sort of way. Burning with embarrassment, Mamah slipped into Frank's office, sank down on a chair, bent over, and put her face in her lap. After that, she wore a large bonnet with a scarf over its crown and tied under her chin, as if she'd just stepped out of an automobile.

Another time, as she emerged from the elevator, she spotted a neighbor, one of his old clients, standing in the hall at the door of Frank's office, taking his leave. She bent her head so her hat hid her face, then walked down the steps to the floor below. Standing there in the stairwell, waiting, she could hear some would-be Paderewski pounding out a piano concerto. From another room, a teacher's voice called out positions above the soft thud of ballet slippers.

Her own heart was thudding by the time she returned to the tenth floor. When she was safe inside his office, he locked the door and pulled the shades down over his windows. They picked up the thread of their almost-life together then, opening up to each other in the darkened room.

They longed to be out in the world, taking it in together. Early in the summer, when they were being extra cautious, they arranged to arrive separately at a downtown nickelodeon where a Tom Mix movie was showing. Sitting a couple of rows from him, she could hear Frank's deep laugh explode throughout the movie, and that sent her into gales. Frank left before she did. The plan was for her to walk to the corner so he could pick her up there. When she got out on the street, she noticed that an enterprising vendor had set up a display of cowboy hats right outside the theater. She stopped and impulsively picked out a wide-brimmed tan hat.

"That's your B.O.P. Stetson, ma'am," the man said, "the best. Stands for 'Boss of the Plains.' "

She laughed. "Perfect."

"It'll run you more," the vendor cautioned. "It's twelve dollars."

"I'll take it." She stuffed money into his hand.

Frank swooped up moments later in his yellow car and could barely conceal his delight. He put on the hat and drove them to the north side, to a tiny German restaurant. What a sight he made, dressed in a duster that hung down to his high boot heels, with the Stetson perched above his driving goggles.

Settled in a booth, she found he wanted to relive each scene from the film. She was amused by how boyish he was, sitting there with the big hat next to him, nearly in convulsions over the memory of desperadoes falling off their horses as Tom Mix chased them down.

SOMETIMES THEY DROVE OUT into the country, the yellow car ripping at terrifying speeds over rutted roads. They stopped along the way for whatever the stands were selling—strawberries, cantaloupe. Frank had a blanket in the car that he spread out, then he took off his shoes and wiggled his toes. "God, that feels good," he said every single time he stripped off his socks.

He loved Whitman. He would lie on his stomach and read *Leaves of Grass* to her. There were long stretches, though, when they didn't talk, just sat near each other. They could have hummed, she thought, and understood each other perfectly.

One day, after they had finished eating, Frank cleaned his hands in ditch water near where they sat, then produced from the car a portfolio full of Japanese woodblock prints. He spread the prints out carefully on the blanket.

"These are by Hiroshige," he said, pointing to three of them. "Pictures of the floating world."

She studied a print of a courtesan fanning herself. "I've never understood what that means—'the floating world.' "

"They're pictures of common people just living for the moment—going to the theater, making love. They're floating along like leaves on a river, not worrying about money or what's going to happen tomorrow.

"I bought these when I was in Japan," he said, taking two landscapes from the portfolio. Mamah remembered Catherine Wright's stories about that trip to Japan. She'd told of how Frank would leave every evening dressed as a local in a straw hat, disappearing with a translator into the back streets of Kyoto, on the prowl for prints.

"Nature is everything to the Japanese," he said. "When they build a house, they face it toward the garden."

"I knew Japan had influenced you," she said. "I didn't realize how much." She thought she saw him flinch. "You don't like the word 'influenced,' do you?"

"Hate it, actually. Beaux Arts snobs—the academics—use it."

"I'm sorry."

"Don't be sorry. But I want you to understand. Nobody's influenced me. Why should I copy the Japanese or the Aztecs or anybody else when I can make something beautiful of my own? It all comes from here." He tapped a finger on one temple. "And from nature."

"I know that," she said. She didn't like the feeling of being chastised by Frank. "It was simply the wrong word." Mamah turned back to the prints. "I love this one." She looked closely at the picture of a courtesan reclining on a bed, reading a book.

"Then it's yours."

She was giddy when she took the print home that day. She put it between the pages of a large picture album where Edwin would never look.

. .

WHEN CATHERINE INVITED MAMAH and Edwin over for dinner in early August, Mamah saw no recourse but to go. She had not seen Catherine in weeks. After dinner, with the men in the studio, the women settled into the living room. They talked about club news and their children and the books they were reading. At one point Catherine got up to retrieve a book from a shelf across the room.

"Did you ever see this?" she asked. She held a copy of *The House Beautiful* in her hands. "You know Reverend Gannett, don't you? Frank illustrated his essays for this book. It must have been back in '96," she mused. "It was our bible in those days."

Catherine paged through the book, reminiscing about the time early in their marriage when Frank was building their house. "He wanted to carve a saying over every doorway. I told him, 'Just one.' Don't ask me where I got the gumption to put my foot down—you know Frank—but it worked. We were young and in love, and he went along with me."

Mamah glanced at the familiar words over the fireplace. LIFE IS TRUTH.

"How did you meet Frank?" she asked impulsively, horrified at once by her own perverse curiosity.

"At a costume dance at his Uncle Jenk's church on the south side," Catherine said, "near where I grew up." A smile spread across her face at the memory. "We were all dressed as characters from *Les Miserables*. Frank was dressed as an officer with epaulets and a sword. I was supposed to be a French maid. It was a reel, I guess, because when everyone changed partners, we just slammed right into each other. Knocked each other right to the floor."

Catherine flipped to the back of the book. "There's this one poem Reverend Gannett quotes, called 'Togetherness,' that is just so beautiful. It was written by a woman who only had eleven years with her husband before he died. Isn't that sad? Here, you read it. I'm going to put out dessert."

Mamah held the book on her lap. She could see herself from the outside, sitting in the same chair she had sat in many times before. The room hadn't changed. Catherine hadn't changed. It was she who had changed into someone who could assess in one cool glance the failings of her lover's household.

She saw now that there was almost no trace of Catherine in the things of the house—every inch of the place was Frank's eye, from the plaster frieze around the top of the room, depicting mythological kings and giants locked in battle, to the moss-colored velvet drapes on either side of the inglenook. But in the commotion of the house, the entrances and exits of children seeking out their mother, in the *sounds* of the house, there was no question who presided.

Mamah scanned the poem quickly to its last verse.

Together greet life's solemn real,
Together own one glad ideal,
Together laugh, together ache,
And think one thought—"Each other's sake,"
And hope one hope—in new-world weather,
To still go on, and go together.

"Tripe," she muttered to herself.

Yet a nausea had taken hold of her belly by the time Catherine arrived with dessert, and she hurried Edwin out the door, pleading sickness.

In the early hours of the morning, she got out of bed and went to the kitchen in search of a cracker to settle her stomach. When she opened the cupboard, a small brown moth flew out. She knew what that meant. If she didn't get rid of the flour and rice and cereal in the cabinet, if she waited until Wednesday, when the cleaning girl came, there would be two dozen moths hanging upside down from the shelves. She held up one bag of grain after another to the kitchen lightbulb, looking for tiny white larvae, tossing anything suspect into a garbage barrel. In the end, she dumped the entire contents of the cabinet, then filled a bowl with hot water and ammonia.

How has it come to this? she wondered as she scrubbed. She had always thought herself a deeply moral person. Not a prude, by any stretch, but someone decent. Honorable. She would no more underline in a library book than allow the butcher to return too much change. How had she come to a point where she could so easily tell herself that adultery with a friend's husband was all right?

The next morning Mamah opened her diary for the first time since the previous winter. Thumbing through the fat little book, she understood why Lizzie and Edwin had been so worried about her. Through much of February, she had simply sat in bed, immobile and half stupid, staring out the bedroom window at the icicles hanging from the eaves.

Now, browsing through the diary, Mamah recognized her own inchoate yearnings in a notation to herself that she'd made while reading during the long winter.

It is not sufficient to be a mother: an oyster can be a mother. Charlotte Perkins Gilman

For as long as Mamah could remember, she had felt a longing inside for something she could not name. She had shoveled everything into that empty place—books, club committees, suffrage work, classes—but nothing filled it.

In college, and for a good period afterward in Port Huron, she'd had big ambitions. She had wanted to be a writer of substance, or maybe a translator of great works. But the years passed. She was nearing thirty when Edwin finally won her over. By the time she married him, she'd put those dreams to rest.

Back in Oak Park, living as a wife, she had done what all the women did: had children. She had truly wanted children—that was the main reason she'd married Ed. But there was a nanny now, and she had reverted to her old habit of retreating into herself, holing up to read and study. When she came out for a burst of socializing, everyone seemed pleased to see her. "Strong-minded" was a word she heard from time to time about herself. It meant brainy. But she heard "lovely," too.

At the Nineteenth Century Woman's Club, she'd occasionally throw an incendiary idea into a conversation. "If nurses get paid for their services, why can't housewives?" Or, "Charlotte Gilman says factory women could have real careers if they lived in communes with shared kitchens and hired cooks and nurses for the children."

The women liked her in spite of her provocations. They thought anyone with studious habits an eccentric, but she was married to Ed Cheney, after all—a splendid regular fellow. Or maybe they simply didn't believe she was serious when she spoke out, for what had she done about all her talk?

Throughout the dark winter, she had berated herself from every angle— some days for being an unfit mother, other days for doing nothing *more* than mothering.

Look at Jane Addams, she wrote to herself, *and Emma Goldman. Look at Grace Trout, the most ordinary of people, taking on the Illinois legislature for the vote. What is the matter with you?*

Louise had come and gone during those weeks, bringing the baby in to see her as if nothing were wrong. By March, Mamah had begun to emerge from her melancholy. One of her first outings was to go hear Frank's talk at the club.

Reading the diary, she wondered if he had seen her vulnerability as she saw it now. *Was I simply low-hanging fruit—easy pickings?*

When she met him next, she asked him outright. They were sitting in his car, parked on a side street on the south side.

"Mamah, something so good has begun here. Don't rub the bloom off of it with talk like that. You can't believe it's wrong, can you?"

"Don't ask me that. Ask me if I'm happy."

"I know the answer to that already."

SHE FELT ALMOST SWOLLEN with a joy that spilled over into every part of her life. She was taken aback by Martha's sweet baby smell and her tiny, nearly translucent fingers. Mamah could play whole afternoons with John and his friend Ellis from next door, hiding behind bushes in the front yard while they hunted for her. She found herself baking cakes, loading the neighborhood kids into the car, and delivering food to people she knew who were ill or had new babies. Once, when Lizzie read to her about a delivery boy who had been injured when his horse collided with a car, Mamah tracked down the boy's house to deliver an envelope with twenty dollars in it.

Edwin was deeply relieved by the change in her. He said she was more beautiful than ever. When his hand found her hip as they lay in bed, she didn't turn away. She let him take his pleasure while her mind drifted elsewhere.

At the beginning of the summer, she had thought, *It can't last; it's impossible. Nine children between us, never mind Catherine and Edwin.* Mamah knew she would never leave her children. But to have something perfect, something utterly one's own for a while . . . who would be the worse for it if they never found out? *One lives but once in the world.*

By the end of the summer, though, she admitted to him what she knew. She loved him with every cell in her body. She found delight in every part of him—his irrepressible laugh, the merry eyes that nearly always looked as if he'd just heard the most amusing punch line, his presence in every waking moment. She loved the way he impulsively brushed the back of his hand across her cheek at unexpected moments.

He made her feel alive and cherished. Rarely did he meet her without bringing some small surprise. He would hold his fist above her outstretched hand and tell her to close her eyes. When she opened them, she might find a foil-wrapped chocolate in her palm, or a small piece of bone from the wing of a bird, its lattice of cartilage stirring a conversation on aerodynamics.

She loved the flexibility of Frank's mind—that he spent his days fitting together geometrical forms, yet could express himself eloquently in writing and play piano with heartfelt beauty. As for his extraordinary soul, one had only to look at the houses he designed to find it laid open for the world to see.

Mamah realized she cared for him for the very reasons he made other people squirm. He was fearlessly outspoken. And he *was* eccentric, but it was the kind of eccentricity she had come to admire in her father. Anyone as attuned as Frank was to nature's order, anyone raised to reason outside the mainstream, was not going to be penned in very well by society's rules. Her father had responded to the order of the natural world, too. He was more interested in the habits of wasps than the politics of Oak Park. He hadn't cared a fig about fashion or the neighbors' opinions about the goats he kept in their suburban backyard. He was a "one-er," as he called stubborn nonconformists like himself, and he had nourished the same independence in his children.

Frank was like that. His ears and eyes and heart were tuned to seek truth in places where other people didn't look. In this, and in so many other ways, she felt a kindred spirit to him.

BELOW THE DARK MUSINGS of the winter, she wrote the date in her diary.

August 20, 1907

I have been standing on the side of life, watching it float by. I want to swim in the river. I want to feel the current.

CHAPTER 6

· ·

"There's something strange going on here," Lizzie said. It was a glorious October morning, a Saturday, and she was standing at the stove while the edge of an egg curled to a brown ruffle in bacon grease.

Mamah glanced up from the newspaper. "What do you mean?" She felt cords in her stomach knotting up.

"It's on page three, I think. There are men going door-to-door selling fake creamery butter. Right here in Oak Park. Did you see that?"

Mamah's shoulders relaxed. "No."

"We need to tell Louise when she comes on Monday so she doesn't open the door."

"What are you doing today?"

"Taking Jessica to a movie," Lizzie said, flipping the egg.

"You're a peach, Liz." They had all taken on the girl after Jessie's death, but it was Lizzie who truly mothered her.

"Do you want to come?"

"No. I'm headed down to the university this afternoon."

Mamah didn't even blink now when she lied. Deception came easily; it was almost routine. Frank would be waiting for her at his office, perhaps with flowers he had bought, or tea and sandwiches brought in from a restaurant.

"Robert Herrick is giving a special program on the New Woman," she said to Lizzie. "Edwin's taking the kids to the zoo."

"CATHERINE KNOWS," Frank said. They were lying on the carpet. Mamah could hear a violinist playing scales somewhere.

She sat up and looked at him. His eyes were closed. "That's why you're quiet."

"She won't say how she found out."

"What did you tell her?"

"I told her the truth. I asked for a divorce."

Mamah took his hand in hers and squeezed it. *This was bound to come.* She reached for her camisole on the floor nearby.

"Don't get up yet," he said. "Stay with me here."

The room was bright and cool. She pulled a folded mover's quilt off the top of a crate close by, covering the length of her body with it. Goose bumps coursed up and down her arms and legs.

"Catherine will keep it quiet," he said grimly. "She's too proud to tell anyone."

Mamah imagined Catherine sobbing. Catherine hurling *The House Beautiful* at her husband's head. Catherine climbing a ladder with a hammer and smashing the lovely figures in the living room frieze. It chilled her to think of what Catherine might want to do to her—a woman she had considered a friend.

Mamah cringed at the thought of the betrayal. *But I didn't steal Frank,* she reasoned. His marriage had been bad for so long, it was possible he'd been intimate with other women before her. She had never pressed him on it because she hadn't wanted to know. Yet that possibility conferred a strange solace just now.

"I'll tell Edwin," she said.

In the past couple of months, she and Frank had talked of simply coming out with it, asking for divorces. It was what both of them wanted, to live honestly. People got divorced these days; it wasn't unheard-of. Sitting in restaurants, walking along Lake Michigan, driving in the country, they had talked of ways it could work, how they could live in Chicago and she could have her children with her somehow. If Edwin agreed, if Catherine agreed . . .

She had rehearsed the speech she would deliver to Edwin a dozen times. But now that the time was here, she couldn't stop herself from shaking.

Standing up and moving around made her feel more resolute. She dressed, then leaned on the edge of the desk, rubbing her arms. "In a way, I'm relieved," she said after a time. Her fingers worked her dark hair into a knot. "We won't have to carry on this charade anymore."

Frank lay with his eyes closed, massaging his temples. After a while, he stood up, his face solemn as he slowly pulled on his clothes. His back was still youthful, not muscled so much as broad for his small frame, and taut, like the back of a strong swimmer.

"She wants a year to see if we can repair it. If it doesn't work, she'll give me a divorce."

Mamah stared at him.

"I know. I know. It's absurd."

"What did you say?"

"I said yes."

Mamah's body started reflexively. "But we agreed when this came—"

"I know what we agreed, Mame. You know how I feel about this. But Catherine . . ." He shrugged and shook his head. "Her heels are dug in. She's fighting for her life. What choice do I have but to wait it out?"

Mamah felt her head wagging, half confused, half angry. Frank put an arm around her back and pulled her face into his neck with the other hand. They stood like that for long minutes, a chasm of silence between them.

In the interminable hours following that afternoon at the Fine Arts Building, she hung suspended in the house on East Avenue, waiting for a telephone call or a note or something. But no word came.

She began to drive around, looking at building sites she knew were his, hoping to catch a glimpse of him. When she heard Frank had finally begun the big house he'd been planning in Hyde Park, she drove to it, parked her car, and waited. After four hours of watching for his yellow auto to appear, she gave up and returned to Oak Park.

On two different nights, coming home from concerts at the opera house after midnight, Edwin and Mamah drove past Frank's Forest Avenue house. Both times his studio was brightly lit. *He's thrown himself into his work,* she told herself.

AS WEEKS PASSED and no word came, Mamah grew more perplexed. She had demanded nothing of Frank when they had last spoken, and he had promised her nothing. In a begrudging way, she admired his sense of honor in abiding by his agreement with Catherine; he could walk away with some shred of integrity. But other times Mamah felt frantic from uncertainty. *How can he stay away,* she wondered, *when I can hardly stop myself from charging through his studio door? How does he* manage *to keep his promise?*

Sometimes her head was so fogged she couldn't concentrate on anything.

She would find her son, John, standing in front of her, patiently saying, "Mama . . . Mama . . . Mama," tugging at her dress, trying to get her attention so he could tell her something. In those moments, when she woke up to the skinny green-eyed boy in front of her, she was seized with remorse, grabbing him into her arms.

Still, she didn't look back and regret what she and Frank had done together. It was the truest love she'd known with a man. But what was their relationship now? More and more in the quiet hours of the day, a fear asserted itself. *He has returned to Catherine.*

NEARLY A YEAR EARLIER, she had agreed to give a presentation on *The Taming of the Shrew* at the Nineteenth Century Woman's Club. As December approached, she wondered what had possessed her to choose that play, of all things.

That was when I was living dangerously, she thought. She had been full of herself, full of indignation about the limits society pressed on women, confident in the rightness of her relationship with Frank, almost daring the world to discover their secret. Now she was hiding in her house most of the time.

A year ago, when she chose Kate's speech on a wife's obedience to her husband, she had imagined a flamboyant, ironic reading, after which she would talk about the changing role of women. Now, as she read the line "Thy husband is thy lord, thy life, thy keeper," she wanted to be in China, Budapest, Africa, anywhere but Oak Park, Illinois.

When the day came, she delivered the reading as she had first imagined it—with great irony—and nearly collapsed with relief when the audience laughed its approval. Strung through her like a thin wire, a streak of old courage had kept her upright long enough to get through it. Catherine had stayed away, but Frank's mother had come. Mamah caught a glimpse of the frowning Anna Wright in the audience and wondered if she knew. Or if anyone knew, for that matter.

The harrowing reading, in the end, seemed to help her turn a corner. She returned to two classes she had begun in the fall at the University of Chicago, both taught by Robert Herrick—a literature class and a course on the writing of novels. She immersed herself in Herrick's novels, attended classes, and wrote furiously.

The gnawing longing she'd felt for Frank was still there, but an uneasiness now matched it. How could she have been so ready to divorce her husband while Frank was so ready to give his wife one more year? She found herself thankful she hadn't told Edwin.

On New Year's Day, she woke to find her husband standing in his striped pajamas at the side of the bed, the thin hair around his ears ruffled like feathers. He bent to kiss her forehead. "Happy 1909, my darling."

Mamah sat up, rubbed her eyes. "Happy New Year," she said groggily.

He pressed into her hands a small wrapped gift. "I couldn't resist."

She opened it to find a gold brooch in the shape of an owl, with two rubies for its eyes.

Years earlier, he had given her a chain with a silver owl pendant on it. *For my scholar,* the note had read. She'd made the mistake of mustering delight, and subsequent owl gifts had followed—-a hooked rug, a carved owl clock, always with a sentimental note.

He had as much acquaintance with the contents of the books she read as she had with the workings of electric transformers. Yet he clearly felt enlarged by the idea that his wife was an intellectual. At dinner parties, he would sometimes direct the conversation toward her, graciously giving her the floor when he knew she had one of her causes to put forth. If talk turned bookish, he stared at her indulgently as she spoke, his forefinger crooked over his chin. When a guest once teased him about his silence during a discussion of an Ibsen play, Edwin had shrugged it off with characteristic modesty. "Mamah tends to Mr. Ibsen in this household. I take care of the car."

"He adores you," the woman seated next to her had said that evening. "You are a very fortunate woman."

"Thank you, Ed," Mamah said now, placing the lid back on the little box. She stretched her arms. "Is that sausage I smell?"

" 'Tis. And eggs. And broiled grapefruit with brown sugar."

"Where are the children?"

"Down in the basement with Lizzie."

"All right. I'm up," she said.

Mamah climbed out of bed, wrapped herself in a robe, and walked into the living room.

"Martha! Johnny! Jessica!" Edwin was hollering from the kitchen.

"Here we come," John called from downstairs.

Mamah corraled Martha, who was toddling happily through the room, and sat her apple-cheeked daughter in the high chair. John came next, then Jessica, who sat patiently waiting for the clamor to end. Even at eight and never having known her own mother, the girl was the picture of composure, so like Jessie it was a bit unnerving.

Louise was off, as was the cook, and Lizzie was joining friends at church. Mamah relished having just the five of them together. After breakfast there would be baths, and games, and dinner to think about later. It would give shape to the day. So many days had been shapeless lately.

She didn't believe in making resolutions on January first, and she hadn't uttered a real prayer for a long time. But she found herself grateful to be present at the table. *It will be all right*, she thought.

IN THE AFTERNOON, with Martha down for a nap and John playing next door, she put her feet up to peruse the events calendar in the *Oak Leaves*. When she spotted the notice WRIGHT TO SPEAK ON THE ART OF THE MACHINE, she felt a tingling all over. Her eyes flew down the column, searching for the location of his talk. She stood up in agitation then. *Goddamn you, Frank. I can't even read the paper.*

Already she could feel the old cloud filling up her head.

CHAPTER 7

· ·

April 12, 1909

Dearest Mamah,

We have survived another winter though it's still frozen here, and I find myself rounding out. I know I am entirely too old to be bouncing another child on my knee. But here I am (happy to boot), due in late September. I'm not looking forward to a summer of confinement, though, as Alden is away much of the time. How did I overlook that little detail when I agreed to marry a mining engineer?

That's where you come in. Why don't you and the children come out for a visit? Boulder is the most beautiful spot on earth in summer. There are outings by rail into the mountains to collect wildflowers, and plenty of interesting lectures over at the Chautauqua camp. You would be entirely in your element. And we could have a grand time catching up. Say you will! I'll make sure you have fun.

Give my love to Edwin, and ask his forgiveness in advance if I steal you away for a couple of weeks. Better still, tell him to come. Kisses all around.

Mattie

Mamah arrived in the field first. She maneuvered the Studebaker along the one road that led to the undeveloped lots just a mile north of town. She and Frank had met there twice the previous spring. The road was surprisingly dry for April.

She drove past the lampposts that had been installed last year in early summer but never lit. The poles were waiting for houses and people and lawns.

"Are you going to class?" Edwin had asked her this morning. He spoke carefully most of the time these days, uncertain what might set her off.

"No."

"But I thought you loved it."

She'd sighed. The thought of climbing on the elevated train and getting out to Hyde Park, then sitting through a two-hour lecture, made her weary rather than eager, as she used to feel.

"Herrick bores me," she said. "How is your grapefruit?"

"Dandy."

"And work?"

"Wagner Electric still stands."

"I'm sorry, Edwin. I haven't asked you a thing about work. I know you've had contract negotiations, and I haven't—"

"It's all right."

Mamah looked out of the dining room window. "It's just that . . . the sky has been so gray lately."

"Not today. You need to get out in the sun. It's glorious out there." He pecked her on the cheek and left.

When Mattie's note had arrived that morning, Mamah was jubilant. She searched the newspaper for train schedules, even though it would be another month before she could leave. Around two, just as she sat down at her secretary to write to Mattie, Louise tapped on the door.

"Mr. Wright is here, ma'am. With another man."

Mamah felt the pen in her hand start to quiver. She walked out into the living room to find Frank and the stranger staring at the row of stained-glass windows along the west side of the room. A wave of anger swept over her.

"The horizontal line is the line of domesticity, of course," Frank was saying.

Mamah cleared her throat, and both men turned toward her.

"Mrs. Cheney," Frank said, bowing elegantly. "Forgive us for intruding upon you. This is Mr. Kuno Francke, a visiting scholar from Germany."

Francke bent low, then kissed her hand.

"He's come from Germany to see my work. I've already traipsed him through three other houses. Do you mind if I show him around your home?"

"Not at all." Mamah shot a furious look at Frank while Mr. Francke gazed at the ceiling.

"Mrs. Cheney speaks fluent German," Frank said.

"Is that so?" the man said in a heavy accent. "Forgive me if I butcher the

English, but I'm practicing. I am trying to convince your architect that his talents are wasted in America. The avant-garde in German architecture is head and shoulders above the Modern architects here. Except for Mr. Wright, who I think leads them all. He would be far better served to practice in Germany right now."

"Well, I can't think of a better place for him," Mamah said. "Now, if you'll excuse me, I was just about to get dressed to go out."

When she headed to the hallway, Frank hurried to catch her. "Meet me in the field tonight. Nine o'clock. Will you?"

She didn't answer him as she slipped into the bedroom and closed the door.

Batter my heart, three-personed God. Stop me in my tracks. Please.

Driving toward the north prairie, she found herself praying in sonnets. She looked around, half expecting to see a flash of bright light. But the sky was black and still.

As much as she could tell in the dark, no foundations had been dug since they had last met. The field remained as it had been, marked off by a few roads, laid out in a grid pattern.

Mamah thought about her departure from home.

"Meeting tonight," she'd called out to Edwin. She wore a simple dress that was neither plain nor fine, a "meeting" dress.

"Go! Get out of the house and enjoy yourself!" he called back.

Now she sat alone in his car in the middle of a dark field. She knew what the prairie looked like by day—patches of grasses and trees. She and Frank had dared to lie there on the ground at sunset last summer. They had felt surprisingly safe, hidden in the maize-colored savannah, the smell of steamy earth wafting over them. But tonight, in the waning moon's light, Mamah could see only the silhouettes of bur oaks spreading their ghoulish arms against the night sky.

It was nine o'clock, and Frank had not appeared. She was considering leaving when she saw the lights of a car turn onto the road leading to the development. A cold excitement swept over her, and she took a blanket from the backseat.

What if it wasn't Frank? What if the developer had decided to come out to the field for some reason? How could she explain herself, sitting out here in the dark? She opened the door and slid from the driver's seat, then hid behind the car, wrapped in the blanket.

Batter my heart. Batter my heart.

The car stopped twenty feet from where she stood. She peeked around the fender again and saw Frank leap from his car and race toward hers. Mamah stepped from behind the auto.

Frank didn't speak to her at all, only held on to her, rocking her back and forth in his arms.

THEY SAT IN THE STUDEBAKER, looking out at the fields around them. Her eyes had adjusted to the darkness. In the dim light, she could discern green shoots pushing up through the brittle shafts of old grasses.

"You look so lovely right now."

"Shhh."

"I mean it."

"Don't try to charm me."

"I thought you understood."

"You could have sent some word, Frank. I've been living inside hell."

"I wanted to come to you. There hasn't been a day . . ."

Mamah felt something surrender inside. She took his hand and brushed her fingers over its familiar shape.

"She's not going to abide by the agreement," he said. "She's off in her own world. Do you know how she spends her days? Filling a scrapbook with sentimental poems about fatherhood and clippings of the children's hair. We have not shared a bedroom for over a year, yet she won't hear a word about divorce."

"It's all so sad."

Frank was silent. When he spoke, his voice was heavy with despair. "Henry Ford was at the studio this week. Monday." He stared out the side window. "It was a disaster."

"Why? What happened?"

"He set up a meeting about a country house. When he showed up, I simply . . . I couldn't gin up an ounce of enthusiasm."

She watched the outline of his face.

"It's not the only commission I've lost lately. I've hit some kind of wall. I just can't live this life anymore. There's this awful doom I feel, that I'll have to spend the rest of my days spitting out houses in Oak Park until I fall over at the table." He emitted a grim sigh, tapped a finger on the steering wheel. "Strange, isn't it, that I have a man of Henry Ford's stature show up at my studio—that some recognition finally comes after all these years—and it means almost nothing."

"I understand."

"You know what'll be built in this field someday? Little boxes iced with stucco that some horse's ass will call 'prairie houses.' Complete with 'Frank Lloyd Wright windows' bought for nothing from some cheap glass company in Chicago. Do you see the irony of it?" When he looked at her, she saw something new, a wounded outrage. "I've been a pariah in this town since I moved here, and now I've got imitators! They think it's just a matter of stripping the frills off, like the dress reformers. The sons of bitches don't have the intelligence to steal the right ideas."

"Clients who understand will pay for the real thing, Frank."

"You know what's wrong?" He moved his fingers through her hair. "I want you, Mame. Next to me. I want to go out into the world and look at things with clear eyes, the way I did when I was twenty. I feel as if I've hardly *lived*. I need time away from here—a spiritual adventure—" He was quiet, as if calculating something. "Kuno Francke isn't the only German who's after me. There's a printer in Berlin named Ernst Wasmuth. He does high-quality art books, and he's convinced we could make good money by publishing a monograph of my work. It would be a statement of what I've done. Hopefully it will generate commissions. I don't know. But I've talked to him about going over to Germany in August."

"Nobody is doing the work you do, Frank. A monograph is your ticket to an international reputation," she said. "You have to go. It's the next step for you."

"You don't understand. It will be enormous work getting the renderings ready. I could be gone a year."

Inside her, sorrow was rising like a wave. She crossed her arms, pressed her fingernails into her flesh.

"Come with me, Mamah. You love Berlin—you've told me so. Take a holiday—women take tours all the time. Call it what you want. Just stay a couple of months so we can be together. We could give it a try and see if it works."

"If only it were that simple." She shook her head. "In a way, it's easier for you that Catherine knows. I nearly told Edwin, but when you didn't contact me, I backed away from it." Mamah felt hot salty tears seep down her cheeks and into her mouth. "I thought you didn't want me anymore."

"Mamah . . ." Frank said. He pulled her toward him.

"There are two of us in this," she said. "Can't you see how impossible it all is? I can't pick up where we left off, sneaking around again. It wears too hard on me." She shifted uneasily on the leather of the seat. "I'm going away for a while to Colorado to stay with some friends, Mattie and Alden Brown. Mattie is due in September, and she needs company. I'm going out there with the children as soon as John finishes school."

Frank looked at her, stunned. "You're not."

"I am."

"Jesus." He sighed. "Look, I'll wait until September if I know that—"

Mamah shook her head. "I need to get away, too, Frank, from Edwin and Oak Park. And you. I need to sort things out." She wiped her eyes and shrugged. "I have to find the path that's right for me."

After a few minutes, Mamah watched him climb disconsolately into his car and wait while she lit her headlights and drove off. She had done the right thing, the hard thing. But there wasn't an ounce of relief in it.

CHAPTER 8

Mamah and Edwin looked up at the same moment when they heard the hammering. The June sun was already blazing at eight A.M., and the concrete stoop was warm under her feet. Leaning against the Belknaps' house was a tall ladder. On it, a carpenter carefully pieced clapboard strips into a second-floor window opening.

"How odd," Edwin said, pulling off his suit coat and flinging it over his arm. "That's a bedroom closet window, isn't it? Why on earth would they want to board it up?"

Mamah gnawed at a cuticle. "I don't know."

He shrugged. "People are strange. A perfectly good window, even if it's in a closet." Edwin kissed her forehead, then walked out to the street.

She slouched on the stoop. A woodpecker drilled a tree somewhere in counterpoint to the hammering. She noticed that tiny box elder seedlings had sprung up in her flower bed from the winged seeds of the neighbors' tree. She bent down and yanked them out of the soil.

I wish you were cruel, Edwin, she thought. *I wish you were devious or lazy or selfish. Anything but kind.*

Mamah looked up at the window and wondered what the neighbor girls had seen last summer. Was it Frank's hand over hers, a kiss, or worse? And why were the Belknaps boarding up the window now? She pictured the girls continuing their watching through the winter, hoping to see more. Had they been caught by their mother and confessed?

Only three days left before she boarded a train for Boulder. Three days. But she saw clearly now what she needed to do. *When Edwin comes home tonight,* she thought, *I'll tell him the truth. Before someone else does.*

Mamah's sister Lizzie appeared from around the corner of the house, headed out somewhere. She came to a halt when she saw Mamah's face. "Are you all right? You look ill."

"No."

"No what? Are you sick?"

"Do you have a minute to talk?"

Lizzie's eyes traveled up the ladder to the boarded-up window. Her face registered guilt when she looked back at Mamah, as if she had been caught in a lie of her own. "Of course, Mame." She put down her satchel and sat down on the stoop.

"I'm not sick, Liz, but I'm not well, either. There's something . . ." Mamah backed up and started over. "Ed and I haven't been happy lately. I suppose you know that."

Lizzie reached into her bag and pulled out her cigarettes. She handed one to Mamah, then took her time lighting it and one for herself. "Is it Frank Wright this is about?"

"So you know." Mamah glanced at Lizzie's face but could tell nothing. Clear of emotion as an alabaster egg. "Does Edwin know, too?"

"I'm not sure how he could miss it." Lizzie's tone was matter-of-fact. "But I suppose it's possible."

Mamah stared at the pavement, her stomach in knots. "I've lost myself, Liz."

Her sister drew deeply on her cigarette. "People make mistakes. You can fix this."

"No. I mean, it's more than Frank. I married Edwin and slowly . . ." She shrugged. "Right now I feel as though if I stay in this house, if I go on pretending much longer, whatever is left of me is going to just smother."

Lizzie looked into her eyes. "Frank Wright isn't helping your situation."

"But he is. Frank made me remember who I was before. I can *talk* to him, Liz. I could never really talk to Ed." Mamah laughed sadly. "Sometimes I think the reason he and I have lasted as long as we have is because you are at the dinner table to keep the conversation going." She wiped an eye with her wrist.

"Go clear out your head, Mamah." Lizzie patted her shoulder. "If you want to leave the children back here with me, go have yourself a vacation."

"No, I want them with me, and they're excited about going. But thanks, Lizzie."

"I have a feeling you'll see things differently with a little distance." Lizzie stubbed out her cigarette, then took the butt back to the alley trash can. When she returned, she ran her hand over Mamah's tousled head. "I'm headed downtown for a while," she said. Her voice was sad.

Mamah watched her sister walk toward the street. When she was out of sight, Mamah looked down at the flower bed along the porch stoop. She and Lizzie had planted it together last spring. Mamah had dug in plants donated by a neighbor—hollyhocks, spiky penstemon, huge-leaved rhubarb. Lizzie had gone out and bought low-growing alyssum plants that made a fragrant white blanket beneath Mamah's raucous giants, somehow managing to pull together the whole crazy quilt with one soft stroke.

The alyssum was pure Lizzie. She was continually moving quietly in the background, making things work. Only three years older than Mamah, she'd always seemed a whole generation beyond her. She was reserved, ladylike, with the kind of cool grace their elder sister, Jessie, had had.

The two of them had been stars in the sky to Mamah when she was small. As the elder children, they'd had their own society, up to the day Jessie died giving birth. After that, when Mamah and Edwin took in Jessie's newborn baby to raise, Mamah and Lizzie became a team. The space below the new house that Frank had envisioned as a built-in garage had become Lizzie's apartment instead.

People shook their heads in puzzlement that Lizzie had not married. They wondered aloud if there was a worm inside that perfect apple, maybe a bitter heart from an early love affair. Mamah knew different.

There had been suitors, all right, but Lizzie preferred her independence. She had acquired a family by happenstance. What need had she of a husband? She liked going off every day to her job as a teacher at the Irving Elementary School. She liked coming home and smoking cigarettes to her heart's content, with no one to apologize to. She did her part—more than her part—in raising little Jessie. After their sister's death, she'd taken on the roles Jessie had played: organizer of holidays, maker of picture albums, rememberer of great-aunts' names, keeper of Borthwick lore.

Lizzie was as grand an auntie to John and Martha and Jessie as any child could hope for. But family life happened upstairs. Without saying a word, she trained all of them to respect her privacy. Her rooms downstairs were sacrosanct—one visited only when invited.

At Christmastime, Mamah loved to enter Lizzie's world. Every square inch of the apartment was covered with ribbons and paper and gift boxes that were wrapped or about to be. She was like that—wildly generous. She had paid for much of Mamah's graduate school out of her meager salary; it was something she was proud of. But she was not the kind of person to loudly demand equal pay, even if she resented that her salary was lower than the male teachers'. She had never been a suffrage marcher, though her heart was in the cause. She guarded her opinions.

No, Lizzie preferred to live unobtrusively, going about her business pleasantly, her delicate antennae cueing her to slip out of a room when talk turned private or uncomfortable. She had lived with Edwin and Mamah nearly all of their married life. It struck Mamah for the first time that other women might have found that trying. But not once had it been a burden. Everybody loved Lizzie, especially the children. Edwin showed her great deference, and she returned it.

She's the one who should have married Edwin, Mamah thought. *Lizzie would have made him a great companion.*

She went inside then and composed a note to Mattie.

Good news. I've decided to stay longer than two weeks. Do you think you can find a boardinghouse for the children and me? If we stay the summer in Boulder, I refuse to burden you with company the whole time. Will you do that for us, dear Mattie? We're all bursting to see you.

Fondly,
Mamah

E dwin stood in a stripe of dusty light on the train platform. Like all the other men, he was dressed in a cool summer suit, but it appeared to Mamah as if he might combust. His scarlet face dripped sweat. His fists clenched and unclenched. He stared past her, down the boarding platform, where porters lifted bags and children up the silver steps of the Rocky Mountain Limited. John leaned against a post a few feet away, eyeing his parents.

"I'm sorry, Ed," Mamah whispered. She held Martha, whose damp head rested on her shoulder. "A few months apart will bring some clarity."

"Why are you doing this to us?" Edwin growled.

Mamah turned her back, but he continued in an angry whisper, talking at the back of her head. "Do you think you're the first woman to fall for that jackass? *For Christ's sake*, come to your senses."

"Please, Ed. I need some time."

"If he shows up out there, so help me God—"

A train whistle blasted. The last passengers were boarding. She pushed Martha into his arms for a hug, watched Edwin's body soften as he kissed her head. He called John and bent down to him.

By the time they reached their seats, the train was moving. The children leaned out the window, waving. With one hand clutching his hat and his other raised in mute farewell, Edwin grew small, then disappeared as they pulled away.

Martha squirmed all over the compartment as the train clattered out of the city, past the stockyards where aproned men dragged on cigarettes outside long buildings. Mamah pointed to a dog lying in the shade of a grocery store awning, a barber pole spinning in the breeze, anything to engage her daughter as the train moved past the outlying suburbs where telephone poles ended and sagging barns buttressed with ricks of straw began, past wooded ravines and hay fields, through the small farm settlements where women stood next to clotheslines of billowing shirts, shading their eyes. When Martha's agitation waned, Mamah sank back in her seat, exhausted.

A half hour out of town, Edwin's stricken wave already haunted her. In the past week, she had punctured her good husband's soul, and the cruelty of it wouldn't go away. She replayed again and again in her mind the moment she had told him. He had nearly fallen over from the blow, the way a soldier might take a cannonball to the belly. He had sunk down on their bed, staring at her in disbelief.

When he began to talk in the following hours, he grilled her, trying to piece it all together. How could such a thing have happened? It didn't make sense to him.

Neither Mamah nor Edwin had slept that night. They'd talked—argued—until midnight, when he stormed over to the liquor shelf, grabbed a bottle, and went out the side door. When she walked into the bedroom around three to get a blanket to sleep on the sofa, she saw the light of his cigar outside, flickering in the dark.

The next morning, they had sat across from each other in the backyard so as to talk in privacy. The children were still at home, though Louise had sniffed a sea change in the house the moment she'd arrived, and was set to take them to the park soon.

Mamah was doing better than he that morning. She'd managed a bath, a fresh shirtwaist, earrings. He was seated in the same garden chair he'd occupied all night, his bearlike shoulders rounded and bent forward, his elbows on his knees. One of his shoes was untied. Stubbed-out Preferidas lay around his chair, ground into leafy pulp.

From time to time he dabbed a handkerchief at his eyes. She had never seen Edwin cry, not once in ten years of marriage, and now he was sobbing intermittently.

"You were in love with me then, I'm sure of it," he said.

Behind him, in the open window of their room, she could see the housekeeper pulling sheets off the bed. Mamah pressed her lips together.

"In college," he said, "I knew I was the clumsy kid, and you were the . . . You were just so beautiful. I'd see you standing on the steps, talking with some other smart girl . . ." He shook his head. "All those years later, when I tracked you down in Port Huron? I really believed it was a new day. I believed I was rescuing you from that backwater town. I wanted to bring you to the city and give you everything you deserved."

Edwin trained his eyes on hers. "Do you remember when we were first married? I'd had a couple of back teeth pulled by the dentist, and I came home and lay down on the couch afterward. I put my head on your lap, and you read to me—an entire book. It was one of the happiest times of my life."

Mamah remained silent. If they were now who they had once been, she might have joked, "You were on morphine." Instead, she breathed evenly, bore it. She owed him this and more.

"I can never remember the name of the book," he went on, "but I remember the story was about a couple who lived on an island, alone. They grew all their own food and built their own house. You said you wanted to do that with me someday." His eyes grew watery again. "I gave you the wrong things, didn't I?" He waved his hand toward the house.

Mamah glanced at her hands in her lap, folded like a penitent's. She unlaced her fingers. "It just happened, Ed. It's not your fault."

From Martha's bedroom window, a shrill giggle echoed against the walls.

Edwin's head was down, across from her knees, as he tied his shoe. The few strands of hair that he always combed back across his tender pate looked absurd now, like strings on a banjo. For a fleeting moment she wanted to put his head in her lap, stroke it. But when he lifted his eyes, he wore a baleful expression.

"You can take them to Colorado with you," he said. "But don't think for a minute you could ever get custody of them."

ROWS OF ILLINOIS CORN fanned out from the horizon like green spokes in a wheel that kept turning. Across acres of farmland west of Chicago, the black earth divided itself from the sky in one flat pencil line.

"On to the Rockies," she said softly.

John held Martha steady as she stood with her nose pressed to the window. He was behaving even more kindly to his sister than usual. Mamah was certain he was aware of the crisis in the house during the past week. At seven, John was the most empathetic, finely tuned creature she had ever known. Even as a baby, he'd been a watcher. Cautious, reserved. When he was six months old, he had sat on her lap, an exclamation of brown curls at the top of his otherwise bald head, and watched. She recalled the time she'd broken her ankle in a fall from a bicycle. John was four at the time. He had come to her room to find her in bed with her foot bandaged and elevated by a pulley. He had stood at the door with a pained look on his face and said simply, "It hurts me."

She reached out and rubbed John's back. "Grandpa was a train man, you know."

"You always say that, " he said. "But what did he do?"

"Well, he wasn't always a train man. First he was an architect, and then a carriage builder." Mamah rallied, injecting cheeriness into her voice. "But when the Chicago and North Western train came through Boone, he took a job with the railroad. He could fix anything, and he got very good at repairing trains. Pretty soon they put him in charge of all the men who repaired North Western trains."

"Is that why you moved away from Iowa?"

"I think so. Papa started working for the railroad around the time I was born. And I was six when we left. Maybe he was in charge of things by then."

"What was Boone like?"

"We lived in an old house in the country. That's where I was born. I remember we had chickens, and I would have to go out and catch one for dinner. I used a long piece of wire that I bent at the end and hooked around the chicken's legs. It was a farm, and we could run free. We caught and skinned copperhead snakes—with my father's help, of course. We weren't afraid of wild things, you see, because we were wild ourselves. My father had a rule: Anything we found, we could raise. One night a mouse had babies—little pink things—and the mother ran off. So we fed them with an eyedropper and tried to keep them, but they ran off, too. My sister was fond of these big, horned tomato caterpillars—oh, they were ugly. But they were her babies. We had a skunk for a while and named her Petunia, but she didn't make a very good pet.

"There seemed to be a big event happening every half hour on that farm. Someone would call 'Come see!' and everyone would run over. Maybe a turtle was laying eggs, or a snake was shedding its skin, or someone had captured the biggest tadpole."

"What else?"

"Well, a day or two before we left Boone, I put a note under a loose floorboard in my bedroom. It said, 'My name is Mamah. I hope you are a girl.' I signed my full name and my age."

"Do you think she found it?"

"Oh, I don't even know if there was a 'she.' But I surely hoped so. I wanted someone to know I had lived there. I was hoping a girl would look out the window at the path through the prairie grass and think, *Maybe Mamah went down that path.* And then perhaps she would follow it and find what I left there."

"What did you leave there?"

"It's a secret."

"No," he groaned.

Mamah laughed. "But I'll tell you. I dragged a piece of old braided rug and a chair out in the field. We left in August, and the prairie was high—over my head. You wouldn't have seen that rug and chair unless you went exploring. But if you did find it, and you sat down, you would discover a private little room there. When the grass got high, it made walls all around."

"Why did you do that?"

"I don't know. Why are children always making hiding places? You tell me."

John pondered it. "Because we like to have secret places that maybe only your best friend knows about."

"Of course," she said. "I had almost forgotten that."

MAMAH COULDN'T RIDE a train without thinking of her father. He had spent forty years keeping the North Western's rolling stock welded together, and moving its thousands of wheel pairs in unison over a vast web of tracks every day, all year round. When he died so suddenly, it took everyone by surprise. The whole company came to his funeral, from the president to the repairmen he oversaw to a half-dozen Pullman porters.

From her earliest years, she had understood that her father was solid and reliable. He had prized those qualities and recognized them in Edwin when he came into the household. Ed and her father had been not just family but good friends. What would Marcus Borthwick think of all this trouble if he were alive?

An image flashed in her mind just then of Lizzie and a bereft Edwin bumping around the empty house on East Avenue. *Will they eat together still?*

When she felt tears coming, she pushed her mind back to where it had been, to the place where she was twelve again, sprung from school and sitting next to a train window, the smell of wheat in her nostrils. A train whistle could make her pulse quicken in those days. It meant strangers with stories, and steak sizzling on heavy white china in the dining car. Now it was enough that the whistle could distract her from the mess she had left behind in Oak Park.

She thought of the Rock Island Line advertisement that had leaped out at her the morning after Mattie's letter had arrived. In the illustration, a young woman reposed thoughtfully, chin in hand, gazing out a train window at mountains and fat white clouds.

Vacation upon the tableland of the continent, the ad had read. *You will earn its cost out of the extra ideas you will gain and the extra vigor you'll feel for the rest of the year.*

Outside, Mamah glimpsed a stand of birches glowing yellow, electrified by the late-afternoon sun. *If anyone ever needed an extra idea,* she thought, *it is I.*

MARTHA WAS RESTLESS STILL, but refused to nap. John produced string from his pocket and indulged her with cat's cradle. When she tired of it, she invented her own amusement. She began by pushing at John until he stood up. He rolled his eyes.

Now Martha was pushing Mamah's legs. "Move, Mama," she insisted. "You move."

"No, I won't move, Martha," Mamah said. "These seats are for all of us."

"You move!" Martha was shrieking now.

Mamah sat stoically as the three-year-old hurled herself at her mother's legs, then rolled around the floor of the compartment in her yellow dress, wailing.

"John," Mamah whispered close to her son's ear. "Just let her be. She'll tire out, and then it will be over."

John smiled, pleased to be the good child.

Martha continued to wail until her small body shook with dry sobs.

"Would you like to come up, Martha?" Mamah asked.

She crawled up onto the seat and put her head in her mother's lap. Mamah closed her burning eyes.

WHEN MARTHA WOKE, Mamah walked the children up to the locomotive, where the engineer pulled the whistle for their benefit. At dinner Martha complained of a stomachache and began crying again. Mamah retreated with her to their car, while John continued playing tic-tac-toe at the dinner table with a boy his size.

In their sleeping compartment, Martha wailed in pain. Mamah searched her memory, trying to remember the last hours at home. Had she moved her bowels before they left? Mamah hadn't paid attention. Only Louise would know, because Martha wasn't saying. Mamah carried her to the toilet compartment. The door latched and unlatched as the train swayed on the tracks. Martha took one look at the dark, smelly hole inside the wooden seat and howled.

What would Louise do?

"It will help you feel better, sweetie," Mamah said, crouching down, securing the door with one foot while she held Martha so she wouldn't fall in, as she feared. She didn't even strain.

"I'll give you a candy. Would you like that?"

Martha only screamed louder, holding on, terrified. When her cries turned to whimpers, Mamah gave up and took her back to bed.

By Nebraska, she felt betrayed by the romantic pull of advertising. She thought of the headline of another ad she'd seen: COLORADO MAKES NEW MEN. When she'd left Chicago, she had entertained a private hope that Colorado had the same effect on women.

The train rocked along, and the children slept through the bleakness of the Great Plains. Mamah had slept that way herself as a child on a train; the bump and clatter and sway of the sleeping car had been rough music to her. Now it kept her awake. Mamah thought about starting over, beginning the trip anew the next morning. She imagined a hearty breakfast for all of them, then fell, finally, into a numbing black sleep.

CHAPTER 10

Off the Rock Island Line at Denver, then onto the Union Pacific to Boulder.

"Are we close to where we are?" Martha asked forlornly as they boarded the train.

"Oh, so close," Mamah said, lifting her up the steps.

She and the children felt pampered in the wide plush seats of the brand-new torpedo-shaped rail car. Martha consented to use the toilet compartment. John opened one of the oval windows and sat smiling with his hair whipping in the wind.

At the Boulder station, a crowd of people milled on the platform. Mamah wasn't sure she would recognize Alden Brown. She hadn't seen him in seven years—not since his marriage to Mattie. All at once a man in a neat suit, with a little pointed beard, let out a shout like a mule skinner, then smothered them in hugs.

"You're not the only celebrity arriving today," Alden said to her as they pushed through the crowd. He picked Martha up and put her on his shoulders. "The Reverend Billy Sunday should be pulling into town any minute now." He winked. "Shall we stick around?"

Mamah laughed. "Absolutely not."

Outside the station, he piled their luggage into his motorcar. Mamah observed Alden as he drove uphill away from the station. He looked more like a banker than a mining engineer, she thought.

There was a time when Mamah believed Mattie was crazy to marry a younger man who seemed all wrong. Alden Brown was accustomed to living in ten-shack gulleys near his latest mine project rather than a town with paved streets and a post office. Mattie had traveled to Paris and New York; she loved the theater. She'd been thirty-two when she'd married him, old enough to know better. How on earth was she to make a life with such a man?

A few years ago, Mattie had sent Mamah a picture of herself and her new husband in front of their house in Boulder. It was a handsome bungalow, clapboard and shingle, in a line of fine new homes. The photo had put Mamah's fears to rest. Now they were pulling up to that very house on Mapleton Street. A towheaded boy and girl leaped from the porch and raced to the curb.

"Mattie's upstairs," Alden said. "She's on doctor's orders to rest in the afternoons." He unloaded the bags. "Get on up there. She's excited."

Mamah vaulted up the steps and found her friend sitting upright in bed, grinning sheepishly. She rubbed her hands over her belly, then threw them up in the air in a "What can I say?" gesture.

"Mattie," Mamah said when she saw her friend. "You look . . ."

"Like Lucretia after the rape?"

"Well, you *are* beginning to . . . ripen."

Mattie leaned back against her pillows, chagrined.

"Poor Mattie." Mamah's brow wrinkled in sympathy. Then she felt herself snort a little laugh, and in an instant they were both weepy with laughter.

"Don't make me wet this bed," Mattie shouted.

"All right, then, down to business. I've brought medicine." Mamah dug into the bag she carried and brought out a box of chocolates.

"How did you do it?"

"Well, persuading the dining car porter to put it on ice was the easy part. Do you know how many times I almost used that candy as a bribe to keep the peace?"

The door creaked, and Mattie's son, Linden, stuck his head around it.

"Come in, sweetheart," Mattie said.

Linden tiptoed in, followed by his sister Anne, and John and Martha.

Mamah lifted her daughter on her lap. "Meet your namesake, Mattie. Miss Martha Cheney."

Mattie beamed. "How old are you?"

"Three," said Martha. The sides and front of her brown hair were tied up in a white ribbon.

"Well, you're big, then. And you look more like your mother than your mother does, child."

"Nature has settled a score," Mamah said. "I'm raising myself."

"And you, young man, you are the picture of your father."

"I know," John said.

"Then you must despise chocolate."

"No." John's eyes widened. "I love it."

"Ah, so there's a little bit of your mother in you, then." Mattie opened the box, swung her legs out of bed, and stood to pass the box of half-melted chocolates around. When everyone had a piece, Mattie sank into a chair near the bed. "No Jessica this trip?"

"She's with her father's parents for a few weeks."

"Linden, will you show John and Martha where they will be sleeping tonight?"

When the children had raced out of the bedroom, Mamah reached into her bag again and produced a book. "More medicine," she said. "I bought it for the title—*The Hermit and the Wild Woman*. It reminded me of you."

"You were the wild woman, as I recall. Does that make me the hermit?" Mattie took the book in her hands. "Short stories . . . perfect. I have the concentration of a flea."

"I'll read them to you."

"Oh, Mamah. Believe it or not, I can still actually read."

"I came to help."

"I know. And you will, just by being here. I'm not an invalid—we can take walks. But I sleep a lot. You'll need some diversions."

"I thought I might hike in the hills."

"There are a million things to do here. I want you to get out and about. My nanny can handle the children."

WHEN MAMAH OPENED her eyes the next morning, she was relieved to find herself alone in Mattie and Alden's guest room. The room was entirely white—walls, sheets, painted furniture. The only color came through the window that her bed faced, and it was the tan of the jagged Flatirons.

She realized she felt at home among these hills. The rises and falls suited her inner landscape, for better or worse. It was the promise of something just over the crest that appealed to her. So unlike the flat prairies of Illinois and Iowa, where everything as far as the eye could see was pretty much evident in a glance.

One day into her stay, life in Boulder was proving to be as she had hoped. Mattie's girl and boy were closer in age to Martha, but John played with them as if he were three again rather than seven. When Mamah heard Alden's auto pull away, she headed downstairs.

It didn't matter where Mattie lived, Mamah reflected, a boarding room or a fine home. She had a way of placing a fern or hanging her landscapes to create a kind of homeyness Mamah envied.

On the stairway landing, she stopped to study two photos she had missed the day before. They were eerie images that appeared at first to be black-and-white paintings. In one, a bright snow-covered mountain gave off an otherworldly glow, in contrast to the deeply shadowed foreground, where a grazing mule was barely discernible. Mamah carried the photo down to the dining room. "Explain this to me."

"Not even hello?" Mattie was eating toast, her blond hair pulled away from her freckled face. It was always this way with them, effortlessly picking up the thread of a years-long conversation they had never dropped. They saved their real talk for each other, sometimes for years.

I believe I have left Edwin, Mamah wanted to say. *I love another man.* Instead, she said, "Good morning, Mattie. Now tell me what this is."

"It's called 'painting with light.' It's what I used to do when we first moved here. When I lived in New York, I studied photography with a man who used this method. After you print a picture, you paint it with a gummy mixture: gum arabic and potassium bichromate. A thick coat of the stuff will make it look grainy, dreamlike. A thin coat will look finer, but unreal still." Mattie sighed. "I love making landscape photographs, but I haven't done any since I had Linden."

"Why not?"

"Too busy, I guess. 'Spoiling my treasures,' as Alden says. Do you think they're spoiled?"

"Your children? Not at all." Mamah held the picture up in the light. "But this. This is wonderful, Mattie. I want to go to this place."

"It's not far from here. I'll take you one of these days."

"You need to find a way to get back to this work. Because you have a gift."

"Thank you."

"It's an admission of total envy. I would love to have some art of my own, something that sails me away."

"Aren't you translating anything?"

"Not lately."

"But you're active in your club."

Mamah rolled her eyes. "Making origami decorations for Valentine's Day."

"Now, stop. Last time you wrote, you were preparing a reading. *Taming of the Shrew?*"

"Yes, for a crowd of women who had lunch on their minds. That's a fine culmination of all those years at the university, isn't it? And let's not forget the paper I delivered last year on Goethe with Catherine Wright."

"Your friend who's married to the architect. Right?"

"That one."

And there it was, the first crumb. Mamah knew that she would keep dropping more crumbs until there was a big pile between them. And then she would probably tell it all, because she had never been able to keep a secret from Mattie. But she had never held a secret so damning. *I might lose the one friendship I cherish most.*

That night she lay alone in the little white bedroom, imagining Mattie's questions. *How did it get to this point?* She explained and reexplained it in her head, but it all sounded wrong.

Because it just did, Mattie. Because some things are inevitable.

CHAPTER 11

"When did it start?"

Mattie was sitting up in her bed. For the past few minutes, she had calmly questioned Mamah. Did Edwin know? Did Frank's wife know? Except for sprigs of frizzy gold hair escaping from barrettes at the sides of her head, she was the picture of composure.

Mattie didn't shock easily. Lightning had hit her so often that by the time she was ten, she'd grown impervious to surprise. Her mother had died when she was two. Then a brother and sister died, leaving her with one brother, a stepmother, and a father who seemed to shock as little as she did. Mamah had spent a good part of her college career trying to get a rise out of her roommate.

She had no desire to do that now. She paced along one wall of the bedroom, framing and reframing the story. "Our friendship just evolved. He would come over to discuss the plans, and we would end up someplace else entirely, talking about anything. He's passionate about so many things—education, literature, architecture, music. He loves Bach."

"Of course." Mattie's pale eyelashes blinked.

"He was easy to talk to, and he opened up. His father had died a couple of weeks before Frank started building our house. He mentioned the death one day in passing, though he didn't seem upset about it. They weren't close, because his father had left the family when Frank was about six or seven. I think his father's passing made him reflective, though, because he talked a great deal to me after that."

"About . . ."

"About his early years, summers, actually, on his uncle's farm in south-western Wisconsin. How he learned to love the prairie and hills there. How he decided to be an architect. And he talked about his marriage to Catherine. It has been bad for a very long time. They simply grew apart—she's immersed in the children, and he in his work. Well, and so it went. I told him about myself, too."

Mamah continued to pace, reliving aloud the day she had brought out the box some five years earlier. When she looked at Mattie, she saw her wince.

"You seduced him with little German readers?"

"No, no, it was another two years before . . ." Mamah collapsed in the chair and buried her face in the sheets at the edge of the bed. "Oh my Lord, Mattie, what a mess I'm in."

"Whew." Mattie whistled. "You are."

"It was so easy to fall into," Mamah said, shaking her head. "Frank has an immense soul. He's so . . ." She smiled to herself. "He's incredibly gentle. Yet very manly and gallant. Some people think he's a colossal egoist, but he's brilliant, and he hates false modesty. With me, though, he's really very humble. And unpretentious." Mamah searched her friend's impassive features. Nothing. "He's a visionary, Mattie, and he's going to be famous someday for developing a true American architecture. He refuses to put up junk he hates, no matter how rich you are. He chooses clients as much as they choose him."

Mattie raised her eyebrows. "Ah, I see how it works," she said. "He makes you feel as if you're brilliant for hiring him."

"It's not flattery, Mattie. He finds out who you are, the way any good architect does. Your habits and your tastes. He takes you on, and then he teaches you. It's a process. Pretty soon you start to see the world through new eyes."

Mattie looked skeptical.

"I know it all sounds like a lot of nonsense to you, but the truth is, he shows you how much better you can live. How much better you can be. You can't have a conversation with Frank about architecture without it turning toward nature. He says nature is the body of God, and it's the closest we're going to get to the Creator in this life." Mamah's hands were tracing lines in the air. "Some of his houses look more like trees than boxes. He cantilevers the roof so it spreads its eaves wide like sheltering branches. He even cantilevers terraces out from the house in the same way, if you can picture it. His walls are bands of windows and doors, the most gorgeous stained-glass designs of abstract prairie flowers. All that glass gives you the sense that you're living free in nature, rather than cut off from it."

She stood up and paced, her hands still moving. "I wish that you could experience one of his houses. He likes to hide the doorway so you have to find it. He leads you in, then surprises you. He calls it 'the path of discovery.' "

Mamah paused, remembering vividly the first time she and Edwin went to visit his studio. He had met them out front, where an etched stone plaque in the wall announced FRANK LLOYD WRIGHT, ARCHITECT, and storklike stone birds stood guard on either side of a recessed portico. A small door on the right opened into a low dark vestibule, with stucco walls of burnished gold and a stained-glass ceiling that let in dim shots of yellow and green light. Ed's head had barely cleared the glass ceiling. Frank had smiled when Edwin reached up and touched it with his palm.

"Why so low?" Edwin asked.

"Suspense before surprise," Frank said. "It's designed for intimacy. So a person who's, say, five foot seven passes through it comfortably."

"Your height?" Ed asked.

"Designer's prerogative," Frank said with a smile.

When they had walked out of the vestibule into the study at the front of the Wrights' house, Mamah was struck by the abrupt opening up of space and light, the "surprise" he had alluded to. It was when they went into the studio, though, with its walls soaring two stories up and a balcony suspended by iron chains, that she knew they would hire Frank Lloyd Wright to design a house for them.

Mamah found herself looking out the window now. "If you saw one of his houses," she said to Mattie, regaining her thread, "you wouldn't laugh when he talks about the hearth as a sort of altar to the family. It's the heart of the house."

"It's the heart of his *dilemma*," Mattie muttered. "The man's values have flown right out his abstract windows."

"I know how it sounds. And I see the seduction of it, Mattie. If I appreciate Frank Lloyd Wright's work, then I am a person of weight and substance. I'm not entirely stupid. I've seen the women whose pulses beat faster when he walks into a room. He excites men just as much. He has a way of waking up your cells."

"Have you mistaken his work for the man?"

"I'm certain I haven't."

Mattie's voice grew tentative as she fiddled with the tatted edge of the sheet. "How long have you been . . ."

"Intimate?" Mamah looked away. When she looked back, she saw the question in her friend's eyes. "Martha is Edwin's child, Mattie." Mamah felt her face burning.

"I'm sorry, Mame. I don't mean to make it any worse than it is."

THE ROOM WAS COOL when Mamah returned. She carried a bowl of soup.

"It's awkward," Mattie said, "knowing Edwin so well."

"I know. It's terrible. Do you hate me?"

"No, but you terrify me. I guess you always have."

"Why?"

"You seemed reckless to me back in college—forever getting into arguments about suffrage and all. I was too busy looking for a husband to be arguing with any of the prospects. You never seemed to care."

"It's not that I didn't want to marry. I *liked* men."

"Liked them? You were infatuated with someone new every other week."

"Only in college. Not in Port Huron. My prospects had slimmed down quite a bit by then, if you recall. But yes, I loved the attention in college. Didn't you? It felt so good."

"Oh, I was looking for some solid ground in those days. You? You were looking for something else."

"Well, can you blame me now? It's wonderful to feel desired. There's a sense of power in it, really."

Mattie stirred the soup slowly. "Don't you see what's happened? You wanted to be in love again. To feel that feeling where a man you hardly know gazes into your eyes and seems to be the only human being who ever understood the real you."

"I love this man more deeply than I ever dreamed possible. He loves me. His marriage has been dead for years."

Mattie narrowed her eyes. "Have you left Edwin?"

"I don't know."

"Have you moved to Boulder without telling me, my friend? Is that why you wanted me to find you a boardinghouse?"

Mamah shook her head disconsolately. "I don't know. All I know is that I'm here and I need to figure it out. A person can get a divorce after two years of separation. Maybe I could find work."

"What happens if you leave Edwin and this man never leaves his family?"

Mamah leaned back and crossed her arms. "Then I shall be living honestly, at least."

Mattie set down her spoon. "What about the children?"

"That's the part—"

"How many does he have?"

"Six."

Mattie flopped back into her pillow. "Have you started the change?"

"No!"

"Well, you surely are acting like it. Women do crazy things. You've seen those stories in the paper where a woman leaves her family to become a missionary, or shoots her husband in a fit of rage."

"I hadn't considered either."

Mattie fell into a silence.

"People are divorcing more nowadays," Mamah said after a while. "It's not impossible."

"No, it's not. But if you think your choices are limited now, imagine being divorced. And who's to say, if you got your way, you would still love him a year from now? You could end up miserable, *without* your children."

"Some women get their children when they divorce. Edwin is furious right now, but given time . . ."

Mattie swung her legs to the side of the bed and stood up. She put her hands on Mamah's shoulders. "Pull yourself back long enough to look at it. Take some walks. Get involved out here. In a few weeks you're going to be saying to yourself, 'What on earth was I thinking?' "

"But I don't love Edwin."

"What about duty? What about honor?" Mattie shook Mamah's shoulders. "I know you. You wouldn't take down two families, Mame. You couldn't live with yourself."

CHAPTER 12

After a week with the Browns, Mamah moved with the children into a boardinghouse run by the organist at Mattie's church. Their little dormer bedroom in the brick and clapboard house was cramped and had only a sliver of a view of the mountains. She found the place appealing anyway. It was kitty-corner across Pine Street from the Carnegie Library, just three blocks from Mattie's, and a short hike away from the stores on Pearl Street.

Marie Brigham was a widow, a big-boned, plain woman with a web of red veins that slid down the ridge of her nose and spread like rivulets across her cheeks. She was the classic boardinghouse landlady—a survivor. Mrs. Brigham went about her business with a cheerful matter-of-factness, changing bed linens and cooking breakfast as if she'd chosen to, as if it were not the only trade a widow could ply.

Good black coffee could be had every morning by seven, and most days Mamah and the children were at the kitchen table by then.

"It's summer that's the best in Boulder. No question about that." Marie wiped her forehead with her sleeve. "There's the annual trip to Ward over the Switzerland Trail." She winked at John. "The train always stops so you can get out and throw snowballs."

"Can we do that?" he asked.

"You bet," Mamah said.

"The circus will be here in a couple of weeks. There's a summer program over at the school. And Clara Savory's got story hour going on every day in the library. The kids can practically . . ."

Marie didn't finish all her sentences. She reached over the stove burners and lifted an iron pan off a hook, humming a little.

"One thing you got to watch for in Boulder, though," Marie said a minute later. "Tuberculars is everywhere. They come here for the cool air, but they bring the phthisis with 'em. People in Boulder like to pretend it ain't a problem. Bad for business, you know. But I warn my guests." She peeled thick strips of bacon into the pan. "You can catch it on your shoe just walking in their spit."

John, the worrier, bent over to have a look at his soles.

"That's why anybody stays here," Marie said, "has got to leave their shoes on the porch."

Mamah and the children had fallen into line on that policy. She felt relief to be away from Oak Park, even if she was surrounded by sick people. In the mornings they walked the flagstone sidewalks, exploring the town, watching their step. The bright summer light of Colorado really did feel healthful. She thought of the streets at home, where workmen would be pouring oil about now to keep the dust clouds down, as they did every summer. Boulder's blue skies made Chicago seem a coal mine by comparison.

She gave herself until July to clear her head. There were plenty of other things to focus on. John came down with a bad sore throat and cold the third week of their visit. His upper lip was rubbed raw from swiping it with a handkerchief.

"I hope I don't have nose fever," he said. He was lying on his cot next to the bed she and Martha shared. "If you drink too much sarsaparilla when you have nose fever, you can die."

Mamah choked back a laugh. "Where did you hear such a thing?"

"Mrs. Brigham."

She felt his forehead. "You know, people don't always say things quite right. Even grown-ups. There's no such thing as nose fever, sweetheart."

Mamah vowed to get them out and around other children. They needed more friends than Linden and Anne, Mattie's kids. A few days later, she enrolled them in the day camp at Mapleton School for a couple of mornings a week. Then she walked across the street to the library and found Clara Savory in a harried state.

"Could you use a volunteer? Maybe I could work on the card catalog?" Mamah asked.

"I would be eternally grateful," the woman said. "I haven't a moment for Melvil Dewey."

Mamah worked at the library two mornings a week after that, spending an hour or two organizing the library's collection. Sometimes she took over story hour and read to the children to give Clara a break.

In the afternoons, with the children ambling behind her, she headed to Mattie's. Her steps always slowed as she passed a bungalow on Mapleton. It had window boxes full of orange poppies, and she found herself picturing Martha and John lolling on its wide front steps.

"LOOK IN THE PAPER," Mattie said to Mamah one afternoon shortly after they had arrived at her house. She was sitting in a heavy oak and leather chair in the living room. "There's a whole circus schedule in there today."

Martha and John ran off in search of Linden and Anne while Mamah collected the newspaper from the kitchen. She had offered to take all the children to the parade and big-top performance the next day. Everyone was wildly pleased by the plan except Mamah, who hadn't mentioned to anyone that she despised the circus. Well, not the entire circus, just the clowns—all that manufactured merriment. She pitied the elephants, too.

"Mattie, have I mentioned how bad this newspaper is?"

"The *Daily Camera?*"

"Since I got here, they've given a front-page column of every issue to Billy Sunday. And they've got one of his followers actually writing the column. Seriously. They put a little disclaimer up at the top, but it's one of his own people giving Billy all this front-page coverage."

"Oh, I know, it's awful," Mattie agreed. "We're such hayseeds out here."

"Listen to this headline," Mamah said incredulously. " 'The dance is a sexual love-feast!' Now I've got to read the thing. Let's see . . . seems the Reverend Sunday met a woman at one of his revivals in New Jersey. Oh, it gets good here.

" 'She had hair like a raven's wing,' said Reverend Sunday, 'a Grecian nose and great big, brown eyes, oval face and olive complexion, and long tapering fingers—a girl that anyone would turn to look at a second time, the prettiest girl that I ever saw, except my wife.' "

"He calls his wife 'Ma.' Isn't that sweet?" Mattie interjected.

"Ma Sunday's no fool." Mamah laughed. "She travels with him. Makes sure he keeps the old tallywhacker tucked in."

"She must know he has a weakness for tapered fingers."

" 'She loved to do it,' " Mamah read on, injecting a lascivious tone. " 'I found her on her knees crying and I said to her: "What is the matter?" She said, "I love to do these things that you preach against." "You mean adultery?" "Oh, no, no!" "You don't drink whiskey, do you?" "Oh, no!" "What is the matter, then?" "Well," she sighed, and said, "I love to dance." ' "

Mattie laughed helplessly. "You know this isn't going to end well."

Mamah's eyes skimmed down to the bottom of the column. "And sure enough, here it is. Seems she went to a dance, went home with a married fellow whose wife was away, and died in his house because he had spliced together the gas stove's rubber hose with a garden hose."

"Not a very bright fella, I'd say."

"It's all that 'Sinners in the hands of an angry God' business I can't bear," Mamah said. "We laugh, but some people read this newspaper and actually believe it."

"Oh, for Pete's sake. Hand me that paper."

Mamah passed the newspaper over to Mattie.

"Two rolls of White Rose toilet paper cost fifteen cents on sale at Crittenden's. I choose to believe that. Wilson Hardware is having a little puzzle contest just for girls." Mattie turned a page. "Hmmm . . . the program at Chautauqua tonight has your name written all over it. They'll be playing opera songs on the Victrola and showing stereopticon pictures of the singers. Sounds wonderful."

"I don't know."

"Ah, here we are. 'Michigan University alumni will swim and feast at Eldorado Springs Saturday. It will be a joint outing of the Rocky Mountain Association and the Woman's U. of M. Club.' " Mattie put down the paper and looked at Mamah. "There. You have no excuses to mope around."

"I haven't been moping, have I?"

"Well, given the circumstances, you could be worse. What I mean is that you're doing what you've always done, darlin'. You ruminate too much. Just go out and do something new. You can leave the children here anytime."

"All right," Mamah said. "All right."

n July, Edwin's letters began to arrive at the boardinghouse. Written on Wagner Electric stationery, they all said the same thing. *I love you. I forgive you. We can overcome anything.*

Mattie's husband Alden arrived home just after the Fourth with fireworks from San Francisco. He held his own independence celebration on July 6, setting off Roman candles and blazing yellow stars that chirped like orioles in the middle of the street. The children hopped up and down on the lawn, squealing while the neighbors cheered wildly. Mamah realized Alden was something of a romantic figure in Boulder, a "dashing" gold miner, if such a type existed.

During the week he was home, Mamah took dinner with him and Mattie. One night when Mattie trundled off to bed early, Alden offered Mamah wine in the den.

"Just a touch," she said.

Alden talked on, regaling her with stories of the wild characters he'd lived with in Jamestown and other mining camps.

"Colombia!" he shouted after a couple of shots of whiskey. "That's the next frontier."

"You mean South America?"

"I do indeed. That's where a man goes these days if he's in my line of work."

"Have you mentioned that to Mattie?"

"Not yet." He laughed. "She has other things on her mind."

Mamah could tell he was serious, and it dawned on her that their married life was more difficult than it appeared on the surface.

"ALDEN'S VOICE CARRIES when he drinks," Mattie said the next day. "Don't worry. He won't run off to Colombia. He couldn't bear to be away from us that long."

She looked enormous that morning, her belly swollen into a great mound. "I can't even see my feet anymore," she moaned.

"I can see them. They look pregnant."

"They get that way every time I carry a child." Mattie sighed. "Do you remember those Port Huron days? We swore we'd be old-maid teachers before we became housewives."

"We almost managed it. I believe you held out longer than I."

"Not on purpose. When Alden showed some interest, I nearly conked him on the head and hauled him off like a cavewoman."

Mamah laughed. "I think Alden did all right for himself." She thought of her own wedding. "It's sad my mother never lived to see me get myself down the aisle—it was what she wanted most in the world. At the end, she rued the day she sent Lizzie and Jessie and me off to college, because none of us was married when she began failing."

"She probably wanted things settled," Mattie said. "She wanted to know you were all safe. I knew your mother. She was proud of you."

"Oh, at first I think she was proud. She wanted us to have the chances she never had. But to tell you the truth? I think at the back of her mind, she believed that having cultivated daughters would mean better marriages for all of us. Instead, off we went to work. She was disappointed at the end, no question about it." Mamah nodded thoughtfully. "She came to think that education had made us unsuited for marriage. And sometimes I think she was right."

"You've grown a bit dark on the subject."

"Well, in those days I thought the world was on the brink of change. But look at us. It's 1909. I couldn't have imagined back then that we wouldn't have suffrage by now."

"These things take time."

"I'm weary of it," Mamah said. "All the talk revolves around getting the vote. That should go without saying. There's so much more personal freedom to gain beyond that. Yet women are part of the problem. We plan dinner parties and make flowers out of crepe paper. Too many of us make small lives for ourselves."

"Does my life look like that to you?"

Mamah was taken aback by the question. "No, Mattie. You do important work in this town. You know what I mean."

MAMAH DROVE MATTIE down the hill that afternoon to a fruit stand she liked.

"So, how were the hordes at the library today?" Mattie asked.

"Lively."

"Clara Savory is divine, isn't she?"

"She has been, until I let it slip that I have a master's degree. She cooled a bit after that."

"Is she intimidated by you?"

"She hasn't any formal training, you know. I've never mentioned that I ran the library in Port Huron, and naturally, I defer to her. But sometimes I'm able to answer questions she can't, and that makes her uncomfortable. Before I left today, out of the blue, she said to me, 'I work from eight in the morning until ten at night. And for that I get eight dollars a month. Along with living quarters, which is a room in a boardinghouse.' "

"Hmm."

"I haven't spoken a word about my situation. Is it obvious that I'm at loose ends?"

"It doesn't matter what Clara Savory thinks. It's what you're thinking that interests me." Mattie's gaze demanded an answer.

"I suppose I'm trying on Boulder. Seeing if it fits."

"You're serious about leaving Edwin, aren't you?"

"I am. But every time I think about starting a life here, I come up against the hard realities." Mamah found a parking place and turned off the car.

"Let's imagine the very best of circumstances. Let's say Edwin agrees to a divorce and, by some miracle, allows me to have the children most of the time. He agrees to allow us to move a thousand miles away, and he even supports us. I am still a marked woman, even in Boulder. The moment I'm no longer a visiting married woman but a divorcée, even my volunteer work will be in jeopardy. No one wants Hester Prynne running the children's story hour."

"Oh, you exaggerate. Boulder isn't that backward."

Mamah helped Mattie down from the car and held her arm as they walked to the fruit stand. "Or," Mamah continued, "let's say that Edwin allows me to keep the children but supports only them, not me. Now, I must work, since my family money would run out in a year, and that's stretching it. Never mind that I wouldn't be invited to the teas you attend. As a librarian, what would I make? Ten dollars a month at best? I've spent that much on a hat."

They waded into the crowd at the stand.

"First of all," Mattie said, "you would make more money than that. Second, you wouldn't have to be a librarian. And third, you might consider buying cheaper hats." Mattie leaned toward Mamah. "There's something I haven't told you yet," she whispered. "There's a woman who heads the German language and literature department over at the U. of C., Mary Rippon. Been there for years. Word is out that she's retiring." Mattie set down the basket she'd brought. "I was feeling hesitant to tell you, but if you really want to move here, then you should apply for the job. The timing is miraculous, and there's no one better qualified than you. Alden and I know the president of the university." Her words were quick with excitement. "And you're not divorced, not yet. You could say your husband will be joining you later, and after a while, if it doesn't get patched up with Edwin, well, it wouldn't matter anymore. You'd be indispensable by then."

The two women stared at each other under the canvas of the fruit stand. A murmur filled the space as people picked up melons and tomatoes, traded gossip. Beyond Mattie, Boulder spread out and up into the hills, unfolding its possibilities—all the shops and schools and people and rugged geography waiting to be discovered.

"You should get over there immediately, though," Mattie said as they returned to the car. "This is a once-in-a-lifetime chance."

They drove back up the hill, Mattie staring pensively out the side window, until they pulled into her driveway.

"A woman can make her own way here," she said. "It's not easy. There are women all over Boulder who do it every day. Mary Rippon's job may be one of the finer ones, but it's still hard work. She hasn't had much of a personal life.

"For the record, Alden works himself ragged. I don't think men have things any easier than women out here. Everyone works hard. I can't recall the last time I made a crepe-paper flower."

"Oh, Mattie! You know I didn't mean—"

"It's just . . . . Sometimes, Mamah, I think you've lived a privileged life since you married Edwin."

Mamah looked down at her shoes, stung.

Mattie patted her elbow. "Living out here will give anyone perspective."

THE FOLLOWING WEEK Mamah bought a dress and jacket on Pearl Street, something that looked appropriate should she manage to get an interview at the university. Mattie had sent off a letter, and they were waiting to hear something. The August heat was stifling as she walked up the hill toward Mapleton carrying the new dress, eager to show it to Mattie. When she arrived at the house, though, the nanny handed her an envelope embossed with Frank's emblem, a red square, and addressed to her in care of Mrs. Alden Brown. Mamah slipped out onto the porch to read it.

Mamah,

I write with some trepidation, given our last conversation. It counts heavily against me that you haven't written, yet I believe your feelings for me have not disappeared. Words were left unspoken when we last met, and my hope now is to clear up any misunderstandings.

I've been so consumed with untangling myself here that it may appear I haven't taken into full account your situation and the high standards of your own intellect and spirit. The fact is, I never thought of you as "following" me to Europe. It is not my intent to seduce you into "breaking free." All along you've told me that freedom is not something that can be conferred on you by someone else anyway. It is something you have inside of you, a way you choose to be.

You've talked about your longing to find that thing—that gift—which makes your heart sing. If it's writing, as you have suggested in the past, might you find inspiration to begin that work in Europe? Consider joining me for a month or two, not as a follower, but as a fellow truth-seeker on her own spiritual adventure.

My plan is to stay in Berlin for as long as it takes me to complete folio drawings for Wasmuth and to make sure that the printing is acceptable. I'm guessing that will be anywhere from nine months to a year. I am leaving here and traveling sometime in late September or early October. You know how I feel. I proceed now, intent upon squaring my life with myself, divorce or no.

My fondest hope is that you will come. I shall happily wait until your friend has had her baby so that you might join me.

If you decide not to come, I won't judge or conclude that you have chosen against freedom. I hold the deepest respect for you.

Please send me some word. I think of you hour to hour.

Frank

Mamah stroked the heavy paper, smelled it. She carried the letter around the rest of the day tucked in her cotton waist.

His voice was in her ear after that. On Friday she walked to the telegraph office and wired Frank a message.

MATTIE DUE SEPTEMBER 25. MBB

"Soon," Mamah said when John asked her when they would be returning home. The boy was agitated often, bored without playmates now that Mattie's children had begun school. Mamah borrowed textbooks from the Mapleton School and began giving him morning lessons.

The children had changed over the summer, almost by the day. Mamah was grateful for the time with only Martha and John. She had rediscovered the pleasant intimacy of bathing and feeding them, rituals she'd handed over to Louise long ago. Martha's tiny feet, such perfect miniatures of Mamah's own, were no longer baby feet. The skin on her soles had grown thick from playing barefoot outside.

John, who'd looked like Edwin from the start, now walked with a bow-legged gait that reminded Mamah of her father. He had begun to roughhouse, sometimes acting tough. At night, though, he was the same as he'd been since he could talk. He crawled into bed with her and Martha and tugged her sleeve. It was a signal between them; it meant "story." And always the stories began in the same way.

"Once upon a time, there was a boy named John, a horse named Ruben, and a dog named Tootie." The stories had started simply enough when he was three or four. Over time they had become more fantastical, peopled with ship captains, sultans and runaway horses, and they always ended with John saving the day in some way. One night in Boulder, when it was clear that Martha was beginning to understand the stories, Mamah had added, "and a little girl named Martha."

"Noooo," John had wailed. His sister's presence in the imaginary world he shared with his mother was too much for him. After that, she took to telling a separate story for Martha.

Perhaps the children's nerves were as frayed as hers, she thought. Edwin's recent letters demanded to know what she would do about John returning to school, and when she planned to come home. She sat down twice to respond, but wrote nothing. She thought she had decided, but she wasn't entirely certain. A tension had been building for weeks, and now her mind changed from moment to moment. It was as if she, too, were waiting to see what would happen.

A short note from Frank arrived on September 20.

I have found a man who is no worry to me who will take over the studio while I am gone, and finish up what is still on the table. The last few weeks have been a rush to assemble drawings to take to Wasmuth. Marion Mahony will stay on to complete drawings to send to me in Germany. I shall be at the Plaza Hotel in New York by the 23rd. Please send some word. I am prepared to wait for you.

Mattie swung slowly on the porch swing opposite Mamah. Her face was white as cream and deadly serious. "What are you thinking of?" she asked.

Mamah didn't want to agitate her now.

"What?" Mattie persisted.

"Don't you see?" Mamah plunged in. "How can I know if this is what I should do if I don't go? If I don't have time to live over there with him, even briefly? You have a happy marriage. I don't. You played your cards right the first time. I didn't. Does that mean I have to play this hand to the bitter end, full of regret? Knowing I might have had the happiest life imaginable with the one man I love more than any other I have ever known?"

Mattie looked exhausted. "You've made up your mind."

"I have."

A hot gust of wind blew dust around in the yard.

"When will you leave?"

"When I know you are safe."

"How long will you be gone?"

"A couple of months. I'll tell Edwin to come and get the children."

Mattie mopped the sweat off her neck with a handkerchief. "You can leave the children here at the house until Edwin collects them. Alden's mother will be here, as well as the nanny."

"It should only be a couple of days."

Her friend nodded.

"Thank you, Mattie. Thank you."

ON THURSDAY MORNING, September 23, Mattie began having pains. Alden, who had returned home a week earlier, held her hand. Mamah remembered a week of such pains before she bore Martha, but Alden's mother, who came daily to look in on her, declared that there would be a baby that day.

"I cannot wait to be free of this bed," Mattie groused when Alden left the room. "This is the last time I shall ever allow myself to get into this condition."

Mamah sponged her friend and changed her nightgown. Mattie was diffi-cult to move. Mamah was worried by the fact that she was swollen all over. Her skin had been mottled pink with white spots, like a slice of bologna, for the past few weeks. Just the pressure of a thumb on her arm left a bloodless white print.

In the past two weeks, Mamah had prepared for the moment by cutting gauze squares and assembling clean sheets, a douche bag, tubes, a ther-mometer, and a clean nightdress. She had been through it twice herself, at-tended a half-dozen other births, knew the routine. But she had also watched her sister Jessie bleed to death. When Mattie's moans grew louder, the doctor appeared and Mamah retreated to the parlor with Alden to wait. Outside the window, maple leaves shimmered gold in the fall sunlight.

By nine that night, Mattie proved her mother-in-law correct. "You have yourself a girl," the doctor said when he fetched Alden. Mamah stayed down-stairs, relieved, while Alden raced up to see his wife. She rocked in her chair, remembering John's birth, how miraculous she'd found such a commonplace moment. She and Edwin had giggled with joy over the boy's miniature blue-veined hands, his tiny, tiny fingernails.

Martha's birth had been different. With the baby wrapped in a blanket and lying on her belly, Mamah had waited until Edwin left the room before she brought the child up to her breast. This time she had not wanted to share the moment with him. She had counted the baby's fingers and toes, moved her palm over the girl's tiny head, savoring that pleasure alone. He could not have understood what she felt, she'd thought at the time. She didn't.

"ALDEN SAYS 'MARY.' Do you think it's too plain?" Mattie lay nursing her day-old baby.

"Let him have his way. We'll give her her real name." Mamah smiled.

"You two look beautiful lying there. She looks just like you." She felt a pang and busied herself folding little clothes so she wouldn't cry.

Mattie looked up. "Have you told Edwin you're leaving?"

"I'm sending a telegram today."

Mattie's brown eyes moved over Mamah's face. "So it's Monday you'll leave."

"Monday." Mamah took a deep breath. "I'll bring the children over here Sunday. We'll stay in the guest room that night, if it's all right with you."

"Yes."

"I expect Edwin will be here in a couple of days. Are you sure your nanny and Alden's mother can manage?"

"Yes. The children are no problem."

"Forgive me for bringing my troubles into your home, especially now. I never intended to make you complicit in this."

Mattie's gaze was on the baby as she shifted her to her other breast. "There's not a word I can say to you that you have not already thought of, Mamah." She gently teased the baby's mouth with her nipple, trying to get her to take it. "There are ways to hold the thing up in the light and see a hundred facets, and knowing you, you've found a hundred and one." She looked up. "Go. See if you're supposed to live with this man. And if he's as enthralling in a nightshirt in two months as you think he is now, then come back and set it right. Do right by Edwin and the children. Allow a decent amount of time, and do a divorce properly."

Mamah leaned down and kissed the infant's forehead, then put her cheek to Mattie's. "Bless you," she whispered.

On Sunday morning, Mamah followed Mapleton down the hill and over to Water Street. At the Union Depot, she went to the Western Union counter.

"Your husband is coming," the clerk said. Mamah realized the man was addressing her. "On Wednesday," he said, cheerfully handing her Edwin's telegram.

A streak of rage shot through her. It was probably impossible not to read the telegrams that came into the office. Still, the content of people's private correspondence was supposed to be inviolate.

"I need to send another." She took a form on the counter and filled it out. "Frank Lloyd Wright, Plaza Hotel, New York. 'Leave tomorrow. M.B.B.' "

The man picked up the message form and read it. He took a pencil from behind his ear and scratched his head. Then he turned to her, his face puzzled.

She fixed him with a cool gaze. "Is there a question?"

"No, ma'am," he said. He turned back to the telegraph machine.

Her ears burned as she waited to see that the message was sent. The man began tapping out her words in irretrievable dots and dashes.

When he was finished, Mamah walked across the lobby to the railroad agent's window and bought a ticket.

BACK IN MATTIE'S SPARE BEDROOM, she composed a letter to Edwin, then slid it into the desk drawer.

"Papa is coming this week," she told the children as she prepared them for bed.

Martha held up her arms to have the nightgown pulled down over her. "I want to go home," she whined.

"He will be so amazed to see how big you are, Martha. You, too, Johnny." Mamah spoke slowly. "Now, listen carefully. I'm going to leave tomorrow to go on a trip to Europe. You will stay here with the Browns until Papa arrives in a couple of days. I'm going on a small vacation."

John burst into tears. "I thought we were on one."

Mamah's heart sank. "One just for me," she said, struggling to stay calm. "Louise and Papa and Aunt Lizzie will take good care of you while I'm gone. And Grandma is visiting there now. Oh, she's going to be so glad to see you again."

John clung to her, whimpering. She rubbed his back, held him. "This has been hard for you. I know that, sweetheart, being away from Papa and Oak Park for so long. But you'll be back in school with your friends in only a couple of days. And I won't be gone long."

Mamah lay down on the bed and pulled their small curled bodies toward her, listening as John's weeping gave way to a soft snore.

At dawn, numb from lack of sleep, she rose to pack her bags. She stumbled around in the dim morning light, trying to make no sound, discarding some things into the wardrobe while stuffing others hurriedly into the jumbled confusion inside her bag. She reached into the desk, removed the sealed letter, and put it next to Martha's shoes on the bedside table where it would be found. Looking back to be certain the children were still asleep, Mamah slipped out the door.

PART TWO

CHAPTER 15

"What are you doing?" Frank asked when he opened his eyes.

Mamah lay just apart from the warm length of his body. She had tried not to wake him as she propped her head up with one hand and wrote in her diary with the other. "Did you know that you laugh in your sleep?" she asked.

His voice was groggy. "Consider it a bonus."

Sometime during the night, they had untangled their limbs and finally gone to sleep. When she'd awakened and turned to Frank, she had found him as he lay now—in fact, as he had lain every night of the voyage—flat on his back without a pillow, his head tilted slightly back, his right hand resting on his chest as if he had pledged himself to slumber.

It seemed to her one of the most intimate of acts—to sleep with another person. Before they met in New York to embark on the trip, she and Frank had never slept together through the night. She had awakened before he did the first morning on the ship and could not take her eyes off him as his eyelids flickered and his chest moved up and down with each shallow breath. Pale light had chiseled his forehead, nose, and chin into such a still, foreign mask, she had felt a sense of panic. *Do I truly know this man?* It was when a smile flitted across Frank's lips that his face had become familiar again. Just moments ago, he'd actually laughed.

How different we are, Mamah thought. This morning she had found her body at the edge of the bed, turned away from him and curled into a ball of blankets and pillows. She had slipped out of bed, put on a fresh gown, brushed her hair, and retrieved her diary before climbing under the covers again.

He was watching her now. "What are you doing?" he asked again.

She smiled. "Oh, I was just thinking about that wonderful puppet theater you designed last year." The minute the words were out of her mouth, she regretted saying them. The little theater had been made for his youngest son. She put her hand on his shoulder. "I'm sorry."

"It's all right."

"I've been trying to remember the words you wrote on it. Something about the moment right before you wake up."

He lifted his head. " 'To fare on—fusing the self that wakes' . . ."

". . . 'and the self that dreams.' That's it. I love that." She penciled the words, then laid her head down again. The ship rose and fell on the swells, causing their bodies to roll gently back and forth. Under the blankets, with the pink sky glowing through the porthole, Mamah felt safe. She didn't want to stand up, or dress, or hear bells or footfalls, or say good morning to the strollers on the deck.

The two of them had stayed huddled this way every morning of the voyage, unwilling to break the peaceful spell that sleep brought. Around nine o'clock, though, Frank's stomach would grow queasy, and they would repair to the dining room to eat at an out-of-the-way table.

Frank had proceeded delicately with her from the moment they'd embraced in New York. At the beginning, none of it had seemed quite real to Mamah. Now, after six days together, the sense of unreality had settled into a solicitous, sometimes awkward dance between them. Before they departed, she had viewed their trip together as a sort of test. How else could two people truly know each other unless they lived together? But she was discovering that there were some things she didn't want to reveal. She found herself sneaking a bit of color onto her cheeks and lips while he was out of the cabin.

Her beauty rituals were easy to conceal, compared to the mood shifts that washed over her out of the blue. The thought of John, so confused at her leaving, seized her with remorse time and again. It happened while she and Frank were waltzing to Schubert one evening; she felt the wind go out of her, and she put her face into his chest. When she confessed what she was feeling, Frank rose to the moment, comforting her with assuring words. But by the middle of the voyage, he was gently making his claim.

"Look," he said one day, glancing up from his book, "Louise will care for the children. And Edwin knows the truth."

"I know, I know. It's just that sometimes I think we should have—"

"Never mind the shoulds." He put his hand on hers. "Don't squander this time, Mame. How long have we talked about having time alone? Five years? Relax. Please. Be with me."

When they went back to their cabin, she kept her eyes closed during their lovemaking. In those moments, forgetfulness freed her mind, and she felt his joy in truly having her to himself.

Later, they dressed warmly and draped blankets over their shoulders and heads to walk around the deck. Their breath puffed white in front of them while black clouds belched out of the three tall smokestacks overhead. The ship's engine roared, and waves crashing against the bow made conversation difficult.

"I'm not even cold," he shouted.

"What is it?"

"Not cold. Are you?"

"No," she lied.

He saw her rattling inside the blankets. "Open your pores, Mamah!" He laughed.

"I take my freedom warm," she shouted, grabbing his hand and pulling him back inside.

At dinner hour, when they had to talk to other people at their table, she was relieved to have an elegant Frenchman on her left. Frank had the misfortune of being between Mamah and a garrulous woman from Kansas City.

"So you've left the brood at home," she heard the woman say. "George and I took a tour when our girls were nine and ten."

"You don't say," Frank muttered, slicing his steak.

"Oh, it was the best thing we could have done. Isn't that right, George?" The woman slapped her husband's knee. "How many children do you love-birds have?"

"Nine," Frank replied.

"Nine!" The woman reared back in her seat. "My goodness. Your wife certainly has kept her figure."

Mamah turned, red-faced, toward Monsieur—Bonnier, was it?—who was critiquing American movies.

"Madame Wright," he was saying, "why do your newspapers scold about smoking and negligees in your films?" He addressed the whole table then. "For a country that claims to be open and free, you Americans are such Puritans."

"You make a point," Frank said, lifting his glass. "A toast to each of our countries' better parts. To cowboy movies," he said, looking around at his companions, "and French lingerie."

Everyone leaned back and laughed.

"Oh, you're a naughty man," said the woman from Kansas City, giggling. "I can tell a naughty one when I see one." She slapped her husband's knee again. "Isn't that right, George?"

When the orchestra played later in the evening, Frank swept Mamah around the floor in a joyful, careless waltz.

Let go of what people think, he had said to her when they'd first set out from New York. Now, near the end of the crossing, she felt she was beginning to.

That night Mamah dreamed she was flying. She saw herself moving like a bird, arms outstretched, across the sky. A small hinged door in her chest opened up, and dark colored shapes fell through the opening to the snow-covered fields below.

CHAPTER 16

٠ ٠

Mamah and Frank were exhausted by their train ride from Paris. They slowly pushed their way out of the station into Berlin's pallid light. *"Eine Gepäckdroscke bitte,"* Mamah said to the porter, who secured a luggage taxi and squeezed their six bags into it, plus the large portfolio Frank had kept at his side throughout most of the trip. Now, as the car moved along Unter den Linden and passed through the Brandenburg Gate, the driver pointed out their hotel in the distance, standing like a fortress guarding the grand boulevard.

Frank had been vague about their accommodations until the moment they climbed into the taxi. It was then that he announced, "The Hotel Adlon." Mysterious, Frank was. How he loved to gift-wrap a moment. "It's new" was all he would say. She liked it that way—the not knowing, the little surprises.

The Adlon, all 250 rooms of it, was as regal as a Bavarian palace. When they stepped out of the car, they were swept along by porters in gold epaulets who spoke English for their benefit. She felt rumpled after a day of train travel, but Frank escorted her into the lobby as if they were visiting royalty.

Mamah had never witnessed such opulence. While Frank registered, her eyes followed red carpeting up the central marble staircase to the gallery above, where plaster goddesses mounted on medallions smiled down on them. No bells sounded, but a system of lights twinkled at the porters' station. Pages swished quietly past the skirts and luggage of new arrivals. Clutches of men and women sat smoking on green mohair banquettes, chatting in Italian, French, and Russian.

Mamah's eye was caught by an exotic figure sitting across from where she stood. The woman was young and beautiful, with wavy black hair and olive skin. She wore a gown draped with filmy red and yellow scarves, and she was speaking soothing Spanish to a parrot on her shoulder. No one stared at the woman the way people would back home, where she'd have been as freakish as the dog-faced girl at the dime museum on State Street. Here she was just a small figure in a big tapestry.

"The whole place was designed by Herr Adlon," the young porter said as he escorted them to the elevator. "Everything, even the face towels. Even this," he said, touching the soutache swirls on his cuff. "He cares about all the little details."

"A man of character," Frank said.

On the third floor, the porter opened the door to their suite. Mamah walked in first and drew a quick breath at the gilded furniture and floor-to-ceiling Palladian windows.

Frank followed her in and looked around. "Headquarters!" He grinned, his eyes glinting with merriment.

The porter led them through the rooms, demonstrating water faucets and curtain pulls. The bed was massive, with a carved headboard and footboard. At the end of it, the boy set up a suitcase stand.

"Will you open the windows?" Frank asked. The young man obliged. Cold air and traffic sounds drifted into the bedroom.

Frank palmed the porter a tip. Once he was out the door, Frank bent over and held his sides, his eyes tearing up from laughter. "Good Lord, the gold leaf alone."

"It's a little bit much," Mamah said, "but I like it." She went to wash up, and when she returned to the sitting room, she found Frank rearranging the furniture. He had already moved several chairs and a small ormolu table over to the window.

"What are you doing?"

"Making this place habitable."

She watched, amused, as he climbed up on the back of a sofa and took down a large portrait of a full-skirted lady in a white wig.

"*Adieu*, Marie Antoinette. Off with your head." He lugged the painting out into the hallway, where he leaned it against the wall. Two more pictures in carved gold frames followed the first. Frank folded his arms, studying the curtains.

"You wouldn't," she whispered as he walked over and fingered the heavy velvet.

"Oh, I would if I could. It's so damn dark in here. But they're attached too high to take them down."

He climbed up on a brocade fauteuil. Heaving an armful of fabric, he tied each panel so the curtains ended in knots five feet off the floor. "Would you hand me my walking stick, my dear?"

Mamah retrieved it from a corner and passed it up to him. She was laughing now, too.

Frank took the stick, placed it beneath one knot, and lobbed the balled material up onto the boxy top of the valance above the window.

"Bravo!" she shouted.

Frank repeated the stick trick with the other curtain. Still standing on the chair, backlit by sunlight, he eyed the crystal chandelier that hung over the center of the sitting room.

"Don't do it!" She laughed. "You'll kill yourself. *Then* you'll have a spiritual adventure, all right."

Frank climbed down from the chair. "I'm not finished yet," he said. He pulled the heavy sofa away from the wall and moved it over so that it faced the window. They collapsed onto it together and watched the city light up as evening fell.

"Welcome home, Mamah." He put an arm around her. "Such as it is."

IN THE MORNING she lay quietly beside his sleeping body. She loved the soap smell of him; the full lower lip perfectly still; the immaculate fingernails trimmed to crescents. She felt safe with him here, as she had on the boat.

They walked the streets together that first full day in Berlin. They had no map, no agenda. Frank said he preferred to simply bump into things. Yet when they found themselves in front of an art gallery on the Kurfürstendamm, Mamah suspected he had conspired from the start to lead her there. Inside, they found wonderful woodblock prints for sale.

Frank was taken with a picture showing a man on horseback riding through a dense stand of trees. *"Waldritt,"* he murmured, reading the penciled title. "What does that mean?"

"Forest ride," she said. The horseman was lit with a beam of ocher-inked sunlight as he came into a clearing. "This figure is probably a knight seeking the Holy Grail," she said after she'd translated the few lines of text next to the print.

"Well, then, I guess that settles it," Frank said. He wore a sheepish grin as he paid for it.

THE NEXT DAY, he left early for his first meeting with Wasmuth.

"It'll be a full day today," he called to her as he headed out the door. "Go have some fun for yourself."

Mamah suppressed the impulse to get out on the street. She spent time unpacking instead, placing the few garments she'd brought in perfect little piles. She wanted to start things right.

She pulled a plain wool dress from the wardrobe and put on a pair of sensible walking shoes. At noon she went down in the elevator and was seated in the dining room.

"May I recommend the bouillabaisse?" the waiter asked when he came to her table. "You won't find it anywhere else in Berlin."

Mamah hesitated. "Bouillabaisse?"

"A seafood soup our chef invented for the kaiser." The waiter bent down as if to show her something on the menu. "Look over there, madam," he said softly. "Kaiser Wilhelm himself."

A group of military officers talked intently around a table across the room. The most decorated of them was clearly the kaiser, holding forth while the others nodded.

"They say he changes uniforms five or six times a day," the waiter whispered.

While Mamah waited for her soup to arrive, she studied the other diners. Several women—wives of diplomats and businessmen, no doubt—ate alone at the white linen–covered tables scattered along a wall of high windows like those in her suite. The sound of silver clinking on china echoed in the cavernous space. Beneath the Rafael-like ceiling mural, women balanced hats like great fruit baskets on their heads. They brought to mind porcelain figurines, with their cinched waists, their breasts thrust forward by S-shaped corsets, as they raised teacups to their lips.

When her food arrived, the saffron broth of the bouillabaisse tasted delicious. She devoured the mussels and lobster as fast as propriety allowed, smiling between bites at the wonderful strangeness of it all. Dining alone in Berlin, dressed like a Quaker. In the midst of a passionate love affair. Sitting right across from Kaiser Wilhelm himself.

Mamah wished at that moment that Mattie or Lizzie were there. She would take either one of them right now, just to laugh. To throw back their heads and howl at the absurdity of the situation. She hoped someday they would forgive her enough that they could do that—laugh together again, about anything.

CHAPTER 17

November 2, 1909

Frank is tense these mornings. He has much invested in making this trip profitable. He wants to be relaxed, but he can't be. He is most happy doing his work, not nego-tiating. Besides the big monograph of perspective drawings of all the buildings he has designed, Wasmuth will be printing a photo book of Frank's completed work. This Sonderheft is small in scale but many pages long, 110 or more. So Frank is doing two projects, and worried as he tries to get the money together still.

Yesterday I went with him to Wasmuth's office. Huge, and a little awe-inspiring. I had no idea the man had 150 people working for him. Frank feels important when he goes to that office, but I didn't enjoy it. Too much pretense.

The hour just after Frank left each day was the difficult time. Dressing to go out that first week in Berlin, voices—Mattie's, Edwin's—filled her mind, argu-ing with her as she pulled on her stockings. She would rush outside onto the streets, where the words in her head dissolved into German conversations all around her.

Mamah fell in step with other people bustling through the Tiergarten. Once before, she had visited Berlin, on her honeymoon with Edwin. When she arrived this time, she had braced herself for something, some pang. But Berlin was devoid of Edwin's ghost. She could recall little of their honeymoon except that they had ventured out from their hotel in a small radius, always returning for a nap after a couple of hours of museums and dining.

Now, with her little red Baedeker guide in hand, she set out each day to ex-plore a new piece of Berlin. It was a big sprawling city that reminded her of Chicago, for it was teeming with Poles, Hungarians, Russians, Scandinavians, Austrians, Italians, French, and Japanese. She used the Stadtbahn when she had to, but preferred walking, poking through shops and art galleries between the official destinations—the royal palace, the Arsenal, the Reichstag.

She quickly tired of warriors on muscled bronze horses. Mamah didn't know what she was after, but she was hungry for something authentic. Wading into crowds as they shopped, she eavesdropped on the conversations and little dramas of the Berliners around her. She was astonished by the potpourri of languages at every turn. She heard an Italian tossing off English slang to a German butcher, and a Russian in high dudgeon hurling French curses at a German taxi driver.

She would walk until her feet were screaming, then rest in cafés where artists buzzed about Modernism at the tables around her. Or she might fall into a bookstore that could be counted on to appear just around the next corner. There she would rest her feet and read the free newspapers.

It was in such a bookstore that she looked up one afternoon and spotted a small volume with "Goethe" printed on its spine. She stretched to retrieve it, then sank down on a bench. Inside the battered leather cover, the pages were edged in black mildew spots, but the text was visible throughout. *Hymn to Nature*, the title page read. She had studied Goethe in college and pursued his works later, on her own. Yet she was unfamiliar with this piece, which appeared to be a long poem. The date on the cover was 1783.

"Is this an original edition?" Mamah asked when she approached the shopkeeper.

"I don't believe so."

"Will you take three marks?"

The man frowned. "You may have something important there." He took the volume in his hamlike hands and studied it. "Twelve," he said.

She lifted the book again and examined it. Then he did. They parried back and forth. In the end, she handed over ten marks.

WITH THE BOOK wrapped in brown paper and tucked in her bag, Mamah hurried back to the Adlon. The moment Frank walked in, she raced to show him her prize.

"It's very old," she said breathlessly. "Over a hundred years."

"It smells that old." He peeled apart pages that were stuck together.

"I'm quite sure it hasn't been translated into English." She glanced into his eyes. "Don't laugh, but I feel as if I was meant to find it."

"Perhaps you were."

"Let's translate it together," she said. "We could actually bring this into English for the first time."

Frank looked skeptical. "But my entire vocabulary is *nein* and *ja.*"

"That's not true. You know *guten Morgen!*"

"*Ja.*"

"It doesn't matter. I'll tell you the literal words, and we'll figure out together how to say it best. It's more important that you're a good writer in your own language. You happen to be a great writer. And the poem happens to be about nature."

"Is that how it works, translating?"

"Well, it's a little bit of alchemy, I think. It helps enormously to understand the culture you're translating from, and then the one you're taking it into."

"And this is a poem."

"Exactly, which makes it harder. Ideally, you're Dryden, sitting there translating Greek poems into perfect English verse. But that's not going to happen here. We'll go for the soul of it."

"I would love that."

"There's a caveat," she teased. "You have to be humble, because no one ever regards it as yours, of course. The translator is merely the filter." She looked at him over her spectacles. "Can you be a filter?"

"Now you're throwing a wrench into the deal."

"Let's start on it over dinner."

"Mmmm," he said, "can't do it tonight." His voice was playful. "I have something even you would prefer to do."

"What? Tell me right now. What is it?"

"Wasmuth and his wife have two extra tickets for the opera. They've invited us to go with them, then to Kempinski's afterward. We're due at the state opera house in about forty-five minutes."

"*You* are willing to go to the opera?"

"Business." He rolled his eyes.

Mamah whooped, swirling around the room in a little dance. "Which opera?" she called to him as she changed quickly into her dark blue evening dress. She couldn't hear what he said. She positioned a jet-studded band around her neck.

"Stunning," Frank said when she emerged.

Out in the hallway, a bald man in a mink-lapeled greatcoat waited for the elevator. When it arrived, he pulled back the folding gate and bowed slightly as Mamah and Frank stepped in. She could smell the man's cologne and felt him studying them.

What picture do we make? she wondered. *Do we look like a married couple, two parts of one machine? Or can he see the truth?*

In the lobby, heads turned to stare. She knew she looked beautiful. But the Adlon was full of beautiful women. It was Frank people thought they should somehow recognize. He was not a tall man, but he was elegant in his black cape, his gray temples and bearing setting him apart and above the other men. The high-heeled leather boots and broad felt hat looked dashing.

They stepped outside just as a cold drizzle ended. Mamah's skin tingled in the charged evening air of Pariser Platz.

"Which opera did you say?" she asked.

"Boito's *Mefistofele.* Chaliapin is singing the lead."

They walked silently for a block. *What can he be thinking?* she wondered.

"Does Wasmuth know?" she asked.

"About our circumstances? No. We've only talked about business."

Mamah composed her face. *I can manage this,* she thought.

"I won't make any more social commitments for us." Frank sensed her disappointment. "I just thought it would be a chance for you to make some sense of what the man has been telling me. He has a fellow who translates, but I think I'm missing a lot.".

At the Opera House, an attendant led them to their seats at the front of the first balcony. Ernst Wasmuth, a smiling, well-fed fellow with an upturned brown mustache, leaped to his feet and kissed Mamah's hand. He introduced them to his wife, a sober little mouse next to her fat Cheshire cat. Mamah settled in the seat at the end of the row, with Frank next to Wasmuth.

As the house lights began to dim, she glanced back at the audience behind her. The shoulders and necks of the women, dressed in velvet, silk, and feathers, glowed softly white in the dark. Some women waved fans like small wings in front of their breasts. The men leaned forward, their crisp shirts gleaming against black coats.

She hadn't seen *Mefistofele* but knew it was a version of the Faust tale, a story she had seen in opera and play form and translated in college. She had wanted to turn around on the street when Frank told her. It had been a bad idea to come.

When the curtain finally rose, the huge chorus—a hundred people, at least—was already onstage. The white-robed heavenly choir sang "Ave

Signor!"—Hail Thee, Lord! Angels and penitents and small cherubim wearing white feathers on their shoulders, arms, and fingertips crowded the stage, their voices swelling in one resounding "Ave!"

Mamah felt as if she were in a great cathedral, her very soul borne up by the achingly sweet voices of the children.

Then, without warning, Mefistofele strode into their midst. Half draped in a red cape and towering above all the others, Chaliapin was bare-chested and menacing, the muscles in his arms flexing with power.

"Do you know of Faust?" the Mystic Chorus sang.

"The strangest lunatic I've ever known!" Mefistofele thundered. "His thirst for knowledge makes him miserable." The devil threw back his head and laughed contemptuously. "Such a feeble creature! I scarcely have the heart to tempt him."

Mamah translated the first few lines in whispers to Frank. She leaned forward as Mefistofele wagered with God to win the soul of the professor.

"*E sia.*" So be it, sang the Mystic Chorus.

In the middle of a village celebration, bookish old Faust appeared used up, as he did in every version of the story, standing amid the beautiful young revelers. A big-bellied tenor sang Faust's role. And what a Faust! His voice was a thrilling counterpoint to the booming basso profundo of Mefistofele.

Yes, he could be tempted, quite easily. Without much protest. Mamah knew well what would tempt Faust, and the tenor sang it poignantly.

> *If you could offer me*
> *One hour of repose*
> *In which my soul might find peace;*
> *If you could reveal to the darkest recesses of my mind*
> *My true self and the truth of the world.*
> *Were it to come to pass, I would say*
> *To the fleeting moment:*
> *Stay, for thou art beautiful!*
> *Then might I die*
> *And let fearsome hell engulf me.*

Mamah glanced at Frank. His face, so handsome, was lit, like those behind them; his forehead glowed.

"*Arrestati, sei bello.*" Stay. For you are so beautiful.

Mamah began to cry. She dabbed tears from her cheeks and blew her nose.

She knew what was coming. Knew that Faust, made young in his bargain with the devil, would love and seduce a peasant girl, Marguerita, then desert her to go off on another adventure with Mefistofele. She knew Faust would return to find the girl in prison for poisoning her mother with a potion he himself had supplied to Marguerita. Only three drops, he had assured her, will plunge your mother into a deep sleep, so that we can be alone. But her mother dies from the potion. In the absence of her lover, Marguerita goes insane, drowning her baby—Faust's baby.

What on earth made me think I could manage it? Mamah thought. She was angry that she had allowed herself to be drawn into attending. Marguerita's madness chilled her, and the familiar old story line hit her like a blow to the sternum. For the past few days, left alone to ruminate, she'd feared that a kind of madness brewed only a step outside the golden circle she and Frank had drawn around themselves.

And yet . . . and yet. How could she, how could *anyone*, condemn Faust, so desperate for a piece of happiness that he would sell his soul in order to say, *Yes, for a brief moment, I was truly alive.*

Mamah slid down in her seat, trying to stop the tears.

Near the end of the opera, Faust fell in love again, this time with the beautiful Helen of Troy, when Mefistofele transported him back in time to ancient Greece. Mamah dabbed her eyes as the tenor sang *"Ogni mia fibra, E'posseduta dall'amor."* My every fiber is possessed by love.

She placed her hand on Frank's. His eyes were closed, and his head swayed with the music. It wasn't his fault. The program was in Italian and German. What could he know? She was the one who had been obsessed with Goethe, after all.

Frank rested his head for a moment on her shoulder. He was humming, unaware of the emotional wreckage in the seat next to him.

KEMPINKSI'S WAS FULL of operagoers drinking champagne and throwing back oysters. There was euphoria in the room as the people around them talked about Boito and Chaliapin. Brilliant. Magnificent. A night to remember. The ache in Mamah's head began to ease.

Wasmuth's wife appeared emboldened by the success of the evening.

"Your eyes are swollen," she said, taking Mamah's hand. "I was moved, too, my dear." Her voice was uncomfortably intimate. "Would you tell your husband, Mrs. Wright, that my husband considers it a privilege to work with a man of his genius?"

The anger Mamah had felt in the theater surged up inexplicably into her throat. Her temples pounded as she translated.

Frank bowed graciously toward the woman, then leaned back, considering the matter before he spoke. "Tell her a genius is merely the man who sees nature, and has the boldness to follow it."

Mamah turned back to Frau Wasmuth and spoke softly to her. The woman's neck began to redden from the collar up, until her face was nearly the hue of the port in her glass. She stood up and spoke privately with her husband. Wasmuth made a quick apology for his wife.

"Is she ill?" Frank asked.

"Yes," said Wasmuth, calling for the check. "Yes. We must go. I'll see you tomorrow."

"Strange," Frank said when they were gone. "Did I say the wrong thing? I suppose I should have returned the compliment . . . some malarkey."

"No, my love," Mamah said, leaning over to kiss his brow. "It's my fault. I told her I am not Mrs. Wright."

CHAPTER 18

A Hymn to Nature

> *Nature!*
> *We are encompassed and enveloped by her, powerless to emerge*
> *and powerless to penetrate deeper.*

They sat on the sofa facing the window. The little Goethe book lay between them. Mamah moved her finger over the third line of the poem, then wrote quickly on the paper in her lap.

" 'Unbid and unforewarned . . . ' " she read.

"Awfully stiff right off the bat," Frank said, scratching his scalp. "How about 'unbidden and unwarned' . . ."

"Sounds better." She wrote the correction above the line, then translated the next line. " 'Into the gyrations of her dance she lifts us, whirling and swirling us onward, until exhausted from her arms we fall.' "

Frank looked over at the paper she held. " 'Gyrations' is harsh, don't you think? It suggests a dervish, that line. I think this whole idea of our dance with life—it's gentler than that, more like a waltz."

Mamah pensively tapped her mouth with the pencil.

"Don't put lead on those lips," he said.

She wrote some words, crossed others out. "How is this?" she said a minute later. " 'Unbidden and unwarned, she takes us up in the round of her dance and sweeps us along, until, exhausted, we fall from her arms.' "

He pushed a long strand of dark hair behind her ear. "Lovely," he said.

SHE WENT WITH FRANK that morning to the office. Ernst Wasmuth seemed flustered to have her there as a translator now that he knew who—*what*—she was. He had stepped into their personal drama, and he didn't want to be there. Wasmuth was refined, just enough, and solicitous—she was an attractive woman. But he was a businessman first. It was clear that he found it difficult to stand firm, let alone bully, through her. He had with him his associate, Herr Dorn, who evidently had no such compunctions.

They wanted nine thousand marks upon delivery of four thousand copies of the smaller project, the book of photographs. The big folio of Frank's perspective drawings would be printed after that—five hundred copies for U.S. distribution, five hundred for European sales. They went back and forth about page counts, type size, duty costs for shipping.

"We have our hands full," Mamah whispered to Frank when they left Wasmuth's office.

"What do you make of Dorn?"

"I wouldn't trust him entirely. Not yet."

They stopped at the office reception desk, where mail was waiting for Frank. Mamah could see a small pile set out for him on the counter. On top was a postcard with a picture of Unity Temple on it.

"Do you have mail for a Mrs. Cheney, Mamah Cheney?" she asked Wasmuth's receptionist.

The woman was dressed like so many others she had seen on the street—small bow at her neck, tiny eyeglasses. "We had some," she said.

"I need to collect that mail," Mamah said.

The woman looked confused, her eyes traveling from Mamah to Frank. "Oh, my," she said, rifling through the basket. "It may have been sent back."

"I forgot to alert them. It's my fault," Frank said. "I wasn't thinking."

Mamah imagined the look on Edwin's face on receiving a returned letter. She had given him the Markgrafenstrasse address of Wasmuth's office.

The woman walked back to the mailroom, and Frank followed her. Mamah reached down and turned over the postcard depicting Unity Temple that sat on top of Frank's pile.

Oct. 20, 1909

My Dear:

*   The children miss you, as do I. We hope your health is good and your work is going well.*

*   Your loving wife,*
*   Catherine L. Wright*

When she looked up, Frank and the woman were walking toward her. Frank still wore a pained expression.

"I'm sorry, Mrs. Wright," the woman said. "Your friend Mrs. Cheney, she is with you?"

"Yes."

The woman handed her two letters, one from Edwin, one from Lizzie.

"There was a man here just a couple of days ago, asking after a Mrs. Cheney. I told him we had her mail but didn't know who she was. I didn't realize she was traveling with you."

"A man?" Mamah felt her throat constrict. "What did he look like?"

The clerk looked at the wall, recollecting. "He wore a big overcoat and was bald, a little brown hair around here." She pointed to the sides of her head. "He spoke English. An American, I believe." She paused, looking first at Frank, then at Mamah. "He asked after Mr. Wright, too."

Mamah and Frank walked out to the hallway and leaned against the wall.

"Edwin," Frank said.

"It has to be." Mamah stared wide-eyed at him. "He must be in Berlin."

"Jesus," Frank muttered, rubbing his forehead with the heel of his palm. "Look, don't go back to the hotel without me. You're touring, right? Just spend the day as you planned, then come back and meet me here." He nodded in the direction of the reception desk. "I'll figure out meantime if she told him where we're staying." He grasped her hands. "If he's in town, we'll both confront him. I don't want you facing him alone."

"He wouldn't harm me in the slightest, you know that. And you? You know Edwin. He's a gentle man at heart—he wouldn't touch you, I don't think." She shook her head. "He's desperate. Still, I can't believe he's come over here."

"Open it," Frank said, gesturing to the letter in her hand.

At that moment Wasmuth emerged from the waiting room. "Frank, I have the others at the table now. Are you ready?"

"Go," Mamah said. "I shall see you this evening at the hotel, not here." She squeezed his arm. "It will be all right."

With the letters in her bag, she walked to the train station. The Charlottenburg line was crammed full of people, so she stood and held on to a pole. In front of her, an old man nodded, then woke in a jerk, nodded, jerked, over and over during the ride. Mamah glanced around the car and squinted at the people on the streets, looking for Edwin's face.

SHE HAD FOUND the Café des Westens in her Baedeker's the previous day when she'd mapped out her day. It was a café where the intellectuals were said to hold court. She had imagined a leisurely hour of soup, thick bread, overheard conversations borrowed from the tables around her.

At ten in the morning, the café was filled with intense-looking men huddled over coffee cups. Mamah searched the restaurant for some private spot where she might open the letter. Opposite her was a red telephone booth with a comical bust of Kaiser Wilhelm balanced on top. She walked over to a table near it. Except for an eccentric-looking woman wearing a lamb's-wool fez and reading a book, the area was empty.

Mamah ordered a cup of tea, then took out the two letters from her bag, ripping open the flap of Edwin's.

Mamah,

I regret that I cannot speak to you in person. Please afford me the dignity of not showing this letter to him.

How I wish I could see your face! Perhaps it would reveal to me what forces could move you to desert Martha and John in Boulder in such circumstances. This is the part I cannot fathom, Mamah. It is so unlike you that I can only assume you are in great mental distress. More than anger, I feel the deepest worry about you. Frank Wright is a liar to his core, and I fear you can't see he has got your mind under his control. I can't believe you are making choices out of your own will. How else can I explain this to myself?

Martha and John and Jessie believe you are on vacation. Louise, Lizzie, and Mother carry on, but none of them is a substitute. The children miss you. I beg you to return to us. I shall do whatever is required to make us a family again.

I haven't stopped loving you.

Edwin

Mamah sighed deeply. He had mailed the letter from Oak Park on October 23. Today was November . . . what? November 10. Time enough for him to catch a train to New York, then a boat over here. What was he doing? Traipsing from hotel to hotel looking for her? Neither Frank nor she had told anyone where they were staying. Only Wasmuth.

Mamah opened the drawing Edwin had included from Martha. It was a crayoned figure of a woman, waving from a boat.

She studied Lizzie's script on the other envelope. *More bitter medicine.* She let the letter sit unopened, glancing instead at the person across from her. The bohemian-looking woman fingered her beaded necklace as she read. She had one booted foot propped on the rung of a chair in front of her.

Mamah sipped her tea, then opened Lizzie's letter.

> Mamah,
>
> *I write with a heavy heart for many reasons, but especially for the terrible news it falls to me to convey. Mattie has died. Word came from Alden in a letter yesterday. Her heart must have begun to give out just after you left. By the time Edwin got to Boulder, her brother Lincoln had been called from Iowa . . .*

No, she thought. This is a hoax.

She imagined Lizzie and Edwin sitting across from each other at the dining table, talking late into the night. Concocting some wrongheaded scheme—letters to get her to come home. Fueled by desperation or love, no doubt, but this . . . And now Edwin, somewhere in Berlin.

Her head began a palsylike shake. *There wasn't a thing wrong with Mattie.*

The edge of a newspaper clipping protruded from Lizzie's envelope. She pulled it out, read the penciled-in date at the top. October 15. Mamah's eyes flew down the column, taking in phrases.

Mrs. Alden H. Brown

> In the death of Mrs. Alden H. Brown yesterday, Boulder loses one of the finest characters among her public-spirited citizens . . . a resident of Boulder since the spring of 1902 . . . Her unusual character and high mental attainments . . . the most devoted wife and mother . . . Her mind was too large to harbor a mean or selfish thought . . . University of

Michigan . . . taught in the high schools of Port
Huron . . . a shock to the entire community, her apparently excellent health giving no warning of this
sudden ending to a useful career . . . Heart disease
with lung involvement . . . Services at 404 Mapleton . . . Interment in Vinton, Iowa.

A moan rose from Mamah's throat. She put her hands over her face. The
woman with the book stood up and came toward her.

"Is there something I can do to help?" The woman's face was next to hers.

"No, no one can help," Mamah stuttered, weeping. "My friend is dead."

CHAPTER 19

Frank sat on the floor of the hotel room with his legs crossed, making notes to himself on small white cards. Spread out in front of him were two rows of four drawings each that he had just received from Marion Mahony. He looked up when he noticed that she was standing next to him.

"Going out?"

"Yes, for a bit."

"Good," he said, standing up. "Good."

"Shall I bring you anything?"

"No. I'll be taking these in to Wasmuth later. I'll get a bite while I'm out." He stood and hugged the wool coat with her inside it. "How are we today?"

"We're putting one foot in front of the other." She managed a wan smile.

He rested his thumb sideways between her brows, then gently stroked the furrows there. "I wish you would talk about it."

She shrugged sadly.

He lifted the brown shawl from her shoulders and wrapped it around her neck. "It's cold out there."

She walked through Pariser Platz onto Unter den Linden. Under the lime trees. The street name seemed a grim joke to Mamah as she walked east alongside the boulevard's naked trees into an angled sheet of freezing rain. She hurried past the aquarium, averting her puffy face when she locked eyes with a haughty woman under an umbrella in front of the Grand Hotel de Rome. When Mamah spotted the copper dome of St. Hedwig's Church, she felt something ease within her. Inside, old women in heavy black shawls fingered rosaries. In the near-darkness, Mamah found the smell she had hoped for, the scent of candle wax burning itself to nothingness in votive cups.

Mamah had wanted to sit alone with Mattie for three days now, ever since the woman from the café had put her into a taxi. Thankfully, Frank had been at the hotel to receive her, to try to comfort her. He would have gladly listened for hours, but he hadn't known Mattie. How could he comprehend it? To spill too much of her sadness to him would be unfair, anyway. The hotel room reeked of worry already. The project was moving too slowly. Letters from Catherine and his mother kept arriving at Wasmuth's. And then there was the specter of Edwin, who might at any moment knock on the door to create God knows what kind of scene. That is, if he was even *in* Berlin.

Their sojourn so far was surely not the spiritual adventure Frank had conjured up six months ago. Nor was it what Mamah had imagined. When she boarded the train to New York, she had expected to feel relief that the thing she had so longed for and worried over had finally *begun,* that at last she was moving out of a tunnel of indecision into the light.

At the moment, though, nothing was clear except that she wanted a few hours in a silent space of her own. Frank was working at a makeshift drafting table in front of the big window. When he was in the room, he was very present.

Mamah needed to say goodbye to Mattie, to somehow *believe* goodbye. But there was no still body to touch. Mattie's cheeks had not been pink when Mamah had left her. But they had not been sallow, either.

For the past three days, Mamah had tried to piece together what might have happened. *Heart disease with lung involvement.* What did that mean? The newspapers never said, *Another woman bled to death giving birth yesterday.* Mattie had been weak after the birth, but women often are. Had she somehow failed to see that Mattie was losing ground? Had Mamah been too wrapped up in herself to look closely?

For the hundredth time, she berated herself. *Had I been there, I would have gone to Denver for a better doctor. I could have saved her.*

It was no use now. No use. She needed to think of Mattie, whole and clean, without her own sickening guilt coating every memory with a gritty film. She wanted to somehow honor Mattie's life, if only in her own mind.

Burrowed deep in wool midday in an empty cathedral, Mamah cried and laughed into her scarf. *Well, Mattie, your hair was a mess, I can admit that now.* Mamah recalled how her friend would drag a brush through her thick mop as she tried to twist it into something stylish. "Why is it," she had moaned once, "that when I walk into a room, somebody always has to say, 'Oh, is it windy outside?' "

Mamah remembered the summer just after their graduation from the university. They'd both landed teaching jobs in Port Huron and had moved their belongings to the boardinghouse there. On a whim, they'd gone to a meeting of the local suffrage association that June, hoping to meet new friends. There was a woman passing out flyers when they arrived. Come to Colorado and help us pass the Women's Suffrage Bill—that was the gist of it. Mamah remembered a phrase from the flyer: *The harvest is white, but the reapers are few.* By the end of the evening, they had signed up for a converting campaign. It was the possibility of hearing their heroes speak that had drawn them in— the likes of Elizabeth Cady Stanton, Carrie Chapman Catt, even Frederick Douglass was scheduled to give a talk. The prospect of high adventure after a month of final exams held considerable appeal as well. Within a couple of weeks, they were going house to house in Denver, passing out pamphlets.

Organizers had put them up at the apartment of a volunteer. She was a thirty-six-year-old widow named Aldine who worked as a factory seamstress to support her three children. The first night there, Mattie and Mamah had stood around a table—there were no chairs—and eaten stale bread with watered-down coffee. They'd walked the poorest areas of town the next day and the days after, knocking on the doors of shacks, handing out pamphlets. At even the worst hovels, they were greeted by people who mostly favored enfranchisement.

But one afternoon, while leafleting on a street with taverns along either side, they were confronted by an angry tavern owner. He had come rushing out of his bar, waving a white towel to shoo them away. "Git!" he screamed at them. Mamah and Mattie had stopped in their tracks, stunned. It now occurred to Mamah that neither of them had ever been told to "git" before. The man's yelling got louder. "We don't need outsiders rilin' people up." Men from across the street came over to have a laugh. Mamah and Mattie soon found themselves surrounded by a circle of hostile men.

"Where you ladies from?" one of the better-dressed men asked. All of them smelled of beer and sweat.

Mamah lifted her chin defiantly. "Michigan."

"You sure traveled a long way." A drunk man spat a wad of tobacco on the ground not far from Mamah's shoes.

"Seems like the ones that make the most ruckus is the ones got no man to keep 'em at home," the first man said, raising his eyebrows, "and happy." The men burst into hoots.

"Sir," Mamah began, but the man pressed on, aiming his finger at her nose.

"And don't tell me about 'taxation without representation,' lady. There's only but one woman for every one hundred who pays taxes."

"Sir," Mamah said, "you are arguing for my cause rather than your own. That is a sign of how few women can find decent employment."

"Pshaw," the man said, waving her off.

Up to that moment Mattie had stood frozen at the center of the group. Prim as a minister's wife in her white gloves and little straw hat, she slowly turned in a circle to look into their eyes. "Gentlemen, you are hardworking men, I can tell." She was twenty-one, and her voice was high-pitched and sweet. "With wives and children you love, I'm sure of it. Is there a man among you who has thought what might be your family's lot if you should die? Do you want your wives to be powerless, to be classed together politically with idiots, and criminals, and the insane? Do you want your wife to work for less money than a man can earn, when she has the mouths of your babies to feed? Look at that child over there." She nodded in the direction of a boy who appeared to be about eight, mopping out a barroom floor across the street. They all turned to look at him. "Do you want your children to be forced out to work at a tender age, like that child?"

The men grumbled and dispersed then, leaving Mamah staring slack-jawed at her gentle friend.

You never lied, Mattie. You spoke from your heart.

Mamah had been nearly mute since she'd read Lizzie's letter. For three days she had played and replayed in her mind what might have happened inside that house on Mapleton. She imagined John and Martha, aware of trouble, scared to death probably, waiting in a sick house for their father to come and take them home. She prayed that the nanny had had the sense to keep the children playing outside. Still, what had they seen or heard?

She pictured Mattie laid out in the parlor where troops of neighbors could examine her pale freckled hands, resting like spotted lilies on her chest. There were probably mourning cakes on the long dining room table, and crepe draped over the mirrors. Alden's mother would have done things the old way. Never mind that Mattie despised funerals.

She could imagine Alden, grief-stricken and confused, suffering the hordes who shook his hand and said, "She's in a better place now."

That's a lie the living tell one another, isn't it, Mattie? What better place could there be for you than in your own living, breathing skin?

There had been no sign of a weak heart. Mattie had the strongest constitution and the greatest will to live of any woman Mamah knew. When

Mamah had kissed her goodbye, Mattie's freckled face was creased with joy, her frizzy blond hair a wild halo. She had been nursing the baby, smiling ear to ear.

Last night Mamah had tossed fitfully, troubled by her dreams. She saw a woman's body in a clean nightdress, laid out as if she were sleeping. Mamah saw herself sit down on the bed and put out a hand to touch her friend's arm. Or was it her sister's? She woke up when she felt the coldness.

She remembered the hour just after Jessie's passing, when she'd gone in to sit next to her sister one last time. The smells of bleach and candle wax had wafted uneasily in the bedroom air. Mamah already knew by then what death looked like. She had seen the lifeless body of her mother. She had touched it, as she touched her sister's body, and she knew Mattie's body would have been the same. When Jessie died, it felt as if her soul just whooshed away. And what was left behind was some empty useless thing, no more sacred a vessel than an old suitcase.

What had stunned Mamah about Jessie's death was how quickly, how utterly, the flesh made that transition from life force to breathless rag. What it had carried inside of it before, that brew of tenderness, wit, fierce loyalty, intelligence—the essence of Jessie—had simply vaporized.

Mamah knew how loss worked. She would ache and grieve for Mattie, as she had for Jessie, and then wake up one morning feeling all right. She would pick up life where she left off. In a year the precious friend she'd mourned so deeply would have disappeared from her everyday thoughts. In two years, without a photo in front of her, she would have a hard time picturing Mattie's nose or mouth. Of all the cruel truths death had to teach, that seemed to her the cruelest one of all.

Mamah stood up and hurried out of the church.

SHE AND FRANK WALKED along Unter den Linden late that afternoon. The rain had stopped. She felt a rush of longing when she noticed a pair of boys about John's age feigning a boxing match outside an apothecary. She stopped to watch them playfully cuff each other, then pose boldly, like skinny little Jack Johnsons.

"The world keeps going," she said as they continued walking. "Everybody who ever lost someone thinks that. It's strange, though. It still comes as a surprise when you see people carrying on."

Frank held her elbow, navigating her along the sidewalk as they stopped in front of one display window or another.

"I remember just after Jessie's death," Mamah said. "I was at a church picnic, and there was a potato-sack race going on. I looked around at all these people hopping crazily along, each with one leg in a potato sack. They were laughing, but they were also quite serious about winning that race. And I remember thinking, *Don't these people know they're going to die?*"

His eyes fixed on hers. "What would she have you do?"

"Mattie?"

"Yes."

"She would have me go home this minute." Mamah looked away, out into the street. "I know that's not the answer you were looking for."

He took her in his arms to comfort her. They were standing in front of the window of a milliner's shop, J. Bister, where colorful scarves were splayed below the hats on stands.

"Come in here for a minute," he said.

He had the salesclerk pull a red scarf out of the window. Frank draped it over her shoulders.

"It looks Spanish," she said, "like the shawls the parrot woman wears." She lifted the price tag, then shook her head. "Too expensive."

"You look beautiful," he said, "and you happen to need it." He handed over twenty-five marks to the shopkeeper. "Now, wear it, won't you, Mamah? For me."

CHAPTER 20

"How long do you think it would take you to pack?"

The question came out of the blue. Frank had been agitated since he'd walked into the hotel room, pacing around in his coat as if he had come back to retrieve something.

When she looked up from her book, she was startled to find his feverish-looking eyes on her, waiting for an answer.

"Now?"

Frank sighed. "It wasn't Edwin looking for us at Wasmuth's office."

"What do you mean?"

"The letter I had from my mother? The day you got news of Mattie? I couldn't tell you then." He stood over her, his fists pushed down hard into his coat pockets. "There's been a reporter snooping around in Oak Park, asking questions. Looking for gossip. I think the *Tribune* put their Berlin reporter on to us. I think that's who was at Wasmuth's asking about you and me."

"Did they tell him where we're staying?"

"The receptionist over there said she didn't give him anything. But I don't believe her. Someone else told me the guy was back again yesterday."

Panic began to expand like a balloon in her chest.

"We've got to leave here. We need to find someplace else. Immediately."

She rose, pulled on her shoes. "I noticed a couple of little places in Wilmersdorf." She could make her voice calm when she was afraid and she did it now. "I'll take the trolley. I'm sure I can find something."

"It won't amount to a hill of beans, because Catherine won't talk."

"They were at your house?"

"And my mother's."

WHEN SHE RETURNED, Frank was already packed. He helped her throw her things into her traveling bags. While he checked out, she walked toward the banquette in the bar, where a group of dandyish young men was drinking and laughing. Mamah slid into a chair near a clutch of other women so as not to be noticed. Two of the men were in high spirits. One of them she recognized as the man in the mink-lapeled coat whom she had seen on the elevator a couple of times. Another man at the end of the banquette dragged on a cigarette, then leaned his head back and made smoke rings for the amusement of the others. She noticed that his shoes were cheap and flashy. Reporters, she thought.

"There's no forwarding address," Frank said loudly over at the reception desk. "We're headed to Japan."

In the taxi, Frank's rage grew. "I'm putting Wasmuth on notice." He craned his neck. "Driver," he said suddenly, "Thirty-five Markgrafen Strasse." He talked intensely to himself. "If he wants this deal to go through, he will tell his employees to keep their mouths shut."

Mamah waited in the taxi while Frank went into Wasmuth's office. When he emerged, he carried two large portfolios and a stack of mail.

"What happened?" she asked. Frank had been inside the building fifteen minutes, at least. "Did you see Wasmuth?"

"No," he said. "He wasn't there."

SHE HAD CHOSEN a residential hotel in a western suburb of the city that rented rooms by the night. It was the least likely place they would be found, she thought. They hauled their bags to the second floor.

"I can't work in these conditions," he said, straining to get the last bag up from the landing. In the room, he thudded into a chair next to a table. "What do I have? A few months to perform a miracle, and already I've lost most of a month."

"It's just temporary. I'll find something better in the morning." It was her brave voice speaking.

He pulled a letter from his mother out of his pocket and slit it open with a fingernail. "What made me think I could escape it?"

Mamah lay down on the bed, still dressed in her coat, and stretched out her arms and legs. In a few minutes she would get up and she would be strong. She could calm him because she had done it before, even when she was afraid. Her muscles ached from lifting the bags. She was bone-weary and knew why: It was the tension that had dogged them from the beginning of the journey.

The sound of shattering plaster caused her to fly up from the mattress.

"Goddammit!" Frank was shouting.

She looked over to see a gaping hole in the wall where his foot had kicked all the way through to furring strips between the studs. Mamah leaped off the bed, confused, to see him sink back down into the chair and put his face in his hands. Her eyes went from his bent head to a letter and clippings on the table.

She stepped tentatively over to look, the words *Chicago Sunday Tribune* becoming visible as she approached. It was from the front page of the November 7 issue.

LEAVE FAMILIES; ELOPE TO EUROPE

ARCHITECT FRANK LLOYD WRIGHT
AND MRS. EDWIN CHENEY
OF OAK PARK STARTLE FRIENDS.

ABANDONED WIFE LOYAL.

SPOUSE VICTIM OF A VAMPIRE, SHE SAYS,
AND WILL RETURN WHEN HE CAN;
OTHER'S HUSBAND SILENT.

Mamah put her hand to her mouth as she read the first paragraph.

A wife pledging faith in a husband gone with another woman . . . two abandoned homes where children play at the hearthsides, and a fly-by-night journey through Germany—these are features which make an affinity tangle of a character unparalleled even in the checkered history of soul mating.

What she saw next caused her to cry out. In the upper-right corner of page seven of the November 9 paper, her own face filled nearly a quarter of the page. Above it, a headline read, WIFE WHO RAN AWAY WITH ARCHITECT. The photograph was the portrait she'd had made for her marriage announcement. It was labeled MRS. E. H. CHENEY.

She pressed her lips together, but the cries kept pushing up from her chest and into her throat, like the screams of an injured animal.

CHAPTER 21

"I can never go back now." Mamah's face was bloated from crying.

"You can and you will. This thing will blow over."

"No," she said, "I'm dead."

"You're not making sense."

Frank left the suite then, and when he returned, he brought soup and a bottle of wine from a restaurant on the block. Mamah didn't eat. Instead, she stared out the window at the leafless trees and drank the wine. After some time, he helped her up and put her to bed. When he left the room, she went to her suitcase and pulled out a bottle of cough syrup. She drank some, then put it beneath the mattress.

Frank was gone when she woke the next day. Mamah got up and stood at the door to the hotel room, listening for his footsteps. Then she went to the table and read the clippings again.

MRS. WRIGHT'S FAITH UNSHAKEN.

"My heart is with him now," Mrs. Wright said to a reporter for the *Tribune* yesterday. "He will come back as soon as he can. I have a faith in Frank Wright that passeth understanding, perhaps, but I know him as no one else knows him. In this instance he is as innocent of real wrongdoing as I am. . . .

"It appears like any ordinary mundane affair, with the trappings of what is low and vulgar. But there is nothing of that sort about Frank Wright. He is hon-

est and sincere. I know him. I tell you I know him. I
have fought side by side with him. My heart is with
him now. I feel certain that he will come back.
When, I don't know. It will be when he has reached
a certain decision with himself."

Mamah could almost see Catherine standing at the door, her golden-red
hair twisted in a Gibson Girl chignon. She was a handsome, dignified-looking
woman.

"The world cannot possibly understand all that is
involved in this affair. Is it not enough to know that I
shall take no action for divorce, that I shall make no
appeal whatever to the courts, that I stand by my
husband right at this moment? I am his wife. He
loves his children tenderly now and has the greatest
anxiety for their welfare. He will come back to them
and live down the publicity to conquer in the end.
They can heap everything they wish to on me and I
will bear it willingly and my place will remain here
in his home."

Frank had been wrong about Catherine. She had talked after all. Mamah
imagined the reporter telling her, "This is your chance to tell your side of it."
Reading down the column, Mamah's eyes found Catherine's pain again and
again.

"His whole life has been a struggle. When he came
here as a young architect he had to fight against
every existing idea in architecture. He did fight, year
after year, against obstacles that would have downed
an ordinary man. . . . He has fought the most
tremendous battles. He is fighting one now and I
know he will win. I have fought it beside him and the
struggle has made me. Whatever I am as a woman,
aside from my good birth, I owe to the example of my
husband. . . . There should not be the same moral
gateway for all of us."

Mamah retrieved the cough syrup and swigged from the bottle. Her eyes fell on the small headline she had seen the night before that caused her to fall back against the pillows.

"SIMPLY A CASE OF A VAMPIRE."

"We have six children. The oldest boy is 19 and he is home from college now. They worship their father and love their mother. If I only could protect them now I would care for nothing else. With regard to Mrs. Cheney, I have nothing to say. I have striven to put her out of my thoughts in connection with the situation. It is simply a force against which we have had to contend. I have never felt that I breathed the same air with her. It was simply a case of a vampire—you have heard of such things."

Mamah climbed into bed. She felt a shame more sickening than anything she had ever known or imagined.

Catherine. Edwin. Lizzie. What horrors had they been subjected to? She imagined Edwin's humiliation at being portrayed as a cuckold. And Lizzie, who had spent most of her life trying not to be noticed, what hell had been visited upon her? One headline had said, simply, MRS. CHENEY'S SISTER IN CHARGE.

It was John she thought of most. Martha wouldn't understand what was going on, but John would know something was terribly amiss; he would be suffering now.

The hands of a small clock on the side table approached the nine o'clock hour. She counted the clock's ticks, waiting for the medicine to dull the terrible ache in her chest. And she thanked God that her parents were dead, especially her mother.

Mamah thought of the day she had bought the cough syrup. Sitting in St. Hedwig's Church, she had picked up a pamphlet on the pew and read about the church's namesake. The saint had worn a hair shirt and slept on the floor, the usual sorts of mortifications. But Hedwig had her own specialties. She surrounded herself with beggars when she traveled—thirteen of them, always thirteen—whose sole purpose was to have their feet washed by her at the end of the day. Good luck for Hedwig was coming upon a leper who allowed her to kiss his ulcers.

A madwoman, Mamah had thought at the time. Now she would welcome the chance to kiss a leper's sores if it meant she could undo the headlines.

Mamah lifted the clipping with her picture in it.

CHENEY CHAMPION OF
RUNAWAY WIFE

OAK PARK MAN HAS NO BLAME
FOR WOMAN WHO ELOPED
WITH FRANK L. WRIGHT.

CABLES MAY HALT THEM.

FRIENDS HOPE TO INTERCEPT
"SOUL MATES" BEFORE THEY GET
ON WAY TO JAPAN.

A new phase of the Wright-Cheney "spiritual hegira" developed yesterday when the husband . . .

They had bushwhacked Edwin at Wagner Electric.

"Mrs. Cheney has been getting the worst end of this deal right along, and it is not fair," he said. "Those of her friends who understand the situation know that she should not be blamed in the way she has been. . . . We would all be grateful if the matter were allowed to drop now. With reference to divorce proceedings or any course I may see fit to pursue in the future I have nothing to say."

Edwin, she thought. *Loyal Edwin.*

Friends said Mr. Cheney for more than a year had suspected Wright, but that family relations had been such that an out-and-out breach would occasion gossip and for that reason he held his peace. Mrs. Cheney has been known to her friends as of a highly temperamental disposition, capricious, and sentimental to a degree. She was a graduate of Ann Arbor and had strong literary inclinations. Mrs. Cheney's sister, who teaches school, lives with them. There is a nursery governess for the two children. Mrs. Cheney is said to have spent little time with them.

Mamah lay flat on the bed. *Mrs. Cheney is said to have spent little time with them.*

Floating pictures of Martha passed across her closed eyes. She saw her at nine months old, with fat tiny feet. She was climbing up Mamah's body as if it were a mountain. She planted a foot on her mother's hip, then pushed herself upward, clutching Mamah's nightgown as she ascended. Up she came, crawling over her belly, then scaling her breasts until she was face-to-face with her mother. The startling blue eyes. Laughs and merriment. The smell of talcum.

A squeaking door hinge roused her.

"You can't hide in there forever." Frank was standing beside the bed. He looked vibrant, almost in good humor.

"Someone has been watching us."

"The Medusa speaks." Frank set down the food he had brought, another bowl of soup. "Eat this. We'll talk when it's down your gullet."

Mamah tipped the bowl and drank the broth. "Everything is lost." Her own voice was dull and faraway.

"You're slurring your words. Just eat." Frank took the empty cough-syrup bottle and tossed it into a wastebasket. "This will pass, Mamah. In a few weeks you can return quietly, if you want, and the thing will have blown over. Those articles were already ten days old by the time they got here."

"What are we going to do?"

"We are going to live our lives. We may have to leave Berlin, but I'm going to finish the portfolio." His composure was stunning. "Do you think I'll hand over my hide so easily?"

Tears began again.

"No more crying. Come on, up you go." He put his hands under her arms and pulled her limp body to the edge of the bed, then helped her walk to the bathroom. "Will you be all right?"

She nodded. He slipped out the door and closed it softly.

Mamah gripped the sink and glimpsed herself in the mirror. *I look insane,* she thought.

She sat on the side of the bathtub, turned on the water, and watched it run and run. When the tub nearly overflowed, she put her arm in to drain out some water, and the skin came up pink. She took off her gown and stepped in, grateful for the burn. Sliding down low into the tub, she let the water fill her open mouth and lap into her nostrils.

Breathe in.

The door opened at that moment, and Frank appeared like a specter in the steam, holding a towel and a clean gown.

"Come on, sweetheart." He lifted her out of the tub. "We're going to make you well."

IN THE MORNING, she rose while he slept, went to the table, and picked up a clipping. To read it would be to peel back another layer of her heart, yet she couldn't stop herself. This article quoted a sermon that was delivered the day after the first headline appeared.

PASTOR REBUKES AFFINITY FOOLS

"Affinity fools" was discussed by the Rev. Frederick E. Hoskins last night in Pilgrim Congregational Church. He spoke about the woman who becomes weary of the hardworking husband and tires of her home life.

Mamah actually remembered Hoskins from her one visit to Pilgrim Church. He had seemed to her a pompous Billy Sunday type who fancied himself amusing but was really a pinched, angry man. Yet the people around her had seemed genuinely moved by him.

"She tries to make herself think she understands a
lot of gab from the platform of her club about the
larger, the fuller life, and her 'sphere.' Along happens a knave. Together they begin to think and talk
about how they understand each other. They look
a long time at each other in silence and breathe
deep, like an old sitting hen. What wonderful things
they discover together, and how different the world
looks through each other's eyes. Thus they proceed
through weeks and months of slush, until one day
there is a splash, and both have tumbled into the
same old hog pen, where thousands have tumbled
before them."

Mamah moaned. No question. It was about her.

When Frank found her holding the article, he ripped it from her hand and
crumpled it. "Mamah," he said. "Please don't do this to yourself." He pressed
his fingers into her shoulders. "Please."

"Don't you see how hopeless this is?"

"You can't buckle!" He stomped away, his arms waving. It was the first
time he had ever directed a shout at her. She felt cowed. "I *need* you now. This
is when you show who you are."

She stared at him, shaken by his anger. "It's the children," she said.
"They'll take them away."

"You don't lose your children because some idiot writes an article in the
newspaper or some preacher talks about affinities. Can one week negate who
you have been to your children for the whole of their lives? How odd for me to
be the one saying these things to you. *You.* Have you forgotten the very things
you've said to me? You can't keep your children by having no life of your own.
You said that once to me. You said, 'They will know. Your own unhappiness
will plant the seeds of unhappiness in your children. And they will blame you
for it someday.' I believed you when you said that."

"I was speaking about my own mother. How she made selflessness her
profession rather than . . . I never dreamed—"

"I know you are suffering. Look, people go through terrible things in their
lives. My mother's family went through years of persecution before they
came over to the States. And do you know what it did to them after a while?
It actually made them tougher. I've told you what their family motto is:

'Truth against the world.' It takes some hard knocks to develop an outlook like that.

"I've never been like other people. Not other fathers, not other business-men. I have never fit into any social norm. And you know what? I don't want to."

Frank seemed tuned to an interior compass. There was no arrogance or braggadocio. This was the wise, fearless man she had fallen in love with.

"So does this mess mean we bow to their rules? That we say 'We're no good, we don't deserve happiness'?" He looked at her squarely. "I don't think we're bad people, Mamah. I hurt like hell for my children. Even for her. But that doesn't mean I'm turning back now.

"We're going to leave this place. Wasmuth is working on lining up some-thing in Florence. In the meantime, we'll go to Paris. It's big and anony-mous. Then Italy. Wasmuth says you can disappear there."

He walked to the bed and pulled her up. "Let's get some breakfast."

"Won't they see us?"

"Who? And do I give a damn?"

IN THE RESTAURANT, Frank was actually smiling. "Give us the full treatment," he said when the waiter arrived. Frank pointed to all the selections on the menu. The young man returned with cereal, cheeses, hard rolls, and a platter of thin-sliced marbled meats.

"We can stop off in Potsdam first. I want to see it. And then on over by train to the Rhine. It's not the best weather, but Dorn says we should experi-ence it. So, we boat down from Cologne to Koblenz. I want to take a little de-tour over to Darmstadt to see Olbrich, if we can. I'm told his work is worth seeing. Then on to Paris." Frank dove into his breakfast with gusto.

She stared at him in disbelief. Frank was talking of their departure from Berlin as if they were going on a jolly holiday.

Frank raised a glass of orange juice to her. " 'Truth against the world,' " he said grimly, quaffing the juice. "Handy motto, isn't it?"

CHAPTER 22

December 1, 1909

N*ancy, France. I am sick at the stomach with what Frank takes to be the flu. I know better. This is what despair makes of your belly. He says we will move on to Paris in a few days when I am feeling well. Then we can decide what we, each of us, will do. But how will I ever feel well again?*

Frank's mother wrote in her letter that young Catherine has been dismissed from the high school because of the "scandal." Frank's anger is murderous. He is wounded by this mess, yet there is something in him, a rock-hard core, that allows him to move forward. His work is his refuge.

Last night I lay awake, desperately worried for the children. How I wish I could simply go back and hold them. How I wish none of this ever happened. I pray Louise holds fast now. There is no fiercer gatekeeper.

I take one hour at a time and wonder at how quickly courage has forsaken me.

"GHASTLY," FRANK MUTTERED. "Sentimental, degenerate crap. What is the matter with these people?" They had been walking the streets of Nancy after a silent dinner, looking at Jugendstil architecture. Now they stood in front of an ornate art nouveau house, the façade of which, with its curving window tops like drooping eyelids, reminded her of the face of a gnome.

A strolling couple paused to see what Frank was looking at as he tapped his cane on the walk indignantly, then jabbed the air as he pointed toward the house. "Dog waste," he sneered.

The man looked at the house, confused, then back at Frank. But the woman clearly understood as she drew her collar up and pulled her husband along.

Mamah was glad for the appearance of the ugly house, for it was taking the full brunt of Frank's outrage. There was a time she'd been mortified when

Frank had stood outside someone's expensive Chicago home and declared it trash. How quaint that sort of embarrassment seemed now.

She walked on and he followed, his eyes panning the street, daring another visual assault. Mamah caught sight of a flyer attached to the side of a newsstand. The words "Ellen Key" appeared in large print at the top. She knew the name; she'd read a book by the Swedish feminist some years before, though she couldn't remember the title.

Mamah pulled the flyer off the shed. "She's speaking here Wednesday night."

"Who's Ellen Key?"

"She's important in the Woman Movement over here. Let's see. She'll be talking on . . ." Mamah translated with her lips moving, her finger following the words on each line. "The morality of woman, love's freedom, free divorce, and a new marriage law."

"Do you suppose she knows we're in town?"

Mamah tried to smile. "I want to see if I can find any of her books."

At a bookstore not far from their hotel, she came upon just one, *Love and Marriage*. Editions in French, English, and German were stacked beside one another. Browsing through them, she could see that, in any language, it was heavy going.

She found Frank among the art books. "The text is very dense in that woolly, scholarly sort of way," she said. "But listen to this."

Frank leaned against the bookcase where they stood, his head down in concentration, while Mamah read from the English version.

> " 'Great love, like great genius, can never be a duty: both are
> life's gracious gifts to the elect. There can be no other standard
> of morality for him who loves more than once than for him who
> loves only one: that of the enhancement of life. He who in a new
> love hears the singing of dried-up springs, feels the sap rising in
> dead boughs, the renewal of life's creative forces; he who is
> prompted anew to magnanimity and truth, to gentleness and
> generosity, he who finds strength as well as intoxication in his
> new love, nourishment as well as a feast—that man has a right
> to the experience.' "

She glanced up to find Frank's eyes on her.

"Have I ever told you that?" His gaze was tender.

"Told me what?"

"Finding you was like finding a safe place to think again. Before I met you, I felt I could soar at the drawing table, but I always came back to the most static prison in my marriage. It set me free to find you, to think that there was the possibility of something more expansive. You make me want to be a better man. A better artist." He put his hand in hers. "I'd be such a sad person if it had never happened."

"Thank you." She put his hand to her face and brushed it across her lips.

"Which version will it be?"

"English, I suppose. Are you buying it for me?"

"Yes."

At the hotel, she sat in the room for hours, reading *Love and Marriage*. So much of what she believed was right there on the page. From the beginning of the book, she sensed that Ellen Key wouldn't be pigeonholed. The woman didn't bother herself with the vote, like other feminists; that was a right she expected without remark. She wasn't an Emma Goldman, or a Socialist-style feminist like Charlotte Perkins Gilman, or a firebrand like Emmeline Pankhurst. Nor was she a subversive saint like Jane Addams. Ellen Key seemed to be something else entirely.

Her style appealed to Mamah—cool and logical, in a scattershot sort of way. She would introduce an argument in one spot and take it up fifty pages later, trusting that those readers who were still with her were the ones she wanted along. She made you travel the paths that her own reasoning took, knocking off one objection after another to her radical views, so that by the time you got to her conclusion, you agreed with her.

Mamah traveled through evolutionary science, Church history, sociological studies, anthropology, Swedish folk customs, critiques of George Sand and other novelists. There were moments during the long afternoon and night of devouring *Love and Marriage* when she felt as if she were a boat pushing through high waves. Just when she reached the top of one line of reasoning, she was plopped down at the base of another.

"It's funny," she said when Frank brought in dinner. "This woman is conservative and wildly radical at the same time."

"How is that?" He was setting up a picnic dinner on the floor. He had gone out and bought a baguette, ham, and a chunk of cheese that he was laying out on butcher paper. Sitting cross-legged on the floor, with his wavy brown hair grown longer since they sailed over, he looked like a young man just then.

"Well," Mamah said thoughtfully, "on one hand, she says women's natures are best suited to raise children, but then she argues that they should be paid for it because it's society's most important job. What I like is that she champions a woman's freedom to realize her personality. For the longest time, it seems there's been almost no discussion of individualism in the Woman Movement. But here is a woman getting at the deeper question of what a woman is and what she can be."

"You look so much better."

"Thank you, my love. I do feel better. Probably because this book is telling me precisely what I want to hear right now."

"Such as?"

"She says that once love leaves a marriage, then the marriage isn't sacred anymore. But if a true, great love happens outside of marriage, it's sacred and has its own rights. She says each fresh couple must prove that their love enhances their lives and the human race by living together. Here, listen. 'Only cohabitation can decide the morality of a particular case.' "

Frank was slicing the bread with a small knife. "You mean we're doing this for the human race?"

"Oh, there's a lot of eugenics in here, to be sure. She claims that as people perfect a culture of love, the human race will evolve to a higher plane where there won't be a need for laws regulating marriage and divorce."

"So if we can just hang on for a millennium or two, it'll all work out."

"You'll like this part. There are some people today—mostly artists—who can handle the freedom of living honestly. Listen: 'Without "criminal" love, the world's creations of beauty would be . . . not only infinitely fewer but poorer.' In fact, artists have a *responsibility* to show others how to live truthfully."

She found his eyes. "Frank, I want to stay to hear this woman."

"Do you think it would help?"

"How I feel? I don't know if anything can help for very long." She shrugged. "Maybe."

"How would you feel if I went on ahead to Paris and met with Wasmuth's contact there?"

"I'll be all right by myself."

Frank looked doubtful.

"Truly," she said. "I will be there in a few days. Just wire me when you get a hotel. I'll find you there."

MAMAH READ ON INTO the night, with Frank sleeping beside her. There were moments when she came upon a sentence so true she wanted to shake him awake. But she couldn't stop reading, couldn't take the time to tell him about it. There would be hours and days for that later. When she got to the chapter on free divorce, she felt as if Ellen Key had interviewed her for the book: *Why is the heart that is broken considered so much more valuable than the one or the two who must cause the pain lest they themselves perish?*

Mamah put down the book sometime before dawn. The only sound that penetrated the walls of the little hotel was the creaking of pines outside their window. In the dark, she could see the giants, their snow-laden branches moving almost imperceptibly in the wind. She pulled the layers of quilts over her face.

Edwin didn't know where she was. Her sister didn't know, either. She had disappeared into a part of Europe that no one's finger would be drawn to on a map. She felt a sense of relief. It was as if Mamah Cheney, the troubled woman in the headlines, had ceased to exist. For the first time in many days, she didn't cry before she slept.

CHAPTER 23

Ellen Key spoke faintly at the front of the room. She was jowly, grand motherly, her thin gray hair parted in the middle and pulled down over her ears into a small bun. She wore a loose dress that hung from her round shoulders like a surplice.

Mamah stared at the nunlike character behind the lectern who was talking, incredibly, about erotic love. She tried to imagine her as a young woman, fresh-faced and infatuated. But there was nothing about Ellen Key to suggest that she had ever lost her senses about anything, least of all a man.

"Love is moral even without legal marriage." Ellen Key's voice rose and broke through the sound of rustling skirts. "But marriage is immoral without love."

The skin on Mamah's arms tingled as she leaned forward in her chair.

"A marriage consummated without mutual love, or continued without mutual love, does not elevate the personal dignity of man or woman. It is instead a criminal counterfeiting of the highest values of life.

"In the new morality, everything exchanged between husband and wife will be a free gift of love, never demanded by one or the other as a right. Such demands are merely a crude survival of the lower periods of culture."

Mamah strained to hear each sentence, her brain fairly twitching. *If I could get to that seat at the front*, she thought. Around her, the women's faces were attentive, but she saw no glimmer of what she felt. Was she the only one being dragged forward by Ellen Key's words, an affinity fool for all to see? Mamah stood, gathered up her coat and bag, and climbed past the knees in her row. She felt her body propelled forward as she swooped down to the front of the auditorium and took the empty seat in the first row.

"The new morality has two types of adversaries," said Ellen Key. "The first is the adherent of conventional morality who pursues something called 'pure love' untouched by sensuality. These people plaster fig leaves over modern art and ban erotic literature."

Laughter rippled through the audience.

"The others, the so-called bohemians, espouse temporary unions that they mistakenly call 'free love.' These people have no idea what soulful devotion is."

Ellen Key's voice was precisely as Mamah had heard it in the book yesterday. The woman exuded the kind of enlightenment Mamah associated with swamis or monks. She was a mixture of wisdom and empathy.

"I want to talk to you today about the noblest type of love—the kind that joins the spiritual with the erotic. When both lovers yearn to become entirely one being, to free each other and to develop each other to the greatest perfection, this is the highest form of love possible between a man and a woman of the same moral and intellectual level.

"To experience such love is to feel oneself doubled. Such feeling liberates and deepens the personality, inspires us to noble deeds and works of genius. When this great love happens—and it is but once in a lifetime—it has a higher right than all other feelings. The perfect love establishes its own right in a life."

Mamah realized that a deep calm had descended upon her. Every part of her body was suffused with warmth. With love. The lurid headlines that had sickened her seemed to recede as she listened to Ellen Key. She felt herself to be in the presence of something bigger and more important than her little footnote of public shaming.

To have her deepest instincts understood—championed!—at this moment of all moments seemed to be a gift from a loving Spirit somewhere.

When Ellen Key finished, women swarmed around the podium, talking intently with the speaker. Mamah remained in her seat, calm. She knew she could wait forever, if need be. When the last woman had pulled away, Ellen Key looked straight into her eyes.

"Come out with it now," she said.

Mamah rose and walked to her. Tears breached her lower lids as she took one of the woman's hands into both of her own. "Thank you" seemed such an inadequate expression.

"Come along," Ellen Key said, patting her back like a mother. "I have an hour before my train. We'll get ourselves some tea."

CHAPTER 24

"Does he give you good sex?"

Mamah's eyes were on the teaspoons of sugar going into the Swedish woman's cup. Three. Four. She looked up, took a breath.

"Frank Lloyd. Does he give you—"

"Yes. Of course, it's much more than that."

"It always is. But it is one measure of a man, if he takes the time."

"He does."

"Good."

They had walked toward the train station from the lecture hall. In the space of four blocks, Mamah had opened her heart for inspection. She had spun the whole complicated web for Ellen Key, beginning with Frank. Frank, then Edwin, John, Martha, Jessica. Tiers of friends. Catherine Wright, too. All the threads that anchored her to a place called Oak Park in the middle of the United States.

The renowned philosopher Key was rummaging in her bag. She pulled out a tin of tea and shook some into the pot on the table. "Sinus cure," she explained. The candles in the train station café were not yet lit, and Mamah squinted to find the woman's features in the shadows.

"You love this man."

"Utterly."

"And his wife refuses him a divorce. Have you asked your husband for one?"

"Not yet."

"What keeps you from it?"

"Uncertainty. If I 'abandoned' Edwin, I couldn't have the children with me. But it doesn't matter anymore. The best lawyer in the world can't help me now."

Ellen Key sat up in her seat, her ponderous bosom like a pillow between her and the table's edge. "I've never been a parent, but I was born to people who loved each other passionately until the last hour of their lives. They were full of joy and interested in everything. Their pleasure in each other nourished my little soul. Everyone has the right to that, don't you think? People who live only for their children make bad company for them." She drank the tea down in one long draft. "Don't misunderstand me. Everything is more delicate in a divorce when children are involved."

"Today you talked about the great loves," Mamah said. "The loves that supersede all others. And you talked about the women—"

"*Les grandes inspiratrices.*" Ellen Key blotted her mouth with a napkin. "It's not an ignoble path for a woman to be a muse. Are you his?"

"Not really," Mamah said thoughtfully. "Frank's drive comes from inside himself. Do I *want* to support him? Yes, of course. He's like all of us—he longs for tenderness." Mamah smiled. "But he has a muse already. Nature."

"I have known you for an hour," the woman said, "so allow me some latitude. It's clear your Frank is not the only one on a spiritual quest here. You are seeking something, too. What might that be?"

Mamah was silent.

"Forgive my bluntness, but leaving a boring man for a stimulating one is only interesting for a while. In time, you are back where you started—still wanting. Better to find your own backbone, the strong thing in you. Clearly, you are educated. What work are you drawn to?"

"I'm not sure," Mamah said. "I used to believe it was writing."

"What do you write?"

"Observations. Essays. Stories sometimes. And little things in my notebook— quotes and such that inspire me."

Ellen slapped the tabletop so the cups rattled. "Then write you must. Something more than little things."

Mamah looked out the window. A drenching rain had begun to fall, and passersby held newspapers over their heads as they hurried along the street. "When I left," she said, "I was reckless. I believed if I came and spent time with Frank, and if it worked, if it *could* work, I would understand what the next step would be." She shook her head. "I never dreamed it would all come crashing in."

Ellen patted her hand. "What would happen if you went back? Faced it head-on?"

"I could go back." There was resignation in her voice. "I could go back. I'd be the humiliated harlot . . . I don't know."

"You need more time." Ellen glanced at her watch, then called for the check. "Your journey has turned into a public shaming. That doesn't erase the need you had in the first place to discover who you are and where you want to go. Let things calm down. Give yourself a couple of months."

"But I worry about the children. And I'll run out of money soon enough. Edwin certainly won't send me any."

"What about Frank?"

"He doesn't talk much about money. But I think he has only enough to support himself through his project."

"Children are always the main issue." Ellen stood up and threw her coat on. "It seems to me, though, that you must find a way to be self-reliant before you commit yourself to a plan."

Mamah bit the inside of her cheek. "I could translate your books."

Ellen Key looked up from her bag. "Oh, I have an English translator in London."

"I know. I read the English translation of *Love and Marriage*. It lacks soul."

The woman stood still, the indignant look on her face giving way to curiosity. "Well."

"I read parts of it to Frank. He said the translation is a poetry crusher. It's too British, too stiff." Mamah held her breath.

Ellen looked amused. "You speak German perfectly. What else?"

"French, Italian, Spanish. I read Greek and Latin as well. I completed a master's degree in language studies."

"And Swedish?"

"No one understands better than I your ideas. No one could translate for an American audience the way I can."

"But Swedish?"

"It's limited. I learned some from a servant girl in the boardinghouse where I lived when I taught school in Michigan. But I could master it—in a heartbeat."

Ellen leaned in closer. "Where are you going next?"

"Paris, then Italy, I think."

Ellen looked at her watch. "Will you walk with me to the gate?"

Mamah lifted her bag and followed her out of the café.

"You know," Ellen said, "you appear before me at an interesting moment, Mamah. I'm at the end of my tour. In a couple of weeks, I will be sixty. My feet swell up whenever I stand at the lectern, and most mornings it takes an hour to get my legs and fingers moving. I'm tired of the nomad life.

"And I'm building a *home* now. Last year the Swedish government gave me a piece of land on a park reservation. It's near a lake not unlike Lago Maggiore. I haven't had a real home of my own since I left my parents' house twenty years ago. Most of the past few years have been spent traveling around lecturing. I've given myself out in little pieces, and there's not much left of me. When my house is completed, I intend to inhabit it."

"How lovely," Mamah said.

"Do you see where I am going? I'm not finished with my work, but my body feels as if it is. I've known for some time that America is next. It's the American woman who is ready to hear what I have to say."

"I have strong connections with the Woman Movement," Mamah said breathlessly. "My heart has been in this fight since I was eighteen. I understand the American woman. I would do outstanding translations of your books. And I would get them distributed."

They stood at a gate while crowds of people snaked around them. Ellen pulled out of her bag typed copies of three essays that she explained would be collected under one title: *The Morality of Woman.*

"Translate these and send them to me. If I like the work you do, I will consider letting you be my American translator."

Mamah threw her arms around her.

"You must agree to one condition, though. I have learned your language already. You must learn Swedish to be a regular translator for me."

Mamah's heart was thudding. "Of course I will."

"The University of Leipzig has a fine language program. I can pay you a small stipend while you bring yourself to full speed. Enough to eat on, at least." Ellen Key scribbled her name and address on a piece of paper. "Here," she said, "send me your translation. And let me know what you want to do."

CHAPTER 25

. .

AWAITING YOU.
CHAMPS-ÉLYSÉES PLAZA, ROOM 15.
FLW JAN. 19, 1910

The terseness of Frank's telegram was a confession: He was miserable without her. She would give herself another whole day, then go to him on Friday. She missed him, too, but leaving Nancy was the last thing she wanted to do. Sitting in the hotel room translating Ellen's essays, she had found more than peace of mind. She had discovered the state of her soul set down in ink.

While she translated, Mamah thought of her father off and on. During the months she and Edwin had lived with him in the old house, he would sit in his study and read the New Testament, a habit he had never bothered with while her mother was alive. From time to time he shuffled out of the smoky study in his slippers, talking and nodding to himself. Mamah had begun to behave in a similar way in her hotel room.

Just this morning she had tried to draft a letter to Ellen Key to thank her. She wanted to say that she truly *understood*. That she would bring Ellen's ideas to America out of gratitude, never mind the compensation. Yet every word she wrote seemed badly chosen. She crossed out the sentence *You have saved my life.* It would probably frighten the woman away.

On Friday morning, a cold drizzle melted the skin of snow on the street as Mamah walked to the train station.

"Are you going to Paris?" a man said to her as she stepped into the ticket line.

"Yes."

"Don't bother waiting. There are no trains to Paris because it's flooding there. Part of the city is underwater now. The stations are all closed."

"But I had a telegram on Wednesday—"

The man shrugged. "It was very sudden. The Seine has filled up the subways, electricity is out. Everything's disrupted. They won't even estimate when the trains will start again."

"Do you know the Champs-Élysées Plaza?"

"Yes," the man said. "It's new." He shook his head. "It's not far from the Seine."

A newsboy on the street hawked papers with the headline INONDATIONS! She had been holed up in her room, unaware.

Frank is resourceful, she thought; *a flood won't rattle him.* Both of them had witnessed the Des Plaines River near Oak Park overflow time and again. If he were struggling, it would be because he was alone, his work disrupted once more.

In the absence of telegrams and trains, there was no choice. She would wait it out in Nancy and continue working. She went back to the hotel and put away the folded clothes.

ON WEDNESDAY MORNING, rain pounded the sidewalks with a fury. It had been five days since the first news of the flooding, and the skies continued their barrage. At breakfast she caught the eye of a businessman with a newspaper who read her question in a glance. He shook his head. "It keeps going up," he said. "There have been some deaths."

She bought a newspaper, sat down in the hotel lobby, and studied the little map on the front page depicting the Seine snaking up from the southeast in a loop around the city. The situation had grown much worse. The basement of the Louvre was filled with water. A photo of the Gare d'Orsay revealed it to be a swimming pool, its locomotives drowned like sunken ships.

Have I grown numb to the point of stupidity? Mamah felt oddly unworried about Frank. A strange new confidence had descended on her.

The peacefulness of Nancy had taken her by surprise. After a few days, she felt as if she had moved back one step and could look at her situation from the outside. At moments she could even imagine that everyone involved—Edwin, Catherine, the children—would someday be happy.

It felt callous to compare her public humiliations with the miseries of the desperate Parisians. Yet the flood's allegory was there for the taking, if it was perspective one wanted.

On January 30 the papers announced that the siege had ended. Parisians were boating about in the sunshine, celebrating. When word came later that trains were scheduled to move again, Mamah raced to the station to buy a ticket.

In the crush of people and luggage along the platform, she held a small valise tightly beneath her arm. Inside were her handwritten translations of *The Morality of Woman*, *The Woman of the Future*, and *The Conventional Woman*. She felt fiercely protective, the way she imagined Frank felt carrying his portfolio of drawings—like a courier with a blueprint that was about to change the world.

The train slugged through Frouard, Commercy, Bar-le-Duc, and Vitry-le-François before it stopped for four hours in Chalons-sur-Marne. Mamah bought food from a man with a cart near the station, then climbed back on board and fell asleep. When she awoke, they were nearly to Paris. As they moved through its eastern suburbs, she saw battered little villages where rowboats were hitched to garden gates and ladders led up to second-floor windows.

Past muddy fields of dun-colored, matted grass, the train lurched forward. Mamah saw large shapes dotting a pasture up ahead in the distance. When the train drew closer, she realized the forms were the bloated carcasses of cows. Farther on, a small cemetery looked as if it had been turned upside down. Headstones and empty caskets lay scattered around a field nearby. She caught sight of what appeared to be the arm of a corpse hanging from one wooden box.

Alarm rippled through the train as passengers moved about to get better views. *"Jesu Christe!"* an old woman cried in a seat nearby. "The dead have been ripped from their graves."

But the calm that had possessed Mamah in Nancy persisted. Sunlight breaking through gray clouds brought the scenes outside her window into sharp focus. She felt a clarity, even more than before, as if she were viewing everything, even herself, from a distance. *How small we humans are,* she thought. *All our scrambling around, trying to buttress ourselves against death. All our efforts to insulate ourselves against uncertainty with codes of behavior and meaningless busyness.*

How ridiculous it all seemed, when life itself was so short, so precious. To live dishonestly seemed a cowardly way to use up one's time. For all the troubles life had meted out to her, she thought, it had given her more extraordinary gifts. Martha and John were that. And then, quite by chance and in the wrong order, life had bestowed on her another kind of love that was both erotic and nourishing. To embrace Frank, to accept the gift, seemed to be an affirmation of life.

How to reconcile the deepest loves of her soul? Staring out the window, she tried to imagine a time in the future when she would explain to her children this understanding. They would have to be adults to comprehend it. But she believed they would see that her choice to leave their father was not meant as a cruel self-indulgence geared to make them unhappy. Rather, it was an act of love for life.

Mamah remembered a line from *Hymn to Nature: She turns everything she gives into a blessing.*

Somehow she would turn this terrible mess into a blessing for the children. She believed it was possible that they could someday feel enlarged by the love all around them. People with children got divorced and remarried; it wasn't the end of the world for them. Martha and John could actually end up better off, with four happy parents.

Mamah's whole life seemed to be of a piece at that moment. Working for Ellen Key was simply more evidence of an impulse inside her that was growing up like a plant, stretching, seeking the light. With every word she translated, she leaned harder toward love and life.

Loud banter turned to whispers as the train pulled into the city. Mamah's eye caught a clock stopped at 10:50. Then she saw another and another. All of the public clocks of Paris had halted at the same instant, marking the eerie moment when the river had rendered schedules irrelevant. The strangeness of the scene snapped her from her reverie.

"Champs-Élysées Plaza!" she said when she got a taxi. "Quickly, please."

At the hotel, she dropped all her bags except the valise in the drenched, smelly lobby and raced up the stairs to the third floor. Her heavy coat tripped her, and she stopped to pull it off. At Room 15, she rapped and waited.

The door opened and Frank, his face unshaven, peered out into the dark hall.

She sighed when she saw him. "Thank you, thank you!"

"May-mah!" He laughed, lifting her off the floor in a swooping bear hug. "What a beautiful sight."

"I would have come sooner if I could have."

"I missed the worst of it. I went out into the country when the river came over the sandbags. I just got back yesterday." He pulled her into the room. "Be careful where you step."

They tiptoed through the drawings that were spread over the floor. Frank was using his portfolio cover as a drawing board on the carpet. A hard half-eaten loaf of bread sat on top of the dresser, along with an apple core and a jug of water. They sat down on the bed.

"I thought you were all right," she said, "but then we got close to Paris, and I was frantic with this fear—"

"But I'm safe. Everything is fine." He put his arm around her shoulders.

"—and I thought, *What would I do if something happened to you?* My life would end."

"You're trembling," he said. "Here, lie down." He drew a blanket over her on the bed.

Mamah eased her back against the pillows and sensed the tension in her body ebb. Light filtered through the window's tracery and cast shadows on gray wallpaper printed with urns and draping vines. The quietness of the city struck her. Not a horse or car or voice could be heard from the sidewalk below.

There was so much to tell Frank, but she felt no hurry. She put her arms around him, then pulled his shirt up in back and slid her hands under it to feel the hot expanse of skin beneath. Her palms moved around to his chest, slowly, feeling the heart beneath the ribs, the rise and fall of muscle under her fingertips. She pressed her mouth to his neck and breast, exploring him unabashedly, gratefully. It was as if they were the first lovers, as if words had no use compared to this.

"I'M STARVING." Frank was awake and getting dressed. She put out a hand, and he pulled her up. As they prepared to go out, he collected his cape and placed a jaunty beret on his head.

"You look wonderful," she said, a little bewildered.

"I found a hatter over at the Place Vendôme," he said. "The man can make anything."

Outside on the street, the low sun yellowed facades and faces. Mamah approached a passerby and got the location of an open café. They walked eight or nine blocks before they found the little place, its white tile walls sparkling. Only the smell of bleach hinted that muddy water had filled it just days before.

The café was packed with diners chatting gaily. "Eggs," the waiter said. "That's all we have. Does that suit you?"

"Yes. Omelets would be marvelous," she said.

When the wine arrived, Frank clicked her glass with his. "To Italy," he said. "If we leave tomorrow, we can be there by Friday."

Mamah's shoulders fell.

He grabbed her hand. "You're tired, aren't you? We'll go the day after. We can sleep late tomorrow."

She saw an omelet pass on a tray and realized she was famished. She couldn't bring herself to tell him about Leipzig just yet; he seemed so happy. She would present the idea tomorrow.

They drank the bottle of wine, Frank regaling her with stories of his Parisian encounters, she talking excitedly about what she had just translated.

On their way back to the hotel, they walked in the street next to the Seine.

"I feel a little woozy," she admitted. Frank grabbed her elbow and navigated her around a large hole where the street had caved in.

"The French are a little woozy right now," he said. "No one will notice."

Naphtha flames lit the river's edge, where workmen struggled to dislodge a wood pier that had wedged itself under a bridge.

"The studio in Florence is all arranged. Lloyd will be coming over to help with the drawings. And a young fellow from Salt Lake who's worked for me—Taylor Woolley—he's coming, too. I need both of them."

"I thought Catherine would never allow Lloyd to leave school. That he couldn't be in the same place I'm staying."

"I've convinced her you won't cross his path. I'll find a room for him and Taylor apart from ours. They're young—they'll want to explore Florence on their own."

"So you've heard from Oak Park."

Frank stopped to squint at something across the river. "I don't want to think about it," he said.

BACK IN THE HOTEL ROOM, he gestured toward the dresser. "You have a letter. Wasmuth forwarded it." Frank delivered the information as carefully as she would have delivered it to him—without emotion. Mamah stepped haltingly across the room and looked at the envelope from a distance. Edwin's Wagner Electric logo was in the upper-left-hand corner. She knew what the envelope held. *How could you? Come to your senses.*

Frank made noise settling her luggage in a corner and kept his eyes averted. She knew he was tendering her a small mercy. It was the first mail she'd had since the newspaper clippings, and he was offering her what little privacy he could. She slit the envelope with her thumbnail, then set it down.

"I'll read it in the morning," she said.

WHEN SHE WOKE, Mamah felt her jaw clamped shut. She had been grinding her teeth, maybe all night. She slipped out of bed while Frank still slept, then pulled Edwin's letter from the envelope. His words hit their mark— the household on East Avenue came into vivid, painful focus. His elderly mother was now living with them, trying to help. Lizzie was bearing up, assisting with Martha and John. Louise had been valiant, chasing away reporters when they showed up on Christmas Day. Edwin added at the end that young Jessie would be leaving the household to live with the Pitkins, her father's family.

Mamah's jaw throbbed. She laid her head down on the desk.

After a time she got up to bathe, pulled on a dress, and went out to find food. Walking along the street, she tried to recapture the peaceful confidence that had filled her the day before. When she returned with bread and coffee, she took up a pen and started a letter to Edwin.

"What time is it?" Frank mumbled from the bed.

"Nine."

"Hmm." He sat up and stretched his arms. "There's a noon train for Milan. I can be ready in an hour if that really is coffee I smell."

She didn't answer.

"Sweetheart?"

She plunged in. "Frank, I'm not going to Italy with you."

"What do you mean?" He stood and wrapped himself in a robe.

"I mean . . . I will come later. I need to go to Leipzig and study Swedish at the university."

"What is it?" His voice was hoarse.

"Ellen says she has mastered my language and she wants me to master hers."

Frank was out of bed, looking down with a puzzled expression as he tied the belt of his robe. "How long?"

"Two months. Maybe three."

"Three *months?*"

"If I master Swedish, Ellen says—"

Frank's hands were suddenly waving. "Jesus Christ! Ellen says *this.* Ellen says *that.* How is it *possible* a woman you didn't know three weeks ago has become more important than I am?"

"She hasn't, Frank. If you understood entirely what she stands for—"

"Don't *do* this to me, Mamah!" He was pacing furiously. "Why can't you study Swedish in Italy?"

"It will go much faster if I attend classes in Leipzig."

"What in hell is happening to us?" He yanked a shirt from the wardrobe. "Have you forgotten why you came here in the first place?"

She pushed the hard nail of her thumb into the flesh of a finger. "Not for a minute."

"Then why are you even talking about this?"

"I need to complete some business of my own."

"For Christ's sake, Mamah. Don't make it more complicated than it already is."

She stood up and walked to the window. Below, men were pulling down the sandbags that were stacked against a building. "Do you remember the words you used when you talked about coming over here?" she asked. "You said you wanted to square your life with yourself. Am I to take it that those words applied only to you?"

"Don't twist things." Frank flung a hairbrush down on the dresser, causing Mamah to jump reflexively at the sharp crack. She turned to look at his face and found it splotchy with anger. Frank seemed a stranger—he'd never been so agitated with her.

She took in a breath, lifted her chin. "This chance means so much, Frank. And right now I need work."

"Nonsense." Frank's voice dripped sarcasm. "You don't need to work."

"Oh, I see," she responded bitterly. "The truth comes out. All this time I've talked about taking possession of my own life, you were only pretending to agree. What you really want is a woman who devotes herself only to you."

He walked into the bathroom and slammed the door. For a minute or two, she heard him crashing around, dropping his razor, cursing.

When he emerged, he was dressed and calmer. He sat on the bed next to her. "I don't want to fight," he said. "But I've felt at loose ends without you. You can't imagine how depressed I've been here, despite appearances. And now you say you're going away again. You seem to be running from the whole situation."

"I'm not."

"Seriously, Mamah. Do you think that if you're not physically with me over here, then somehow your accusers can't fault you? That if we're living apart, then we're not really lovers?"

Mamah flinched. The thought had not occurred to her. Maybe there was some truth in it, but she could not think about that now. "Stop, Frank," she pleaded softly. "Please listen. Here's the offer Ellen made me. She has agreed to name me her official English translator on the condition that I study Swedish and become fluent in it. I can translate two more books of hers from German, but for the rest I have to master Swedish so there won't be any more watering down of her texts. That seems like a fair proposition to me. It would mean that I would attend the University of Leipzig now, study Swedish, and maybe teach a little English. You can go get settled in Florence and start your portfolio work. In June I'll come and meet you in Italy to spend the rest of the summer." She took his face in her hands. "I love you so much. I love you enough that I want to stay *separate* from you. You're an extraordinary man, Frank Wright. I could so easily lose myself in your world and never make a world of my own. And where would that leave us? We'd both be bored stupid."

Frank smiled faintly. He reached up and took her hands in his.

"Am I asking too much? You tell me, Frank. Because it feels that my whole life, I have never asked enough of love or work or myself. Except for the last two weeks, during which I have actually used my brain."

He sighed. "What choice do I have?"

"You can spend a couple of months with Lloyd and not have to worry about me being there. And I'll be relatively close to Wasmuth. I can go into the city and act as your agent with him while you're in Italy."

"Just beware of panaceas," he said, as if he had not heard her last remark.

"Meaning?"

"Don't fool yourself into believing Ellen Key can change the reviews we've been getting from the Chicago papers. Her books are never going to reach the little minds who read that crap and believe it."

"How do you know? You've never read her books."

"No, I haven't. I only know what you've told me. But I can see how irresistible her thinking is to you. Look, it's vindication. I like it, too. All I'm saying is, I don't want to lose the lovely woman I'm mad for to some feminist ideology. Don't forget who Mamah Borthwick is. That's all."

Frank got up and shuffled around the room, picking up his things, brooding. Mamah moved over to an armchair and closed her eyes. Her right hand felt like a burning ball in her lap. For two weeks she had copied and recopied her translations until her fingers wouldn't move properly. Her whole body, in fact, felt sore, for some reason, but her mind was still clear. She knew what she had to do. She would write to Edwin today, officially requesting a divorce. And she would write to Lizzie, asking her to help with the children a while longer.

A note to Martha would be easy. But what to say to an eight-year-old boy?

Mamah took out a piece of stationery from her suitcase and moved over to the writing desk. She stared at the paper for a long while before she wrote.

Dear John,

I am in Paris now. Did you know there was a big flood here? Water from the river rose up to the second floor of buildings in some places. I was not here during the worst of it, but was told that people rode around in boats through the streets. The water has gone down, though, and the sun is shining. People are on the streets smiling again.

I hope you are smiling, too, my love. I miss you terribly. It seems every time I turn a corner, I am reminded of you. I see so many things you would enjoy, and someday I will bring you here to see them for yourself.

It would make me so happy to be with you and Martha. I will be back, but not quite yet. For a few months, I will be a student just like you. I plan to study Swedish in Germany so I can translate some books. It will be my new job.

Everything is going to be all right, Johnny. I know your papa and Aunt Lizzie and Louise are taking good care of you. Do not think that I don't love you, or that you have done something wrong. You are a good and brave boy, my darling. You are the very best son anyone could have. Be kind to your little sister. But then, I know you will.

I love you,
Mama

In Leipzig, Mamah was twice the age of the other students. She sat upright, intently scribbling Swedish phrases into a notebook, while all around her, young men lolled in their seats, intoxicated by the approach of spring and the promise of beer in the evening.

Her professor, an ebullient fellow in his fifties, was an acquaintance of Ellen Key's. He addressed his lessons to the dark-haired woman in the front row, pleased to have someone respond to his questions.

Twice Mamah traveled to Berlin to visit with Wasmuth, to assess the state of the portfolio's printing, and to report to Frank her findings. Otherwise, she lived quietly in Leipzig, allowing herself few indulgences. Her pleasure came from growing confident in Swedish.

In late May, as she prepared to depart for Italy, she received a letter from Ellen inviting her to visit her new home on Lake Vattern. Mamah carefully worded a telegram to Frank asking his indulgence once more.

Take what time you need, he replied. Within a few days, she was on her way.

Arriving in Alvastra, she was met by an elderly gentleman whose words were incomprehensible, thanks to a considerable wad of chewing tobacco in his cheek. He ferried Mamah by wagon to Ellen's house, which was set just above Lake Vattern, then led her into the front door, where she stood in a hallway with white walls, a redbrick floor, and rows of freshly painted red doors along its sides. Near the ceiling ran a stenciled frieze of green garland. Above the front door, painted in red, were the words MEMENTO VIVERE. Remember to live.

At that moment Mamah was nearly toppled by a Saint Bernard who came roaring from the end of the hallway.

"Wild," Ellen Key said when she found Mamah wiping her wet hands on her skirt. "That's his name. He's an affectionate fellow, but sloppy." Ellen embraced her heartily. "Welcome to Strand, my dear. Now sign my guest book. You're one of the first."

THAT A WOMAN could make a house like this, on her own, was a wonder Mamah pondered over the next five days. She had not read Ellen's book *Beauty for Everyone*, but in the rooms, she saw her "light and healthy" aesthetic. Gustavian furniture painted pearly gray. Every window in the house open to the June breeze. Folk crafts scattered all around.

"Why did you name your home Strand?" she asked Ellen once the young housekeeper had brought tea.

"Come over here." Ellen led Mamah back out into the hallway and pointed to a framed map of the Vattern area. Painted in blue and yellow letters above it were the words DÄR LIVETS HAV OSS GETT EN STRAND.

" 'Where life's sea has given us a strand,' " Mamah translated.

"That came quite easily. You've been working at it, haven't you?"

"IT *IS* MY QUIET STRAND," Ellen said later. They were sitting near the lake on a bench in a circular columned portico that perched atop some rocks just above the waterline. Wild rested at Ellen's feet. "It's so beautiful here, especially in the morning." She stopped to reconsider. "No, especially at night under the stars. Well, you'll see. I've been sitting out here lately, thinking that I want to make Strand a kind of legacy once I'm gone. I'm just drawing up a will now that spells it out. What it will be is a haven for workingwomen who need a rest. They can actually have a holiday."

Mamah smiled. "Am I the first?"

"I suppose you are." Ellen grinned as if the idea pleased her. "It has been a hard go of it, yes?"

The question caused Mamah to close her eyes.

"Come along, dear," Ellen said. "Let's have a swim."

They changed into bathing suits, black baggy things, and swam out into Lake Vattern. Mamah floated on her back, studying the cloud formations. From time to time she saw Ellen dive under the surface with her broad back arched, then reappear seconds later some distance away, her head popping up like a seal's.

"Please, Ellen Key," she called to her friend, "no more talk of wills. I want you to live here forever."

"I'll do my best," Ellen called back.

During the next four days, Ellen's small, womanly kindnesses moved Mamah deeply. Gerda, the house girl, brought her breakfast in bed with flowers on the tray every morning. The sheets smelled as if lilacs had been pressed into them.

In the hours they spent together, talking of so many things, she watched Ellen's face. Ellen was calm here, less dogmatic. In fact, she was maternal. Mamah wondered what sadness she had experienced in her own life. How had she ended up alone? The professor of Swedish in Leipzig had spoken of a married man in her life for many years, who had failed to leave his wife. Mamah wanted desperately to ask if this were true, but she held her tongue. Ellen Key was like her sister Lizzie in that way. There was deep vein of goodness in her, but she kept most people at arm's length.

Still, Mamah could see that her visit pleased Ellen. To her surprise, she also discovered that the great philosopher was a little vain. At one point she showed Mamah a magazine cut of an official portrait that had been painted by a Norwegian artist.

"What do you think of the likeness?" she asked.

Mamah examined the picture. "He's depicted you as a seer, hasn't he? A sort of high priestess. It's a very lovely likeness."

Ellen beamed.

"But these curtains," Mamah said playfully, pointing to the abstract drapes that curved over the top two corners of the painting. "Can't you talk him into painting them out? My goodness. They look like two ugly blobs on either side of your head."

Ellen shot her an offended look. Then she burst into laughter. "I like someone who speaks her mind."

LATE IN THE DAY, walking down to the water, Mamah felt the dry ferns brush against her ankles. She sat down cross-legged on the floor of the portico and listened to the waves lap against the rocks beneath her. She wanted a home like this of her own. In the past, she had thought only in the abstract about a house for herself and Frank, but now she could picture some details. It would be out in the country, near water, but close to a city, as this place was close to Stockholm. A home that guests would remember for its small indulgences. Frank would make it a miracle of light and space. And she would make it feel the way this place felt.

They spent their mornings in Ellen's study, talking. Mamah guessed the pile of letters on Ellen's desk could be from any of the famous figures she said she corresponded with. Sitting in the sun-filled room, a lake breeze quivering the beech leaves outside, she was struck by the honor of being among the first guests at Strand. How strange to be sitting across from a woman her countrymen regarded as Ibsen and Strindberg's equal.

Photos of Ellen's famous friends—Rilke, Bjornsen—hung on the wall above her desk, interspersed among the colorful prints of family life painted by her friend Carl Larsson. Mamah tried to imagine what gift she might contribute to the house that could possibly measure up to the personal objects Ellen had already assembled. Then it struck her. She would ask Frank for one of his beloved Hiroshiges to send to Ellen.

"WOMEN NEED TO DEVELOP their personalities from within," Ellen said. They had been talking for hours about how Mamah might get Ellen's essays into *The American* magazine, how different pieces might be edited down, how best to reach women readers in the United States.

"It's hard to say how *The Morality of Woman* will be received once it's published there," Mamah said. "The focus of the Woman Movement in America is the vote and equal pay."

Gerda came into the study and set down their dinner: rib roast and potatoes.

"To free women from conventionalism—*that* should be the aim of the struggle." Ellen's tone was agitated. "What good does it do if woman is emancipated but has little education and no courage to act?"

"But there are many women—" Mamah began.

Ellen either ignored her or didn't hear. "Men have always been *trained* to have the courage to dare." She chewed meat off a rib bone. "Women, on the other hand, are stuck being the keepers of memories and traditions. We've become the great conservators. Oh, I suppose we're suppler, as a result, because we've learned to see many sides. But what a price has been paid. It has kept us from greatness! And most women are happy just to repeat opinions and judgments they've heard, as if they thought of the ideas themselves. It's dangerous!" She poked the air with the white bone. "Women need to understand evolutionary science, philosophy, art. They need to expand their knowledge and stop assassinating each others' characters."

"This has been a personal struggle for you," Mamah said gently.

"They say I'm licentious, all sorts of sordid things." Ellen's proud, full face took on a haggard expression. The deep lines beside her mouth made her look like a bitter old warhorse. "It's a very effective method: Attack the personal character of the thinker, and you will kill her ideas. I have been forced to live a careful life as a result."

Gerda came in to clear their plates, then returned with generous slices of butter cake. Ellen's whole countenance changed. "Oh," she said, lacing her fingers together like a child at an unexpected treat. While Mamah picked at her dessert, she watched Ellen eat her slice with abandon, then chase the remaining crumbs around her plate with a fork.

Mamah felt a pang of pity for the solitary life Ellen had ended up with. She searched her mind for some little kindness to bestow. "You remind me of Frank," she said.

Ellen's eyebrows went up. She leaned back in her chair.

"You each have made a reputation with your aesthetic ideas about making a home. You both seem to take great pleasure in writing sayings on your walls," Mamah teased. "And you're both ornery as can be."

Ellen Key's earthy laugh filled the room. "I shall have to meet this man."

THE NEXT MORNING as Mamah prepared to depart, Ellen embraced her at the front door. "You know, you were wound tight as a top when you arrived here," she said. "Stay the course, daughter. But show yourself some kindness along the way."

Mamah climbed up into the wagon.

"And get your picture made," Ellen called to her, waving. "I'll want it for my study."

CHAPTER 27

The convent bell across the street from Villino Belvedere was pealing the hour when Mamah stepped into the garden. It was one of the morning sounds in Fiesole that she was growing accustomed to. Horse hooves clomping on stone, bakers' trays thudding on a table a few doors away, an anvil clanking somewhere meant the workday had begun. From the apartment at the opposite side of the house, she heard the first sounds of bow on string from the Russian cellist and violinist who practiced every morning.

Frank was stretched out in a garden chair, eyes closed, face slanted up to the sun. "Another perfect day," he said when he heard her footfall.

Frank had said the same thing every morning since she'd joined him, whether the village was fogged in or baking white in the sun. Everything about the hill town pleased him.

"Aren't you working today?" she asked.

"Just for a couple of hours."

"Let's look at some old gardens. What do you say?"

"Haven't we seen them all?"

"We haven't seen Villa Medici yet. Estero says no one is there right now, and she knows the gardener." Estero, the sweet-faced woman who cooked for them, had friends in every corner of Fiesole who were willing to help the nice couple from America.

"Is it far?"

"We can walk. I'll see if she can get us in."

"Eleven o'clock," he called as he went down the steps to the lower level of the house where he had his studio.

The days shaped themselves in just this way, their cadence tuned to the sun's rise and the midday meal. By eight-thirty they were both at their own posts, though some mornings Mamah slipped into the studio room to watch

Frank and Taylor Woolley delicately tracing drawings onto thin paper with crow quills dipped in ink.

She did her own work in the smaller of the house's two gardens, this one sheltered under an arbor heavy with yellow roses that ran along the edge of the terrace. From the round garden table situated next to a wall that separated her from a terrifying drop-off, she could look out upon the red tile roofs of Florence.

She took her time translating *Love and Ethics*. She toyed with phrases, consulted her dictionary, framed and reframed sentences. She wanted to honor the work by getting it right. And when she did, when she poured the German translation of Ellen's wisdom through the filter of her own soul, when it distilled into elegant, persuasive English sentences right there on the paper, something very much like ecstasy came over her.

She lived outside as much as she could, leaving her translating some mornings to hike up Via San Francesco to the ancient church and monastery at the top of the hill. The spot was one of a dozen destinations she had, though her hikes through poppy-covered meadows all seemed to culminate in the same way. She would find a place to sit and stare out at the hills until calm swept over her like a stupor. When half-moons of brown skin appeared on her back and chest from her hours in the sun, she found a hat with a broader brim.

"Mamah of the Hills!" Frank saluted her one morning when she emerged from the house into the garden wearing the floppy hiking hat. Henceforth, it was his pet name for her.

Mamah's June arrival in Fiesole had coincided with Taylor Woolley's return there. He and Frank's son Lloyd had both worked on the portfolio during late winter and spring, first in Florence and then in Fiesole, where Frank rented Villino Belvedere from an Englishwoman who owned several places in town. When Lloyd and Taylor had finished the bulk of their drawings, Frank set the two of them free with money in their pockets for sightseeing. At the end of their tour, Lloyd had gone home (probably to avoid her, she thought), but Taylor returned to Fiesole to work.

She found Taylor Woolley the gentlest and most discreet of young men. He was a Mormon boy of twenty-six, with a slender build and a pronounced limp. Fifteen years separated them, but she discovered in the young architect from Salt Lake a fit companion for her walks in the hills.

Often the three of them took the tram down into the city to wan-

through the great cathedrals. They spent whole days in the Uffizi Gal-
y, studying the statues of Donatello and Michelangelo, thirteenth-century
paintings of the Virgin, portraits of red-garbed cardinals with backgrounds of
Tuscan landscapes. They collapsed on benches, let their heads fall back, only
to see gilded ceilings flocked with angels, before they had to leave, exhausted
from sheer satiety.

Taylor carried a small camera but rarely pointed it at the churches of Florence. Instead, he photographed the city's loose patchwork pattern from
above, capturing the edges of rectangles fringed with cypress trees. He was
taken with the ancient Roman roads and the houses that clung to hills so
steep the steps leading to their doors looked like ladders. Mamah went with
him sometimes, seeking out the most hair-raising precipices near Villino
Belvedere from which to photograph the city below.

One afternoon he took her out to an overlook and taught her how to oper-
ate the camera. From where they stood, Florence seemed awash in a white
river that shifted and swirled, revealing a street here, a tall building there,
before it covered over everything. Taylor and Mamah took turns peering
through his viewfinder, waiting for the fog to open and reveal a particular
villa they had noticed before. The great house rose from time to time, like an
island, out of the roiling mist.

"Let me take your photograph," Mamah said. Taylor posed patiently on a
stone wall while she shifted the camera to compose the picture. All the while,
they talked about their childhoods. She noticed how careful Taylor was not to
touch on her more recent history. Nor did he ask to photograph her.

MAMAH AND FRANK set out from the heavy green door of Villino Belvedere as
the morning heated up, carrying a knapsack containing a lunch prepared by
Estero. By now they were a familiar sight to the locals as they walked hand in
hand up and down the ancient roads, he with a walking stick tucked under
his sleeve, she in the wide-brimmed hat. By noon they stood in the upper terraced garden of Villa Medici.

It was a grand, faded place, bound on one side by a long rose-laden pergola next to the hillside, and on the other side by a sweeping view of the River
Arno meandering through Florence. The terraced garden was one of three
green rooms that stepped down the hillside. There was no central outdoor
staircase connecting the garden tiers. One entered each garden from the
house or from the sides via little paths.

"Gardens say so much about a culture, don't they?" Mamah was thinking out loud and breathing heavily from climbing. "You really see what the people value."

Frank stood within earshot when she spoke, but he didn't respond. She knew he was gone somewhere else, lost in absorbing the space. She had learned to leave him alone at these moments.

He walked the pebble paths, climbed up and down the hillside, paced through the separate outdoor rooms around the villa, studied the house from a distance. The stucco looked golden. Up close, though, it appeared moments from collapse.

No one was home, and the gardener insisted they take their lunch under the pergola.

"See those trees?" Mamah said, gesturing out toward a pair of cypress trees framing the view of the hills beyond. "They've been placed there purposely, like exclamation points, as if to say, 'Look at this! Isn't it something?' "

Frank was observing the hill opposite them. "Mmm. I was noticing those little houses hanging on to the hillside. They seem as natural there as the trees and rocks."

"How characteristic," Mamah said, "that I am agog over this glorious house and garden, and you're eyeing the mud huts."

"I see the garden." Frank smiled. "It reminds me of Japan."

She pretended to glower at him. "I brought you up here thinking you would look at these terraces. That you would sit under a pergola just like this one, and you would talk about how these terraces blur the line between house and nature. I thought I was rather clever, engineering this little outing."

"You did, did you?"

"Yes, I figured you would say, 'Mamah, this is where I want to live with you forever. Let me build a villa for us on that hill over there.' And I would swoon and say yes. Instead, you say it reminds you of Japan."

He laughed. "But I was thinking about something else. I was noticing how the farmers till the land here. And it brought to mind the Japanese farmers, who make the most beautiful lined terraces for their crops, which step down, similar to this. So you look around you from your beautiful home, and you see the hand of man on the land."

"You don't see wilderness? Isn't that what Frank Lloyd Wright wants to see?"

"I want to see some wild land, yes. But . . ."

"But man is part of nature," she said.

"Yes, as much as any living thing. These patterns we make in farming and using the land—they're ancient images, really, ingrained in our psyches, I think, so we just naturally see them as beautiful. The farmer doesn't start out planting crops to be artistic. He's practical. He's going to work with the contours of his fields. But the rhythm of the land finds a way of asserting itself, making the farmer create beautiful wavy lines with his wheat fields in Umbria, or grids somewhere else. If you do the land's bidding, you can build a house that's organic to it."

"How do you feel about *this* place?"

"I think a man who loved buildings made these gardens rather than a gardener. I admire it—to a degree."

"I mean Italy. How do you feel about Italy?"

"Can't you tell? You'd be a fool not to feel the magic of it. The hills . . ."

"Let me guess. They remind you of Wisconsin."

"They do." He shrugged, smiling. "Very much."

THE NEXT DAY they took the tram that ran down the pine-scented road into Florence. Once they reached the town, they decided to forgo the museums and climb up the hill that led to Piazzale Michelangelo. Frank walked her by Villino Fortuna, the first house he had rented when he arrived in Florence.

"We were freezing in there," he said. "Lloyd and Taylor and I had to warm our fingers over a fire just to get them working." Only three or four months had elapsed since he'd inhabited the house, but he painted the picture as if it had happened long ago. Frank did that. He could make a legend out of a happenstance.

Near the top, they rested on a bench by a small church. Frank walked over to stand next to the building, watching workmen dye the stucco with an ocher color. Jasmine climbed up and around the door, but through the vine, Mamah could read words carved in stone.

"There's a phrase over the door," she called to him. " '*Haec est porta coeli.*' "

A browned workman with a kerchief around his forehead looked up from his stucco, trying to understand their conversation.

"My Latin's rusty," Frank called back. "What does it say? We're all going to hell?"

"No, no," she shouted back. " 'Here is the gate to heaven.' "

They were too tired to return to Fiesole in the afternoon, so they took a room at an inn near the Piazza della Repubblica. That evening they ate dinner in a café on the plaza. She and Frank watched the early-evening strollers. A well-dressed couple promenaded elegantly; an old man pushing a cart full of rubble hurled himself forward, the echoes of his cart's wheels clapping against the surrounding buildings. Near them, another pair of travelers huddled over a small table, their dialogue a low hum.

"Take your time, madam, and enjoy the pageant," the waiter said when Mamah told him they were not ready to order yet. "This is my favorite part of the day."

"Have you worked here in the piazza long?"

"*Sí, signora.* Twelve years at this hotel. I never tire of it. I have a small place, a room near here," he said. "It's all I need. The piazza is the Italian's parlor. I receive my friends here."

"Have you traveled away at all?"

"No. Why should I? The world eventually comes to me, right here in the piazza."

Mamah laughed and translated the conversation for Frank.

"Now ask the gentleman if I may buy this white tablecloth, as I am about to draw on it."

The waiter shrugged. *"Non c'e problema."*

Mamah ordered soup for them.

"Ask him to hold off serving it, would you?" Frank moved the glasses aside. He took from a small bag a blue colored pencil he'd bought to add to a collection he'd begun in Berlin. He quickly sharpened it with a small knife he carried in his breast pocket, then drew an irregularly curving line on the white cloth and sketched some rectangles pressed into the curve. He was drawing upside down for her benefit, but the geometric forms were clearly parts of a house set into the side of a hill. More curving lines appeared, outlining a river and more hills.

"Villa Medici had three levels, didn't it?" she asked.

Frank continued to draw, penciling in trees and roads. On one hill, he covered the curves with patchwork gardens. "This isn't Villa Medici."

"Oh." Mamah's finger traced the curving line at the bottom of the drawing. "I thought this was the Arno."

"You're close," he said. "It's a river, but not the Arno. It's the Wisconsin River."

She bent her head toward the drawing.

"There is a hill," he said, "one I visited often as a boy, near my grandfather's homestead, where my aunts run their school. That hill was a magical place for me then. Summers, when I was working my uncle's farm, I would go there to get away from everyone and just sit, looking down on the treetops. The hill is big and round—like the top of a head. I want to put a house just below the crown of that hill, Mamah. Our house."

Mamah felt a sinking sensation inside.

"I dream about this house all the time," he said. "It backs itself up into that hillside and has wings that embrace the hill. It's made of the same limestone that pushes out of the earth all over Wisconsin, so it looks like a great outcrop of rock. And it has a courtyard like the one we saw at Villa Medici. You'll have gardens all around you, Mamah. You'll walk from indoor room to outdoor room and never even feel where the house ends and the fresh air begins."

There was a fierce excitement in his eyes. "I want to farm there," he said. "I want to cover these other hills with fruit trees. Just allow yourself for one minute to imagine the perfume of a hundred apple trees. Can you smell it? And vegetables—tons of them. We'll grow our own food in ribbons across the hills."

Mamah stared at him sadly.

"I'm not crazy, Mamah. It's within our reach. I've already written to my mother about it."

"You have?"

"I think she would buy the land for me. No one will be the wiser until it's built."

"You've never said you'd—"

"We can live in peace there. I'll run my practice from up there, maybe keep a small office in Chicago, and you can translate, garden, do what you love. Yes, there are mostly farm folks there, but we'll figure out a way to bring some culture to Spring Green. We'll get the world to come to us."

"There's no place for me back there right now," Mamah said. "Not even in Wisconsin. Anyway, I've put it all out of my mind. Please, Frank, we're in Italy—"

"Look," he said. "My family goes back three generations in that valley. That counts for something—people will be civil. It's utterly private, only three hours by train from Chicago. Our children will come to stay with us."

She watched pigeons swoop across the piazza. "I know how you love Wisconsin, Frank. But . . ." She sat up and looked him in the eye. "Just for me," she began, "would you design a house for us in *this* place? The children could live with us part of the year here. Maybe your children could come during the other part."

"Mamah." Frank stroked her hand tenderly. "You're dreaming. Italy is no more my home than—"

Mamah pulled her hand away. "Is Oak Park *my* home? Or Wisconsin? I don't have a home anymore. At least in Italy I'm anonymous."

The waiter arrived at the table with two large bowls of soup. He looked at the drawing, then tentatively at Mamah and Frank, waiting for some signal. Finally, Frank motioned to him, and he put the bowls down, covering the pencil sketch.

CHAPTER 28

At Villino Belvedere, late evenings were given over to books. Sometimes Frank read aloud, then talked with her about the passages.

" 'Blue color,' " he read from Ruskin one evening, " 'is everlastingly appointed by the Deity to be a source of delight.' " Back and forth they went, debating the best blues—azure, cobalt, cornflower, the blue of the Mediterranean. Or the subtle differences of orange-reds—Venetian versus Chinese versus Cherokee red.

If the translating had gone well that day, Frank was treated to nuggets from *Love and Ethics*. But they avoided any more talk of Wisconsin or the hill crown.

One morning when the sun was particularly hot, Mamah stepped down into the make-do studio to cool off. Frank had furnished it sparsely with objects that pleased him—a wool scarf laid over a table, topped by a fat glazed pot full of tree branches, architectural drawings pinned to the floral wallpaper, a small shelf lined with simple Italian vases. He and Taylor were quietly working at separate tables.

She walked over to Frank, putting one hand on his shoulder to glance at what he was working on.

"Well, you've caught me," he said.

She laughed. "Caught you doing what?"

"Just look for a moment."

He was working on a pair of drawings arranged on a single page, one above the other.

"It's my house," she said of the top picture. Marion Mahony's elaborately drawn foliage curled around the corners of the picture and spilled over the terrace wall. It was the very drawing that had sold her and Edwin on Frank's design back in 1903.

She stared at the rendering below. It showed a rectilinear house with wide terrace walls that stood proudly against a steep hillside. Lettering under the drawing read VILLA FOR ARTIST.

"I want these two drawings together on one lithograph plate," he said.

"Why is that?"

"Because I designed both of them for you."

She cocked her head, confused, then looked at the lower drawing again.

Taylor stood up and stretched. "I believe I'll take a break," he said, and walked out into the garden.

"That bottom one is just an experiment," Frank said. "I was exploring how a house might fit into the hillside here . . . an organic house."

"You drew a house for Fiesole?"

"Yes."

"Oh, Frank!" she shouted, "I love it. Is that a walled garden?"

He nodded.

She threw her arms around his shoulders. "It's not such an outrageous idea, truly it isn't. We wouldn't be the first people to live abroad for a while." She squeezed him tightly. "There are expatriates sheltering in villas all over these hills right now. Just think of all the artists who have used this place to hide out—Shelley, Proust, Ruskin."

She took the rendering over to the window and held it up in the light. "It's wonderful. Wonderful." When she looked back at him, she found that he was watching her. "Don't you see, Frank? We wouldn't be freaks here. We could have friends, a community. There's so much culture here. And working in Europe for a while might actually be good for your career. Once the portfolio is published, there will be Europeans pounding a path to your door."

"We'll have to see," he said vaguely.

She stopped, careful not to press the idea further.

Mamah's walks in the hills took on purpose after that. Frank had made no promises. Still, it was the end of July, and his work was nearly finished. His plan all along had been to return to Chicago by September or October. If they were to stay, they would need to find a place to live quickly. Perhaps to build.

On a Friday morning when Frank had gone into the city to get the mail and run a few errands, she set out on her customary walk up Via Verdi with a sketch pad under her arm, intent upon mapping out the unbuilt places in the distant hills.

"*Buon giorno!*" Taylor Woolley called out to her, skipping to compensate for his game leg. "I didn't know you sketched," he said when he reached her.

"Oh, I only draw things to remember them. Frank is in the city. Do you want to come with me?"

"I really shouldn't today. I leave tomorrow for Germany, you know."

"Is that possible? I thought you were leaving next week."

"I decided to polish things off so I can do a little more traveling before I have to return."

"Oh, Taylor, how I'll miss you. I know what we must do this evening, then. We'll all have a farewell supper together."

"I'd like that." He waved goodbye as he let himself into the garden. "See you tonight!"

Walking toward town, she stopped by Estero's house and requested a special dinner for that evening.

SETTLED IN A SPOT at the top of the hill, Mamah scanned the undulating slopes around Fiesole, looking for spots in the distance where an angular stucco house might fit into a hill's tawny folds. She drew the shape of the mountains on her pad, then made irregular circles where the empty spots were.

Mamah allowed herself to imagine a life with Frank in Italy. She pictured her children spending half the year with them. That was the best situation her imagination would permit, but she could see it quite clearly—how John and Martha might crouch around a patch of dirt, playing marbles with other children, their familiar voices interspersed with others, all of them speaking Italian.

It would not be a permanent arrangement, but a voluntary exile for a couple of years. In the interim, hopefully, Edwin and Catherine would agree to divorces. She would bring Frank to this spot, maybe tomorrow, to show him the places where he might build.

"IT'S A HOT ONE." Taylor pressed his sleeve against his sweat-beaded forehead. "This drawing is the last one, and I'm terrified I'm going to drip on it."

Mamah stood a few feet from him. She bent over and squinted at the spines of books lining the shelves in Frank's studio. She was looking for Vasari's *Lives*, which she'd seen Frank reading not a week ago, but she couldn't find it. Straightening up, she patted her pockets, then put on the eyeglasses she habitually misplaced and promptly saw it: *The Lives of the Most Excellent*

Painters, Sculptors, and Architects. Frank had talked admiringly of Vasari's accounts of Giotto and Brunelleschi and the other Italians who transcended the bounds between painting and sculture and architecture.

When she pulled the book from the case, a piece of stationery tucked inside the cover fell out. It was an unsent letter written by Frank to someone named Walter, dated June 10, 1910, Fiesole, Italy. *The very day I signed Ellen's guest book,* she mused.

Mamah read the letter quickly, trying to puzzle out its meaning. In his tight script, Frank was shaming a Walter for rumors that Frank had short-changed him in some deal. She realized it was Walter Griffin he was addressing. It appeared that Frank had repaid a debt to Griffin with Japanese prints rather than cash, and Walter was unhappy with the prints.

She tried to picture Walter Griffin. He had been working at the studio in 1903 when Frank designed the house for her and Edwin. She remembered him as a soft-spoken but intense landscape architect who was passionate about his field.

It was the tone of the letter that disturbed her. Frank was deeply anguished by Griffin's betrayal. He had written the letter only a week or so before she had arrived in Fiesole, yet he had never mentioned the matter to her.

"Taylor," Mamah asked, "do you know anything about a debt between Mr. Wright and Walter Griffin?"

Taylor's eyes shot from her face to the letter in her hand. He looked worried.

"I realize this is awkward, Taylor, and I don't want to put you in a bad spot. But I need to understand some things."

"Well," he said tentatively, "I heard some talk."

"Yes?"

"How much of it was true, I couldn't say."

"Yes?"

He looked out the window. "It happened before I arrived at the studio, when Walt Griffin and Mr. Wright were business partners. I guess Mr. Wright wanted to go to Japan with—uh—Mrs. Wright. He borrowed five thousand dollars from Walter. He also put him in charge of the studio while he was gone. I'm not sure what year that would have been."

"It was 1905." She remembered exactly the time—a year after Frank had built the house for her and Edwin. The year she became pregnant with Martha.

"Five years ago, then," Taylor said. "Anyway, it seems Mr. Wright repaid

Walter with some woodblock prints he brought back from Japan, and Walter was upset with them. I guess he would have rather had his cash. As for Mr. Wright, they say he was angry with Walter for losing a big commission while he was gone. And for altering some of his plans that Walter was supposed to be overseeing."

"Mr. Wright does that sometimes, doesn't he? I mean, use his prints as collateral for loans. Use them as money." She knew perfectly well that Frank did. He had told her himself that he'd sold some of his collection to pay for his time in Europe. The check from that sale to an art collector had arrived just a few days before.

"I couldn't really say, ma'am."

"But Frank says in the letter that Walter never told him he was unhappy about being paid in prints."

"That I don't know."

It didn't involve her, but the whole thing made Mamah feel embarrassed and uncomfortable. Had Frank acted improperly? The tone of his letter was so injured, it seemed more likely that it was a painful misunderstanding. She felt bad for Frank—one more humiliation in a string of them. She wondered why he hadn't sent it, and it occurred to her that it might be because he couldn't even pay the interest he had offered in the letter.

"Did Mr. Wright pay his people on time back in Oak Park?"

"There were times," Taylor said carefully, "when we didn't get our pay on time. A client might take his time, or something could go wrong with a job, slow down. There were occasions . . ." He moved about, putting away tools. "I'd better be going now."

"Taylor . . ."

"Yes?"

"I trust you can be honest with me. How is it, working for Mr. Wright? Is he sometimes difficult?"

"That depends on what you mean by 'difficult.' Is he demanding? Yes. There were stories." A private smile spread across his face.

"Tell me the stories."

Taylor paused, considering. "Well, there was a draftsman who was newly married. I never knew the man, I only heard the story. And he was working long hours for Mr. Wright. Sometimes the draftsmen slept on the studio floor when we had a big deadline and then got up early the next morning to keep on working. It seems this fella's wife got pretty mad because her husband was never home. The story was that she came over and screamed at Mr. Wright and popped him one right in the nose." Taylor laughed. "The reason I can't believe that story is because Mr. Wright would never force somebody to stay. He can be persuasive, though, I'll grant you that. Does he want it done his way? Yes, ma'am. Is he cranky? Well, I suppose Thomas Jefferson was cranky sometimes, too.

"Most of the men I knew who worked for him wanted to be there. Some got worn out or mad because they felt they weren't getting proper credit, so they left. But that's how an architecture firm works—one man gets the credit, and you know that going in. As for me, I consider myself blessed. Not everyone gets to work for a genius.

"Mr. Wright is way ahead of other architects. People just think 'prairie house' when they hear his name. But he's so much more than that. If you listen to what he says about organic architecture, you can go build natural houses anywhere in the world. People don't understand that now, but they will someday."

He took down his hat from a hook near the door. "What I'm trying to say is, he's a prophet. What he shows in this portfolio here has never been seen by the Europeans, as far as I know. It's going to change the way architecture is practiced. Period."

Mamah smiled, and Taylor grinned back. "With Mr. Wright, you just grab hold of the tail of the kite. If you can hang on, you're going to go places you never thought possible."

"Thanks, Taylor." She squeezed his arm as he left. "See you at eight."

FRANK'S FACE WAS RED and dripping sweat when he arrived home from the tram. He found her in the garden, where she had gone to sit after bathing. He was in high spirits and wore a new beige linen jacket. Under both arms, he carried packages that he dropped on a chair as he bent down to kiss her.

"I love how beautifully they wrap things here." He mopped his brow with a handkerchief and untied the string on one package. Inside were trousers that matched his jacket. Right there he unbuttoned the ones he was wearing and slipped on the new pants, which buttoned snugly at his ankles. Then he strutted through the garden, modeling the whole ensemble and posing with his cane like a dandy. "Exquisite, isn't it?" He took off the jacket and showed her the little wonders of the thing—the FLW embroidered in curling Florentine script on the silk lining of the coat. "The tailor I've found is a genius. You can't find this sort of thing in Chicago."

"Taylor is coming for dinner tonight."

"Perfect. I bought him a little going-away gift. But do you like this jacket? It's not too narrow, is it?"

"No, it fits beautifully. Who are all these packages for?"

"My children. Plus a little something for you." He put a large wrapped package on the table in front of her.

Mamah stared at the brown paper imprinted with lilies. "You shouldn't be spending money on me," she said softly.

"Open it, sweetheart."

"I need to talk to you about something." She reached into her pocket and pulled out the letter. "I found this today."

She hated seeing the gaiety drain from his face.

"What about it?"

"What does it mean?"

"Walter Griffin doesn't deserve a civil word from me."

"Why didn't you send it?"

He studied her face. "Why are you asking?"

"Because I'm afraid."

"Of what?"

"That you don't have money to send to Griffin. That you're in trouble financially and somehow protecting me."

"The portfolio is going to change everything."

"I was just thinking . . ." She gestured toward the packages.

"Mamah. Relax a little!"

She looked at him skeptically. "So I shouldn't worry about money."

Frank sighed. "No, it always comes. It's never been the reason I practice architecture. But money can buy beautiful things, and I *need* beautiful things around me. I'm an artist, Mame. You more than anyone should comprehend that. Beautiful objects stimulate me, they inspire me. Look at this." He pointed to the delicate hand stitching on the lapels. "I don't buy junk. When I buy something, it's got to be perfection or I don't want it," he said. "You won't find me coming home with five cheap suits, one for each day of the week. I'd rather have one perfect suit or none. This suit wasn't even that expensive. You see, I happened upon this tailor a couple of weeks ago, before you got here. If I tried to have this made in Chicago . . ." Frank threw up his arms. "Jesus, Mamah, we're in Italy. We'd be *insane* not to buy clothes here!"

"I was only asking."

He nudged her arm gently. "Now, go on, have a look."

She unwrapped the paper and felt something soft inside. It was a dress—two, actually, a paper-thin satin chemise with tiny straps and an overdress of the sheerest, gauziest embroidered and beaded cream silk she had ever seen.

"It's exquisite, Frank."

"Wear it tonight."

"But this is a dress for the opera."

"And this is a festive occasion. We're finished with the portfolio. I want to celebrate."

IN THE EVENING Estero brought dinner. She spread a white cloth on the garden table, set it with dishes, then laid out the food on a small table nearby.

"*Fettunta . . . bistecca . . .*" The tiny gray-haired woman named each dish, from the bread to the beef surrounded by small grilled onions, and all of it rubbed or soaked or roasted or otherwise imbued with olive oil and garlic. She put out a bowl of cooked spinach, then the individual caramel custards she had made for dessert. As she did so, Estero shook her head. It was not how she would choose to serve the food—all at once—but she knew they wished to be alone.

Mamah guessed Frank had told Taylor how to dress, because he arrived in a suit and tie. Frank wore his new suit. He bowed elegantly to Mamah when she appeared in the garden in the dress he had bought her.

She was amused by his grand manners. He was playing the role of the most gracious of hosts, seating her and Taylor formally, then serving them Estero's dinner with the exaggerated seriousness of an English butler.

Next door the Russians began their evening session. "Ah," Frank said, pausing in his serving to sniff the air, as if to smell the notes cascading from the side window. "The Boccherini minuet."

"SIMPLE FOOD," he said, tearing apart a piece of crusty bread, "is the only good food. My mother knew this, and the Italian peasant knows this. Have you noticed the Italians apply the same instincts to building their houses?" He dipped his bread in some oil. "Or have you missed that fact during your forays into gilded cathedrals, Woolley?"

"I have noticed it, sir."

"And what have you found?"

"Organic architecture, sir."

"You found houses made out of the same mud the Etruscans used," Frank said. "Buildings that spring naturally from the earth where they stand." He pointed his fork in Taylor's direction. "Mud huts are the people's architectural folk tales. Pay attention to the folk tales, Woolley."

"Yes, sir."

"You're going back to the desert. Where will you look for inspiration there?" Frank didn't wait for an answer. "You'll look to the desert, the mountains. What form has true spell power there? Are the mountains in the distance triangular, for instance? That big Mormon temple won't give you an ounce of help. Every landscape has its own latent poetry. Let the contours of the land and the plants reveal to you the geometry of its soul. Then dig your hands into the earth and get acquainted with its properties."

"Yes, sir."

"I'm not worried about you, Woolley."

"Thank you, sir."

"Now, tell me this. Are you up to the task of seeing Wasmuth?" Frank turned to Mamah. "I'm having him pay a call on the old bastard. They're dragging their heels, I'm persuaded. Only twelve plates have been pulled out of seventy-six." He flicked his hand as if he were batting away an insect. "I don't want to think about Wasmuth tonight."

They ate and drank, and Frank held forth. The Russians switched to bohemian dances.

"Most of these cathedrals we've visited have no soul," Frank said.

"Don't you find any of them beautiful?" Mamah asked.

"I'd rather look at a pine tree for inspiration. It teaches me more about architecture than all the marble in St. Peter's. A pine tree speaks to my soul. As for *saving* my soul, you know where I fall on that topic."

"Here it comes, Taylor. 'Mariolatry!' " Mamah pounded her fist on the table for emphasis, imitating Frank in full tirade. It was a favorite word of Frank's these days, and they all laughed. Both she and Taylor had been lectured by him several times on the Renaissance artists' obsession with the Virgin.

"It's everywhere, is it not? I understand why. But I'm confounded by the end result of it all—people bowing down before statues. Where's the God in that?" He stood up and opened another bottle of wine. She took note of it because she had stopped drinking, and Taylor, a devout Mormon, had partaken only of water all evening. Frank usually drank very little, if at all.

"It's pretty much settled here in Italy," he said as he poured the wine. "It would be hard indeed to practice modern architecture in a country with traditions as set as Italy's. But in America this is the moment. The landscape is yours for the building. You're a young man in architecture, Woolley, no obligations."

"You're not exactly old, Mr. Wright."

"No," Frank mused, "and I have no plans of rolling over, though I can count on two hands the people who wish I would. But if we're ever going to achieve an architecture of our own in America—a democratic architecture that expresses the spirit of the place—then we have to change the way we teach young minds. Is there a university-trained architect in America today whose head hasn't been filled with Beaux Arts crap? They're all decorators, for Christ's sake!" Frank was pacing now. "We need to show young people there's more to design than the Greek column. What happened to the spirit of individualism? My God, isn't that what our democracy is supposed to be about? Yet what are America's architects doing? They're mimicking the architectural traditions of monarchies!"

He stopped in his tracks, his eyes wide. "I could change all that. I really could. Give me a handful of young unschooled minds, and we'll change the face of America. Never mind classrooms with blackboards. And the only book they'd need would be Viollet-le-Duc's. *Discourses on Architecture*—they could read it themselves. That's what I did. Beyond that, my drafting table would be the classroom. I would take them through the process of discovery. Let them *watch* me. When they're true problem solvers, they'll be worthy of the title 'architect.' And they will go out and change the world."

Frank sat down and talked on, with Taylor listening intently, but Mamah drifted on the edge of the conversation. The music from next door was softer now. She wanted to remember every detail of the night—the food and music and camaraderie, Frank's white shirt glowing in the candlelight, the black valley below them twinkling with lights. It was almost eleven when she realized she'd forgotten Taylor's gifts.

She fetched two slim packages she had wrapped up—her dog-eared Italian and German dictionaries, each with a different inscription. She presented them to him, and he seemed pleasantly embarrassed. Frank gave him a fine pen.

The candles burned down, and they grew quieter. No one seemed to want to leave the table. When she looked across at Frank, though, she saw tears dripping down his cheeks.

Mamah stood up. "I hate to say good night, but I'm so tired, Taylor. Will I see you in the morning?" She helped Frank to his feet. He slid away from her hands, then stumbled inside without a word.

"Did I say something wrong?"

"No, no, Taylor, it's all right. He's exhausted, I think."

She found Frank hunched over the upright piano in the parlor, picking out some old tune on the keys. She approached him and put her hand on his shoulder.

"I'm going back," he said. He stopped playing.

Mamah stood still, waited.

He began to rub his eyes. It was something he did, a tic, when he had something hard to say. "Not to Catherine. But to the children. Do you understand?"

She couldn't speak.

"My practice is in shambles. The people I trained are stealing my work, passing off my ideas as theirs." His face was more agonized than angry. "If any of them ever wanted to do work of their own, I encouraged them, gave them a place to draft after hours. I swore when I started the studio that I would never punish anybody for being ambitious, the way I was fired by Sullivan for doing after-hours work. But this isn't ambition. It's theft."

He looked up at her. "I haven't visited a work site or had honest dirt under my fingernails in a year. It's against my nature," he said softly. "I need to build. It's ludicrous—my sitting here in an Italian villa, talking about democratic architecture. Staying here is impossible for me."

"Why did you let me believe?" She felt a fury rising inside.

Frank began to weep. "I can't live with myself. Their letters . . ."

He was talking of his children's letters. She had seen them, and they weren't very different from the ones she got—sweetly scrawled childish words, misspelled sometimes. *I am seven years old,* John had last written. As if she had forgotten.

"I've received the same letters," she said. She hated the bitterness in her own voice.

"I never meant to harm them. I always hated the sound of the word 'Papa.' Now . . ." Frank's shoulders shook as he sobbed. "I thought if they could just see a life lived out in front of them that was honest, that was dedicated to something—it would be the best I could do for them." He dabbed a tear with his thumb. "I never dreamed it would come to this."

Her whole body ached with anger. And shame at being angry. "Neither did I," she said.

MAMAH SLEPT LITTLE that night. Before daylight, she tiptoed downstairs to his studio and went to his drafting table. When she found Frank's first simple sketch of the Italian villa tucked underneath the more detailed version he had shown her, she pulled it out of the stack, rolled it up, and set it aside.

Taylor would be there in a couple of hours to collect the last of his items and be on his way. She wanted to memorize this place before Frank began to pack up, before it became one more disassembled camp. She knew where Frank kept his correspondence, in a cigar box in the corner. The twinge of guilt she felt perusing his letters was overruled by the anger still simmering inside.

Looking through the box, she found no evidence that Catherine had written to him. Mamah supposed Frank had thrown those letters away, for there had been some. But he had kept his children's notes. And a letter from his mother expressing her sorrow that he hadn't replied to her many letters.

Mamah noticed another long letter from a minister in Sewanee, Tennessee, dated May 14, 1910. Mamah couldn't discern the signature, but the tone was that of an old friend. He was answering Frank's request for advice; point by point, he explained to Frank why he must abandon his foolish rebellion with Mamah.

The minister knew Frank well enough not to use scripture on him. Instead, he seemed to be challenging Ellen Key's ideas, which Frank had obviously outlined in a letter to him. The minister talked of how wrong it was for the exceptional individual to go against the social order. If an ordinary man does, it has few long-term consequences. But for Frank it would be disastrous, as his God-given gifts would be used up in his fight with society. And *that* would be a great loss to the world.

Even if Mamah were the most heavenly of beings, he said, even if they both secured divorces and managed to create a wonderful new home together, Frank would be robbing his children of his full presence in their lives. It would be better to carry on a carnal relationship in secrecy than to try to change society to accommodate such an affair.

Mamah put the minister's letter into the cigar box along with the others. *So this is how it is.*

Until last night Frank had revealed little of the conflict raging inside himself. He had shown such brave resolve in Berlin when the hideous scandal arrived in an envelope. He had been her loving protector when she might have destroyed herself. He'd been the one most insistent about pursuing a life together. She'd never seen him happier than he was here in Fiesole.

What he had kept from her, though, was what she kept from him—the terrible weight of remorse and doubt that daily, hourly sometimes, shifted inside like cargo. Last night Frank had listed decisively to the side that would pull him back home to his family.

Maybe designing a villa in Fiesole had been only an exercise for him. Why had she expected the dream to be any more than that, a fantasy, given the odds against it? Now he said he was going back to his children, not Catherine. But how could he sustain that resolve in the face of so much opposition?

Mamah didn't know if *she* could sustain it. If she returned right now, there was a good chance she would be sucked back into being Edwin Cheney's wife. As much as she longed for her children, she knew if she got close to Oak Park, the work she had begun would be put aside.

Ellen had told Mamah about a friend in Berlin who could secure a teaching position for her if she chose to stay in Europe. There was no hope of finding a job in the United States in the wake of the scandal, and she would need one now. She counted the months she had been gone. Fourteen since she boarded the train to Boulder. If she could stay on the continent ten more months, she could get a divorce from Edwin even if he didn't want one. By then it would be two years since she'd lived under the same roof with him.

Mamah would have to lean on Lizzie longer than she had expected. It was a lot to ask. Maybe she could manage to stay only until spring—another six months—but that might be enough.

When Frank came into the garden that morning, he sat across from her. "What will you do?" he asked. The skin below his eyes was brown and puffy.

"I've been thinking about that." She looked out over the fog in the valley that was just beginning to burn off. "I've decided to stay over here, at least until spring."

Frank stirred milk into his coffee and avoided her eyes. "But you haven't got a friend here."

"I'm going to ask Edwin to allow the children to come over. Louise could bring them." She couldn't keep her shoulders from sagging a little at the thought of the furor that idea would ignite back in Oak Park.

Frank crossed his arms and confronted her gaze. "I told you from the start I would only stay over here for a year."

"I know that."

"Why don't you come back, take an apartment in Chicago?"

"Why don't you say 'I love you, Mamah.'?" Her voice quivered with anger. "Why don't you say 'Keep the faith. We will find a way.'? Why can't you say that to me?"

Frank swept the back of his hand gently across her cheek. "Of course I love you. You know what I want for us. But what can I promise? I am going back nearly broke to a place where I am despised. And the worst of it? I'm worried sick about leaving you here unprotected. How will you fend for yourself?"

"Ellen says she knows people at a girls' seminary school who will hire me to teach English." Her infuriating frustration began to dissipate. "I'll take more Swedish classes." She tried to brighten her voice. "Once Ellen authorizes me to begin *The Woman Movement,* it has to come straight from the Swedish. I persuaded her I could do it, but it's going to take total immersion."

Mamah could tell her bravado was not fooling him. "I dread being alone over here," she admitted. "But the truth is, I'm not ready to face the yellow press. When I go back, I shall be stronger, for everyone concerned."

During breakfast they talked of their remaining weeks together. If they lived cheaply, they could make a quick tour through Austria and Germany, perhaps take up Wasmuth on his offer to arrange a meeting with the Austrian artist Gustav Klimt. On his way back to the States, Frank would stop in England to persuade his friend Ashbee to write an introduction to the volume of photographs Wasmuth was preparing. He would also take Mamah's translations of *The Morality of Woman* and *Love and Ethics* back to his friend Ralph Seymour, to see if he'd publish them.

He talked about his plans to divide up the house on Forest Avenue. He would renovate his studio into living quarters for Catherine and the children, then eventually, rent out the other half so they would have a regular income in addition to what he gave them. It would take time to lay the groundwork. But it wouldn't be long before he and Mamah could have a home of their own together, maybe in the city.

When Taylor knocked at the gate, Frank ushered him into the garden. Mamah greeted him, then stepped into the studio to fetch the rolled-up drawing of the villa. In the early-morning hours, she had covered it in the lily-patterned wrapping paper Frank had discarded the night before.

"May I give this to you for safekeeping, Taylor?" she asked, putting it into his hands.

He and Frank looked puzzled. "Of course," Taylor said.

"A little memento of our time here in Italy." She smiled at his earnest face. "Proof that we all didn't dream it. If you hold it for me, Taylor, then I know I'll see you again."

CHAPTER 29

October 28, 1910

Ellen talks about living a "terrifyingly earnest life." She says moral law is not written upon tablets of stone, but on tablets of flesh and blood. In one year I have traveled from Oak Park to Boulder, New York, Berlin, Paris, Leipzig, Florence, and back to Berlin. I'm tired. I don't want to be anyone's tablet of truth.

Mamah set aside her journal and readied herself to go out. Bundled in her coat, she tiptoed down the hall past the closed door of Frau Boehm, past the parlor crammed full of heavy, dark furniture that reeked of polish, and through the front door of the Pension Gottschalk. On the street, she wrapped a scarf around her neck against the October chill, walked to the end of the block, then turned north toward the Wilmersdorf district police station. Anyone staying longer than two weeks in Berlin was required to register with the police. She was late getting to it, and annoyed now at having to give over perhaps an hour to waiting in line.

"MAMA—" THE SERGEANT tripped on her first name as he read from her passport.

"May-muh. It's a difficult one, no matter what language," she said.

He didn't look up. "May-muh Borthwick Cheney. Oak Park, Illinois. U.S.A."

"Yes."

"Father's full name?"

"Marcus S. Borthwick."

"Occupation?"

"Do you mean my occupation?"

The man looked up at her through smudged glasses. "No, his."

"Train repairman."

"His place of birth?"

"New York."

The sergeant straightened in his seat and rotated his shoulders, then slumped down again, drew on his cigarette. "Are you married?"

She swallowed. "Yes."

"Husband's full name?"

"Edwin H. Cheney."

"Occupation?"

"President of an electric company."

"Birthplace?"

"Mine?"

"His."

Mamah felt her ears growing hot. "Illinois."

The man's eyebrows rose above the spectacles. "Is he with you?"

"No."

"Your religion?"

"Why do you need to know that?"

The man looked up and frowned. "It is the law, madam."

"Protestant."

"Number of times in Germany?"

"*Dreimal.*" Three times.

"Purpose of your visit?"

"To translate sex manuals," she muttered in English. "To drive house-wives to mayhem."

"Eh?"

"*Um zu studieren.*" To study.

"How long will you stay?"

"Three or four months."

He handed over her passport. "You are free to go."

Oh, Frank, where are you when I need you? She would have made him laugh, telling him about the pompous sergeant. But there wasn't anyone with whom to share a real conversation. Frank had been back in Oak Park for a month and had his own struggles, far worse than hers. His one letter had been short and devastating. *It's official, my dear. Not a soul on my side. Friends cross the street rather than speak.*

Standing on the steps of the police station, Mamah felt her enthusiasm for her list of chores draining. It could all wait. She dropped her letters to Frank and Lizzie at the post office, then headed back to the boardinghouse.

She had arrived at Pension Gottschalk thanks to Ellen, who knew the landlady. Frau Boehm was a well-heeled widow who gave generously to the Woman Movement. She was bighearted and bigheaded, with her hair rolled into heavy puffs over each ear, the sort of outspoken woman who might have been a colorful friend had their paths crossed back in Oak Park. But here in Berlin, there was a class distinction between landlady and boarder, especially since Mamah had chosen to rent a room on the top floor of the pension, the cheapest room in the house.

She suspected she was one of the landlady's causes, that the woman fancied she was "harboring" her. And while Mamah offered no details of her personal life, she guessed Frau Boehm had gotten her personal history from Ellen Key.

At dinner the landlady sat at the end of the table, dressed in unfortunate copies of French gowns, with her great head floating like a dirigible above her shoulders. From time to time she paused midbite to pose discussion topics to her three female boarders. Is motherhood the right of every unmarried woman? Should girls be allowed to exercise naked at the gymnasiums? Mamah endured the dinners in silence. She had little money for food outside the fare that came with her room.

Except for the enforced intimacy at the pension, Mamah felt invisible in Berlin. She was grateful for the anonymity. Neither the professor of Swedish at the university, nor the headmistress at the girls' seminary where she taught, knew her full story. She'd passed herself off as an unmarried American scholar when she applied for the teaching position. That she was a foreigner was far less troubling than that she was a married woman living apart from her husband.

When Frank left her in Berlin in September, Mamah had looked forward to the solitude ahead, because Ellen's work required more than singleness of purpose. It required surrender. In Nancy, when she'd given herself over to *Love and Marriage,* she had come away from the book with her soul fed as it had never been fed before.

If she could lead other women to experience the same intense recognition she'd felt, if she could manage to make Ellen Key comprehensible to American women, who knew what might happen? Maybe a revolution in the Woman Movement. To tease from Swedish into English the delicate shadings of phrase and argument would take every drop of concentration she could squeeze from herself. Solitude was a requirement. More than anything, she wanted to feel again the calm confidence she'd felt in Nancy.

But what had been clear in September became fuzzy by October. After working six days a week at the girls' seminary from seven in the morning to one in the afternoon, she often returned to her room to study Swedish until nine or ten at night. Translating some of *The Woman Movement*, Mamah discovered little of the excitement she'd found in other texts.

She was exhausted, distracted. And for the first time in months, she found herself questioning the trail of decisions that had led her to the tiny room at Pension Gottschalk. The longing for her children was almost too much to bear. At night she lay in bed, trying to recall the exact smell of Martha when she was a baby. What had it been? Lilac talcum? Milk on her breath? Mamah couldn't conjure up the mix of smells she had so loved, but she could almost hear the sound of Martha's chatter rippling down the hall from her crib.

And John at four. Coming in from outside, time and again, carrying his bug jar. "I am the daddy of this worm," he'd announced once, then he'd taken it for a walk in his wagon. Another time he'd come up to her when she was standing in the living room, leaned in to her side, and said, "I love you as much as a bomb could explode."

Awake at night in Berlin, she cried and laughed.

When sleep came, the children were in her dreams. The whorls of dark hair at the nape of John's neck. The constellation of moles sprinkled across his back like the Little Dipper. She saw Martha's small fingers wrapped around one of her own; the delicate indentation in her chin, the bottle-blue eyes. Regret filled her when she woke. Or sometimes terror. One night she saw John batting at a wasp's nest while she looked down on him from a window she could not open. A particularly horrible nightmare came two nights in a row. John appeared to her and said, "A man is burying Martha in sand." When Mamah tried to rise from her chair in the dream, her limbs wouldn't move.

She began taking long walks, cutting through the zoological garden that lay like a wonderland between her pension and the heart of Berlin. She stood among the crowds of children in front of the animal cages, imagining John and Martha agog at the whimsical animal shelters where pelicans lived in a Japanese temple and antelopes in a Moorish house decorated with colorful majolica tiles.

When she wrote to Edwin begging him to allow Louise to bring the

children for a visit, he responded with a swift no. His letter threw her into a
downward spiral, but it was Lizzie's letter in late September that put her at the
bottom of a dark pit.

> Dearest Mamah,
>
> I write to you today with a hopeful heart that what I have to say will help
> you see the truth.
>
> Frank Wright returned to Oak Park last week in his usual way, making a
> spectacle of himself. I am told he enlisted poor William Martin to collect him
> and his belongings at the train station, then came along Chicago Avenue like a
> politician on the 4th of July, waving his hat and calling out to anyone he saw on
> the street. It would almost be amusing were this family not part of the humili-
> ating attention that has been stirred up by his return.
>
> People who never spoke to me in the past about your situation have come for-
> ward recently. Did you know that when Frank Wright departed for Europe, he
> left Catherine Wright with a $900 grocery bill? I am told Catherine has been
> hounded by debt collectors of all kinds throughout his absence, including the
> sheriff. Now that he is back, the entire town believes Frank has returned to
> Catherine, because that is what he is telling people. Yet your letters give me no
> reason to believe you and he have parted ways. Can you possibly believe a man
> who behaves this way?
>
> As for Edwin, he is mightily hurt. Yet I am convinced that if you saw your
> way back here, he would welcome you with open arms.
>
> Contrary to what you wrote in your last letter, Mamah, people remember
> you for the good and kind person you are. They are more forgiving than you
> think.
>
> > Faithfully,
> > Lizzie

Returned from her outing to the police station, Mamah hung up her coat
in the small wardrobe in her room and sat down at her desk. It was cold in the
room and quiet except for the sound of a streetcar squealing around a corner.

She hadn't known what to make of Lizzie's letter. Frank had struggled financially in the past; it might be true about the grocery debt. But his money
troubles never seemed to last, because work always came along. Now,

though, he was trying to perform a miracle on a shoestring—restart his practice, get the portfolio printed—and he hadn't had a new commission in a very
long time.

The letter she had just mailed to Lizzie was as truthful as she could manage without admitting the gnawing doubts left by her sister's words.

Dear Lizzie,

*I cannot speak for Frank. I know him well enough to understand that his re-
turn in the manner you describe was the bravado of a man in great pain. His
friends and clients have abandoned him. I deeply regret that you are suffering
anew as a result of his return. Yet he is there because he is the sole provider for
his family. Whatever his debts may be—I do not know of any "grocer's bill,"
but I suspect exaggeration in the remark made to you—he has returned to support his children out of loyalty and obligation.*

*And how can I not do the same, you may wonder. I struggle with this ques-
tion throughout each day here. I cannot explain except to say that the pressing
need continues to be that I be alone to study, to work as I can, to sort things out
unaffected by Frank's influence or, in truth, the influence of my own family. It is
not a need that I welcome, but it does not go away.*

*This much I know: I can stay here because of you, my darling Liz. It would
be impossible otherwise. This gift of time to strengthen myself away from judging eyes is the greatest of the many kindnesses you have showered upon me. I
hold you to your word that you will wire me immediately if any emergency
arises. I will be on the next ship. In the meantime, it is not lost upon me that my
absence is an ongoing sadness for the children. You understand, as no one else
seems to, that every day away from John and Martha is an arrow in my heart,
knowing it is I who causes their pain. I know you are the one who sits with them
as they compose their precious letters. I live for their arrival, and I thank you.*

Your loving sister,
Mamah

In the letter to Lizzie, Mamah had revealed half her true situation. She
was desperately lonely and nearly broke. She couldn't afford decent stationery, using instead school paper cadged from the seminary to write the letter. She had holes in her shoes and would need a new pair by winter, though
she hadn't any idea where that money would come from. Thankfully, her

winter things—two wool suits and a good coat—had held up. No one looking at her would guess her underwear was threadbare.

Living a spartan life was not so hard; Mamah embraced it. For the first time since Port Huron, she was self-reliant. She found pleasure in having a work schedule again, and in teaching the eager young women who wanted to be teachers themselves. Far more troubling than poverty were the panics that came over her in the morning when she woke to find herself in the rented room.

Then her heart tripped so madly that it frightened her. Had Frank gone back to Oak Park and realized how impossible their hopes were? Had he returned to the open arms of his children and regretted more deeply his absence? Mamah struggled to steady herself when the terror hit. She had doubted him two years earlier, when he'd obliged Catherine by giving her the year she'd asked for. But Frank had come back to Mamah then.

What assurances did she have that he would return to her this time? And if he didn't, how could she fault him? She didn't doubt that he loved her. She was certain he did. But he was human.

In her panics, she tallied the cost of what they had done. Two families ripped apart. The children hurt cruelly. Frank's business wrecked. Her reputation so universally ruined that her prospects for self-support were nil if she returned. And all for what? Perhaps nothing. Perhaps it was already over with in Frank's mind. Maybe he felt as Mamah was beginning to feel—that the price for their relationship was too dear to continue paying.

She didn't blame Frank. This was a self-imposed exile. *Why did I feel so compelled to stay?*

She got up from the desk, knelt beside the bed, and put her forehead down on the covers. She was not practiced at prayer anymore. The only word that came to mind was "please."

For a long time she had believed that a gardener prayed when she dug a hole; that a carpenter prayed when he pounded a nail. Now that notion seemed the attitude of a naive and lucky person. In the past, it had felt wrong, given the tragedies in the world, to ask for her own problems to be solved. But she asked it now.

When a prayer came, she wasn't surprised that it came as a poem, one she'd learned long ago.

If I stoop into a dark tremendous sea of cloud,
It is but for a time; I press God's lamp

Close to my breast; its splendour, soon or late
    Will pierce the gloom: I shall emerge one day.

Her knees were stiff when she finally stood up. She went back to her desk to write the one letter she'd been so reluctant to compose. Sentences appeared on the paper so fast it was as if they had been waiting inside her fingers to trail out.

Ellen Key, most beloved Lady,

I have meant for some time to write to you and tell you just how important you are in my life. Before I attended your lecture in Nancy, I had met you as a true friend on the printed page. In fact, you have been a greater influence on my life than any other person except for Frank Lloyd Wright. You cannot imagine the light your words shed on me during the dark days before I met you. I shall never forget the brightness of your torch, the warmth of your companionship, as I struggled to follow a path I had come to fear was mine alone.

In truth, I struggle even now. I don't know if I have the strength required to pursue this path of living freely and openly with the one real love of my life. Just now I feel as if the price may be too terrible for everyone involved if I continue on in this direction. There is only one thing certain. Your words will light my way and help me find the path I should pursue.

Your loving disciple,
Mamah Bouton Borthwick
October 28, 1910

On Monday morning, when the headmistress stopped her in the hall out-side her classroom, she grabbed Mamah's wrist. *The end of the ruse,* Mamah thought. Something in her demeanor had undoubtedly raised the woman's suspicions. Butterflies fluttered around her stomach when the headmistress stared intently at her. "Do you belong to a church?" she asked.

Mamah took in a quick breath. "I—"

"Because if you don't, my church could surely use your services. We send volunteers over to a doss-house in the Wedding District on Sunday after-noons."

"What do you do there?" Mamah felt the tension ebb.

The headmistress shrugged. "What we can."

"You need a translator?"

"Yes." The woman's voice warmed a degree. "To write letters. It's factory workers, you know. Poor. They all have long-lost cousins in America. That's where they want to go." She laughed. "They think all their problems will be solved if they can just get over to Minnesota."

ONE EGG. A length of ribbon. An embroidered handkerchief. *Pfeffernüsse.* The items they brought were not gifts, Mamah realized, but barter for her services. By the middle of November, word was out on the street that there was an American woman at a doss-house in the neighborhood who would translate letters. The small lobby was usually full of people when she arrived. Whole families arrived together, debated over what to include in their letters, ate food they'd brought. The room smelled of cooked cabbage and soiled diapers. Small children toddled around, their noses running. Coughs hacked through the air.

All of them wanted their letters written in English, though they could have been understood in German by their recipients. It dawned on Mamah that many of these people couldn't write in their own language and did not want to admit it. One woman would leave the table, and another would take her place. Often there was a girl of fourteen or fifteen in tow. During the first week, Mamah saw the pattern. These were the "domestics" who made any number of things possible for American women of a certain class: clean houses, meals, child care while they attended club meetings. The girls slept in attic bedrooms and sent home whatever they made.

"Wisconsin," said the peasant woman who sat next to her daughter.

"Where in Wisconsin, Frau Westergren? Do you have the address?"

The woman took Mamah's pen in her raw, knobby fingers and wrote out six letters. "R-A-C-I-N-E."

"Is that all you have?" Mamah spoke in German. She'd just written a letter to the woman's brother asking if her daughter might work in his house as a nanny or maid.

"Yes."

"But you say you haven't seen your brother in fifteen years. How do you know he's alive? You can't just send her over there without knowing."

The woman pursed her lips. Mamah understood that she had stepped over a line. She examined the girl. All of fifteen, with a fifth-grade education, she was wan from her work as a spooler in a factory. The girl stared heavily at her lap. That a mother would catapult her only child two thousand miles across an ocean to the Wisconsin farm of a brother she didn't know anymore was some measure of the woman's desperation. Or hope.

"Then we shall send the letter to Mr. Adolph Westergren in Racine, Wisconsin," Mamah said finally when it became apparent that the woman would not speak again. "Let's just see what happens."

The next day she asked the headmistress if she knew Frau Westergren. "Yes, I know which one she is," she said. "And her daughter." She shot Mamah a knowing look. "Illegitimate," she said softly.

Mamah was ashamed she had thought ill of the mother. To have a love so great for her child that she would give her up—she was stunned by it. The girl was doomed to poverty in Germany. In America she stood a chance. She could reinvent herself.

MAMAH FELT BETTER when she came home from the doss-house. It was comforting to help people fling their hopes out into the ether on the long chance that something good would come back. And it did sometimes. Relatives occasionally replied, offering to sponsor them. One man, a bricklayer, found a Catholic parish in Chicago willing to employ him in building their new church.

She came to look forward to Sundays. The fusty smell of the tenements grew on her, and the occasional drunk urinating in the gutter ceased to rattle her. She arrived in the Wedding District curious to see what the day held.

One Sunday afternoon Mamah came home so exhausted she fell into bed without eating dinner. When she woke, she found herself still dressed in her street clothes and realized she had slept for nearly twelve hours. She rose and went to the window. Dawn was just breaking, the sun pushing pink veins through a sky that wanted to rain. Watching the light come up, she felt oddly hopeful. She was sick to death of uncertainty, weary of fear and remorse.

She missed Frank. He wasn't a perfect man, but she loved him so deeply, she hardly knew how her body contained it. Someday, she was almost certain, they would look back on all this and say, *Yes, it was harrowing, but it's over, and we're stronger for it.*

There was another way it could unfold, though, and she forced herself to think of it. There were no guarantees. Frank might have already said goodbye to her. She could be drifting on an ice floe and just not know it yet.

What would she do if that were true? Edwin had not responded to her request for a divorce. If he would take her back, as Lizzie said, would she return to him? She tried to picture it, and she knew then and there that no matter how desperate she might be, she would never go back to Ed. That knowledge offered a strange comfort. She had left not only because of Frank but because her marriage had been all wrong.

Before Mamah came over to Germany, Mattie had said to her, "What will you do if Frank returns to his wife? You'll have nothing." But Mamah felt now that if that came to be, she had more than nothing. She had whatever it was inside herself that made her survive. The past few months had boiled her down to her very essence. All the rest, it seemed, had just floated away.

She had never believed, as Edwin did, that if a person simply acted happy, he would be happy. But it seemed futile to hang on to sorrow at this point. What good did it do anyone for her to continue grieving, as if it were the only proper emotion, given the situation?

Children need happy people around them. That thought alone was reason enough to let go of all the misery she had held on to. She resolved then that, come hell or high water, she would have John and Martha with her when she went back—for as much time as she could negotiate, beg, or steal.

As Christmas approached, Mamah bought gifts for the children from the vendors who set up booths along the streets. She chose a set of miniature painted soldiers for John and a small sapphire ring for Martha, to match her eyes. Mamah packed these and a few other wrapped toys into a parcel that she posted in mid-November.

In December Frau Boehm erected a towering Christmas tree in the parlor and strung garlands of fir and gilded nutshells throughout the house. For three weeks the fragrance of pine punished Mamah's emotions. On Christmas Day, when the inmates of Pension Gottschalk sat down to smoked goose, she excused herself. She slipped out the front door onto Schaper Strasse and walked a few blocks up Joachimstaler Strasse toward Kurfürstendamm and the Café des Westens, where the evening could be passed uncelebrated among the Jewish artists.

CHAPTER 31

On a small platform stage at Café des Westens, a costumed woman stood motionless with her head bent, a flute to her lips, waiting for the room to quiet. Every table of the smoke-filled café was occupied. A standing throng leaned against the poster-papered walls, holding glasses of beer.

Mamah turned to leave when she saw no table available, but a waiter appeared at that moment and escorted her to an empty chair. The four men at the table stood when she sat down, while the women acknowledged her with nods. The man next to her leaned intently toward Mamah. He was small, with a body tense as a coil about to spring. His round spectacles magnified intelligent eyes. "Wine?" he asked.

"Yes, thank you," she said. He said something else to her, but she couldn't understand it because of the noise in the room.

Mamah wasn't sure what the performer's costume was intended to portray. The woman wore black satin pantaloons that stopped at her delicate ankles, just above stylish feminine boots. A short matching jacket, wrapped around her like a kimono, was held closed by a wide belt covered in seashells. Her straight black hair was cut just below her jaw. The face—lovely, with eyes as dark as her hair—was eerily familiar.

"My wife the poet." The man next to her cocked his head toward the stage. "Else Lasker-Schüler. Or Jussef, prince of Thebes, depending upon her mood. She enjoys fantasy." He extended a hand. "Herwarth Walden," he said.

"Mamah Borthwick."

"American?"

"Yes."

When the waiter asked for her dinner order, Mamah scanned the menu for some small item.

"Have the pheasant and cranberries," Herwarth said. He turned to the waiter. "Red, give her the pheasant." Mamah fingered the cloth purse in her lap. It would take nearly every cent in it to pay for such a dinner. The man was merely being friendly; still, his familiarity annoyed her. She began to speak, but the waiter dashed off as the shrill sound of the flute pierced the noise, and the room fell silent. The poet handed away the flute, then surveyed the crowd through the smoke.

"Farewell," she announced. She paused, her eyes focused on the man who sat next to Mamah.

" 'But you never came with the evening,' " she began, " 'I sat in a cape of stars.' "

Mamah shifted uneasily in her seat.

" 'When I heard someone knocking,' " the woman said, her voice hoarse with a gravelly despair, " 'it was my own heart.

" 'Now it hangs on every door post,
even yours—
among ferns a burnt-out fire-rose
in garland brown.
For you I stained heaven blackberry
with my own heart's blood.
But you never came with the evening—
I stood in golden shoes.' "

The intimacy of the woman's words, so clearly directed at her husband, created in Mamah a profound urge to get out of the room. "Excuse me," she said as she got up and pushed past people clapping and shouting, "Jussef! Jussef!" She navigated her way through the crowd and stepped out onto the sidewalk, where the air hit her face like a cold cloth on sunburned skin. She wanted to leave but realized she'd foolishly left her wrap slung over the back of her chair. She would have to wade back in, pay the waiter, then plead illness to her tablemates just so she could retrieve her coat and be gone.

"Slumming tonight, are we?" a voice said.

Mamah almost jumped when she saw the poet standing not two feet from her on the sidewalk, her red mouth turned downward.

"I know you," Mamah said.

"A lot of people know me."

"You helped me one day—the only other time I was at this café. I had just gotten word that my friend had died, and . . ."

The woman stepped back and stared at Mamah's face. "And you fell over,

is what you did. I wondered whatever happened to you. You cried and cried."
She put an arm around her and patted her shoulder.

"Thank you for that day," Mamah said. "I don't know if I said it then."

The woman took a cigarette packet from beneath the shell belt. Into her
palm she emptied its contents—two cigarettes and one chocolate cookie.
"Choose," she said.

Mamah took a cigarette.

"Call me Else." She struck a match. "What is a well-dressed American
woman doing loose on the streets of Berlin on Christmas night? You look
nothing like the other strays we get here at Café Megalomania."

"My name is Mamah Borthwick."

"You speak fine German, Mamah Borthwick."

"Thank you. I'm here to study languages for a while—Swedish, actually. I
am Ellen Key's American translator." Mamah instantly regretted the preten-
sion in the remark. "I am waiting here until I can obtain a divorce from my
husband." Now she regretted spilling such personal information.

"Well." Else raised her eyebrows and flicked a bit of tobacco from her finger. "Where are you from?"

"Chicago."

"Chicago! I have a sister there!"

Else took her hand and led her back to the table. "Dearest Moderns," she
addressed the group, "we have among us a new friend. This is Mamah Borthwick of Chicago. She is the English translator for Ellen Key."

"To free sex!" one of the women shouted, lifting her glass.

"These are my playmates." Else went around the table. "Hedwig, Minn the
Warrior, Lucretia Borzia, Little Kurt, Martha the Sorceress, and Caius-Maius
the Emperor." She paused. "And my husband, whom you appear to have
met."

"Let her eat her pheasant," Herwarth said, his voice sour. "It's already
cold."

Else pulled up a chair next to Mamah. "Oh, I love cold pheasant," she said.

Sharing her plate, Mamah listened as the group talked about which artists
might show their work at Herwarth's new gallery when it opened. Mamah
had heard of some of them and had actually seen the canvases of others. It
seemed Herwarth was the editor of *Der Sturm* as well. She had read the
weekly a couple of times since she'd been back in Berlin. In fact, she had relished his editorials, in which he picked fights with the kaiser over his antedilu-

vian taste in art. As Mamah followed her tablemates' conversation, it dawned on her that she was sitting very near the center of the German Modernist movement.

"Does this talk bore you?" Else asked her at one point.

"Not at all. I'm very interested in modern art."

"Then you've come to the right place. Modernists, Expressionists, Secessionists. Cubists. Berlin is full of '-ists.' Writers and painters flock here and pollinate each other. Quite literally." She flicked her head toward a couple in the corner, where a man held a pretty young woman's hand as if it were a small bird. "He's probably seducing her with Rudolph Steiner quotes right now."

Mamah leaned back in her chair and laughed. "Ah, it's such a relief."

"What is that?"

"To laugh. To be among people who are irreverent. I come from a different kind of place."

"Isn't Chicago cosmopolitan?"

"I'm speaking of a village I come from which is near Chicago. And yes, there are artists in Chicago who believe the same thing these people do, that art is going to save the world. It's the architects who are the Moderns over there. They call themselves the Chicago School. They're tossing up buildings that would take your breath away. The best is Frank Lloyd Wright."

The poet assessed her. "Is he like Olbrich or Adolf Loos?"

"He's like no one else."

Else questioned her. In small pieces, Mamah let go of the truth, relieved to be opening up to someone who did not judge.

WHEN SHE RETURNED to the café a couple of days later, Mamah took a table near the window. She glanced toward the corner, where two of the men she'd met on Christmas night were huddled over their playing cards. They nodded when they spotted her. The waiter with the copper-colored hair delivered her tea, then presented a copy of *Der Sturm* with a friendly little flourish.

Was it her imagination, or had something changed in the space of two days? Because she certainly felt a difference. Even now people walking through the door acknowledged her.

She suspected Else's sudden friendship had stamped her as "approved" among the artists. Mamah was amused by it. Back in Chicago, no one had heard of Ellen Key. Her name wouldn't have bought Mamah a cup of coffee. Here at Café des Westens, it was her passport.

Outside the window, scores of office girls walked by arm in arm. Military men in epaulets passed, along with hordes of others: fresh-faced farm boys turned factory workers carrying tin lunch pails; businessmen in homburg hats; gray-braided grandmothers in black dresses; nurses, shopgirls, society women out for tea. And then a woman like none of the others emerged from the crowd and stepped into the café.

"You sit down in this café, and the devil has you," Else huffed as she took a chair across from Mamah. She was wearing a purple cape. Scattered over it were cameo pins with tiny photographs of faces inside each one.

"Your family?" Mamah asked, pointing toward a picture of an old-fashioned couple.

"Oh, no. I found them in a pawnshop. They were all begging to get out of the place." Else ordered coffee, and when it came, she said, "I come from a village like yours. I was married to a doctor." She pressed her coffee cup against her cheek to warm it. "I had fine china. Lovely rugs on the floor." The serious brown eyes were flecked with gold. "One day I woke up and thought, *What have you done with your gifts? You've traded them for furniture.*" She moved the cup to the other cheek. "As you can see, I joined a different tribe. I have almost no furniture now, by the way. I owe the morning waiter and the midnight waiter, and I'm wondering how I'll pay the rent now that Herwarth's going. Still . . ." Her voice trailed off.

"Where is your husband going?"

Else put down the cup and looked away. When she turned back, her eyes were narrowed. "This is what I know of you, Mamah Borthwick of Chicago. You are a translator for Ellen Key's sex philosophies. And you have left your husband for an artistic lover. Yet you live among the bourgeoisie here in Berlin. You're a puzzle to me."

Mamah stiffened as if she'd just discovered someone snooping around in her drawers. She crossed her arms. "My room is the cheapest one in the pension," she said.

"You don't have to defend yourself."

Mamah felt embarrassed. "I admire the way you inhabit your life. You don't seem to care whether other people approve."

Else shrugged. "We all have our little battles going on inside." That thought seemed to spark something, because she jumped up from her seat. "Work to do," she said, then drifted off to her own table. She took out a notebook and began writing.

DURING THE WEEK of her holiday that followed, Mamah returned to the café every day. She had always loved the smell of coffee in the morning, and the aroma in the café did not disappoint. The place was nearly empty when she arrived, and the hard morning light revealed it to be a tawdry mess. The bust of the kaiser still leaned drunkenly on top of the battered phone booth. The edges of posters curled up at their corners on walls dirty with fingerprints. But the round marble tabletops were cleaned of beer-glass rings by eight A.M., when Mamah happily settled at a table near the front window.

She wrote postcards to her children and translated until people filtered in. Sometimes a new friend would sit with her for a few minutes to chat, but mostly, the regulars drank coffee behind their newspapers. It was when the poets and writers began arriving around lunchtime that the place filled up with laughter, arguments, ideas.

Else got there by two in the afternoon and settled at her own table in a back corner, where she held court when she wasn't writing. Most days she brought her son, Paul, a boy of four who seemed content to color in a book across from her. Mamah was touched by the two of them huddled together.

"He's left her," the woman named Hedwig said to Mamah one afternoon, glancing over at Else.

"Herwarth?"

"Yes, he moved out. There's a Swedish woman, someone said."

Mamah was stricken almost sick by the statement.

"Herwarth has been good to the boy, but he hasn't any obligation, really. He's not his father," Hedwig said. "Else claims the father is a sheik or something."

When Mamah looked over again, she was seared by the pained little society in the corner.

As the afternoon wore on, she listened to the people around her. Liebermann, Kokoschka, Franz Marc, Kandinsky—the names rolled off their tongues like a litany of Secessionist saints. When the day grew dark, Red circulated through the café lighting candles. "The world is changing," someone said. "It is, it is," the others agreed.

The room grew blue from smoke and pulsed with excitement by four, as people ordered bottles of wine and beer. They talked of Italian Futurism, of Gaudi in Barcelona, of mathematics as "the way God thinks." They talked of who was sleeping with whom, of politics, war, magic, socialism.

One evening Mamah joined a table where Else was holding forth to a group of fellow artists. "That's your sacred office," she was saying heatedly. Her son was nowhere in sight. "To continue the act of creation where God left off on the last day. To unlock the secret language of nature. I truly believe that every time I go deep enough to bring back a nugget of truth or beauty, God is making use of me." Else looked around at her tablemates. "Artists can redeem the world. But we can't tarry, my friends. You and I are the salvation of this country, not the generals."

Mamah drank in the pleasure of the words around her, the camaraderie. She had two glasses of wine that night, then another, and felt as if she had never been so comfortable among a group of people. She had arrived in Berlin from someplace else where she felt she didn't belong, just as they had.

The night before Mamah was to return to work, a snowstorm blanketed Berlin. She woke to the news that whole sections of the city were without power and that her school had been closed for the day. She bundled up and went out to a newsstand. With a paper under her arm, she moved on to the post office, which she found open, though eerily empty. In her box, one envelope waited. The letterhead belonged to a Chicago law firm she knew to be the one used by Wagner Electric. Inside, she found what she expected. Edwin Cheney was suing Mamah Borthwick Cheney for divorce. *Grounds for Suit: Desertion.*

She put the letter in her handbag and walked back toward the pension. It didn't seem quite real that a major piece of her future had just fallen into place. She wanted to tell Else, but when Mamah looked in at the café, she saw that the place had only one other patron in it. She sat down at her table near the window and stared out at the street.

"I love a good snowstorm," Red said to her when he brought a newspaper and a cup of coffee. "Stops people in their tracks."

At the top of the front page, she saw the familiar words that Red stamped every morning on every newspaper that came into the place—STOLEN FROM CAFÉ DES WESTENS. She took a pencil from her handbag and wrote a note to Frank in the small section of empty white space at the top of the page.

January 10, 1911

It's official. Got divorce notice today.

Loving you, Mamah.

"Is there an envelope anywhere around?" she asked Red, ripping her note off the top of the newspaper.

When he brought her one, she addressed it, slipped the folded note in, and sealed the envelope, then headed back out into the snow toward the post office.

CHAPTER 32

"There's a man downstairs to see you."

Mamah looked over her eyeglasses at Frau Boehm, who rarely made the climb to the third floor. "Who is it?"

"A Mr. Wright."

Mamah leaped up from her chair and raced past the startled woman, taking the steps two at a time.

Frank was standing in the parlor in an overcoat, his hat in his hands.

"You didn't tell me!" She threw her arms around him.

"I thought if I did, you would say not to come."

She put her hands on his cold face. "You look as if you walked from Chicago. Have you had any sleep in the past ten days?"

"Not to speak of."

"Seasickness?"

His nostrils flared at the word. "Don't remind me." He took her hand. "I got a room," he said softly. "At a little hotel not far from here."

"I'll get a bag," she said, grinning like a madwoman. "It will take me five minutes."

They walked through the Tiergarten on the way to the hotel. Frank was sober, his wicked wit nowhere in evidence. He had come to surprise Wasmuth, he told her, who had stopped printing the portfolio because of a disagreement between them. "The printing of the photo book is terrible, and he has misidentified at least two of the buildings on the plates. I told Wasmuth flat out I would not accept it. So what has he done? Stopped the whole damn project. He won't do another thing on the folio until I accept the photo book." Frank's voice was raw with hurt at the unfairness of it. "I'm too far into this now. I will have to fight him for another contract."

There were troubles back in Chicago, too, besides the fact that he was a pariah and no one would hire him. He was about to sue Herman von Holst for cheating him out of his rightful commissions for the work he had left behind. A light snow had just fallen. She watched two people ahead of them leave dark footprints on the stone sidewalk as Frank listed the litany of struggles.

"They hate me." He was talking of his children now.

"But you wrote that they were ecstatic to see you."

"Oh, it didn't take long for the truth to out. She's turned them against me." He swallowed hard and regained his voice. "All the bloody recriminations, the public shaming . . . none of it was necessary. If only she had agreed to a divorce."

"Edwin has agreed to a divorce," Mamah said abruptly. "Did you know that? I wrote a letter, but you probably—"

His face registered surprise. "No, I didn't get it."

"It's true. He agreed to meet me in August to settle the details. I feel as if I can go back now." She looked at him. "Maybe when Catherine learns that Edwin has agreed . . ."

"Don't even think maybe," Frank said. "It's not going to happen."

"You came here to tell me something, didn't you? The thing you want to say has to do with a house. In Wisconsin."

"Am I so transparent?"

"It's what you've wanted all along."

"My mother has agreed to buy land in her name for me. Thirty acres at Hillside, near my grandfather's farm. Exactly the spot I told you about." He stopped on the sidewalk. "It's time, Mamah. It will be the most beautiful place you've ever lived. You won't care if you can't go out and see a play."

He looked beyond her at the lines of naked trees in the park. "The main thing is, we won't have to live these fragmented lives anymore. Who we are, what we do, what we love, everything we've said to each other about spreading Ellen's ideals, teaching—it's going to be in the mortar. It will be all one thing in that place."

"But you haven't had any work."

"If Darwin Martin gives me a loan—and he will—I can begin construction this summer. Once it's built, we can be self-sufficient. Grow our own food. Whatever it takes." He turned and caught her nervously biting her upper lip. "Look, in Italy all you could think of was building a retreat there, away from it all. Well, this is a retreat, and every bit as beautiful as Fiesole. I'll pay Martin back, don't worry about that. As for the farmers around there, I won't lie. They're not going to be very friendly at first. They'll want us to roast on the spit for a while. But I swear to you, we will live true. We'll be the very model of living true."

"Are you asking me?"

Frank had removed a glove and was crouching. With his forefinger, he made three lines in the snow. They looked to her like a child's drawing of light rays beaming down from the sun.

"That's the Druid symbol for 'Truth against the world.'" He looked up at her. "It's a tough row to hoe, to live for the true and the beautiful. Most people would laugh at me for speaking those words out loud. But it's all I want now." He paused. "If you will go there with me, Mame, we can do it. If you will live with me there."

She smiled. "Are you asking me?" she repeated.

"I am."

"Yes," she said. "I will."

PART THREE

Martha's dour little face turned in the direction her mother was pointing. "Do you see him?" Mamah whispered. "He's bright yellow."

The girl stared into the woods.

They were both kneeling on pine needles in a small clearing. She extended the binoculars to her daughter. "Up there on that branch."

Martha pushed away the field glasses, turning a blank stare back into the trees. "Papa is the bird teller," she said.

Mamah stiffened, then counted the words Martha had uttered. *Five,* she thought. *That's progress.*

BACK IN BERLIN, the idea of a summer at a Canadian camp with the children seemed the perfect scenario for the reunion. They would be her own—no Louise, no Lizzie. Edwin would bring them up and stay for a day to negotiate the terms of their divorce. Mamah had expected it to be hard for all of them, but they would be away from prying eyes. They would take their time.

For the past two years, she had inundated the children with letters and, recently, a portrait of herself. But they didn't seem to remember her.

Two years in a child's life is the distance between stars, she thought. She remembered being a child herself, lolling luxuriously in a bathtub at the age of eight and contemplating the vastness of the summer ahead. And it had turned out to be that—a millennium, it seemed, of fireflies and kick the can, of nights and days strung together by one long, pulsing cricket song.

Martha had been three when Mamah left, John almost seven. In Italy and in Berlin, she had watched children of the same ages, noticed how they moved. Listened to their words. But here in the flesh, John and Martha were strangers.

John remembered her some. He was almost the same little boy who used to leap into her arms the minute he saw her. He was still Peter Pan, but taller, and with a stick now. The boy had carried some kind of stick from the moment she'd encountered him in front of the cabin. He had been pushing it into the dirt when she'd walked up. John had just stood there beaming, allowing himself to be hugged.

"Are you afraid of spiders?" were the first words out of his mouth. He went inside and returned with a mason jar housing a brown-striped thing. "Found it in the cabin," he'd said with obvious pleasure.

Martha, on the other hand, had stood next to Edwin when Mamah arrived, connected to her father by the piece of trouser fabric she held between her thumb and forefinger. She was wearing a fat ribbon at the top of her head. Her face was entirely new. The baby fullness of her cheeks was almost gone. Martha was taking on the face she would carry from here on out, and it was a Borthwick face. High cheekbones, square jaw, a dark brushstroke of brows just like Mamah's own. At that moment, standing in front of the cabin, the eyebrows had been clouds, black and low-hanging. Martha had slid behind Edwin when her mother approached her, and refused to come out. Edwin stood stiff and unmoving as Mamah backed off.

That night, with the children in bed, Mamah and Edwin sat in the front porch rockers, whispering.

"They will live with me," he said.

"I want to see them."

"You can see them at appropriate intervals."

"How often is that?" She looked at him suspiciously.

"I don't object to their visiting you for a couple of weeks in the summer."

"Why not a couple of months?"

"Perhaps four weeks," he said. "We will have to see how it works out. I don't know what the children will be willing to do. They're both afraid of things."

Katydids screeched their squeaky pulley sound out in the woods.

"I never meant to cause so much suffering," she said.

It came out as a paltry understatement. Still, her words seemed to reach Edwin, who had been exceedingly formal since she'd arrived.

"Martha didn't understand any of it then. It was John who took the brunt of it. There were times . . ." Edwin stopped himself.

Mamah drew in a breath. "Go ahead."

"In Boulder, after you left, he got lost. Mattie had taken sick by then. There were people in and out of that house—doctors, neighbors—nobody noticed that he'd gone missing. I wasn't due until the end of that week to pick them up. When the nanny discovered that he'd disappeared, she was frantic."

Mamah felt as if her chest had been slugged.

"He didn't run away, it turned out. They found him that night wandering around in Boulder, miles from the house. He was looking for you."

She pressed her lips together and put a hand across her mouth to suppress the sob that was pushing up inside. She had no right to weep.

After Edwin departed for the main lodge, she lay awake past midnight, listening to the breathing of the children across the room. John was on the top bunk, Martha on the bottom.

Four weeks, Mamah could have them. That was what Edwin had finally agreed to. Four weeks, no more, until Christmas, when she would be allowed two days of visitation in Oak Park before the holiday. After that she could have them for a few weeks in Wisconsin every summer, and could visit them when she wanted to in Oak Park.

Now they would have only a month together. How could anyone fix what had happened in one month?

"Nooooo!" Martha had howled when Edwin left in the morning. She had to be pried from his leg as he got into the waiting car. The man who ran the counter at the lodge had come out to have a look. "That's some set of pipes," he said.

Bird-watching. What was I thinking? What child ever really cared about bird-watching? Mamah stood in the brittle clearing, a resinous smell wafting around them. Martha was a sullen heap at her feet.

"What's next?" John asked.

Mamah hadn't made an alternative plan. She looked at her watch. Ten o'clock. John walked over to the nearest pine and thwacked the trunk with his stick.

"Let's go back to the lodge," she said. "We might just hitch a canoe ride for you."

SHE HADN'T PLANNED to put them into the daylong classes the other children at the camp attended. She had hoped, selfishly, to have them to herself. She was desperate for the feel of their skin on hers—it was the one sensation she had most missed about them. In Europe she had dreamed about the feel of Martha's fat little legs pressing on her arm as she held her. But that wasn't going to happen. Not yet. Maybe not for a long time.

John wanted to please her, though. He didn't initiate hugs, but he put himself in Mamah's proximity so she could wrap her arms around him. She would pull him to her and feel his ribs and the bony little buttocks punching into her lap. At one of those moments, when he lingered, she tried to talk with him.

"I'm sorry it took me so long to get home," she said. He leaped up before she could say another word, and ran off to join some children across the clearing.

Some days she watched them from the shore of the lake. Other parents were on their own expeditions while their children swam with the young activity leaders. Mamah felt like a spy, lurching around in the trees, trying to watch them play without their knowing she was there. John seemed comfortable with himself, she thought, chattering away as he floated in a rubber tire, then getting into water fights when he bumped into other kids. Martha, though, looked so lonesome sitting in the black rubber float, wearing the same worried look among other children that she wore around her mother.

Crouched at the edge of the water, Mamah thought of the remark some "acquaintance" had made in one of the *Tribune* articles about how she'd spent little time with her children. That remark, as much as anything, had infuriated her, because it wasn't true. She had loved her children passionately and had spent plenty of time with them, more than a lot of mothers whose children were raised entirely by nannies. But there was a deeper truth that she had not wanted to face, and now she couldn't avoid it.

Carrying on a love affair had been work. It had consumed her energy and preoccupied her mind all those years in Oak Park. Even in the presence of the children, her thoughts were about Frank—how they would manage to meet next, or what he had meant by a remark the last time they were together. It had been an obsession for so long that she had taken it to be normal. The children had been pushed aside, not physically, maybe, but certainly in her mind.

It hadn't always been that way. She and John were exceptionally close before her relationship with Frank began. It wasn't John who'd been most neglected during those years of the affair, she thought. No, it was Martha. Mamah realized she had been mentally gone since Martha was born. First with depression, then with Frank. Martha had been a year old when the affair began.

The reality of her absence hit Mamah like a flying brick. Usually, the guilt centered on the same frozen image—the moment she had walked out of the bedroom in Boulder while John and Martha slept. Always, whenever she thought of it, she asked herself the same horrified question: *Did I even look back at them?*

Now she saw that she had removed herself from them long before that morning. For extended stretches in those early years, her eyes and ears and full delight—so rightfully theirs—had been focused on someone else.

Mamah sat stripping needles from a pine tassel. Somehow, she didn't know how, she would have to make it right again. Apologies wouldn't matter one whit to John and Martha. It would take time, maybe years, to set things right with them.

She remembered the awful days just after she'd told Edwin she loved Frank. "All your goddamn ideas ruined you, Mamah," he'd shouted at her. "Even your children are abstract to you."

She would never tell him she could see the kernel of truth in those words. Sitting in the woods, she said it to herself. *I wasn't there when I should have been. Not nearly enough.*

ONE AFTERNOON NEAR the end of July, Mamah and the children stayed on at the lodge when everyone else had gone out after lunch. Someone had taught the children to tie knots, and both had made a jumble of their projects. They were sitting under a ceiling fan watching their mother undo the twine when a dog wandered into the dining hall. The only other person around was an aproned kitchen helper who was putting dirty dishes into a sink. When he saw the animal, he moved to shoo it away.

John was on his feet and went over to greet the dog. He was medium-sized and all black, with a long snout and long ears and stringy hair hanging from his chin like a beard.

"Do you know whose dog this is?" Mamah asked the kitchen man. She felt suddenly protective of the children.

"No, ma'am," he said, "never seen him before."

She and Martha walked over to have a look. "Don't get too close to him," Mamah cautioned. But John was already on his knees, and the dog was licking him.

"He's thirsty," the boy said. He went over to a pile of dirty dishes and retrieved two bowls. In one he put water; in the other, leftover meat loaf from someone's plate.

"He's hot," Martha said, keeping her distance.

"Well, he's got a big heavy coat on, hasn't he?" Mamah said. "Why don't

we go and ask if the manager knows him? He looks pretty clean. I bet someone is missing him right now."

John pulled out a string of his knotting twine and made a leash of it.
Walking over to the lodge, the dog trotted next to the boy, as if they were old
friends.

"Never seen him," the manager said. "And he doesn't belong to any of the
folks here right now, 'cause I've seen all their pets."

"What about the neighbors?"

"Not that I know of. But there's plenty of farms about. Coulda strayed
from one of 'em."

"Can we put a sign up at the lodge?"

"Sure. In fact, the driver'll take you around, if you want to check with the
neighbors."

Martha crooked a small finger toward her mother. Mamah, taken by surprise, bent down quickly. "Can we keep him in our cabin tonight?" Martha
whispered.

Mamah stood up. "We'll be keeping him in our cabin tonight," she said to
the manager.

He shrugged. "I don't mind if you don't mind."

They took the dog with them as they tacked signs to telephone poles along
the road. Later, the lodge's chauffeur took them to three neighboring farms to
inquire if anyone was missing a pet. No one knew the black dog.

"Might be a huntin' dog got loose, though it's not the season yet," the last
farmer speculated. "Or somebody let him out on the road, maybe. People from
the city do that, bring 'em out here and let 'em go."

The children were kneeling again, petting him. The farmer lifted up the
ears of the hound, opened his mouth and looked around inside, raised his tail
to peer at his anus, then inspected his paws. Martha and John's eyes followed
the proceedings.

"He's a pup," the farmer said. "Healthy enough—no worms or sores I can
see. Going to be a big fella."

"I think there's some wolfhound in him," Mamah said.

"I'd take him if nobody claims him," the man said.

On the way back to the lodge, John spoke what they were all thinking.
"Papa won't let us keep a dog."

Edwin had never wanted a dog in the house. They made him sneeze and
left hair all over the place.

"Honey, this fellow belongs to someone," Mamah said. "He's too clean to have been living out in the open." She hated to burst John's bubble, but it seemed crueler to let him hope.

That evening they made a bed for the dog on the floor of the cabin. They found straw and a blanket to put inside a large box they got from behind the lodge. Then they all lay down around the dog and smothered him with strokes and kisses. The dog panted patiently while Martha clung to his neck, cooing, "You're a good dog."

Watching the children, Mamah could see already what she would do. She would let the signs stay up for another two days. Maybe one. And if no one claimed him (*please, God, don't let anyone claim him*), she would quietly go around and take them down.

There were still two weeks ahead of them, fourteen whole days to swim with the dog, teach him to catch, name him, sleep with him. When they had to leave in August, the dog could go with them on the train. If Edwin didn't want him, and she knew he wouldn't, then he would go to Wisconsin with her.

Maybe it was unfair to make the dog's home Wisconsin as an enticement to her children to visit. Edwin would call it calculating, a ploy to buy her way back into their hearts. She didn't care what he thought. To her, the dog was an opportunity for a second chance. She would take her grace where she found it.

CHAPTER 34

Frank's car bumped along Highway 14. He pointed out the landmarks to Mamah, the old farmhouses or trees that signified that Spring Green was fifty or sixty miles up ahead. The car was loaded with suitcases and boxes. Squeezed into a corner, the dog the children had named Lucky hung his head out the window despite the drizzle.

"Can you see that sign?" Frank gestured toward a barn in the distance.

Someone had painted an advertisement across one entire side of it. As they got closer, she could see that it was a realistic-looking bare foot. Only two words accompanied the picture: ATHLETE'S FOOT.

"Are they for it or against it?" she asked.

Frank laughed. "Welcome to Wisconsin."

"I swear you developed an accent when we left Illinois."

"Oh, you'll have it in a month."

For much of the drive, Frank regaled her with stories about his mother's family. "Radical Unitarians," he called them. "Real reformers." His grandfather had settled in the Helena Valley just south of the Wisconsin River some fifty years before. Three of his mother's brothers—Enos, James, and John—all had farms near the hill where Frank was building the new house. Only Jenkin Lloyd Jones had gone to the city to make his career as a Unitarian minister. He was living in Chicago and was quite well-known now, but even Uncle Jenk had bought land up here—a few acres on the Wisconsin River that he called Tower Hill, where he ran a Chautauqua-type camp every summer. They were all accomplished, the whole lot of his aunts and uncles. They might argue among themselves, but they were loyal to one another. His relatives had been his first architectural clients. Early on he had designed a chapel for his grandfather's old homestead and, later, for his schoolteacher aunts, a school.

Mamah's anxiety grew as the family stories layered one upon another. *Oh Lord*, she thought, *what am I getting myself into?*

Frank had promised her one spectacular milestone before they reached Spring Green. Now he pointed toward a vast wall of sedimentary rock stretching across a field in the distance. "There it is—God in stripes," he said. "We're ten miles from home."

They fell into silence. Outside, the rainy landscape was a charcoal lesson in perspective, with the road curling like a black ribbon through the fields ahead. In the foreground, growing in ditches, sumac trees raised their rusty deltoid fingertips, while in the far distance, hills receded in deepening grays. Horses grazed midground in pastures of pale grass. From time to time the entire vista disappeared behind towering hunks of rock, shaggy with white pine upstarts rooted in their cracks.

Southwestern Wisconsin, with its rolling unglaciated hills, seemed to her to be the very stuff of Frank's brain. Always Wisconsin had been there in his imaginings, an undulating canvas waiting for him to draw a fitting house into its contours. In the grayness of the August rain, though, the hills had a brooding feeling.

How different from Germany, she thought. In Berlin her eye had never traveled farther than the row of shops or houses across any given street. Nature seemed to be somewhere outside the city limits. But it hadn't mattered. Even the dust of the crumbling brick and stone had been invigorating.

"Are you afraid?"

"Some."

"Truly?"

"Not afraid of living with you. But if you mean living near your mother and sister and cousins, yes. It makes me nervous."

"You'll win them over." Frank reached across the seat and squeezed her hand. "Just be who you are, and the rest will come."

"You forget I know your mother. From the Nineteenth Century Club. She's . . ."

"Fierce?"

Mamah thought about the few times she had seen Anna Wright in action. She was smart, influential, and an umbrage taker. "Well . . . formidable," she said. When she glanced sidelong at his face, she saw that he was wearing a wicked smile. "You seem to enjoy the idea that she might be fierce."

"It's not a bad thing to have someone fierce on your side. She's intense about a lot of things, especially loyalty. She's been forced to take sides. And when push comes to shove with her, it's her people and her land. Give her time. She will adjust to you."

"What about your aunts who run the school?"

"Oh, they're wonderful. Huge hearts. But they're probably squirming right now."

"Afraid for their school's reputation, now that we're moving next door?"

"Don't let it frighten you. These farmers can be sanctimonious, but they're decent. We'll be fattening up on their cookies before you know it."

In that moment Mamah's eye caught sight of a broad roof, limestone walls, and the sand-gold rectangles of stucco. The house nestled into the hill, wrapping itself around the area just below the rounded crown. Frank pulled the car over to the side of the road. He walked around to open the door for her, and they stood in the tall grass together. Mamah felt the goose bumps rising on her skin.

"I'd like to call it Taliesin, if it's all right with you. Do you know Richard Hovey's play *Taliesin*? About the Welsh bard who was part of King Arthur's court? He was a truth-seeker and a prophet, Taliesin was. His name meant 'shining brow.' I think it's quite appropriate."

"Taliesin." She tried the word in her mouth as she studied the house in the distance.

Indeed, the building glowed, in spite of the gray light. It was a shocking contrast to the little farmhouses she had seen on the way up to Spring Green. This house—the word seemed somehow wrong—was like nothing else she had ever seen. It looked so modern, so architected. Yet it was harmonious with the hills, its overhanging roofs echoing the pitch of the ridge. Elevated and isolated, away from other houses and set into this great golden vista, Taliesin was more like the villas around Fiesole than anything Frank had built in Oak Park.

"It's brilliant," she whispered. She took off her glasses, squinted, then put them on again.

"It's for you," he said.

Back in the car, Frank was jittery as he nosed up the hill toward the entrance driveway.

"Romeo and Juliet," he said, pointing to a windmill in the distance he had built for his aunts' school building. "See how one part leans in to the other?"

"It seems such a romantic name for a pair of teachers to choose."

Frank laughed. "Oh, I chose the name. There's not a Lloyd Jones who would admit to being a romantic. We prefer to be seen as hard-bitten." He nodded at structures dotting the hills around the new house. "At one time, when I was young, there were sixty or seventy family members living on these hills around here. There's Tan-Y-Deri."

Tan-Y-Deri was his sister Jennie's house. Mamah knew that story, too. Jennie had insisted on a prairie house for her family, like the kind he had built in Oak Park. Frank had wanted to build her a "natural" house, more in keeping with these hills. Persuasive as he was, Frank had failed to sell his younger sister on the idea. Jennie must be as stubborn as he, Mamah mused.

"Tan-Y-Deri is Welsh for 'under the oaks,' " he was saying. He pointed off to the southeast. "That way is Uncle Enos's place."

"Why am I thinking of Italy right now?"

"You tell me."

"I have this sense that each of your uncles' homesteads is almost a little fiefdom, the way it was in the past in Tuscany."

"You're not far off," Frank said. "People don't call this place the Valley of the God-Almighty Joneses for nothing."

The car crept up to a heavy entry column of roughly stacked stone blocks. Standing on top of the pier was a soaring statue of a classic-looking nude. The voluptuous curves of her body melded in white plaster with the straight lines of a skyscraper in front of her. The woman's head was bent, and her hand was placing a capstone at the top of the building.

"Flower in the Crannied Wall," Frank said, nodding toward the figure. "I had Bock make one for Taliesin." It was the statue Mamah had seen the sculptor working on during one of her first visits to Frank's studio in Oak Park.

"She looks magnificent here—like an angel guarding the place."

The drive led the car under the roof of the porte cochere, then continued between the house on one side and an incline on the other. Mamah could already imagine clumps of daffodils climbing up that little hill. Ahead, at the end of the driveway, she saw workers coming and going in a courtyard. As she and Frank drew closer, she noticed that windows all along the back of the house faced out toward it. A private courtyard!

Workmen stopped to shade their eyes as the car inched along. When Frank opened the car door, they returned to their work, furiously mortaring and hammering as if they hadn't noticed the new arrivals. Mamah wanted to race along the drive into the courtyard, but she stood stock-still instead. No one looked at her.

"Billy!" Frank called to the foreman, who was walking toward them now. The man was short, with a weathered brown face. Frank had told Mamah about the carpenter, how he could take one of Frank's shorthand sketches in his battered hands and pace out its perimeter almost exactly without real drawings.

"Billy, I want you to meet someone. This is the lady of the house."

Billy Weston's pants were worn at the knees and in the place where he slung a hammer from a loop. He was not old, perhaps thirty-five, but everything about him had a faded quality. Even his blue eyes looked like pale eggs in an old nest. Mamah watched as the eyes registered confusion. Frank had obviously not explained anything in advance.

"How d'ya do, ma'am," Billy mumbled, nodding.

"She will be the person to go to when I'm not here."

Billy's eyes flicked suspiciously on hers for a moment before he nodded again. Frank had said Billy didn't always take instructions from him gladly. How could he possibly be happy about taking orders from her?

"Yessir." Billy scratched behind his ear and shifted from foot to foot.

"You two ought to know each other pretty well by the time this place is done."

"Done?" Billy grinned. "Nothin's ever really done with you, Mr. Wright."

Frank let out a belly laugh. "Billy's as good as they come," he said to Mamah as the man walked away. "You won't find another carpenter like him out here."

He walked Mamah through the length of the one-story building. The house was really three horizontal rectangles joined together into one U-shaped form that wrapped its arms around the hill. One arm of the U was a wing of bedrooms; the arm on the opposite side included barns for horses and cows, plus a garage. In between was the social and working space, a string of rooms with windows that faced out onto vast views of the valley below. In many places, glass doors led from the rooms onto terraces surrounding the house.

Frank toured her through the living room, their bedroom, then the bedroom that would be her children's when they visited. He envisioned for her how each room would look. The house was exactly as he had described it, a place where shelter and nature were fused. She could picture how it would be when it was finished. How guests would walk through the entryway with its low ceiling that compressed down the space, making them feel a kind of tension. How they would suddenly, physically, feel that tension lift and joy replace it as they entered the expansive living room with its wide-open vistas of sky and green land as far as the eye could see.

What the eye saw now, though, was bare studs and lath board. Holes where doors and windows were to be placed. Vats for mixing plaster. Bags of sand. Sawhorses. And, everywhere, dust. Wood dust. Plaster dust. Dirt dust.

Frank saw the question on her face. "In a few weeks . . ."

"Where will we sleep?"

"At Jennie's."

"But . . ." She didn't speak out loud what she was thinking. *Stay in the house where Jennie's children are, where their Aunt Catherine usually stayed when she came with Frank? In the same house with Anna Wright?*

As if on cue, Frank's sister Jennie stepped through one of the openings, carrying a basket of lunch. She set it down on the floor, then came over and extended her hand.

"Mamah," she said warmly, "how good to meet you."

Mamah's knees nearly buckled in gratitude. Frank had said Jennie would be kind. She was a pretty version of Frank's mother, her dark hair parted and pulled tight at the nape of her neck. No one would mistake her for Frank's sister, though. She had a shy manner, countered by penetrating dark eyes that stared at the speaker a moment too long, as if there were a deeper meaning to be had just below the surface of a remark.

"I have a room all ready for you up at the house," she said.

"I think tonight we will stay here," Frank said.

"On the floor? Are you sure?" Jennie's eyes studied his.

"I'll set up the bed I've got stored in the shed."

"All right, then, if you insist. We'll see you in the morning."

Watching Frank's sister step through piles of lumber as she headed back to her house, Mamah felt relief. "That wasn't so hard," she said. "It has to be strange for her."

"Count her as a friend."

Mamah and Frank walked down to the Wisconsin River below the house, followed by the dog. The rain had stopped. Along the river, peeling white birches shed bark like dead skin, revealing patches of pink underneath. Mamah and Frank ate the sandwiches Jennie had brought them, and watched the men load wheelbarrows full of sand.

After a time, they walked back up the hill behind the workmen. Out in the courtyard, men stirred sand, lime, and water into a brown "mud" mix. A young plasterer carried a bucket inside and spread some onto a stretch of wall in the living room as an undercoat. While it was drying, Frank went to the car and retrieved some pigments he had bought in the city. He poured ocher and umber in varying amounts in different buckets of plaster, making an array of shades for use on different walls, "depending on the light they get," he told the plasterer, who had watched the mixing cautiously.

"How will you get the same color again if you don't measure and write it down?" the plasterer asked. "You've got six formulas going there."

"I don't have to fall into a vat of dye to know what color it is," Frank said. "I can look at the shade on the wall and remix it."

The plasterer raised his eyebrows, impressed.

Mamah spent the rest of the day helping move her boxes into a shed for storage, then cleaning, cleaning, trying to get the dust and debris out of the bedroom they were to sleep in. There were no windows in it yet. "Organic, indeed," she teased Frank as she made up the bed.

That night when they lay down, Frank put out his arm to hold her. He pointed out Orion's Belt through the open hole in the wall, then fell almost immediately to sleep. During the night, she got up to use the bucket he had placed by her side of the bed. As she lifted her nightgown to crouch, a bat whipped by within inches of her shoulder. She leaped back into bed and covered her head with the blanket.

Frank turned in his sleep, muttered, "Heigh-ho," then commenced snoring.

CHAPTER 35

"Well, shit. If that don't beat all."

"That's what he said. She's the one in charge when he ain't here."

"He ain't here a *lot.*"

"He'll be around more now she's here. She's a looker."

"Shit, Murphy, you better not be lookin'."

Mamah could hear the men moving around in the living room. Something dragged across the wood floor.

"Gad, I overslept." Frank sat up and swung his legs around. "They don't know we're here," he said as he reached for his trousers.

She grabbed his arm. "Shhh. It's all right," she whispered. "Don't say a word to them." She knew Billy's voice but had no faces for the other two.

"I don't need a woman telling me how to drive a fuckin' nail."

Sawing drowned out their voices before they rose again.

"Don't saw when you're mad, Billy. You're gonna cut off another finger."

"Oh, he ain't done that in near a month." Laughter.

"At least my pecker ain't been cut off, like some I know."

THERE ARE THIRTY-SIX of them now," Jennie Porter said. "It changes up or down, depending on what Frank's working on. During the week, they sleep in shacks around here, then they go home on weekends."

The two women stood between the kitchen table and the cooking range. Jennie and her son, Frankie, rolled chunks of beef in flour, then tossed them into sizzling oil in an iron pot. "Frank hired a woman from town to do the cooking, but it's too much for one person," Jennie said. "Somebody has to get things half ready for her, so the big meal can go on around one."

"Frankie," she said, "show Miz Borthwick where the carrots are, will you?"

That one sentence confirmed what Mamah had suspected. She was the somebody who would be taking over food duty from Jennie.

It was only right, of course. It wasn't Jennie's house they were building, Mamah thought as she pulled up carrots and potatoes from the big garden next to the Porters' house. She didn't mind the idea of riding herd over the operation, but she knew almost nothing about cooking.

"It's written down," Jennie assured her. "All my recipes feed forty now."

AS A TEN-YEAR-OLD returning to Boone for a visit, Mamah had gone with a cousin and aunt out into the fields during harvest. They rode in a wagon laden with bowls covered by dish towels. When they found the men, they set up the pots and jugs along the back of the wagon so the farmhands could fill their own plates. Mamah remembered her job that day—ladeling stew into tin cups. Even as a young girl, she had been stunned by how much food went into those men's mouths.

"Harvest" was all her mother had said when Mamah described the scene once she got home. In Iowa everyone knew what that meant—men bent over pulling and hacking, tending horses, working their hands raw. Women doing the same in the kitchen—cooking, cooking, and then cooking some more.

Mamah ran Jennie Porter's kitchen as if it were harvest time at Taliesin. There were two main meals, not one, as it turned out. The men ate oatmeal for breakfast, with plenty of coffee. At midday they ate heaps of stew and biscuits. At night they consumed another big meal—chicken, mashed potatoes, something green. Seconds of everything, and then dessert.

Lil, the tired-looking Spring Green cook, arrived from town every day with fresh supplies from the grocer. Only occasionally did they raid Jennie's garden—there weren't enough potatoes or greens in the plot for so many people. Mamah began dessert before Lil arrived. Usually, it was coconut cake or yellow cake with cocoa frosting, the two items she had mastered as a housewife. She had never been expected—none of the women she knew in Oak Park were expected—to have more than one specialty. A married woman in Mamah's circle needed to master just one dish to trot out at dinner parties or to deliver to ailing friends. Everything else was done by a cook or house girl.

Lil taught Mamah the subtleties of pie crust—how you forked the lard, salt, and flour into just the right crumbly mix before you added very cold water. How you pressed your left thumb up and your index fingers down to make a handsome crimped edge.

The first week of meals, the workmen hardly spoke to her. Mamah, Lil, and Jennie hung back, watching as the men devoured one large pot of victuals after another. Mamah had placed a glass vase of flowers on the table and was pained by the amused looks the men shot at one another upon discovering the new frivolity. They ate the cakes and grunted their approval nonetheless, always saying "thank you" when they stood up. But that was all.

"Pie crusts," she would say to Frank weeks later when he asked her at what point the men had begun actually conversing with her. It went without explanation, like "harvest." Frank knew the value of a good pie crust in the Wisconsin countryside. A woman didn't want to be known for making a bad one. But a woman who could make a really good one—now, *that* was worth something.

"LAST SUNDAY OUR preacher warned about consorting with people who live in sin. He didn't name no names, but . . ."

Mamah stood in the kitchen at the new house. In the days since her arrival, the kitchen had become a higher priority. It had been cleaned up, and she'd found a block of marble for a pastry board. She was rolling out her crusts there when the voices outside the window began. This time she recognized the young one. It belonged to a sweet-faced workman from a town a few miles over, newly married.

"You worry about the damnedest things," she heard Murphy say in his thick Irish brogue.

"Well, people are talking."

"You're gone five days a week from that little girl of yours, Jimmy. She's over there alone in Mineral Point with all them Cornish stonemasons. I'd be worryin' about that, if I was you. Any man knows what a new bride wants. A good stiff prick as far-r-r-r as it will go."

Men laughed wildly out in the yard.

People are talking. It was to be expected. She had slipped into their midst, and not without notice. Frank had purposely resisted introducing her by name, even to Billy. But the men had only to observe how Frank treated her to know she was more than a housekeeper to him. They addressed her as "ma'am," if they spoke to her at all.

"I'm sorry it has to be this way. You understand, don't you?" Frank said to her later. "A newspaper story would be disastrous at this point. It's not just our hides. Aunt Nell and Aunt Jennie are sensitive about publicity, what with their school nearby. I'm sure that's why they and the rest of the Lloyd Joneses are keeping their distance."

The locals probably knew there was a stranger among them—a particular stranger. Once, while riding out in the fields on Frank's horse, Mamah had come upon two farmers cutting across the property. They had stopped to look at her, and she'd pulled her hat down and ridden off rather than greet them, for fear of making her identity known.

There would come a time when she would have to be presented officially in the community. In the back of her mind, she kept hoping that Catherine would agree to a divorce. Then Mamah and Frank would marry, though they both said it was not a necessity. But how much easier it would make life to have that piece of parchment.

For the time being, she avoided any car trips into Spring Green. When she decided work shoes were the only solution for the mud around the construction site, Frank took one of her shoes into town and bought a pair of men's heavy boots for her.

The second week of her stay at Taliesin, Frank departed for his Chicago office. He had a project on his drawing table, a summerhouse in Minnesota for old clients, the Littles, that would bring in desperately needed money.

He left on a Saturday, so as to visit his children. On Sunday morning Mamah rose to have breakfast with Jennie and her husband Andrew, their children, and Anna Wright. Frank's mother had avoided Mamah as much as possible, disappearing into her room at the Porters' house for long periods during the day. Now they sat across the table from each other as Jennie slid eggs onto their plates.

"She won't eat eggs," Anna Wright said. She was thin, erect, and stern-looking, with steel-gray hair wrapped in a tight bun at her neck. Everything about her was sour, even her breath.

Mamah realized Anna was talking about her. The woman's lips were pressed together in a thin line. The puckered skin just below the corners of her mouth was a measure of the offense Anna took at her presence.

"Oh, I will today," Mamah said quickly.

Anna looked just to the side of her face as she spoke. "There's too much work not to eat."

Feeling chastised, Mamah salted and peppered the eggs on her plate.

"I don't believe in pepper," Anna said. "*Frank* won't touch pepper. It's bad for the digestion."

At least she didn't call me Mrs. Cheney, Mamah later reflected, the way she had the first week whenever Frank was out of earshot.

"Anna, I have changed my name legally to Borthwick," Mamah told her when it happened the third time. Now the old woman, like the workers, didn't call her anything.

It didn't take much cleverness to understand how the Wright family worked. Anna treated Jennie with a matter-of-fact familiarity. But when Frank entered the room, something in her seemed to brighten. She asked him questions as if he were a visiting celebrity, her cheeks—those sagging pockets—lifting at the sight of him.

Mamah knew her to be an intelligent woman, even witty; she had seen her present at the club in Oak Park. *That* Anna, cofounder of the Nineteenth Century Woman's Club, "Madame Wright," as she introduced herself, inhabited her body when Frank appeared. She pampered him, making up special plates of food for him, pointing out articles she'd read and wanted to share with him. And she told endless anecdotes about his childhood while he sat at the table chuckling at the old stories as if he were genuinely amused. Frank's sisters, Jennie and Maginel, usually appeared as accessories in the tales, yet even Jennie smiled at the old stories.

Frank had grown up among women, and they all adored him. His sisters and Anna—especially Anna—had doted on him since he'd first appeared. Mamah felt like a mature bride coming into a household where the groom has long been the apple of the mother's eye. It was a new experience, since Edwin's mother had always deferred to her, for some reason.

Frank had prepared Mamah to be accepted by his mother, but that was clearly wishful thinking on his part. Even Mamah had imagined better relations, though. She had romanticized Anna as a wise mother—the kind of woman who let her child's temperament and interests guide how she educated him. Having spent only a few hours with Anna, though, she wondered how on earth she was going to tolerate sharing a house with her, for Frank had earmarked one of the bedrooms in their home for his mother.

THE NEXT DAY, Monday, was so humid and witheringly hot, it put everyone in a bad temper. Mamah was making bread and pies when Frank's mother appeared in the kitchen. She landed a long cold stare on Mamah when she saw her rolling out crust. Anna didn't believe in sugar except as it could be used in some home remedy, cough syrup, perhaps. She had expressed more than once the notion that "people" harmed others' health by baking pies and cakes. Mamah had thought the grainy bread would please her, since it was from one of her own recipes. But the old woman gave no sign of approval when she saw it go into the oven.

Anna was boiling coffee when Lil arrived with the day's supplies from town. When Mamah and the cook carried six boxes of produce into the house, Frank's mother went straight to the vegetables to examine them.

"You can't have paid actual money for this terrible cabbage," she said, her voice as caustic as acid. "It's full of bugs."

"It's all they had," Lil said. "It's a Monday. The food came in on Saturday."

"You didn't pay full price for that, did you?"

"Yes."

"You bargain when it's like this," Anna snapped, "or you don't buy it."

Lil stopped in her tracks. "That's all there was. What would the men eat if I didn't buy it?"

Anna didn't respond. She poked around the boxes further. "What is *this*?" She held up some onions. "They're *damp*, like they've been sitting in water." She picked up a bunch of small turnips with wilted greens. "How did you manage to find old vegetables in September? These have *mold* on them."

Lil glared at the old woman. "Then we'll peel off the skins."

The remark infuriated Anna, who threw the turnips into the garbage barrel. "Anybody knows the skin's the most important part."

Lil's eyes were puffy little slits that gave her face a dull look, but Mamah knew she wasn't stupid. She was like a lot of country women, red-knuckled from a life of soapsuds and bone-grinding work. Tired out, maybe, but not someone you could push over. Lil pulled out the grocery bill from her pocket and slammed it on the counter. "You owe me five dollars." She met Anna's seething look with one of her own.

"Well," Anna replied, "we shall see what Mr. Wright has to say about that. I, for one, don't reimburse bad judgment."

Lil took off her apron and threw it on the floor. She stormed out the door and leaped into her truck. Mamah watched as the battered vehicle trailed a funnel cloud of brown dust down the road and out to the highway.

"Good riddance," Anna muttered when Mamah came back into the kitchen. She put on an old apron and began moving briskly around the stifling room. "We'll have chicken stew tonight for dinner," she said with the slightest hint of cheer in her voice. She went out into the dooryard, lifted a hatchet from its hook, then headed for the chicken coop. When she returned a half hour later, she carried six headless carcasses in the sling of her bloody apron, which she held with one hand. A fistful of herbs was in the other. The contretemps with Lil seemed to have elevated her spirits, because she began talking, apparently to Mamah, as she was the only other person in the kitchen.

"People will take advantage of you when they can, even in the country," Anna said, her voice thick still with a Welsh accent. "Especially if they take you for an outsider." Anna smirked as she ripped feathers out of the birds. "That woman doesn't know who she's talking to." She wiped sweat off her upper lip with her sleeve. "If she did, she wouldn't try to get away with that nonsense. She probably got a decent price and is trying to gouge us."

Mamah cleared her throat and tried to change the subject. "Frank told me your father settled this land."

Anna looked up from her work and gazed past Mamah's face again. "My father . . ." She paused, as if deciding whether to sully her father's story by telling it to Mamah. "My father had nothing when he came here." Her head was shaking a little, as if palsied by indignation. "*Nothing.* Except a wife and passel of children who could work. They were driven out of Wales by religious persecution."

"They were Unitarian preachers, weren't they?"

"You couldn't live by just that. The Lloyd Joneses were farmers, some of them. A hatmaker, my father was. Great men. Brilliant men. But they were misunderstood back in Wales, treated like heretics by their own people. Because they weren't afraid to think for themselves. My father was forced to leave the village church because he questioned the divinity of Christ. Most doctrines can't abide questioners. And my father opened his mouth. He spoke what he believed." She shook her head. "Oh, the persecution he and Mother endured."

"So they left," Mamah said.

"My father had a sister in Wisconsin. At first all we had was our hands and backs. One baby didn't make it—died on the trip out here from New York." Anna was washing the blood from the apron in cold water. "In time the Lloyd Joneses owned this whole valley."

Anna went out of the kitchen, leaving the big pot steaming.

THERE WAS NO REASON to expect Frank's mother to ever come around. Mamah remembered Catherine's story of her wedding day. Anna Wright had behaved as if she were at a funeral, fainting during the ceremony. She'd been at constant odds with her daughter-in-law ever since. Yet she had stayed near Frank the whole time. When he set off from Wisconsin as a young man to seek his fortune in Chicago, Anna had followed him within a year or so, moving with her two daughters to live nearby. Actually, to be supported by him.

He'd built a home for himself and his new bride on Chicago Avenue, next door to the house his mother and sisters occupied. Settled in Oak Park, Anna had carved out a life for herself as Madame Wright, mother of the brilliant architect.

It occurred to Mamah that Frank had never been without his mother close by, except for the one year in Europe. For all the adoration Frank enjoyed in his family, he'd been a beast of burden since he was nineteen or twenty. Standing in the kitchen peeling potatoes, Mamah could easily piece together how things had unfolded recently. Anna Wright had come up here and bought this land for Frank because she knew him well enough to see that he wasn't going to stay with Catherine. Where would that leave her, living next door to the daughter-in-law he had left behind? No, the mother had to throw her lot in with the son once more, out of loyalty, surely, but also because she had no other options.

To judge by what Mamah could glean from Frank's meager details, Anna Wright had made a bad bet in the one big gamble of her life. When she'd married, she had settled on a widowed preacher with a charming personality and a gift for music. Anna had ended up sending away his children to live with their dead mother's family once she had her own children with William Wright. But Frank's father turned out to be a rambling man, skipping across the country from one low-paying congregation to the next. One day when she'd had enough, Anna cut William out of her life. Banished him to an attic bed and stopped taking care of him, prompting him to file for divorce.

How humiliating for a woman like Anna to have to go back to the handouts of her brothers, the ones who owned the land. Following Frank to Chicago, Anna traded one kind of dependency for another. Now, once again, she was in the valley of the God-Almighty Joneses.

Maybe Anna was finding some respite up here after the newspaper scandal. Mamah had seen Anna's letters to Frank, knew how deeply pained she had been by the public humiliation. To return to her family's beloved valley, this time owning a piece of it—at least Frank owning a piece of it—must have restored a little dignity for her. And with Jennie only a stone's throw away, she must have felt satisfaction in at last laying claim to a part of the Jones dynasty.

Back in Berlin, listening to Frank conjure up images of life at Taliesin,

Mamah had not inserted Anna Wright into the picture. Now it dawned on her that Madame Wright could be a very present fact in her life, once Taliesin was completed.

WHEN ANNA APPEARED in the kitchen to check on the stew, Mamah tried again. "Frank says you are the one who really led him to architecture."

"I put pictures of cathedrals on the walls around his crib," Anna said. She stirred the steaming pot with a slotted spoon. "And, of course, I introduced him to the Froebel building blocks that he played with growing up."

Mamah remembered a remark Catherine had made at the housewarming party long ago: "His mother takes credit for his genius. It just burns me up."

"That's not the usual thing a mother does," Mamah said solicitously to Anna. "It was quite enlightened."

"Well, it certainly wasn't ordinary in 1867, when he was born, but I had a sense from the beginning that this child saw things other people didn't."

"Did you say 1867?"

"Yes. In Richland Center."

Mamah did not press her, but Frank had said he was born in 1869. She studied the woman's face. *Anna must be at least seventy-five,* she thought. *It's possible she's entering senility; that would explain her constant crankiness.* Mamah remembered the onset of her grandmother's forgetfulness, the confusion of time and dates, the bursts of temper. In that moment she felt some tenderness for Anna Wright.

CHAPTER 36

September 1911

Frank Wright—what a joy and a puzzle you are. Evenings and mornings I catch you sitting on the window seat, studying the valley. I know what you are doing. You're observing the progression of colors as the leaves change. You're thinking about plum trees and vineyards. About cows on the hillsides. Which ones are the most picturesque? We can't have just any cows at Taliesin. Oh my, no. "Only Guernseys against these emerald hills," you tell me.

The next moment you are up on your feet, dragging me down to the river. Never mind dinner. Let's go fishing. You pull up two fish and you are twelve again.

By day you dash around here looking like a country squire who has fallen into a pig trough. You sashay out into the middle of construction in your suit, just off the train from Chicago. When you should dress up, you don't. A couple of weeks ago, when we drove into Spring Green, you actually went into the bank barefoot. I sat in the car, trying to go unnoticed, while you went to see your banker dressed as Huck Finn.

Was that a test? To see if I have the stuff to ride the raft with you? Or were you simply pushing up against the rules because you feel more alive when you have a foe to fight?

You are in the middle of reliving every boyhood fantasy you ever had, Frank. You've told me time and again about sitting on this hill after your uncle had worked you near to death in the fields, and dreaming about building a house right in this place. Well, you have done it. You've proven yourself.

One of these days I will find the courage to say to you what I write here. That you don't have to test the loyalty of the people in this place. You are already testing sorely the love of your family by coming here with me. Let us live shoed lives for a while.

Frank was pacing around the kitchen, holding a flyswatter. His eyes followed a large black fly as it circled the kitchen table, then landed on a leftover piece of toast.

"Griffin!" Frank shouted, whacking the fly with such ferocity that the plate slid across the table and would have fallen off had he not grabbed it just in time. He took a moment to swipe the dead fly onto the plate, collect the toast from the floor, and toss the mess into the garbage. In the blink of an eye, he was leaping through the air, hollering, "Harriet Monroe!" Whack. The swatter came down on the kitchen window. When he lifted it, a fat black smudge remained on the glass.

"What has Harriet Monroe ever done to you?" Mamah asked.

"She wrote a nasty review in the *Tribune*."

"You didn't mention it. When?"

"Four years ago." Frank was creeping toward a cabinet speckled with flies. "William Drummond!" he muttered. Smack. "Elmslie. Purcell." Smack. Smack. He knocked over a chair while dispatching the last two flies, named for former draftsmen she'd heard him mention in moments of despair—men he once trusted who now copied his work.

"I'm going into town."

Frank stopped his swatting. "What prompts your recklessness, my dear?"

"Your mother. I'm going to take Lil the five dollars we owe her, and hopefully talk her into coming back, because I really don't want to do this cooking job by myself."

Frank put down the swatter and walked over to her. He stood behind Mamah and rubbed her shoulders. "She lives above the general store," he said, kissing her ear. "Will you get a couple of other things?"

"Give me a list and some money."

Frank scribbled down a few items on a scrap of paper. He reached into his right pocket and pulled out its contents in handfuls. Crumpled together were dollar bills, envelopes, old uncashed checks, a couple of pencils, and an eraser. He flattened out four five-dollar bills. "Is this enough?"

"It should be. I'll buy some groceries, too."

Mamah put on her sun hat and climbed into the car. It was the autumn equinox and still blazing hot. Black flies swirled outside as the workmen began to arrive at the house.

"CAN YOU TELL ME how I can find Lil Sullivan?" Mamah asked. She was standing in front of the fabric counter when the owner appeared.

"Just go around back and climb up the steps," he said. "She should be there."

When Lil answered the door, she was wearing a rumpled robe. Somewhere in the background, a child was crying. She looked stunned to find Mamah standing there.

"I want to apologize to you. I should have gotten here sooner to give you this money, but . . . Well, here it is." Mamah handed her the five.

"Thank you."

"You shouldn't have been treated the way you were that day. I should have spoken up, and I haven't forgiven myself for not doing it. I was thinking, Lil, if you came back—if you were willing to come back—I would do my best to keep her out of the kitchen. I will speak to Mr. Wright about it, and we will find a way."

"Who is that?" A man's voice came from somewhere inside the apartment.

"I can come back," Lil said. "Is tomorrow all right?"

"Tomorrow is wonderful. Tomorrow is perfect. Thank you."

Mamah felt so elated, she nearly forgot to stop downstairs to buy supplies. She waited her turn behind a couple of farmers who were discreet enough not to stare at a new face in the store. When it was her turn, she handed over the list Frank had scribbled—so many pounds of black galvanized nails, lengths of pipe, and other jottings the nature of which she couldn't interpret. The man went in the back and returned with the supplies.

"Do you have an account with us, ma'am?" He was a big man with deep, vertical furrows in his long face.

"We do." The store was now blessedly empty. "It's the account of Frank Lloyd Wright." She held her breath and looked at the man straight on. If he had heard about "the woman" out at Taliesin living with Frank, he did not betray it. He turned his back to her, bent down to get out his account book, opened it, then pointed to a page titled WRIGHT, F.

"Mr. Wright owes money on his account," he said. His attitude cooled. "He paid half of his balance in June and has not paid the rest since. He owes fifty-eight dollars."

Mamah's eyes began to burn. "I'll just get the supplies another day," she said. She took out the remaining fifteen dollars Frank had given her, added to the money the few dollars of her own she was carrying, and handed them over to the man. "We shall get the other forty to you promptly," she said. She walked out of the store and kept her head bent as she climbed into the car.

Behind the steering wheel, Mamah slowly drove out of town. When she got to the county road, she pressed the pedal to the floor and constructed one withering sentence after another to deliver to Frank when she got home.

As she pulled into the driveway, she saw him and the workmen crouched around something, probably plans. When she got closer, she saw that they were circled around an array of eggs, standing, every last one of them, on end.

"Mamah!" Frank called out when he saw her. "You're just in time. This only lasts for a short while."

The carpenters and plasterers stood around the eggs with grins on their faces, feeling a little silly, perhaps, but clearly delighted by Frank's artful spin on the old equinox trick. For he had taken the time to decorate every egg in its own complex geometrical pattern with colored pencils. The results were dazzling; the eggs looked like brilliant, faceted jewels.

"How often is the world in perfect balance, gentlemen?" Frank said. "Enjoy it."

"I don't believe you!" she said when she had him alone. "To experience that kind of humiliation and then to come home . . ." She threw up her arms in exasperation. "What were you thinking, sending me to the general store when you knew you owed them money?"

Frank shrugged. "Look, help me. I'm terrible at the business part of this thing."

"I won't live this way, Frank. You have to pay your bills. The *whole* bill. *Every* bill. Or just pay cash."

"I do. Often."

"And if you can't afford it, then *don't buy it.*"

"We have to get this place closed in before winter," he said. "I need the supplies, and I need them now."

"I would rather freeze than buy things on credit."

"Look, if you're willing to, you can take over the bill paying." He was scratching his back against the door frame.

"Will you sit down, please, and talk to me?"

He sank into a chair.

"Frank, this is no way to start things up here, I'm telling you. There are people who *want* us to fail."

"I know," he said, "I know."

She pulled a chair up and sat with her knees nearly touching his. "Let's not give them the satisfaction. What do you say?"

He lowered his eyes.

"And something else."

Frank shifted in his chair, as if he knew he would be held there for a while.

"Lil is coming back."

"Congratulations. How did you do that?"

"I told her your mother would not be coming into the kitchen."

He bent his head and put a thumb and forefinger over his closed eyes. "Shall I put Mother in charge of cow roping?" He sighed when he looked up. "Or hay stacking?"

"I'm serious. Would you arrange for her to keep away from Lil?"

"We'll figure it out."

"I'm not done."

"Yes, ma'am," he said boyishly.

"Frank." She hesitated. "What year were you born?"

"Ah, Mamah." Frank fell against the back of the chair he was sitting on and threw up his hands in a "caught me" gesture. "1867." There was some defiance in his voice.

"You told me you were born the same year I was, 1869."

"And there it is," he said.

"What do you mean, 'And there it is'?"

"I was a man in love. What can I say? It was a soul confession. I thought that finding you was damn near miraculous. Still think so. It didn't seem such a big . . ."

"Lie?"

"I just said it. I didn't think about it before it came out, and you seemed so happy about it. I felt that even though it wasn't precisely true, it *should* be true."

So odd an untruth, she thought when she was alone. About something so inconsequential. Yet it wasn't the first time she had caught him in a lie or distortion. He romanticized things. He couldn't resist enlarging his clients into heroes and heroines, making them gallant figures in his own King Arthur–size imagination. Today, out in the courtyard, he had been Merlin, dazzling the men with a show of magic. He loved imbuing everything with a little drama. It made life so much more interesting.

It was hard to get angry with Frank Wright. Somehow she would have to find a way to make him understand that there was no need to exaggerate anything. That he was extraordinary enough already.

CHAPTER 37

October 28, 1911

Frank presented me with bad news last night. He showed me an article about us that ran in the Chicago Examiner *in early September. It was lurid—"love nest" and Catherine "left in the lurch" and all that. That no other newspapers jumped on board to make it a full-blown scandal is miraculous, I guess. In this case, I don't begrudge Frank for keeping the whole thing from me until now. It's not so awful to receive one's bad news late, when the time for the other shoe to drop is well past. Lizzie, if she knew of it, made no mention to me.*

On we go. Wasmuth has finally sent the monograph to Frank's Chicago office. It has only sold a few copies in the U.S., but Frank is relieved and optimistic. Taliesin marks our new beginning. The monograph marks a new start for Frank's career. No time to toast milestones. Too busy.

It weighs heavily on me daily that I have written but one letter to Ellen since I came to Taliesin. That I have been too burdened with the house to even think of writing seems a poor excuse. Thank goodness I have good news to deliver to her now— Love and Ethics *is nearly published. Ellen doesn't understand how provincial people are here in the States. She doesn't fully comprehend why Frank had to put up the money for Ralph Seymour to print* Love and Ethics *and* The Morality of Woman. *I have tried to explain kindly that no other publisher would touch either of them. I am reluctant to tell her how badly I was treated at Putnam's last summer when I stopped over in New York. They wanted no part of my proposal to publish her "personal freedom" essays. Their excuse was that their London office does all of her English translating. Obviously, she hasn't told them I will translate for the American audience. In truth, though, I could smell something else in their lack of interest— fear. Too controversial.*

Last week in the mail I received a disturbing letter from a man in New York named Huebsch who insists Ellen Key gave him exclusive rights to publish Love and Ethics *in America. How very strange. Who knew that the translating business was as low-down as bootlegging? One makes so little money from it, it seems hardly worth the effort to steal.*

Frank has begun building a dam to create a source of power here on the property. He says we will also have a pond for waterfowl. Taliesin is taking shape. Soon I shall have my own study!

Frank rose at dawn that morning, as he always did. He went outside to bring in wood while the sky was still a pink ceiling over the pale horizon. The furnace was not functioning yet—some parts of the behemoth were still missing—and Mamah didn't think Frank cared a whit. He loved getting the stove and fire-places roaring. She stayed in bed until she felt guilty, then stuck a foot out to test the air. Freezing. In a little while he would bring her the socks and dress and wool underwear she'd set out the night before. For the past week, he had been warming her clothes by the fire. When he brought them in to her, she would leap up, dance around the cold floor as she dressed, then go put the per-colator on the stove.

Around eight-thirty, as he departed for the train to the city, she watched him move down the road. When his car passed a ditch full of cattails, it star-tled a flock of sandhill cranes. They flew up crying, straightened their long necks and beaks into perfect arrows, then turned southward, along with Frank.

Intent on settling in completely while Frank was gone, Mamah went to the shed to bring her remaining belongings into the house. She took a candle into the dark little building, pushing the door wide to get what daylight she could. Mamah moaned when the candlelight revealed the chaos inside. Shreds of paper and fabric lay around the chewed-up boxes where animals had been devouring their contents.

She sank to her knees to go through what was left of a box of old pho-tographs. Raccoons, judging by the scat on the floor, had chewed the corners off of the pictures. She could save them, she thought, by trimming and re-framing them, but as she sorted through the contents, her heart sank. She found a twenty-year-old family portrait shredded beyond repair, the legs of her parents and sisters chewed off.

Mamah felt ill as she carried the remains of her possessions into the house. She didn't care so much for her clothes, but she ached over the loss of the portrait. And she was terrified to open the box with the half-finished translations in it.

Ten months had elapsed since Frank had appeared in Berlin, so full of hope and plans for their future in Wisconsin. At the time she had pictured herself as happy as a queen, translating at her own desk in a room with a vast view of the hills—an image she might have captioned THE VOICE FOR ELLEN KEY IN AMERICA, AT WORK. Now, when she opened the box containing the manuscripts, she was elated simply to find that they had not been eaten.

THE CLOSE CALL shook Mamah. She resolved to return to translating at once, and sat down to write Ellen Key the letter she'd already composed in her head. She promised to send some essays to *The American* magazine, where they could be read by the general public, and she included the strange Huebsch letter. At the end Mamah assured Ellen she was back to work again.

She was just folding up the letter when one of the workmen knocked at the end of the hallway to get her attention. "Mrs. Borthwick?" someone called out. The men had begun to call her that name, at her own request, but it still sounded strange to her.

"Josiah's come back today," It was Billy's voice. "Do you want to talk with him, or should I?"

"I will," Mamah said. "Tell him to meet me in the living room."

Josiah was a young carpenter's apprentice who had revealed, during his brief employment with them, a considerable talent and a weakness for drink. In August and September, he had failed to show up on the occasional Monday. But by the end of October, he was missing two in five workdays, yesterday being the latest.

Josiah was small and wiry, a handsome boy with white-blond hair and a shy manner. He held his hat in his hands, his head bent as his contrite gray eyes peered up at her under the bushy blond eyebrows.

"We missed you sorely yesterday, Josiah."

"I'm sorry about that, ma'am," he said. "I was awful sick. Musta laid into something spoilt."

Mamah studied the young man's red face. Beneath one eye, the skin was swollen and yellow-green—suggestive of another barroom brawl. She hated the prospect of Frank having to fire him, if it came to that.

"Well, Josiah, the truth is, we need you desperately here. You're one of the best carpenter's apprentices Mr. Wright has had the pleasure of working with."

The young man hung his head. "I'll do better."

"I know you will. I'm sure of it."

The exchange left Mamah feeling enervated. It occurred to her that if she were to keep Ellen's faith in her, she would have to find a way to separate from the day-to-day decisions and chores at Taliesin. The crews had shrunk enough for Lil to handle the food preparation by herself. It wouldn't be premature to withdraw a bit now.

Taliesin had come a long way since Mamah had arrived that first August day. There were windows in—large clear panes, with no stained glass because there was no need to block out the views. There was plaster on the walls. Rough-cut oak beams thrust out from interior walls of stacked limestone.

How different from the house on East Avenue, she thought. In Oak Park, the kind of building Frank had put up, despite being called a "prairie house," turned inward toward the hearth and family life and turned its back on the street, because there was no real prairie beyond the door, only other houses.

Here, Taliesin opened its arms to what was outside—the sun and sky and green hills and black earth. Far more than the house on East Avenue, this house promised good times. It was truly for her, with its terraces and courtyard and gardens so like the Italian villas she had loved. Yet it wasn't an Italian villa. It had elements of the prairie house but it was not one. Taliesin was original, unlike anything else she had ever been in—a truly organic house that was *of* the hill.

Most astounding to Mamah was the space within; it was a dimension unto itself. What could be more expressive of the American ideal than a home where a person could feel sheltered and free at the same time? She loved sitting near the fireplace and looking out through the spacious living room to the fields and sky beyond. It was as if there were no walls to limit her view or thoughts or spirit as they expanded out and out. This was the "democratic architecture" Frank had been straining to achieve since she'd known him. Often she had heard him say that the reality of a building is the space within. And what you put into that space will affect how you live in it and what you become. Here at Taliesin he didn't want to clutter the place with stuff that did not ennoble them. She felt the same.

Mamah could picture Frank when he came to this hill with the idea of Taliesin brewing in his mind. Unrestrained by a suburban lot, he was free here to scoop up the sun and breezes and views. She could see him standing with his nose in the air, sniffing like a bird dog, taking in the place the way he often did when an idea began to form in his mind. Pretty soon the squares and rectangles, the circles and triangles, would be arranging and rearranging themselves in his mind. This could go on for weeks before pencil touched paper. When it did, he might sketch furiously for only an hour before a brilliant design appeared. How often she had heard him say with a bit of bravado, "I shook it out of my sleeve," as if it were the easiest thing, when in reality the design had been stewing for weeks inside his head. Other times he would take out his compass and T square and play on paper for long hours, designing and revising an idea, just as he'd done as a boy with his Froebel blocks.

She could understand his creative process only to a point. "It's a mystery," he'd once said, "even to me." Proof of that was the boyish joy he took in one of his buildings when it was finished. He seemed as delighted as a total stranger might be coming upon it for the first time.

There was no question that the men who had worked on Taliesin were immensely proud of it. To the man, they were devoted to Frank, probably because he would never ask them to do something he himself would not do. He honored what they knew and who they were, and they returned the sentiment. It was always "Mr. Wright," never "Frank." But they weren't afraid to complain about the lack of working drawings or how he kept changing plans on the spot. They weren't so respectful that they didn't ask him to leave when he hovered around them as they worked. Any skeptics among them had been won over as they beheld the strange beauty of Taliesin, the "organic" house they had shaped with their own hands out of Wisconsin rock, sand, and timber.

By November the living room had taken on the feel of a camp lodge. Most nights, away from their families, the workmen gathered around the main fireplace, still wearing their coats and caps to keep warm. A shy fellow who assisted the Norwegian stonemason always brought his pennywhistle to play.

One evening Mamah set up Frank's camera in the living room and had the men pose. It was hard to get them to sit still. They kept up their banter, laughing and teasing the young man who had recently married, saying he would look fat in the picture. "He may be pinin' for the new missus," someone said, "but it don't put him off his feed none." Their jokes were a measure of how relaxed the men had become in her presence. Yet they were respectful, even protective of her. If one of them launched into an off-color story within her earshot, he was quickly cut off.

When she peered through the camera, she regretted what the shutter couldn't capture: the accents of Ireland and Norway and backwoods Wisconsin. The sweet, high longing of the flute. The smell of tobacco on the men, and sweat muffled under layers of wool. But the camera would see their smoking pipes and calloused hands. It would catch the twinkling eyes and puckish grins on their faces. Mamah knew then what she wanted to give

Frank for Christmas. The men's portrait would be one of a whole series of pictures for a photo album that would tell the story of Taliesin.

There wasn't much time; snow was coming on. She made a mental list of what she wanted: long views from every direction, then close views of Frank's studio, the bunk room, bedrooms, and living room. To capture the expanse of the living room, she would take three photos and splice them together in a triptych, like a Japanese screen. He would love that. She would photograph the simple oak tables and chairs and beds Frank had commissioned. And, of course, "Flower in the Crannied Wall," looming like a guardian angel at the gate.

THE SECOND WEEK of November, Frank's sister Jennie called to say that a letter from Ellen Key had been delivered to her house. Mamah ran up the hill to Tan-Y-Deri, embraced Jennie, then hurried back to her own house to read the letter. When she opened it, she found that it was long and sprawling, like Ellen's essays.

Dear Mamah:

I have not heard from you in some time and wish to know the progress of the subjects we touched upon when you were at Strand in June. In your last letter you indicated that Mr. Putnam was not in his office and you had to speak to his representative when you were in New York. You said there was not much interest in the "personal freedom" selection. Might we regroup some other essays and give them to Putnam under another title? I would consider such a change in selection. Did you look up my friend Miss Emmy Sanders while you were in New York? Have you sent anything to the Atlantic Monthly? *To* The American? *Also, you said at the time that Mr. Seymour had the manuscript in hand for* Lieb und Ethik, *but I have had no word on the progress of its publication.*

Mamah cringed as she read down the list of questions. She would have to write back to Ellen immediately and reassure her, point by point.

The next paragraph, by contrast, made her nearly leap for joy. *I authorize you to commence translating* "Missbrauchte Frauenkraft" *and* "Frauenbewegung" *right away.*

The prospect of new work meant that Ellen had not given up on her. Near the end of the letter, she inquired about Mamah's life at Taliesin.

I was sorry to learn that your situation with Mr. Wright has garnered un-favorable publicity. In reading the account of your departure from the United States two years ago, I find myself much concerned about the manner in which you have chosen to pursue certain choices. It has been my belief and expressed philosophy that the very legitimate right of a free love can never be acceptable if it is enjoyed at the expense of maternal love. It distresses me deeply that my words to you have been misinterpreted. I urge you to reconsider this matter and return to your children if there is any question of their happiness.

You know the esteem I hold for you. I trust you will make a choice in harmony with your own soul.

Ellen Key

Mamah had to sit down. She took the letter into the newly stuccoed study and sat with it on her lap, trying to catch her breath. The smell of lime from the wet plaster, or perhaps the letter itself, created a sour taste in her mouth. Perched on the chair, squeezing her eyes shut, she felt like such a stupid, selfish fool. She had made a mess of so many lives. If she had waited a few more years . . . if she had simply moved to Boulder with the children . . . But how would they have survived? She felt as if she were butting her head against the same old wall.

Anger welled up in her. It struck her that Ellen Key's ideas were inherently self-contradictory. Mamah had found inconsistencies as she had translated, but none so disheartening or confusing as this. What did Ellen want her to do? Return to Edwin for the sake of the children? How ironic, in light of what she had written about staying in an unloving marriage—that it was tantamount to prostitution.

"I FEEL LIKE I just lost a friend," Frank said when Mamah read the letter aloud to him. He was tired from the train ride from Chicago and had stretched his feet out in front of the fireplace. "You know, you're right. It *does* sound as if she would have you return to Edwin."

"What's strange is that I thought I had made my situation clear to her. I thought she knew I was not going to do that."

"Did you tell her you were coming to Wisconsin after you left Europe?"

"No. She didn't ask. We talked almost entirely about business that last time I was at Strand. She was giving me all kinds of instructions and new responsibilities. She was very positive. She said, 'You will be the mouthpiece for me in America.' The mouthpiece. I remember that because it seemed such a funny word to come from her. We were planning a whole strategy for bringing her ideas to this country, and it was incredibly exciting."

"Someone got to her. Maybe Huebsch sent her the *Examiner* article to discredit you."

"Well, I can understand that it may not look good for Ellen to have me as her translator. There are other things lately, though, that I haven't wanted to admit to myself. For example, she hints in her letters that somehow you and I are making money off her books that we aren't reporting to her. It's laughable, isn't it? I've explained that it's you who has lost money out of your pocket. And then there's Huebsch. Did she really give him translating rights? I'm not sure she can remember exactly what she has promised to whom. I know for certain she can't keep straight what she has given *me* permission to do." Mamah shook her head. "It makes me question if I know her well at all. Before I even met her, just reading her books, I felt closer to her than I have ever been to almost anyone in my life, except you. And then to be welcomed by her in Sweden, almost as a daughter—it was wonderful. Now, though, I feel as though I've fallen from grace with her."

Frank shook his head. "Now, wait. She asked you to do more translating. She told you when you were there before that you were her mouthpiece. Do you still want to be her sole translator in America?"

"More than anything. I've told her all along that it wasn't the money I cared about. You know all this, Frank. I truly feel no one else understands her work quite the way I do. And it has always been about getting her ideas into the mainstream."

"Then don't let this slip away. And anyway, you adore Ellen Key. Even I adore her, and I've never clapped eyes on the woman."

"Ah, Frank," Mamah said sadly.

Frank had been feeding the fire with fragrant fresh-split wood. He used a log to poke the others, and the fire spat red cinders back at his feet.

"Do you mind if I just go and write her this minute?"

"Go," he said. "I'll finish making dinner."

DEAR ELLEN KEY. Mamah did not begin with *Beloved Lady*, as she usually did. She started with business issues, itemizing each point of concern and reiterating what they had agreed to, while reminding Ellen that she had named

Mamah her sole authorized English translator in America. Mamah told her about the pirated translation of Huebsch, which the publisher claimed Ellen had authorized. She paused to consider how to word what she had to say next. She had not been forthcoming about her plans when she'd been at Strand with Ellen last June, and it had come back to bite her. Now was not the time to mince words, whatever the consequences might be.

I have as you hope "made a choice in harmony with my own soul"—the choice as far as my own life was concerned was made long since—that is, absolute separation from Mr. Cheney. A divorce was obtained last summer and my maiden name is now legally mine. Also I have since made a choice in harmony with my own soul and what I believe to be Frank Wright's happiness and I am now keeping his house for him. In this very beautiful Hillside, as beautiful in its way as the country about Strand, he has been building a summer house, Taliesin, the combination of site and dwelling quite the most beautiful I have seen any place in the world. We are hoping to have some photographs to send you soon. I believe it is a house founded upon Ellen Key's ideal of love. The nearest neighbor half a mile away is Frank's sister, where I visited when I first came here. She has championed our love most loyally, believing it her brother's happiness. . . . My children I hope to have at times, but that cannot be just yet. I had a good summer alone with them camping in the Canadian woods. . . .

I will wish you now a very happy Christmas and tell you that Frank is sending you a little Hiroshige, which we hope you may care to hang in your new house.

I am grateful indeed for your words of friendship and I trust I may live my life and I believe I am living it so that you may not be ashamed of it as a testimony of faith in the beauty and purity and nobility of Ellen Key's wonderful words.

> *Your loving disciple,*
> *Mamah Bouton Borthwick*
>
> *Taliesin*
> *Spring Green, Wisconsin*
> *U.S.A.*

December 23, 1911

Such a painful "early Christmas" with the children in Chicago last week. Every-one uncomfortable in the hotel room. And then Edwin, suddenly friendly, pulling me aside at the end of my allotted day and a half to confide so happily his secret. He has not even told the children yet that he plans to marry this Elinor Millor woman next August. If she is one of Lizzie's best friends, how is it I have never once heard men-tion of her? How magnanimous Edwin thought himself, offering to allow me to have the children an extra month while he is on his honeymoon next summer.

I should feel glad for him. I should be happy when Edwin says she shows only the tenderest concern for the children. Instead, I am ashamed to admit, I feel stupidly betrayed. Replaced, more like it. Cannot think on it much or I will surely go mad.

Frank had his own "holiday"—ate his sliced turkey downtown with his children and Catherine, then took them all shopping. He won't go back to Oak Park on Christ-mas Day, says it will only encourage Catherine in her fantasies. So it will be just the two of us here for a quiet Christmas—our first at Taliesin.

Icicles have made the most beautiful, glassy veil around the house. They hang from the roof edge all the way down to the snow on the ground. Frank has hung some Japanese prints and the pictures we bought in Berlin. This place is taking on the feel of a real home. No rugs or much furniture, but here and there he has made assemblages of things from nature—rocks, pine boughs, and branches with berries. So lovely.

Mamah noticed the horse first. She was making coffee when she heard neigh-ing outside. The roads had been impassable around Taliesin for the past week, and the workmen came in on horseback now. But today was Saturday, two days before Christmas. Everyone was gone, even Frank's mother, who had de-cided to pass the week in Oak Park.

When Mamah went to the door, she found a red-cheeked young man peering in, his fist poised to rap on the glass.

"Good morning," he called cheerfully. She looked him up and down, opened the door. He was clean and well-spoken. "Is Mr. Wright here?"

"Come in," she said.

"Say, something smells good." She couldn't place his face, but his manner made her think he was a workman's son come back home for the holiday and looking for work.

"He's here. I'll be right back." Mamah found Frank in front of the fireplace. "There's someone here to see you."

Frank got up from his knees and went into the kitchen, wiping his hands on his pants.

"The name is Lester Cowden," the visitor said, extending his hand. "I'm from the *Chicago Journal.*"

Frank withdrew his hand. "What is it you want?"

"Sir, we had a report that Mrs. Cheney is living here, and I was sent out to confirm it." The young man seemed without shame in stating his business.

"I won't say a word!" Frank shouted. He yanked open the door and pulled the man's coat sleeve until he was outside. "Go on, get out of here." He slammed the door and waited until the man had mounted his horse and turned down the driveway. "The invidious sons of bitches," he muttered.

"I wasn't thinking. He seemed to know you."

"Don't talk to any of them, Mamah. Don't let anyone you don't know into this house."

Later that afternoon, while Frank was out in the barn tending to the horses, the telephone rang.

"Mamah?" A man's voice. "Mrs. Cheney?"

She hung up, threw on her coat, and went to the barn to tell Frank.

"The vermin are back," he said.

THEY HALFHEARTEDLY ate the lamb and greens she had cooked that night. When the phone jangled again, they both started. Frank got up and answered it. "All right," he said. "Just read it to me."

Mamah knew this meant a telegram. That was how they had to handle telegrams sent to them at Taliesin, unless they wanted to travel into the train station in Spring Green. It was an unsatisfactory system for all purposes, business and personal, as the telegraph office was patched through by the telephone operator on a rural party line. "You might as well just put an ad in the *Weekly Home News*," Frank would grumble after such a transaction.

"The *Chicago Tribune*, you say, not the *Journal*?" He was pressing a finger against his free ear. "No. No. Wait a minute, Selma. Just a minute." He looked over at Mamah. "The *Tribune*'s on to it now. What do you want to do?"

Mamah bit down on the inside of her cheek. "Call them back later."

"I'll call you back, Selma . . . What is it? Well, I don't give a damn about their deadline." Frank hung up the receiver and slumped into a chair.

"So they all know I'm here," she said.

"It was only a matter of time."

"Now what?"

"Just carry on with our lives. You can't let them rattle your footings every time they show up."

"Why don't you say some small thing, Frank? Tell them I'm divorced. Say we are living quietly together and wish not to be disturbed. Something like that. Then they've gotten their quote and it's over with."

He picked up the phone and called the telegraph office. "It's Frank Wright," he said. "Look, about that telegram from the *Tribune*. Just send one back to them from me. Say this: 'Let there be no misunderstanding. A Mrs. E. H. Cheney never existed for me and now is no more, in fact. But Mamah Borthwick is here, and I intend to take care of her.'"

Frank listened to the woman on the other end reading it back to him. "B-O-R-T-H-W-I-C-K," he said. "No, that's all. Just sign my whole name."

The next day Frank stood at the window of her study, brooding and waiting. From where he was positioned, he had a commanding view of the driveway. At ten o'clock, a party of three men on horseback turned off the highway and rode toward the house.

"Stay here," Frank instructed her.

When the knock came at the kitchen door, he answered it. The men included the reporter from the *Journal*, one from the *Chicago Record Herald*, and the other from the *Tribune*. The *Journal* reporter had been chosen spokesman.

Mamah crept down the hall to better hear what they were saying.

"Not a man here wants to be spending his holiday this way, Mr. Wright. Personally, you have our respect and sympathy. But the fact is, the editors think the only way to sell papers is with sensational news stories. That's what the people want."

"I won't be a part of it," Frank said.

"Sir, you already are. Here are today's papers."

She heard Frank cursing.

"Mr. Wright, why don't you tell your side of the story? I honestly think people would be sympathetic, and it could put an end to this."

"That's right," the other ones said.

She heard the door shut hard, and watched Frank walk disconsolately into the living room carrying the newspapers. When she joined him and picked up the top paper on the stack, it was ice-cold. Like a familiar bad dream, there was her portrait on the front page of the *Journal*. Next to her head, black letters shouted the "news."

MRS. CHENEY AND WRIGHT ELOPE AGAIN
FAMOUS CHICAGO ARCHITECT LIVES WITH
DIVORCEE IN SECLUSION AT HILLSIDE, WIS.;
LEAVES WIFE AT HOME
FORGIVEN AFTER FIRST ESCAPADE,
HE NOW TACKS RENT SIGN ON RESIDENCE

She looked at the Sunday *Chicago Tribune*. Running down the middle of the front page was a similar headline. Mamah shuddered as she read accounts of their love affair rehashed from two years before. But the *Tribune*, on a tip, had gone to the office of the Wrights' lawyer, Sherman Booth, and had come upon Catherine, who insisted that the woman up in Wisconsin was Frank's mother and not Mamah. Asked about the wall Frank had built between the studio and the house, Catherine insisted Frank was renting out one part of the house because he thought it had become too large.

It occurred to Mamah that Catherine might be mentally unstable. Why else would she carry on with this fiction?

"The bastards bushwhacked my daughter," Frank growled. His voice was murderous.

Mamah read the paragraph he pointed to in the *Tribune*.

At the bungalow, Wright's 17-year-old daughter
met all inquiries with the flat statement, "We have
nothing to say." When shown a copy of the report
exploiting her father's latest fall from grace she
seemed surprised and amused.

"We have become hardened to the sensational features of this case," she said, finally with a smile,
"and we really don't pay much attention, one way or
the other. Just say for Mr. Wright and Mrs. Wright,
and all the little Wrights, that we don't know anything about this awful story, and that it must be un-
true."

It was young Catherine's bravado in the last paragraph that pierced
Mamah's heart. She remembered the pretty blond girl as deeply shy.

"Frank, are your children really expecting you for Christmas?"

"I made it very clear to Catherine that I would not be back there for Christmas."

"But did *you* tell your children?"

Frank threw up his hands. "I have tried to talk with my children."

"Catherine *does* know you live with me here, right? She doesn't actually
believe you built this house for your mother—"

"Oh, for Chrissakes. Of course not. She's pulling us all down with her insanity. There won't be a client left after all this."

Mamah looked through the kitchen window and confirmed what she suspected: the reporters had not left. "Come sit down with me for a minute," she
said when she returned. "Let's think this out together. I believe the reporter
could be right. There's a part of me that feels we should lock the door and
never speak to those people again. But I keep thinking maybe it's time to tell
our side of the story once and for all." Now it was Mamah who paced. "Just
imagine for a minute what would happen if we dignified this whole witch
hunt with an explanation spoken from our hearts. I believe it would help."

"You think rather highly of the man on the street."

"Seriously, how many times have we talked about exposing people to
Ellen's ideals—our ideals? If I stand up on a podium and talk about living an
honest, authentic life, no newspaper is going to cover it. But now, at this moment, in the context of this absurd situation, it may be the one chance we get
to explain ourselves."

"Beat them at their own game?"

"I don't want to use Ellen's name at all. It would be our own thoughts."

Frank sat for a while, considering, then got up and went into the kitchen.
Mamah could hear the relief in the reporters' voices as they piled through the

kitchen door. They were probably nearly frozen. "Come back tomorrow," she could hear Frank telling them. "I'll talk to you tomorrow. Be here at ten." He let them stay for a few minutes to warm themselves, then sent them packing.

"Do you think it's wise to have them come back on Christmas Day?" she asked when they were gone. "Maybe we should wait until the day after."

"If we're going to talk, we can't take the hand railing down the stair on this. If it means a press conference on Christmas Day, then so be it."

DURING THE AFTERNOON and into the late evening, they struggled to put words on paper.

"I'll talk," he said. "They'll crucify you if you speak out."

He was trying to protect her. When she looked at him sitting there with his arms crossed, she knew he would not be budged on this point. "Then say I am in accord with all your remarks."

"Agreed."

He read the sentences to her as he composed, and Mamah was the editor, responding to the words he had chosen about squaring one's life with one's self. By nine o'clock Frank was depleted. In bed, she stared into the dark, waiting for the blankness of sleep.

In the morning Frank built fires and bathed. He emerged from the bathroom wearing his bright red robe over a white shirt and pajama bottoms. "We're going to have Christmas, even if it's for ten minutes," he said. She bathed, dressed, and hurried down the hall. There wasn't much time before the reporters were scheduled to arrive. When she saw a gift waiting for her under the tree, she dashed back and pulled from beneath the bed the wrapped picture album she'd made for him.

They took their ten minutes, he studying her photo story of Taliesin, she examining the Genroku kimono he'd bought for her. It was exquisitely dyed and embroidered with pine trees, wisteria, and jagged rocks.

She carried it back to their bedroom and laid it out on the bed. On any other Christmas morning, she would have put it on to please him. And to please herself, really. She hesitated, then held it up and viewed herself in front of the long closet mirror. In the space of a few seconds, she was pulling off her dress and wrapping the kimono around herself.

In the kitchen she made two pots of coffee, briefly considered biscuits, and then thought better of it. She was not willing to stoop that low.

Frank sat at the table while she prepared oatmeal, poring over the Christmas Day newspapers Jennie's husband, Andrew, had brought from the Spring Green train station that morning. "Thank God for Mrs. Upton Sinclair," he said. "She's knocked us off the front page."

Mamah looked over his shoulder. There was a portrait of the unfortunate woman next to a headline that read, AFFINITY OF POET DECLARES SHE WANTS ONLY FREEDOM IN HER ACTIONS. Mamah cringed at the word affinity. The yellow journals had turned a lovely word into a weapon—a code for "ridiculous whore."

"Atta girl," Frank muttered.

"What is it?"

"She let 'em have it. Listen. ' "I don't give a d— about marriage, divorce, reports of courts or the findings of referees," declared Mrs. Upton Sinclair, wife of the novelist. "I am so exhausted by the worries of the divorce suit that I have decided to live my own life with Harry Kemp as I see fit. Here we are hid away in a little insignificant bungalow, away from the outside world. . . . It is here in the wilds with our sacred feelings in perfect accord. . . ." ' " Frank looked up at Mamah. "Dear God, did all these hack writers go to the same lousy school?"

"No one talks like that," Mamah said. "No one says, 'Here we are hid away in a little insignificant bungalow.' "

"Didn't you know? All affinities talk alike. And they all live in bungalows. It's the only way the editors will have it."

"I think she's made a mistake."

"Mrs. Sinclair?"

"To come out swinging like that. I understand it, but there's a more dignified way." Mamah went and retrieved the notes they had composed the night before. "Do it as we said, darling, will you?" she said, handing him the paper.

"I'm no good at recitation." He sighed, but when he saw her worried look, he muttered, "All right. I'll read the darn thing."

At ten there were six reporters gathered around the fireplace, from papers in Chicago, Milwaukee, Madison, and Spring Green. For reporters who were supposed to be fiercely competitive, the men were behaving like old chums. They seemed to have formed a quick camaraderie, the way travelers do when they find themselves thrown together in a strange place. Frank assumed a position in front of them, standing in his long red robe with one arm propped on the mantel. When Mamah entered the room, they turned en masse, then jotted madly in their notebooks. Mamah took a chair as Frank began to speak.

"In the first place, I haven't abandoned my children or deserted any woman, nor have I eloped with any man's wife. There has been nothing clandestine about this affair in any of its aspects. I have been trying to live honestly. I *have* been living honestly.

"Mrs. E. H. Cheney never existed for me. She was always Mamah Borthwick to me, an individual separate and distinct, who was not any man's possession."

Frank glanced toward Mamah, and she nodded in return. He seemed to be in full command of his faculties, almost glad to be in front of an audience.

"The children, my children, are as well provided for as they ever were. I love them as much as any father could, but I suppose I haven't been a good father to them.

"Certainly, I regard it as a tragedy that things should have come about as they have, but I could not act differently if I had it all to do over again. Mrs. Wright wanted children, loved children, and understood children. She had her life in them. She played with them and enjoyed them. But . . . I found *my* life in my work."

Frank set down his notes on the mantel. "You see, I started out to give expression to certain ideals in architecture. I wanted to create something organic—something sound and wholesome. American in spirit and beautiful if might be. I think I have succeeded in that. In a way, my buildings are my children."

Mamah winced. She knew what he meant, but the newspaper readers would not, she was certain. And how would his children feel, reading it? She cleared her throat. Frank looked over at her, then continued on.

"If I could have put aside the desire to live my life as I build my buildings—from within outward—if I could have persuaded myself that human beings are benefited by the sacrifices others make for them . . . if I could have *lied* to myself, I might have been able to stay."

The *Journal* reporter jumped in. "How can you justify leaving when you have children?"

Frank kept his calm. "I believe we can't be useful to the progress of society without a stubborn selfhood. . . . I wanted to be honestly myself first and take care of everything else afterward. I can do better by my children now than I could have done had I sacrificed that which was life itself to me. I believe in them, but no parent can live his children's lives for them. More are ruined that way than saved. I don't want to be a pattern for them. I want them to have room in which to grow up to be themselves.

"I have taken nothing and shall take nothing from them. My earning capacity is as rightfully at their service as ever. I hope to be something helpful and suggestive of better things to them. When they get a little older, I hope they will see me in another light."

"And Mrs. Wright?"

"Mrs. Wright has a soul of her own and much greater matters than this to occupy her heart and mind. It's not for me to say what she may do."

Frank looked away, thoughtful, then turned his face to the men again. "Look," he said, "it will be a waste of something socially precious if this thing robs me of my work. I have struggled to express something *real* in American architecture. I have something to give. It will be a misfortune if the world decides not to receive what I have to give.

"As for the general aspect of this thing, I want to say this: Laws and rules are made for the average man."

Mamah stood up abruptly. She knew what was coming next. She tried to get his attention, but Frank kept talking.

"The ordinary man cannot live without rules to guide his conduct. It is infinitely more difficult to live *without* rules, but that is what the really honest, sincere, thinking man is compelled to do. And I think when a man has displayed some spiritual power, has given concrete evidence of his ability to see and to feel the *higher* and *better* things of life, we ought to go slow in deciding that he has acted badly."

Mamah glared at him. Had he not heard what she'd said to him this morning? That nothing made better copy than someone who thinks himself more important than the common man? It was like throwing meat to lions.

"That's all I care to say to you, gentlemen," he said when she finally caught his eye. "If you want to see what I have done here, I'll take you around Taliesin."

While Frank went to change his clothes, the men stood waiting in the foyer. She could tell he was keeping them waiting on purpose, probably to prevent them from making their deadlines. Mamah collected coffee cups and stood on the other side of the wall to listen.

At first they didn't speak, and then she heard their schoolboy snickers. She stood frozen, listening. She heard "kimono" and "red" as their titters escalated to choked laughter.

Mamah hurried out into the kitchen.

"I thought the interview went rather well," Frank said quietly to her when he appeared at last.

She looked at him standing there with his regal bearing in the suit he had designed for himself. She saw him then as the reporters had viewed him—an eccentric figure of a man, all too self-serious. She knew at that moment that they would not be spared.

"Just get rid of them," she said.

CHAPTER 39

T he morning of December 26 began with a gaggle of reporters at the gate. Josiah brought in the newspapers that the men had shoved at him when he arrived. Mamah skimmed down, pausing at the hurtful parts.

> Apparently Mr. Wright did not feel any regret he was not present in the Oak Park house where his lawful wife and their six children were spending their Christmas and Mamah Borthwick seemed to have forgotten the Christmases of the past which she had spent with her husband and children.

"What do you want us to do?" Josiah asked.

"Ignore the mutts and go on with your work," Frank said. "And do not talk to them, do you understand? Tell all the men that I said so."

"Yes, sir."

"On second thought, escort the lot of them out of here."

"Yes, sir."

Mamah stood up to watch Josiah approach the reporters. He opened the gate and spoke to them. After a while, he took to feinting and lunging forward like a boxer before he closed the gate and retreated, looking fiercely frustrated. The men climbed on their horses and rode down the driveway only to dismount at the entrance from the road to Taliesin.

When the phone rang, she answered it cautiously. It was Jennie, saying that some reporters had already been to her house and over to Hillside School to besiege Frank's aunts as they began classes. Aunt Jennie and Aunt Nell were frantic and begging Frank to come immediately to Hillside.

Frank had dressed that morning in his riding clothes and saddled his horse, intent on getting some fresh air. He mounted Champion and rode the mile to the school. When he returned an hour later, he was wild with anger. "They're terrified. They had parents show up this morning, threatening to pull their children out of the school if something isn't settled."

"Do you think—"

"Yes, I think it could happen. Aunt Jenny and Nell's finances are shaky anyway. They're trying to buy back the school from Uncle Jenk. He bailed them out when they went bankrupt a couple of years ago, but this could be the end of everything for them." Frank turned around and headed out the door again.

"Where are you going?"

"I'm going to find the gun."

"*What* gun?"

"I have a rifle somewhere. In the shed, I think."

Mamah went to her study and looked out the window. The cluster of men out near the entrance had grown, and a party of them was mounting their horses. She watched in horror as they headed up the driveway toward the house. She ran out to the shed, where she found Frank trying to put together a disassembled old firearm.

"If you love me, Frank, you will keep your head. Listen to me—put that thing back in the box."

"Oh, hell, Mamah, the damn thing doesn't work anyway."

"Just come into the house with me. The reporters are headed up here again."

Frank leaped to his feet, grabbed his battered old Stetson off a hook, and charged out of the shed. He placed himself in front of the gate, arms folded. "Get out of here, you boobs," he shouted when they were in earshot.

The reporters kept coming. When they reached him, they appeared to be pleading their case to Frank. Mamah stood outside the kitchen door, straining to hear their words. "If you continue to intrude on me," she heard him shout, "I shall have only one recourse, and that is my revolver." He turned on his heel and came back to the house.

"We've got big problems," he said when he slipped into the kitchen. "They say people in Spring Green are up in arms, and somebody has filed a complaint with the sheriff. They're telling me Pengally over in Dodgeville is coming here to arrest me."

Mamah steadied herself by holding on to a chair back.

"Let him come," Frank said, furiously scratching the back of his neck. He paced around the kitchen, red-faced. "There's not a chance in hell he's going to arrest anybody."

"You have a revolver, too?" Mamah asked.

"Of course not," Frank said. "I haven't even got a decent slingshot."

They retreated into the bedroom. She climbed under the bedcovers, shaking. Frank had let the fires go out.

"You see what they did, don't you?" he said. "They wrote their stories, ran to the train station to wire them to their editors yesterday, then went straight to goading the Iowa County sheriff to do something. One of them told me a petition was going around, trying to get us to leave. Now, who do you think started the goddamn petition? One of those asses outside right now, that's who. They're making money hand over fist on us because *we* sell their papers. *We* are the fodder in their circulation wars."

"There's enough food in the house to stay in here for a few days." She shivered. "If we don't go out, they will go away."

He was sitting on the edge of the bed, his head hanging. "My family has lived in this valley for fifty years. My aunts . . ."

She shook his shoulders. "Frank," she said gently. "Frank. Have you talked to Sheriff Pengally yourself?"

"No."

"Then call him right now, for goodness' sake."

LATER, WHEN SHE REMEMBERED these days, she would think of Josiah, lunging and feinting, lunging and feinting. It was the same dance she and Frank had been drawn into as they attempted to make the men disappear. Each day a new development caused one side to retreat, only to lunge forward the next day with some new ploy or response. Pengally confirmed by phone that reporters had been nagging him. They had gone after the district attorney to search the state statutes, but the harried man found nothing to put before a grand jury. "Don't worry," the sheriff told Frank, "I'll shoo them off." Yet the headlines persisted. SOUL HEGIRA HEADS TOWARD SORDID JAIL. Another called Taliesin a "love jungle." Another claimed a posse had raided "F. L. Wright's Den of Love."

There had been no posse after all. At the time, though, not even the men who worked for Frank knew whether to believe a posse was headed toward Taliesin. During the worst of it, the workmen had brought firearms from home and taken it upon themselves to patrol the perimeter of the property. The thought of these loyal country men, whose lives were rooted in family and church, trying to protect her and Frank had made Mamah feel grateful and, at the same time, deeply embarrassed.

In despair, Frank wrote another public statement of their position, passed it to the press, then announced that he would ask Catherine and Edwin for a "family caucus" to sign an agreement that everyone was at peace with the situation. The day before New Year's, as he was preparing to go to Oak Park to get their signatures, the morning newspaper rendered the trip unnecessary. Catherine Wright made it very clear that she knew nothing of a caucus and had no intention of signing anything. "I shall not divorce my husband," she said, "and I shall not allow him to marry another. He will always be welcome in his home; I shall always be glad to see him."

Mamah hadn't heard Catherine's voice for some time, but this sounded like the woman she once knew. The statement, Mamah felt certain, was meant for her. It dawned on her that the newspapers had become a messenger service between them.

Once again she found herself a character in a morality play, cast by the dailies and watched by the public. Nowhere was that more evident than in an interview with Frank's former secretary, Grace Majors, that ran the next day. She described Catherine as a woman of not only extraordinary character but great beauty. Radiantly lovely with pink and white coloring, Catherine looked particularly stunning in a chiffon gown Frank had designed for her that matched her auburn hair. When people complimented her on her appearance, according to the secretary, Catherine always said, "The credit for the beauty of this gown is all due Mr. Wright."

Miss Majors did not remark on Mamah's looks but did dismiss her as a devotee of Ibsen, whom Mamah regarded as her spiritual and physical director. That part caused Mamah to laugh bitterly. She'd never met the secretary. True, she had read some Ibsen, but to describe him as her spiritual and physical director? What did that even mean?

But it didn't have to mean anything for readers to catch the message of the article. *Catherine is the angel,* Mamah thought. *And I am the devil.*

For a full week the newspaper scandal raged on. A few parents took their children out of Hillside School for fear they would be tainted by the nearness of Taliesin. Clergymen of every stripe from Madison to Chicago railed against Frank and Mamah from their pulpits. The church Mamah had attended in Oak Park dropped her from its rolls.

In the early part of the siege, the reporters had placed the latest papers outside their door, like bait. She and Frank had taken in the papers each day. The reporters got what they wanted—a distressed response that ran the following day.

Now that the workmen were patrolling the property, the papers had stopped appearing. Frank was relieved, but she missed them. Maybe Mrs. Upton Sinclair was strong enough to refuse to read the dailies, but Mamah couldn't stop herself. The articles were saturated with distortions, but there were nuggets of truth in them, too—correct chronologies, real quotes.

She asked Josiah to bring her any Chicago papers he could get from the train station. He looked at her mournfully. "They're full of lies," she said, "but it would be worse to not know what's being said."

ON JANUARY 3, a bitter cold seized southwest Wisconsin. They woke to find Lucky's bowl of water frozen solid in the kitchen. Dressed in layers of wool, Frank cursed the useless furnace and went out to get more wood. She watched through the window as he bent down, gathered snow in his hands, and washed his face with it. He collected an armful of logs, came inside, then started up the stove and built a roaring fire in the living room.

She kept the oven door open until her fingers could function properly. Sitting in the kitchen, Mamah took stock. The stove had unwiped spills on it. In the living room, she'd noticed footprints through gray ashes all around the fireplace. The sheets needed to be changed and the bathroom scrubbed.

When she felt warm enough, she opened the door to see that Josiah had left her a newspaper. They had not had any press for two days, and she'd begun to believe the assault was over. But there in the middle column of the *Chicago Journal*'s front page, some editor had fired his parting shot.

HEGIRA TEARS CHILD HEARTS

MRS. CHENEY'S OFFSPRING PRAY
SHE MAY RETURN,
BUT ONLY ONE HAS HOPE

Mamah dropped the paper on the kitchen table, crossed her arms, and squeezed her ribs as she read down the column.

The three children of Edwin H. Cheney and Mamah Bouton Borthwick, his divorced wife, have given up hope of having their mother again.

"I guess she is not coming back," said 9-year-old John today as he plodded from his home to the Holmes School in Oak Park.

"Us three kids pray for her every night, but I guess God can't hear us, or something, for none of us except Martha believes she will come back.

"Jessie and I have read a lot about her in the newspapers whenever we get a chance, but they keep them away from us most of the time, and there is a lot of it we don't understand. Martha is too young to read the papers, so she just keeps wishing for Mamma. She talks about her nearly all the time."

Mamah's anguished cry brought Frank in from the living room. He read down the column and said, "They've made it up. It's hard to imagine such cruelty, but they've put words in John's mouth."

"How do you know that?"

"Does he speak like that?"

She looked at him fearfully. "No, but there are some things right in it. The name of Holmes School."

Mamah read one section after another. CHILDREN TAUNT LITTLE CHENEYS. CHENEY CHILDREN GAIN LOVE OF THEIR AUNT. "They talked to Lizzie," she said.

"Now I *know* it's made up," Frank said. "She's never talked to anyone."

"Read this." Mamah pointed to a section on the second page, where her portrait once again loomed midpage.

MAMAH BRILLIANT AS A CHILD

"There is really nothing to say," declared Miss Borthwick. "I educated my sister, I still love her—I couldn't help doing that; nobody could, because everybody who knows her loves her. And I will be a mother to her children. Mr. Cheney never has uttered a word against his former wife, even to his closest friends, and if he does not condemn her, why should I?

"Mamah was always brilliant, even as a little child, and was mistress of three languages at an age when some children can scarcely construct a correct sentence in their own language. I taught school and paid for her education at Ann Arbor."

Frank looked up. "Is that true?"

"Yes," Mamah said, pressing her fingers into her flesh.

"She graduated from that institution with honors. Later Mamah became librarian at Port Huron. She was regarded not only as brilliant, but as one of the best-read women in America and an efficient librarian. But there isn't anything to say.

"All I can do is the woman's part—that is, do my duty, love and care for my unhappy, misguided sister's little boy and girl and help them fill the aching void left there to both Mr. Cheney and the children by the absence of the mother."

"Words in her mouth," Frank said. "Don't finish it."

When he tried to take away the paper, Mamah grabbed it tight and held on. For a moment there was an angry tug-of-war, until Frank let go. Sighing, he walked back into the living room while she read and reread the terrible story.

No, Lizzie didn't talk that way. But some parts were things only Lizzie and a few others knew. Three languages by kindergarten. That Lizzie had helped pay Mamah's way through graduate school. And the comment about being well-read. What was missing was the familiar remark Lizzie always added: "So why can't you remember where you put your glasses?"

Mamah got up and banged pots around in the sink. She could imagine the taunts the children had suffered. For John to have his mother portrayed on the front page as a whore was the cruelest thing she could think of. Children could be hideous on the playground. What did her own pain amount to, compared to what John and Martha and Jessie had endured?

At that moment, if she could have, she would have taken one of the workmen's guns and shot dead the reporter who had tracked John down to poke at his wounds.

She remembered the moment when they were in Canada, when she had tried to explain to John what divorce meant. He had squirmed out of her arms and slipped away to play. That was the thing about children. Even if John had nodded, even if he had said he understood, he wouldn't have. *He is nine years old,* she thought. *All he knows is the feeling inside himself, the terrible longing. What could the word "divorce" really mean to a child that young? Or to Martha?* The image of the girl waiting, hoping, believing, was horrifying to Mamah. What must it be like for Martha to bear?

She wanted to leap on the next train to Chicago, to hold her children in her arms. She wanted to tell Martha and Jessie over and over that everything would be all right. She was desperate to feel John's warm, skinny body, to stroke his head and let him know that he meant everything, more than the world itself, to her.

Mamah stood at the kitchen window and considered the driveway. It was a sheet of ice. The car would surely not start. It was too cold and slippery to try to make any real distance on horseback.

But if she did go, if she found a way to get there, who would it serve?
Only me.

She understood something new just then. That the greatest measure of her love would be to leave them alone. To rush back to Oak Park would be to poke her own stick in their wounds, because once the reunion was over, she would leave again. What they needed now, in order to heal, was distance from her and all this drama. They needed a normal household and the steady, present love of Edwin and Louise and Lizzie. And Elinor Millor.

Mamah saw clearly now just what she had lost. She had given up her right to keep her place as the children's most beloved. The small, daily offices of love that had connected her to the children before—the shoe tying, the hair combing, the nightly storytelling—were no longer hers to claim. How dare she seek from them the comfort that had once so nourished her? To keep them yearning for a mother who was rarely with them, through her own choice, would be to sentence them to whole lifetimes of sorrow.

What she had to do was secure for them some sense of privacy so they could begin to accept that she was not coming home. She would not inflict herself upon them in the flesh. To go see them now, even if she could, would be to visit the press upon them once more.

Instead, she could write to them and pour out her love for them in letters. She could ask their forgiveness. She could try once more to explain. Words lasted longer on paper than when they were spoken into a child's ear. *Someday*, she prayed, *someday when they are grown, let them understand.*

CHAPTER 40

Mamah sat in her study with the new translation of the *Taliesin* poem on her lap. She had ordered the book months ago as a Christmas gift for Frank. But it had arrived only yesterday, and Christmas was an agonizing memory she preferred not to think of.

It was February, yet she felt they were both still tender as new bruises. Frank had been right. Clients and prospects had fallen away in the wake of the newspaper stories. He had spent a good deal of time since December writing letters to those whose projects were on the drawing board, urging them to stay with him.

To her, he'd shown a despair she'd never seen in him. In the worst of the onslaught, he had entertained the fear that he might actually die at the hands of lynchers. At the end of December, Frank had taken out a fifty-thousand-dollar life insurance policy, naming Mamah as the beneficiary. He'd talked of it in terms of protecting her, but there was also another part of it, a deep sense of doom—the flipped-over side of his powerful sense of destiny as an artist.

Mamah read a passage of the poem.

> I was a hero in trouble:
> I was a great current on the slopes:
> I was a boat in the destructive spread of the flood:
> I was a captive on the cross . . .

The words would only darken Frank's outlook. Mamah closed the volume and put it on her shelf. She had to be careful. Maybe in a couple of months she would give it to him. Now it would only cause him to fall deeper into depression.

"I can't sit around and design indefinitely," he said more than once during the long days of February. "There are mouths to feed." He would go out and split wood until he couldn't lift his arms anymore, then come back inside, still furious.

He needed to build, he would say, slamming more logs into a pile in the living room. Who *was* he otherwise? He had to have partners in his work, people who would pay for the materials of his art, who would provide themselves and their dreams as material to inspire him. To lose clients meant so much more than losing income. It meant the loss of an essential dynamic. He would continue to design; he couldn't really stop himself. But to build, to interact with a place and its materials, to make the decisions along the way that breathed life into a space . . .

It will be a misfortune if the world decides not to receive what I have to give. She was haunted by the words he'd said to the reporters.

At night he brooded aloud in front of the fire, gauging the loyalty of old clients. Darwin Martin. The Littles. The Coonleys. People who'd had the courage in the past to dream along with Frank. They meant more than money to him. They were the true believers, former and current. Now, in his troubled evenings, he tallied his enemies and friends.

"I should have listened to my instincts," Mamah told him one night. The dog lay on top of her feet beside the fireplace.

"I wish you wouldn't do that," Frank said when he saw that she'd brought table scraps from dinner and was sneaking bits of beef to the dog. "He has a bowl."

"I blame myself."

Frank waved away the remark. "I thought you believed that woman's intuition was fiction, anyway."

She did. The expression annoyed her, as if women didn't use intelligence and experience—just as men did—to make wise decisions. Frank, even Edwin, had accused her of thinking a thing to death. But sometimes she just listened to her instincts. This time she wished she had listened to what they were telling her: Lock the door and don't talk. She'd encouraged Frank to speak openly to the newspapermen, then watched in horror as he stepped into a perverse dance with the press. It was as if he couldn't stop himself once the thing had begun. In the end, it was he who had been made a fool of, more than she.

There was nothing to be done about it. The past month had been a nightmare she wanted to forget. Only one shred of good had come of it. When Anna had returned from Oak Park, she'd taken up residence at her daughter Jennie's house rather than with Frank and Mamah.

"What is happening at the office?" Mamah asked him.

"Well, Sherman hasn't given up on me. He's going ahead with the house in Glencoe. There are a couple of stalwarts left. Fred is sending out the mono-graph to the booksellers who ordered it, but it's very slow-going." Fred was the office manager in Chicago. She wondered how Frank managed to pay the rent at Orchestra Hall, let alone the young architect, given all his other finan-cial obligations.

"And the children?" she asked him. He had not mentioned them since he'd come back.

"They still hate me some."

She suspected he was meting out in doses the time he spent with them or reflected on them. It was how she got through a day. To take John's and Martha's letters out of her secretary whenever she felt the impulse was too dangerous. She would exist as a useless heap on the floor if she did.

"When do you see them now?"

"It depends on how you mean 'see.' In a week I might visit with them once." He fell quiet.

"Yes?" She put her hand over his on the armrest.

"But there have been times . . . at night, when it's dark . . . I take the train out to Oak Park."

She waited, listened to the wet wood hiss in the grate.

"The lights are always on, and if I stand on the terrace, I can see them through the windows. Llewellyn and Frances, they're such wild little things. They're usually running around. Sometimes I just go stand there and watch them." He shook his head and fell silent.

OUTSIDE THE WINDOW of her study, the February sky was dove gray. Nothing moved. Even the dry grasses poking up through the snow had ceased shiver-ing in the wind. They were stooped over, frozen stiff by the last ice storm. She put on her glasses and scanned the landscape. Where were the hares she had seen in profusion last fall? Dreaming in their holes, she supposed.

Sitting at her desk, she had a clear view to the south and west; she could see who was coming and going. Now it was only workmen or Jennie's family. Still, it was a useful thing, to command a long view. She thought again of the fortresslike houses on the hills around Siena, situated so that no enemy could approach without being seen.

Had Frank suspected that they would come under siege? Had he thought of Taliesin as some sort of fortress? The idea seemed utterly contrary to the openness of the place. A year ago, when he had appeared in Berlin so full of passion about building Taliesin, he had understood something she hadn't comprehended at that point. He had gotten a mouthful of the intractable hatred some people felt for him. No wonder he was so adamant about starting to build *right then*. He couldn't have seen ahead to the cruelty of the past couple of months. But he had prepared for it nonetheless.

At least we have heat now, she thought. It was a vast improvement. A real gift, actually. Heat was something people took for granted until it suddenly wasn't there. What did a person need to survive? Food. Water. Shelter. Warmth in cold weather. Those simple things were helping both of them heal.

And something else—books. In January Frank had hired Josiah to build bookshelves for Mamah's new study. The young man was working on a job elsewhere but had come out to Taliesin evenings and weekends until the shelves were finished. She had unpacked her books, dusting and arranging them by subject and author on the beautiful new shelves, all the while thinking about what volumes she could buy when she had a little money. She arranged in a row her journals, scribbled edge to edge with thoughts and quotes, and stuffed fat with slips of papers on which she'd copied more thoughts and quotes. She'd barely had time to dip into her subscription magazines, sent in care of Frank's sister Jennie during the past half year. Now they were piled neatly in a basket—six months' worth of thought on women's issues, as well as fiction stories, waiting to be savored like expensive chocolates.

There was almost no money. But the pleasure of sitting among the goldlettered spines in the company of George Eliot, Ibsen, Shakespeare, Plato, Emerson, Freud, and Emma Goldman brought some relief.

Frank had found his own kind of relief. When he was not in Chicago, he was at Taliesin with her, but his mind was somewhere in the countryside beyond Kyoto, wandering over bridges and through the snowy mountains of Hiroshige landscapes. He would go into the vault, take out the prints, and pore over them in his studio, rising from time to time to crank up his Victrola and listen to the structured clarity of Mozart or Bach. The prints and music were better than nerve medicine for him.

"You should write about Japanese art," she told him one evening. They were seated once more in front of the fireplace. His resting spot was a Morris chair with wide, flat armrests; hers was smaller in scale, with the back and arms upholstered in old wine-colored velvet. "You're an expert by now," she went on. "This is a chance to educate other people. You may never again have the time to do it."

He rubbed the day's bristly growth on his chin, considering. His face in profile reminded her of a handsome bust of Beethoven—the fine nose and mouth, the thoughtful brow met by a mane of long, backswept hair. In the eight years she had known him, he had grown more handsome, the increasingly gray hair giving him new dignity and power.

"You keep saying you'll lose money if you sell the prints now—that you have to hold them for a while to make a profit," she said. "Well, I see another way to make them profitable. *Japonism* is all the rage. Why don't you write a book about how to understand the Japanese print?"

Within the hour, he had embarked upon the project.

SETTLED AND ORGANIZED, Mamah returned to her own work. Along with the painful letter Ellen had sent last November, she had included two essays for Mamah to translate. The one Mamah had begun was "Missbrauchte Frauenkraft"—"The Misuse of Woman's Strength." Ellen had published it in Sweden seventeen years earlier, in 1895. Mamah knew very little of it. A few pages into translating, she felt a growing sense of unease.

Ellen was arguing that women's energy should be used for child rearing, that suffragists were wrongheaded to focus so intently on jobs and equal pay when motherhood was their legitimate work. For a woman to rush out seeking men's work was to abandon her post by the cradle as the shaper of the human race. Far better, Ellen argued, that the emancipators worked toward rewarding and enhancing the job of "mother."

It was not the first time Mamah had come upon the argument. Ellen had leveled it in *Love and Ethics*, too. But it had not been the main focus.

"She's taking potshots at suffragists in this 'Misuse of Woman's Strength' essay." Mamah was frying onions at the stove. Frank sat at the kitchen table, shaving into perfect points the soft lead of his drawing pencils.

"It's funny," Mamah said. "I remember when I first met Else at the café in Berlin. One of the women at the table—a woman named Hedwig—called Ellen Key 'the wise fool of the Woman Movement.' I was puzzled when she said it, but so much was happening that night . . .

"About a month later, I ran into Hedwig. I sat down with her in the café and asked her what she had meant. She explained to me that Ellen is revered in Europe for being the champion of the new morality, but she is despised by suffragists for something she did back in 1896. It seems she made a speech to a women's congress and attacked the whole suffrage movement because she thought they placed equal pay and the vote above the mother function, which she stated is the only truly legitimate work for women. Apparently, the speech sent shock waves throughout Europe. Ellen had loads of devout followers, and the speech turned many of them away from the suffrage cause. Hedwig said she set back the movement in Germany by a decade."

"Ellen Key?" Frank looked at Mamah incredulously.

"Yes. I guess Ellen came to Berlin a few years after that and endorsed suffrage, but the damage had been done. The movement is still trying to recover from the schism she created.

"And here's the interesting part. That speech she delivered back in 1896? It was called 'Missbrauchte Frauenkraft'—'The Misuse of Woman's Strength.' The very document I have on my desk. The very thing she wants me to translate and communicate to the women of America."

"So you're afraid if you publish it, it will set back the movement here."

"Absolutely. I'd love to just throw the thing away, but she clearly wants me to get it out to the public. What amazes me is that she can still believe it in 1912."

"People have blind spots."

"But it's so antithetical to everything she's written about personal freedom. And she holds some sway now. That's what I've been meaning to tell you. Women are actually reading Ellen Key now."

"Really? That's big news. How do you know?"

"From a couple of magazine articles I've been reading. It's astonishing, isn't it? She's quite fashionable. All kinds of people are buzzing about her because she's taken on Charlotte Perkins Gilman over this motherhood-versus-jobs issue. Gilman has always argued that women should be out in the workforce. She has been a major spokeswoman for the suffrage movement for a very long time. But Ellen Key is suddenly the new darling of the literati."

"And we did it?"

"We must have. How else would they know about her?"

"Then why are book sales so bad? I paid Ralph Seymour good money to publish them, and I haven't gotten a dime back."

"Well, maybe the masses didn't purchase *Morality of Woman* or *Love and Ethics.* But the magazine writers did. At least her ideas are getting exposure. It's what we set out to do, and it's happening."

"I think that calls for some kind of toast."

"I'd gladly celebrate if I weren't so appalled by this essay."

"You don't need to agree with her on everything."

"No. But I'm perplexed. Ellen came into my life when I was at the bottom of a well, and she threw a rope down to me. Ever since, all I've wanted to do is get her books into the hands of American women. This essay, though . . . it's Ellen's romantic eugenics in florid bloom. She paints a picture of women in a hundred years as fully realized personalities who want nothing more than to be breeder hens of a superior race. I'm almost embarrassed to send it out to anyone."

Frank sighed. "But Ellen Key is not you. You are not Ellen Key. You are her translator. You can decide to take it or leave it, but you can't censor her. I say, let the chips fall where they may."

Mamah shook her head. "I don't know. It's ironic that Ellen has never been married or had children, yet she feels free to expound upon motherhood. I think that's rather arrogant."

"Bad trait, arrogance." He wore a wry smile as he whittled at another pencil.

"Look at the fine time Ellen's having being a famous intellectual. She dines with heads of state. Corresponds with some of the most famous people in the world. She mourns her bad luck in love because it kept her from having babies. But my goodness. She's had a rather glorious career for herself—a career she wouldn't have had if she'd been the kind of full-time mother she glorifies."

"You sound almost angry at her."

THAT NIGHT, lying in bed, Mamah wondered how she had managed to turn a deaf ear to what Hedwig had told her about Ellen. She had heard it, then filed it away somewhere in her mind. It disturbed her to think that she'd done that.

Frank's remark about her being merely Ellen's translator had stirred Mamah, too. Had her own identity gotten all tangled up in Ellen's? She was such a powerful force. Ellen Key had a mind like a honed steel ax. It would be hard to argue with her about the damage this article might do in the United States, just at a moment when factions in the Woman Movement were putting aside differences to unite for the vote. For years before she met Frank, Mamah had been a passionate suffrage supporter. She wondered what had happened to that young woman.

Back in her study, she closed the Swedish version of *The Misuse of Woman's*

Strength. Maybe she would drag her heels on translating it. Maybe she'd even tell Ellen no editor wanted it. She searched the bookshelves, looking for a place to put it, and ended up setting the booklet on its side—not quite put away.

Outside, the sun had burned away the gray clouds. Through the icicles glittering like wet crystals, the sky had turned blue as a robin's egg. Mamah thought she saw a white shape move among the frozen grasses in the field. It was probably a hare, foraging for bark or twigs or buds on branches. Frank had said hares turned completely white in winter to conceal themselves from predators. But they had to come out for food.

Mamah took down her field glasses from the bookshelf, put on her boots and coat, and hurried out into the snow. Slipping, nearly skating, down the icy driveway, she stopped once to look back. Taliesin's fringe of icicles glinted. Oh, it felt grand to be out in the air. When she went back to the house, she would bring Frank out to show him how his "shining brow" was shining.

She headed into the field, breaking the icy crust with each step, then sinking to her knees in snow. She walked head down, the field glasses swinging from her neck. When she looked up to get her bearings, her face met the sun. In that moment her pupils contracted from the blazing light. She could see only throbbing waves of white. No clear outline appeared as she looked back at the house. Nothing distinct anywhere, really. She couldn't even see her feet. *You fool,* she thought, laughing out loud. *Knee-deep and snow-blind.*

She closed her eyes and waited for it to pass.

CHAPTER 41

Near the end of April, spring pushed out through stiff branches and spiked up from the mud. Tiny green fists unfurled themselves. Mamah hoped against hope that spring wouldn't suck in its fragrance and retreat.

Seed catalogs had arrived in February. When the few packets she'd ordered appeared in mid-March with the mail, she planted the seeds in coffee tins and arranged them along the south-facing windows in her study.

Whenever she and Frank got a moment together throughout February and March, they talked about planting. Frank hovered over his own catalogs of plum and apple tree varieties. "This Yellow Transparent here?" Frank said once. "We called it the 'harvest apple' when I was a kid, because it ripens during wheat-threshing time." He was off then, recounting memories of the pies his aunts had made during harvest, and of the migrant threshers who ate them.

Planting fever was not new to Mamah. Even in the Berlin boardinghouse, without a square foot of her own dirt, she had entertained herself by imagining what she'd pick if she had but one choice. She'd settled on a Japanese peony she'd seen in a book, the kind with heart-stopping white flowers that had a fragrance straight from heaven.

Now the plant dreaming was on a colossal scale—thirty-one acres to think of, including an orchard and a vineyard. Then there was the terraced garden that rose to the hilltop, where Frank had encircled two majestic oaks with a low limestone wall, creating a sloping hill garden and the "tea circle." Along with these, there were planting beds scattered all around the house.

Frank had consulted with his friend Jens Jensen about the orchard and vineyard. He trusted the list of apple trees and grape varieties Jensen suggested, and added his own favorites. But Mamah had her own authorities— Gertrude Jekyll, the English plantswoman, chief among them. Mamah knew Jensen's prairie-style landscaping, even admired it. But grasses didn't make her heart thump the way roses did. As more catalogs arrived, she became giddy reading about county-fair first-place winners.

"Aren't these little striped carnations adorable?" she said in a moment of surrender. She pointed to a watercolor picture on the cover of a catalog.

"Freaks," he said.

"But hollyhocks might look handsome standing against the stucco," she ventured.

He gritted his teeth as if he'd backed into thorns. "I don't like foundation plantings."

She shifted in her seat and took another tack. "I know, but hollyhocks are architectural, really. Big plants give a garden *form,* like wonderful pieces of sculpture. Gertrude Jekyll uses them a lot."

He didn't respond. She knew what he wanted. Plants in the native vernacular. From the beginning he'd said that Taliesin should be all of a piece. That the woods, the fields, the orchard and garden and house should be one seamless, continuous cloth.

"It's not that I just want sumac all over the place," he said, "but—"

"But the detail expresses the whole. I know that. Don't you think I understand after all this time?"

"There are design considerations."

"Have I no taste? I once hired you, you know."

He ran a hand through his hair.

"I think you're just afraid to cede control," she said.

He looked crestfallen. "I built this place for you, Mamah."

"Then think of your client, my dear. She is a woman who has seen England in summer. I don't understand why we can't have flowers *and* prairie grasses." Mamah got up and embraced him. "Does everything have to be exactly right? Can't we play? Can't I make a few mistakes while I'm figuring things out?"

He allowed a smile. "Nothing pink. And limit the foreigners, will you?"

"Reds and yellows would be gorgeous."

"You're the gardener," he said, heading into the studio.

MAMAH THOUGHT ABOUT the planting beds from every angle. She watched the changing light on the hill leading up to the tea circle. She pondered the catalog descriptions, struggling to hold in her mind at one time the flowers, foliage, and berries of various plants. Poring over Frank's plans for the whole of Taliesin, she made her own diagrams of flower beds and seasons, trying to create progressive waves of color.

Overwhelmed, she ended up picking old favorites and some she didn't know a thing about. She chose phlox Coquelicot—twelve of them—because its flower was the color of orange poppies; then she picked another three varieties as much for their names as for their colors, hoping Fräulein G. von Lassburg would bring out the best in General von Heutsze. She ordered twenty rugosa roses, twenty mock oranges, ten snowball viburnums with white ruffled flowers the size of plates. Multiples of flowering plants were added, mostly in hues of red and orange.

She thought she had ordered too much until she saw Frank's orchard list. Two hundred and eighty-five apple trees in twelve varieties, not to mention twenty each of plum and pear trees, three hundred gooseberries, two hundred blackberries, and a hundred and seventy-five raspberries, plus two hundred currant and grape plants for the vineyard. Her eyebrows went up. "Did a drunken sailor with a taste for pies fill out this form?"

"We're laying the foundation," he said. "It means self-sufficiency." There was impatience in his voice. "Anyway, Jensen gets these things cheap. They're just little saplings, and if we don't plant them now . . ."

He looked over her choices, then added twenty sumac trees to the list.

FRANK MENTIONED one afternoon in the middle of May that the plants were due in a day or two. He'd hired a couple of trucks to bring the shipment over from the Spring Green train station when it arrived, and they would need extra hands to unload.

"There are two boys over at the Barton place," Josiah offered.

"Do you know them?" she asked.

"Nice family," Josiah said. "Boys'll be in school till afternoon. But I'd get 'em over here now to start digging holes."

"Will you arrange it?"

"Yes, ma'am." Josiah went to make the phone call from the kitchen.

"Tell them I will come to pick up the boys tomorrow," she whispered as he was calling.

"I can get them," he said.

"Thank you, Josiah, but I'll go."

Mamah had observed the little farmstead every time she drove along County Road C. It was like almost every other country farmhouse in the area—a whitewashed clapboard house with a swatch of cut grass in front of it, a barn, a windbreak to the north, and fields of crops that ran right up to the yard. She remembered the first time she'd taken real notice of this one. Driving past, she had caught sight of a small girl balanced over the top rung of the white fence, dangling a string toward a cat below her. A few feet away, rabbit skins were stretched out on the fence, drying.

Mamah had told Josiah to make her identity clear to the mother who answered the phone. Miss Mamah Borthwick from over at the Wright place would be coming to pick up her sons if they could be spared for some planting work at Taliesin. Standing next to the telephone as he spoke, Mamah waited for a polite refusal.

"They'll be ready for you at three o'clock," Josiah said.

Mamah let out the breath trapped in her lungs. "Oh," she said with some wonder. "Isn't that grand?"

"GLAD TO MEET YOU." A stocky woman younger than Mamah answered the front door, wiping her hands on her apron. "I'm Dorothea Barton. Come on in." She led Mamah into a tiny parlor, where she handed over two mason jars of blackberry preserves with bows around their necks. "I've been meaning to get over to your place to welcome you."

Mamah stood in the tiny parlor, struck dumb by the woman's friendliness.

"Did the flu get you folks this winter?" the woman asked.

The press got us, Mamah wanted to say, but this woman was not like Mattie or Else or even Lizzie. "No, thank goodness."

As Dorothea Barton went out into the yard and hallooed for her sons, Mamah glanced around the parlor. There were mismatched blue-patterned china dishes arranged on a rack above a sideboard. An ancient studio portrait of an old-time family. A battered organ with a fringed shawl thrown over it. A shiny black horsehair sofa. Above the organ, an embroidered hanging read, DILIGENCE IS THE MOTHER OF GOOD LUCK.

When Dorothea returned, she was followed by two gangly boys in their teens who announced themselves as Leo and Fred.

"Did you see my Emma when you came in?" The woman had a young girl by the hand. "Emma, tell Miz Borthwick how old you are."

"Six."

"You have a daughter about her age, don't you?" Dorothea asked Mamah.

"I do." *She's read about Martha and John,* Mamah thought. "She will be here for the whole summer. I know she would love to meet you."

Heading down the driveway of the farm, she saw that Dorothea Barton's cutting garden was already sprouting flowers. Nearby, circle-patterned trellises braced luxurious grapevines. "Where did you get those supports?" she asked the boys.

"Pop makes 'em out of barrel hoops," Leo said. "He can do a hundred things with a barrel."

When she got home, she went looking for Frank. She called out to him, but he was nowhere nearby. She took off her coat and went back into her study. There she found her coffee tins and seedlings placed on the floor. For a moment she felt puzzled, and then she understood. Frank had taken them down from the window because of how they looked, she was sure of it. They cluttered the lines of the windows and had probably driven him mad for weeks.

It hurt her, almost like a slap on the hand, but she put the slight aside. It was warm enough now to harden off the seedlings. She gathered the cans onto a tray and carried them outside. She wouldn't mention the barrel-hoop idea to Frank. He would think she had taken leave of her senses.

MAMAH CALLED THE Barton boys when the truck with the plants arrived the next day. Their father, Samuel, drove them over and got out of the car to have a look. He was a tall, emaciated man with a bottlebrush mustache.

"Rotted," he said as the boys unloaded the perennials first. The chrysanthemums, physostegia, and coreopsis were all dead. Of the sixty phlox plants she'd ordered, only fourteen had survived the trip. Fraülein von Lassburg and General von Heutsze were among the corpses. All twenty rosebushes were dried out and useless.

"I can't help you with those," he said, "but if we work quick, we can save the berries and apple trees. How many men have you got here?"

There were Josiah, Billy Weston and his son, the Barton boys, and eventually, there would be Frank, who had gone to Madison for building supplies. Mamah went into the house and brought out the drawing of the whole property, with its tiny Xs showing how the trees would form grids diagonally down the hills. She didn't mention the grid's inspiration, how the trees in the Arno Valley below Fiesole had been marked off into squares by cypress trees. She knew better than to mention the undulating crops of Umbria or how the Japanese so artfully terraced their crops.

Samuel walked down the slope with Mamah beside him. He stood midhill with his hands in his back pockets. "Doing some big farming, are you?" he said.

With the truck fully unloaded, Mamah and the men stood in a forest of saplings. She was relieved when Frank appeared. He seemed glad to have a neighbor giving directions on how to plant the trees. Would Frank have known to prune them before they went into the ground, the way Samuel Barton was instructing everyone? In his feverish dreams of self-sufficiency for Taliesin, Frank had bitten off more than he could chew. He had not anticipated the Herculean job now at hand, but he would never admit it. He changed clothes and joined the men in the field.

For three days they planted. Mamah asked for help from Lil, who cooked two pot roasts for the men when they came in from the fields, while Mamah set about planting those things that had survived. When Dorothea Barton arrived with her family the morning of the second day, she and her sons began unloading boxes crammed full of plants she had dug up from her garden. "Sam said you lost some of yours, so here's a few to plug in. The daisies are from the Wilkins' garden. They're the next farm past us. Oh, she has a garden. I'll take you over there when it gets blooming." The women worked beside each other, talking about gardens and children as they dug in the plants.

"Your sons are such fine young men, Dorothea," Mamah said.

The woman looked up from her work, beaming. "Thank you," she said.

At the end of the last day of planting, Dorothea and her little family toured the house. They took off their shoes at the door and walked through the house as if it were a peculiar cathedral. Dorothea seemed puzzled by Frank's arrangements of mosses and rocks, and she called the Ming vase he had filled with willow branches "sweet."

Samuel remained closemouthed until he reached the bedroom window. "She's a beaut, all right," he said, staring out at the view.

Mamah thought he was talking about the fields they had just planted. The little trees, laid out like black cross-stitches on a rustic quilt, were already charming and full of promise. How extraordinary it would be in six or seven years to look down upon them and see clouds of blooms.

When she saw the dampness in his eyes, though, she knew he was talking about his own farm. "I've never seen her look so pretty," he said.

CHAPTER 42

Taylor Woolley pulled a drawing from a cardboard tube and spread it out on the drafting table. He smoothed the edges, then set a pencil box on one corner and weighed down the others with things he found around the studio—a T square, a vase. Emil Brodelle, the young draftsman working at the other table, drifted over to have a look.

" 'Villa for an Artist,' " he said, reading aloud the label at the bottom. "I saw this in the portfolio."

The three of them stood staring at the drawing.

"I see Taliesin in it," Emil said. "The way it fits into the hill. The terraces, too."

Mamah smiled at Taylor when they were alone. "You didn't forget."

"It was the first thing I packed."

"I can smell the pines around Fiesole just looking at that drawing," she said.

"Do you miss it?"

"Oh, I miss the time we had. But I love this place. Isn't it funny? I hated the idea of Wisconsin, and now all I want to do is stay put."

"Sink some roots?"

"Deep ones," she said. "Since we've been back from Japan, I look around and see all kinds of things crying out for attention. My garden, for instance. I can't tell you how good it feels to have a place that needs me." She rolled up the drawing and put it back in the tube. "Come with me. I want to store this in the vault, and there are some other things to show you."

She led him to the stone vault in the studio where Frank kept his prize Japanese prints. "Pictures of the floating world," Mamah said with a little flourish of her hand. Taylor stared, agog, as she opened one box after another. She showed him colorful pictures of Kabuki actors with drawn swords, geishas with parasols, views of snowy Mount Fuji.

"Mr. Wright has transformed himself into a print merchant," she said.

"I always knew he was wild for the things, but—"

"More than wild. He will have to explain to you their meanings. Oh, how he loves to have a print party. We'll have one tonight, just the three of us. And he'll tell you all about every one of these. You'll wish you hadn't asked."

"My stars, there must be a thousand of them."

"And this is what's left over. The bulk of them have been shipped off to Boston."

"He mentioned some collectors."

"Yes," she said, closing the vault door. "The Spaulding brothers in Boston. They're really the reason we could afford to be over there for so long. They gave Frank carte blanche to buy what he saw fit." She didn't tell him the dollar amount the brothers had turned over to Frank—twenty-five thousand. The figure would seem preposterous to a young man struggling to get by as an architect. Taylor had come to help Frank prepare drawings for an exhibit, and she was sure he wouldn't be making much money during his stay.

"Do you want to take a walk around while we wait for Frank? His train gets in about an hour and a half from now."

"I can't think of anything better."

"It was a stroke of luck," Mamah said as they headed out to the gardens. "We were planning to go to Japan in January anyway, so Frank could talk to government people about the Imperial Hotel. You know that part of the story, right?"

"I heard he was under consideration. It's a huge commission."

"Well, it's still up in the air, but we have very high hopes. It went well on that front. And it couldn't come at a better time, if it comes." She stopped walking for a moment and looked Taylor in the eyes. "I hate pretending with you. The truth is, Frank's work has practically dried up. It seems there's always something on the drafting table, but when it comes to getting a project built. . . ." Taylor didn't speak but took her elbow for a moment. He was a young man, Frank's employee. She shouldn't be talking to him about money.

"Anyway, these Spauldings got wind that Frank was traveling to Japan. He was going to look for prints anyway. You know him. But suddenly, there was money to spend on behalf of these brothers. It seems Frank is considered something of an expert on Japanese prints. *And* at ferreting them out." She aimed an amused look at him over her spectacles.

"Quite an adventure you had?" Taylor had a knowing smile on his face. He'd been on a couple of Frank's shopping sprees in Italy.

"I never knew what the next day would bring," she said. "One moment we'd be chatting with a print seller in a perfectly dignified office over tea, and the next moment Frank would be disappearing down into smoky basements in the merchant's quarters—'go-downs,' he calls them—where people had stockpiled the most amazing collections of *ukiyo-e* prints. Mind you, these weren't the pristine pictures we found at the high end. But Frank doesn't care if the edges are torn or if the prints are dirty. He is absolutely taken with the art and geometry of these things, which I suppose is what makes him so good at choosing them. He says they are more modern than Modernism."

They sat down on the arc of stone around the tea circle.

"How has it been here?" Taylor might have been inquiring about the weather. Mamah knew he was asking about the press debacle.

"Did you hear about it out there?"

He nodded. "Only through a friend in Chicago. I didn't read any of it myself. It wasn't news in Salt Lake."

Mamah sighed. "Thank you, Taylor." She patted his hand. "People have been surprisingly generous. No one mentions it. Those who speak to us, that is."

"And you? How are you?"

"I'm all right. Just trying to get my bearings since we returned."

"Still translating?"

"Not at the moment. It's too long a story."

"And your children have visited?"

Mamah's face broke into a broad smile. "They did. I had worried so much after all the publicity. But my daughter Martha instantly struck up a friendship with a girl named Emma from the next farm over, and she has a boy cousin who is my John's age. It went better than I had expected. They ended up caring very much for Frank, I think, by the end of the summer. He took them riding and fishing and spoiled them, of course.

"We had so many visitors last summer. People would see the house from the highway and drive up the road out of curiosity. There were organized trips, too. We had a group of normal school students come with their teachers. And a Sunday school class. Can you believe it?"

"Interesting how people adapt with a little time."

"Even people like me. This is my home now, Taylor."

"What will you do if you have to go back to Japan?"

She shifted thoughtfully on the bench. "I'll cross that bridge when I have to, I guess."

They sat in the sun, soaking up the pleasure of the warm air and each other's company. After a time Taylor went to the studio to settle in, and Mamah remained in the garden. It was the most perfect time of year in Wisconsin—the second week of May. When she and Frank had returned to Taliesin in April, she'd been thrilled to be home in time to see the first asparagus-like plugs of peonies rise out of the ground, and to smell the lilacs when they first popped open. Nearly all the fruit trees had survived and were leafing out. The house looked more beautiful than ever. Frank had brought home vases and screens and gorgeous silk kimonos that he arranged artfully throughout the rooms. The Far East melded into the American Middle West without a peep of protest. Mamah and Frank's common history—the prairie house, Italy, Japan, even a bit of Germany—seemed to permeate every square inch of Taliesin.

Some of the harder parts about this place had not changed. Mamah couldn't look out at the driveway without remembering the reporters coming up to the house. And Frank's mother, who'd vacated her bedroom when they returned from Japan, now sulked around Jennie's house when Mamah appeared, barely speaking to her. But Mamah had come back to Jennie as well, as sunny and kind a friend as she could hope for. She had also come back to the prospect of her children's summer visit a few weeks away, and to a small circle of friends that was beginning to grow.

There was work to get back to if she decided to go forward with it. *Frauen-bewegung, The Woman Movement*, was waiting. She'd done no translating for Ellen while in Japan. In fact, she had left the States truly upset with Ellen. She and Frank had been set to depart in early January for California, where their ship would embark for Japan. When word came that the Spaulding brothers wanted to see Frank before he sailed, a quick trip to the East Coast was arranged. The bulk of the week was spent in Boston, but at Mamah's request, she and Frank traveled to New York to confront Mr. Huebsch, the man who was publishing the pirated translation of *Love and Ethics*. It was the principle of the thing that had pushed Mamah to get the conflict settled, but a practical matter as well. The audience for *Love and Ethics* was so small, there wasn't room for two translations on the market. Huebsch's version was almost certainly causing the slow sales of her own translation. Frank had encouraged her to confront him.

What a disappointment it had been to track Huebsch down only to have the man Mamah had so demonized produce a check from Ellen Key that proved she had not only authorized but paid him for his translation.

There was no use pretending now. Ellen had simply lied to her. But even more disconcerting was a remark by Heubsch's fawning assistant, just as they were departing. "I mean no offense, Miss Borthwick," said the ascetic-looking man whose pants were belted across his chest, "but I have an associate over at Putnam's who says Ellen Key prefers our translations of her work above all others. Putnam's office in London feels the same way."

"You pathetic worm," Frank had shot back, his mouth nearly frothing. "You inconsequential—"

"We'll go now," Mamah said, pulling him along and out the door of the office.

They had caught the next train home, repacked quickly, and departed for California the next morning. Distraught, she took Heubsch's translation of *Love and Ethics* and her own on the journey west. As it turned out, she had plenty of time to study them, since they missed their boat to Japan and had to remain an extra two weeks in California. She and Frank compared the two translations line by line during their wait. In some places she had to admit that Heubsch's version was superior, while in other areas she felt she'd bested him. In the end, Mamah left the two translations on the writing desk of their hotel room and boarded the ship, intent on not thinking about Ellen Key for another six months.

And she had nearly managed. Every day on the ship was devoted to distracting Frank from his terrible seasickness. Once his feet hit the ground in Tokyo, though, he was immersed in meetings with government officials and, in his free moments, on the hunt for prints.

Frank had as his guide a remarkable man, Shugio Hiromichi, an Oxford-educated businessman with exquisite manners and connections to all levels of Japanese society, from highly placed officials to humble artisans. After a while Mamah stopped going along on the print hunts in the merchants' quarters, especially at night. It made her uncomfortable to see Frank's glassy gaze as he paused for a few words with Shugio on the steps of a go-down just before he went in, his heart clearly racing like a wolf's outside a chicken coop. Mamah's presence complicated the transactions, anyway. She was a woman, a well-dressed Westerner, who only gentrified the proceedings. "No bargains are going to be had in my presence," she'd told the men after a few forays. "It's best if you two go alone."

Without her along, Frank could get dressed up in one of the costumes he fancied would help him pass as . . . what? An artist? Certainly not a native. No one she'd seen on the streets of Tokyo dressed as he did, in the full button-cuffed pants and puffy Dutch-boy hat he'd had styled by a local tailor. Where did he find shoes with wood heels so high? They made him taller, but they were as extreme in their way as the wooden platforms geishas wore in the tea-houses. To see him decked out in a costume she once would have found charming now made her feel embarrassed and inexplicably angry.

The last transaction she'd witnessed had convinced her she didn't have the stomach for commerce. They had been standing in a go-down, waiting for a merchant to retrieve his prints from a back room, when Frank spotted a large vase he admired on a table along the wall. He walked over to it and tapped it with a bamboo cane he had picked up in Tokyo. The tap nearly caused the vase to topple. "How much for this?" Frank had asked the man's wife, who stood horror-stricken as she watched the pot sway, then right itself. The woman bowed her head and muttered. "It's not for sale," Shugio translated. "It has been in her family for many generations."

The dramatics of the print negotiating that followed made Mamah squirm even more. Frank pretending high offense at an asking price. The poor old seller going off to the back of the room to consult with the wife. Frank wheedling, making small jokes, ingratiating himself, all through the translating finesse of Shugio, who seemed to smooth over the awkwardness. Then coming away with prints for almost nothing compared to what the Spaulding brothers would pay Frank. There was a mercenary quality to the proceedings that left a bad taste in Mamah's mouth.

"These prints are not high art to the Japanese," Frank reassured her one day as he prepared to send off another telegram to the Spauldings asking for more money. "It's the common man's art. The sellers don't feel they're sacrificing anything. In fact, they believe they're getting the better of *me.*"

Despite her queasiness during Frank's nighttime forays, she couldn't help laughing when he came back so full of good cheer and interesting stories. Only once did he return deeply sobered. He'd been followed back to the hotel by a fearsome-looking man who appeared to be waiting for the right moment to pounce. Word was clearly out on the street that there was a wild print buyer in town with cash in his pockets. Shugio and Frank had wanted the word to pass to print owners, but it had passed to the pickpockets, too. After that, Mamah worried until he was safely ensconced in their room.

"When do I get my architect back?" she said gently one night when he returned ill-humored and empty-handed after an outing.

His whole body seemed disappointed in her when he spoke. "It weighs on me, Mamah, that as bright as you are, you persist in not wanting to understand this part of my life." He wiped his mouth with a napkin and pushed his chair back.

"I understand, it's just that—"

Frank raised his hand dismissively. "It's our bread and butter right now. But pretty soon it won't matter. I believe I've nearly cleaned out Japan of its best old prints. They get harder to find by the day."

Without the focus of translating, or any real purpose of her own, Mamah felt rudderless in Japan after a few weeks. She was careful not to show her unhappiness to Frank. She didn't want to play the miserable Griselda, as Catherine Wright had on her trip to Japan with Frank, patiently sitting alone in the hotel, wondering when he would return. There had been suggestions in Catherine's stories of "disappointments," which Mamah had taken to mean visits by Frank to the pleasure quarters during his absences. Had Frank done that to her this time? Had he been lying with a white-faced, red-lipped woman all afternoon? She knew how smitten he was by the erotic woodblock prints of geishas he had turned up. She had to admit that it was possible. Lately, he was so preoccupied, he barely spoke to her.

"Let's go out to the countryside today, just the two of us," she'd proposed one morning.

"Can't," he said. "Shugio has found a man—"

"Frank." She put her hands on his shoulders. "We're drifting. I've hardly seen you in the past two weeks."

He groaned in exasperation. "I've been obsessed, I admit it. But my God, the things I've found! You've got to be patient."

"I'm trying."

He rubbed her temples with his fingertips. "What's going on in here?"

"Only bad things, I'm afraid." She tried to keep her voice light.

"Such as?"

"Oh, Frank. I keep thinking about the things I've done wrong. One minute I think about what Heubsch said about Ellen's unhappiness with my translating—"

"You're going to believe that bullcrap? If you have any doubts, ask Ellen outright."

"And then the next minute . . ."

"Yes?"

"I think about how long I will have been gone from the children by the time this trip is over with. Six months is just too much."

"But how many times could you have seen them during that six months? A few weekends?"

"I keep thinking about Martha."

"What about Martha?"

"That weekend I went into Chicago just before the trip out east? Before we traveled to California?"

"Yes?"

"When I got up on Sunday morning and dressed, you know, getting ready to meet Edwin down in the lobby and hand them over, I couldn't find my shoes. I looked all over the room, and then I found them in the bathroom behind a radiator. Martha had hidden them." Mamah's eyes filled with tears. "She didn't want me to go away again. And look what I've done."

Frank wrapped her in his arms and rocked her.

"I know what I said before." The tears were coming now. "That the children need some distance from me to heal. But I can't help thinking, what will happen if you do get this job? What will happen if I come back to Japan with you and I am gone from them for a whole year? Can they take that much distance? Because I don't think I can."

"You're getting way ahead of yourself. Now, listen. I'm coming home early today, and we'll plan out a trip to Kyoto. You will love it there."

"What I'm trying to say to you is a good thing, Frank. That Taliesin is my home now. After all these months and years of not knowing where I would be, or where I even *wanted* to be, all I can think about is going back there."

"Patience." He kissed her forehead. "The print trading will keep us afloat until the hotel comes through. It's going to be a seven-million-dollar project. Four or five hundred thousand in architect's fees. Now, who do you want to get the job?"

"You," she said, "of course."

CHAPTER 43

"Let's have a picnic before Taylor leaves," Frank said one morning.

He had talked about fishing in the river since they'd been back from Japan. She smiled at the sight of him ahead of her now, conversing with his two young draftsmen, who hung on his every word.

When Frank found a spot he liked, they spread out the blankets and took off their shoes. She unloaded the cheese and sausages, passed out four plates.

Frank was peeling off his socks. "So what's happened in the world of American architecture in my absence, gentlemen?" he asked. "Tell me there's been a coup in the palace."

Mamah half listened as names were mentioned, buildings described. The day was as perfect as any she'd passed in Wisconsin. Low clouds were racing over the hills, flickering sun on and off the green field grass like light in a moving picture. She lay down on her side and closed her eyes, following the hum of the conversation more than its substance. She noticed how reverently Taylor and Emil addressed him, how they laughed at his stories. She didn't have to see him to know he was happy. This was what he'd imagined in Italy when he'd told her how he would school young architects. No classrooms, only his drawing board. And picnics. He had forgotten to add picnics.

In Japan, he had fallen into a dark reverie one evening over how some employees had betrayed him. In a fit of anger, he'd said he would never again use any draftsman who had worked for him before. It would be only Germans and Austrians from here on out, young people who could handle the apprentice system. Yet here was Taylor, his one exception, she supposed. And Emil Brodelle, a Milwaukee boy whose background she suspected was neither German nor Austrian.

But they were audience enough. Soon it was only Frank's voice holding forth uninterrupted, talking of architecture in Europe and Japan and America. She became aware that when one of the others squeezed in a few words,

Frank barely acknowledged him. Nor did he laugh at their jokes. He only half listened while he seemed to be formulating his next witticism.

Emil jumped in when Frank paused. "What do you think of Walter Griffin winning the contest to design Canberra? I heard he and Marion Mahony have already moved to Australia. It's something, isn't it? To design the capitol of an entire country?"

Mamah opened her eyes and caught Taylor's glance. Frank knew Marion had married Walter Griffin. She looked in Frank's direction, but he made no move to show he'd heard a word. He was buttering a piece of bread.

Emil squirmed in the silence. "They both worked with you at one time, didn't they, sir?"

Frank chewed his bread thoughtfully. "Griffin was a student of mine briefly; he's been sucking my eggs ever since. As for her, she was an illustrator more than architect."

Mamah flinched. The complaint about Griffin was old hat. But it pained her to hear Frank deny Marion her due. She had an actual architecture degree from MIT. She had been with Frank in the Oak Park office almost from the beginning. In fact, it was Marion's presentation drawing, with its luscious foliage and tree trunks, that had convinced Mamah and Edwin to hire Frank in the first place.

"*Frank,*" Mamah humored him, "now, Frank. You know she was your right hand. Marion is every *inch* an architect."

Frank looked out over the river. He stood up and fetched his fishing pole. "Who's getting the first one, boys?"

The men strung themselves along the riverbank and sank their hooks. After ten or fifteen minutes, there were cheers and congratulations. Frank had caught a fish.

BACK AT THE HOUSE, Mamah walked into the kitchen while Frank was at the counter, gutting the paddlefish he'd caught. When she approached and stood nearby, he stopped what he was doing. He waited, his sharp knife frozen in midair over the wet carcass until she instinctively moved a step back. Then he sank the blade again into the tumid flesh of the fish and finished the job.

Mamah felt confused. It had seemed in that moment that he was furious with her. She assumed he was angry because she had contradicted him in front of his draftsmen. It wasn't the first time she had felt as if he couldn't bear her nearness, though. Sometimes her foot would touch his under the table during dinner, and he would make a great show of moving his foot away, adjusting his position in relation to her, as if to say, *Are you quite finished arranging yourself?*

He seemed to feel space and objects with the sensitivity of a bat. She remembered many evenings when he'd sat down to dinner and promptly swept aside his silverware. It was a habit that struck Mamah as crude, almost contemptuous, since she had just set the table only moments before.

"Why do you do that?" she'd asked him once.

"Do what?"

"Push aside your silver that way, as if you're angry."

"I hate clutter."

"Silverware is clutter?" she asked.

"Until I'm ready to use it, yes."

That night, though, as they spooned together, the skin of his chest warm upon her back, she decided she had misread him. He had simply needed elbow room this afternoon. *One more new wrinkle to adapt to, but not worth trying to change,* she thought. *I might as well try to alter his eye color or reshape his nose.*

CHAPTER 44

Darby and Joan were hitched up when Mamah came out in the morning. Frank must have asked the handyman, Tom Brunker, to do it before he left, because the wagon was all ready to go.

"Might rain," Tom said to Mamah, running his hand over the haunch of one of the sorrels. "Plan to be out long?"

"A few hours. I don't want to miss the wildflowers this year. I heard there's a whole stretch of them in the woods over near the Paulson place."

Mamah took the reins and guided the horses down the drive and onto the road. Out in the country, the appearance of the wildflowers was like a theater debut in the city. She was reminded of another day years before, when Mattie had persuaded her to take the Switzerland Trail train ride outside Boulder. She and the children had come back with bouquets of flowers.

She spotted the spread of pink gaywings when she approached the woods. Mamah climbed down from the rig and walked carefully, bending to examine the winglike petals and the soft little flowers that had sprung up through a carpet of brittle leaves faded to beige by winter. She would not pick any of them; they were too perfect right here. She sat down in a grassy spot and thought about Mattie. What would she make of how everything had worked out?

A year ago Mamah had written to Alden to inquire about his well-being and that of the children. She had not heard back from him. When she'd finally gotten a reply, it was from Mattie's brother, Lincoln, who was raising the children in Iowa. *Alden is working at a mine in Colombia,* he had written to her. *South America.*

Alden had done what so many widowed men did—passed on his children to a relative's home where there was an able-bodied woman. Would Mattie be sorely disappointed in her husband? For a long while after her death, Mattie's voice was the one Mamah had heard in her head, the judging voice. It struck her, hunched among the flowers, that she hadn't heard it in a long while.

Mamah took her time driving home. Frank and Taylor had taken the train into Chicago, where Taylor would board another one and return to Salt Lake. "You got your villa," he'd said when he hugged her goodbye. She had felt a rush of sadness as he pulled away.

She had no obligations except for a brief meeting this evening, when a couple of local churchwomen were scheduled to come to the house. Mamah had offered, through Dorothea, to give English lessons to the Swedish and German house girls around the area. To her astonishment, they had agreed to her idea.

When she drove the wagon through the porte cochere, Mamah saw a delivery truck pulled up in the driveway behind the house. It was like the one that had delivered the plants a year before, and her first thought was that Frank had ordered more trees, though he hadn't mentioned it.

"Why the truck?" she asked Billy, who was standing next to it.

"A delivery from Marshall Field's."

"I don't know anything about a delivery."

"Paid in full, it says." He handed her the bill of lading. "By Mr. Wright."

"What is it?"

"Furniture." Billy shifted from foot to foot and looked at the ground. "I hope you don't mind, but they went ahead and did what he asked. Mr. Wright drew out a sketch of where to put it all."

All? She entered the foyer, then stepped around into the living room. A large Chinese carpet covered the middle of the floor. Another rested beneath the dining table where—*one, two, three,* she counted . . . six—new chairs surrounded it. Another six chairs were scattered around the room. In the corner, she saw a gleaming grand piano.

Billy had come in behind her. "Do you want me to lay out those rugs over there?" He pointed to a stack of nine or ten rolled-up rugs in varying sizes. "The drawing didn't show where those went."

Mamah felt her face burning. "No, Billy. Thank you. Would you ask Tom to put the horses away?"

"Yes, ma'am."

"And may I have that?"

He handed her the slip of paper and went out.

There was nothing on it to show the cost of the goods—just the items shipped were listed. Frank would not be back from Chicago for two days. He had talked as he left about the possibility—*possibility*—of a huge job he was scheduled to discuss with a contact. An enormous beer garden, an entertainment center, he'd said. It might be three days before he got home, depending upon meetings.

Mamah walked over to the pile of rugs and opened the smallest one. It was a red and blue Turkoman with a pattern of a square rotated within a square—a pattern Frank himself had used. She understood immediately why he had chosen the rug. She rolled it up again, then took off her shoes and walked across the Chinese carpet. She knew why he had picked this one, too—for its indigo-blue field and pattern of ivory cranes and vines winding around its border.

She sat down on the window seat and looked around the room. She could see what he had envisioned when he selected each piece. The chairs were simple oak with leather-upholstered seats that could be used for dining or moved around to accommodate a large group. Twelve of them, all the same—a great luxury—and as suited to the room as if he had designed them himself. The rugs added the depth he was after, and echoed the colors of the kimono on the wall.

And the piano. She could see Frank standing in front of the piano, hearing Beethoven and Mozart. He would have pictured himself leaving his drawing table to play Bach while he worked through a problem in his head. He would have imagined special invited guests—traveling musicians who'd come to Madison to perform, perhaps—who would be honored to visit the famous architect and his already-famous Taliesin, to sit down at his gorgeous Steinway piano and play for the women and men in evening clothes, fascinating guests upon whom the moment would not be lost. Frank would have been filled with the most profound sense of rightness about all of the things he had bought.

She could imagine the look in his eyes as he went through Marshall Field's, acquiring the furniture and rugs as quickly as he bought prints in Japan. Feverish with the excitement of taking possession of beautiful found objects.

What she could not imagine was how he had paid for them.

A light summer rain had begun to fall. She flung open the living room windows to air out the strange smells of the new furnishings. Then she went and telephoned the two churchwomen to cancel the meeting, pleading illness. It was impossible to have them to Taliesin. When she did meet with them, it would be at one of their homes. How could she have country people who lived in tiny farmhouses enter this place now?

When a rap came on the door, it startled her.

"Josiah!" she said when she opened it. "I wasn't expecting anyone. It's so good to see you. Come in."

The young man stepped through the foyer into the living room. "Mrs. Borthwick," he said, nodding his head.

"Sit down. I haven't seen you in a long while."

Josiah took his hat off but declined a seat. He was quiet for a moment, looking first at the ceiling, then running his hand along the oiled oak of the living room door frame.

She smiled. "It looks beautiful, doesn't it? You men did a fine job."

"I reckon we did." He kneaded his hat in his hands. "Is Mr. Wright around?"

"No, he's not. He's in Chicago until tomorrow. What is it you need? Maybe I can help you."

Josiah looked away, and in that moment he spotted the new piano. He let out an admiring whistle. She noticed him sway slightly and could tell that he had been drinking.

"He owes me money," he said, "for the bookcases."

"The bookcases in my study?"

"Yes, ma'am."

"But that was a year ago, Josiah."

"Over a year."

"Are you sure?"

"Oh, I'm sure, all right. Never paid me a dime."

"So you've spoken to him about this?"

"Three times."

"And what did he say?"

Josiah snorted. "The first two times he said he just forgot to pay me. But the last time he said I should feel privileged to work for him. How did he put it?" Josiah squinted and looked across the room. "To add my *creativity* to Taliesin. He said that should be payment enough. And then"—he began to laugh—"he thanked me for my *contribution*."

Mamah's stomach throbbed. "I'll talk to him when he returns. You'll get your money, Josiah."

"Thank you, ma'am."

THAT NIGHT SHE WOKE in a panic. She had no idea how much or how little money they had. Frank had said their finances were in good shape since the trip to Japan. She realized now that she did not trust him.

Months ago she'd set up an account book for him, for the Taliesin studio and the household. She had kept tabs on groceries and studio expenses. But there had been little business coming in, and then they'd gone to Japan for six months. How much had they spent in order to live in Japan, never mind the art and textiles they had bought? She hadn't any real notion.

Lying in bed, she tried to calculate their income and expenses, but she could think only of how much everything had cost. She knew there were loan payments to be made to Darwin Martin for Taliesin and a mortgage on the house in Oak Park; college tuition for two of his children, plus everything else that his family needed—shoes, clothes, food, school things, doctor visits. Rent for the office he had taken at Orchestra Hall. Salary for his office manager there and for Emil here, as well as the workmen at Taliesin. She thought of Billy and the others and shuddered at the prospect that there were probably times they had not been paid on time. But would they be here if they hadn't been paid at all?

There were also the exhibits Frank participated in, which always cost money to prepare for. That was where dollars were going now, models and drawings for a show of his work at the Art Institute. Beyond that, she suspected he gave money to his mother to live on. And he was talking about buying thirty more acres for Taliesin from Jennie and her husband. Had he done that already? She didn't know.

And the things he had done for her, such as pay Ralph Seymour the cost of publishing the first three translations of Ellen's books—they'd never made money back on those. Plus, he fed her. My God, he had to feed so many people. Animals, too—horses and cows. She didn't want to count the mouths that depended on him.

But what was there to count of income? The Littles' summer house. Sherman Booth's house. There was the chance of a bank in Madison. That was all, except for the prints. Frank had received a commission from the Spauldings for his work, which he was to split with Shugio. The dollar amounts had kept changing as Frank wired back to the brothers in Boston for more money, and she assumed his commission had gone up as the Spauldings' investment increased. What had he ended up with? She had been reluctant to ask. There were so many deals she knew nothing about. Meetings happened at his office in Chicago, contacts came and went. She had seen money go in and out of his pockets like a bank teller's drawer, with no accounting at the end of the day. One time she'd found four-month-old checks crumpled together with dollar bills in his winter coat.

Mamah looked at the brass alarm clock by her bed. Three o'clock. She got up, threw a shawl over her nightgown, and went to his studio. Frank used a long table with a cloth on top as a desk. Underneath it were boxes full of correspondence and a few files marked with the names of clients and other people to whom he frequently wrote. Darwin Martin had his own box. She read a number of Martin's letters. In most of them, he was responding to Frank's request for loans, or to buy prints, or to take prints as collateral on a loan. Mamah was struck by Martin's capitulation time and again to Frank's requests, but also by his condescending tone, how free he felt to dispense advice and scold Frank about his personal life.

For the next three hours, she waded through the boxes, trying to make sense of the contents. For a man who worshipped order, Frank's papers were in chaos, much like his pants pockets. In one box, wedged between files, were IOUs with dates from five years back, canceled checks, letters from his children and clients, and official-looking loan documents. And bills, bills, bills. Another box contained mostly lumberyard and building supply bills. She divided these into two piles—those paid in full and those partially paid or unpaid. She shivered as she dealt out the bills, watching the unpaid stack grow. Some of them went back to the summer they'd broken ground for Taliesin. Many of them bore handwritten notes begging for payment.

The angriest letters were posted from towns nearby. They were the oldest bills. Spring Green, Richland Center. There appeared to be a pattern. The more recent bills came from Mineral Point, from Madison. She suspected he was sending his men farther and farther out to buy lumber because he hadn't paid his suppliers in nearby towns.

The scale of his debt took her breath away. The thought that she was as culpable as he—occupying this extraordinary house, traveling abroad, living a privileged life while their creditors were stuck holding the bag—made her want to hide in one moment and smash something in the next.

Frank was excavating a hole they'd never climb out of. What seemed worst of all to her was the fact that so many of the betrayed lenders were his friends. In a file marked SHUGIO, she found a recent letter from the Japanese guide asking for more money, saying, in the kindest terms, that he'd been shortchanged.

If Frank were in this room, she thought, *I would strangle him with my own hands.*

ON FRIDAY MORNING, when Billy showed up, she went out into the driveway.

"There's something weighing on me I must talk to you about, Billy."

The carpenter, usually unflappable, looked taken aback.

"You buy supplies all the time for Frank, don't you?"

"Yes, ma'am."

"I found some bills last night, a lot of them, for lumber and supplies. They appear to be unpaid. I need you to tell me the truth. Is Frank not paying his bills?"

He tilted his head to the side, massaged the tough cords that ran up the front of his neck like ropes. "He always pays me on time."

"I know you know, Billy. I don't want to make you uncomfortable, but it's too late for that. Just say yes or no. When you go back to buy more, will they give you credit?"

"I can't . . ." He looked up at her. "It's not my place."

That evening she waited. When Frank traveled to Chicago, he left his car at the train station in Spring Green. It would be around seven by the time he drove back to Taliesin from the station. Most Fridays she had dinner in the oven. In winter they sat in their chairs in front of the fireplace and talked about their time apart, what had happened, before they sat down to eat. In summer she had begun to wait out in the tea circle for him to come home. But tonight she would remain inside. She sat on the window seat in the living room and smoked one cigarette after another.

When Frank walked through the door, he grasped the situation in a glance.

"I wanted to be here when it arrived," he said, "but they flatly refused to give me an exact delivery day." He set down his briefcase and began pacing around, looking at the rolled-up carpets and the piano. He stopped moving and stared at her. He was not accustomed to seeing her smoke. When he approached her to kiss the top of her head, as he always did when he returned, her hand flew up to block him.

He drew back. "I know what you're thinking, but it's paid for. All of it." His face was furrowed. "We've been here two years now. Don't you think it's time for some rugs?"

"And a grand piano?"

"I need a good piano. It helps me work." Frank looked bewildered. He pointed to the Chinese rug. "I thought you would love it."

Mamah got up and went to his studio, returning with a fistful of unpaid bills. She threw them on the floor, then bent down and picked one up. "Why don't we invite Mr. Howard Fuller in for a party? Let's ask him if he finds the rug beautiful. After all, you owe him two hundred dollars. I'd say he's an investor in it."

"Mamah—"

"How could you squander what little goodwill we have among these people? Are you incapable of shame?"

He turned away. "I'll talk to you when you're ready to discuss this calmly."

Mamah grabbed his shoulder and swung him around with a force that stunned both of them. "You will talk to me now." Her voice came through clenched teeth. "You will fix this. *Fix* this!" She swept her arm around the room. "You will return all this, and you will pay the people you owe money to. And you will ask their forgiveness for your arrogance in not doing it sooner. Starting with Josiah. Do you understand me?"

He stared at her, his face pinched in disbelief.

"Do you?" she shouted.

Frank let out a sigh and put up both palms. "Fine."

"Catherine knew what I didn't know. That you don't pay people. That's why she won't divorce you, isn't it? She's afraid, isn't she, that once you're free, she won't get a red cent out of you?"

His silence made her angrier.

"How dare you talk about 'democratic architecture.' You hypocrite! You have nothing but contempt for the little man and you cheat him whenever you get a chance. I cannot imagine how you could cheat Josiah after all he's done for us." She swiped at tears running down her face. "But then I suppose I can. You are a man of such *refined* sensibilities. You must have your beautiful things."

Mamah turned and walked back to the bedroom. She lay down and flung an arm over her face. Sobs welled up in great waves.

After a while he was standing at the door. "Mame," he pleaded.

"I've made a terrible mistake," she cried. "I left my children for a liar."

"I don't know why—"

"Get out. Go sleep at Jennie's. I'll be gone tomorrow morning."

"Where are you going?"

"I don't know." She covered her face with her arm again.

"Please don't . . ."

She would not speak anymore. He could stand there all night, but she would not open her mouth. Finally she heard him shuffle down the hall and go out the door.

IN THE MORNING, Mamah packed a bag. She would get the key from him for the coach house in Chicago where he slept when he was working there. It struck her that she had nowhere else to go. She hadn't a single close friend left to whom she could turn.

When she walked out into the living room, he was standing there, freshly shaved.

"Can we talk?" he asked.

"In the car. You can take me to the train."

"Are you going into Chicago?"

"Yes. I need the key to your place."

Frank drove toward Spring Green slowly. "If I have not been good at managing money," he said, "if I have left some fellow holding the bag, it was not out of malice."

"Why do you go out and buy things you can't afford? Because it makes you feel bigger?"

He shook his head sadly. "For a sense of completeness."

"For God's sake, Frank."

"When I find beautiful things, it feels as if they are necessary *tools* for my life. I can't bear to have old junk around, disturbing the peace. Better a space be empty. But we have been here two years, and when I saw the chairs and rugs, I had to buy them—for my sanity, Mamah. Can you possibly understand that? It's part of finishing a piece of art."

She stared out the window. "Where did the money come from?"

Frank exhaled heavily.

"The truth or nothing."

"I owed back rent at Orchestra Hall."

"How much?"

"Fifteen hundred. They'd been after me, and then, about ten days ago, the sheriff came around and was threatening to . . ." Frank ran his hand over his mouth. "Well, what do you know, William Spaulding came through the front door of the office at that moment. So John—my son was there—he kept the sheriff busy while I sold William a set of woodblock prints."

"How much did he give you for the prints?"

Frank paused and cleared his throat.

"You have one chance to tell me the story, Frank, and if you don't give the whole of it, it's over with."

"Ten thousand. He gave me ten thousand dollars for the prints. They were rare ones."

"And then?"

"I gave the manager at Orchestra Hall fifteen hundred dollars and settled the debt." Frank paused and adjusted the side mirror. "Then John and I went out. I wanted to pay off some other bills. We poked around Lyon and Healy, just looking. And before I knew it, I had bought the pianos."

"There was *more than one* piano?"

His voice cracked. "I bought three. Two had to be ordered."

"Three grand pianos." She felt a chilling urge to laugh. "Did you spend the rest of the money at Marshall Field's?"

"Yes." He was quiet for a while. "I haven't had a chance to tell you. There's going to be big money coming in soon. I'm going to be doing a huge hurry-up job in Chicago. It's an enormous concert garden, like the beer gardens we saw in Berlin. But much bigger. Midway Gardens. I've started on it already."

"Have you been paid for it?"

"No, not yet."

Mamah stared out the car window.

"I know," he said, "it's madness." He shook his head. "You can't imagine. I hold off, and then this pent-up desire to buy things comes on. I don't expect you to understand it, but it all springs from the same place—the good and the bad. This impulse to arrange things in space, to make harmony out of the right objects in relation to each other. What can I say? It's an insatiable—"

"Affliction," she said. "It's a sickness, Frank. You cannot use your gifts to justify cheating other people. There's no harmony to be had when you cheat the lumberman so that you can have a grand piano. Do you think genius somehow trumps responsibility? You're not helpless in this."

They didn't speak for the remainder of the drive. When she opened the car door at the station, he grasped her hand. "Nothing like this will ever happen again."

She climbed out of the car. "It's more than the spending. It's so many things in you. And I don't know if they're things you can change." She closed the door and turned away.

"Mamah," he called after her, but she walked into the station house entrance and couldn't hear him anymore.

CHAPTER 45

When Mamah arrived in Chicago, she bought two boxes of candy in the train station, took a taxi to the Cedar Street pied-à-terre, where she left her bag, then returned to the waiting taxi. "Wabash and Washington, please," she said.

She climbed up to the El platform and rode the train out to Oak Park, watching as the west side of Chicago sped by. There were so many changes since she'd last taken the train. New apartment buildings. Gorgeous gardens around Garfield Park Conservatory. As the train entered the suburb of Oak Park, she could see that it had changed, too. The elms and oaks lining the streets were as lovely as she remembered them, but everywhere, new houses had sprouted up between the old ones. She looked toward the north prairie where she had taken John every June to pick strawberries, where she had lain once under the moon with Frank. It was dotted now with new roofs.

Mamah walked briskly toward East Avenue, glancing furtively at the people who passed. For four years she'd feared this moment, but she saw not one familiar face. In the past she couldn't walk down the street without being hailed by someone.

Lizzie was on summer vacation from school and might not be home. Mamah stood in front of the house. Everything was just as she had left it, even the gardens. She glanced up at the window where the Belknap girls had stood, probably watching her and Frank as they'd made love. She shuddered. It was still boarded up. The carpenter had done a fair job, but there was no disguising it. She looked down quickly, fearful that Lulu Belknap might be staring at her right now.

Mamah let herself through the gate and walked on the path to the rear of the house. She rapped on the glass doors, but Lizzie didn't answer. She could see for herself that Lizzie wasn't in the apartment. Inside, nothing looked different. Mamah went back around to the side of the house, summoned her courage, and knocked on the screen door. In a minute a pretty blond woman appeared.

Elinor Millor, the new Mrs. Cheney, nearly fell backward. "Mamah?"

"Yes, I'm Mamah."

"Come in." She held the door open.

"You must be Elinor."

"I am." The woman fingered the little pleats at her collar, her face dumbstruck.

"I don't mean to bother you. I was only here to see Lizzie, and the children, if they are around. I know I should have called you."

"Lizzie was here just a half hour ago. She lives downstairs."

"I know."

"Oh, of course you know. What am I thinking?" The woman pushed fine strands of hair from her forehead. "The children are not here. Martha is with her father. They've gone to the lake. John had a baseball game. He's over at the school field."

"I see."

"Let me go look for Lizzie. Please sit down."

Mamah glanced around. The living room was spotless and nearly exactly as it had been when she'd left. There were a few new touches. An unfamiliar lace tablecloth on the dining table. White eyelet curtains on the library windows.

"She must have gone off to the grocery store. She said earlier that was what she was going to do. You can wait. It's no trouble at all. In fact, I just made lemonade."

"Thank you."

When Elinor returned, she sat across from Mamah in front of the fireplace. She busied herself with the glasses and napkins, taking a long draft from her drink before settling on something to say. "The garden you planted is very lovely."

"Elinor," Mamah began, "it's kind of you to invite me in. Lizzie and Edwin have spoken so lovingly of you. I want you to know that I appreciate how good you have been to my children."

Elinor shook her head. "Oh, no, please. It's so easy. I love them." She seemed about to say something more, her mouth half open, but she produced no sound. An awkwardness hung in the air.

"I brought something for John and Martha," Mamah said. "Just the gumdrops they like. May I put these on their beds?"

If Elinor saw through her feeble ruse to go into the children's rooms, she didn't reveal it. "Absolutely. Go right ahead."

Mamah walked down the hall to John's room first. She stepped inside and let her eyes adjust to the afternoon dimness. The space had changed. This was an eleven-year-old boy's room now, with baseball pennants on the wall and a paperboy's bag hanging by its strap over his desk chair. There was no evidence of the colorful train set that had once enchanted him, or any sign of the dozens of gifts she had sent him from Germany and Italy. As she looked around, a warm breeze lifted the curtains to reveal a row of fossil-encrusted sandstone chunks placed along the windowsill. Her throat ached with gladness. The few fossils they had gathered together when he was six had expanded into a collection.

"El!" Mamah heard Lizzie's voice at that moment, calling from somewhere outside. "Can you please open the screen? My arms are full."

"Coming," Elinor called back.

Mamah felt like an intruder, yet she hurried to Martha's door. She dropped the box of candy on the frilly bedcover. Her daughter's room was wallpapered now in a sunny flower print. Dolls were everywhere.

Mamah slipped out of the room and walked down the hall into the kitchen, where Lizzie was unloading food from two large bags of groceries. The corners of her mouth fell when she saw her sister.

"Let me help you," Mamah said.

THEY WENT OUT the front sidewalk and up East Avenue. "I've been desperate to see you, Liz. We haven't talked in so long." Her sister remained taciturn. "I've missed you so."

Lizzie walked along slowly, not returning Mamah's glance. She looked older. What softness there had been in her strong, chiseled face had been filed away by the past few years. She was all angle and bone.

"The truth is, I came to apologize to you for all the trouble I've put you through. I've told you before, but I cannot say it enough. I bless you every day for stepping in and taking care of the children. I never could have stayed in Berlin without your help."

"It was for John and Martha, whatever I did."

Mamah inhaled. Lizzie's square jaw, so like her own, was set hard.

"Do you think I don't know how they suffered?"

"I don't know what you know anymore, Mamah."

"I know that you suffered, too, Liz. You've always been so private and dignified. I can only imagine the harassment you have endured. It was unremitting for us. We had reporters looking in the windows up at Taliesin—"

"Oh, *did* you?" The sarcasm in Lizzie's voice was lacerating.

"I never meant to bring all of it upon you. Surely you understand that. I have loved you and admired you all my life. You are the only true hero I have. I owe you everything."

Lizzie reached out and stripped leaves off a twig. "You always wanted to do something big. Something *important.*"

"Is that such a terrible thing? You're the one who told me once that the world can't forgive ambition in a woman."

"I never got to find out. My ambitions never seemed to figure into things. You were away at the university when Mother got sick, so it fell to Jessie and me. And you were already married by the time Jessie passed. Your life was set. Suddenly, there was a niece to raise, and then . . ." Lizzie paused. "Then you had your personality to go discover." She tossed away a fistful of leaves. "You had everything. You had a wonderful man who adored you, beautiful healthy children. Freedom. No money worries. A nanny and a housekeeper. You didn't have to work, and Edwin never asked a thing of you. Do you realize what you gave up for Frank Wright? The kind of life most women—most *feminists*—dream of."

They walked on in silence. Mamah was desperate to shift the direction of their words. "How is Jessie doing with her father's people?" she said finally.

"Jessie is . . . trying to adapt. I thought it better that she be with them, for the present, anyway. She's not Edwin's blood. I work all day. And now, without Louise . . ."

"What do you mean?"

Lizzie looked at her, puzzled. "Louise is no longer with us. I thought you knew that. Elinor didn't think she was needed. She let her go."

Mamah caught her breath. *Oh, Louise, you must be dead from sorrow someplace.* How could the woman turn Louise out? She had been the sun and the moon to John since he was a baby. To Martha too. "Where did she go?"

"She went to live with her brother. She's looking for another family. I'm hoping she finds something, but Louise is fifty-one now. She may have to live at the mercy of her brother." Lizzie wiped her forehead with a square of handkerchief. "I'll move out eventually, too. They haven't asked me to, but Elinor deserves her privacy." They had circled the block and stood now at the side gate. Lizzie's eyes narrowed. "What is it you want from me?"

Mamah reached out and took her sister's hand. "I know it's a lot to ask, Lizzie, but don't cut me off, I beg of you. Please forgive me for not considering your feelings more." Lizzie's hand felt limp, noncommittal.

Elinor appeared, smiling. "Well," she said, "isn't it a fine day? I had hardly noticed."

When Mamah turned to leave, she saw John come loping across lawns toward the house, his head down, his lips moving as if he were singing to himself. He seemed even taller now than he had when she'd seen him in April, when she was just home from Japan. As his head came up, his dark eyes grew saucerlike when he spotted her in the yard. He stopped in his tracks.

"Johnny!" Mamah walked over to him and pulled his stiff body to her in an awkward hug. "I almost missed seeing you. Will you go out with me for ice cream?"

The boy looked confused. It pained her to see him glance first at Lizzie, then at Elinor. Mamah turned to see them nodding.

"Okay." He tossed his glove to Lizzie.

"Shall we walk to Peterson's?"

"No," he said, shifting from one foot to the other. "That's too far."

Too embarrassing, Mamah thought. It was probably where his friends gathered.

"There's a grocery store that has ice cream," he said. "It's just two blocks. You know that one?"

"I do. Let's go there."

They walked south. John caught Mamah glancing up at the Belknaps'. He said, "Ellis doesn't live there anymore. His family moved to Wisconsin."

"You don't say."

"They invited me to Waukesha to visit for a week this summer. Papa said I could take the train from there to Spring Green when I come see you." His eyes lit up. "By myself."

The image of John alone on the train disturbed her. She swallowed hard and struggled to put brightness in her voice. "That sounds so grown-up."

Once more she glanced at the hulking Victorian, now empty of her nemesis. Over the past four years, whenever she'd thought of Oak Park, she could hear Lulu Belknap next door on a Sunday evening, leading her girls at the piano as they sang "Jesus, Savior, pilot me." How strange to know the Belknaps were gone. And Louise, too.

"I understand you've become quite a rock collector," Mamah said, touching her son's arm lightly as they walked.

"Uh-huh," he said, his head down. Subtly, he put another foot of sidewalk between them as they moved along. "Aunt Lizzie takes us."

MAMAH'S HEAD THROBBED all the way back to Chicago. The ache had started when she had said goodbye to John and watched him go into the house. A shapeless anger had come over her in that moment. By the time she got on the El and found a place to sit, she wanted to hammer the seat with her fist until the leather split.

She propped her elbow on the open window and pressed her knuckles against her mouth. Below, on a wet lawn, children in bathing suits sprayed each other with a hose.

So many things she hadn't wanted to think about. But there were pictures in her mind now that wouldn't go away.

Elinor Millor had slipped into Mamah's old life as if it were a comfortable dress. She looked like she had been there forever, standing on the stoop, smiling and chatting with Lizzie, tousling John's hair as he raced into the house, the sound of a banging screen door echoing behind him.

You always wanted to do something big. Lizzie's words burned between her ears. It was true. She *had* always wanted to make a mark, to inhabit a bigger world than Boone or Port Huron or Oak Park.

But what had she done with all that ambition? Attached herself to two colossal personalities. Spent herself on Frank Lloyd Wright and Ellen Key, who would have done great work without ever having known her. Poured her soul into defending the sanctity of the individual while John and Martha slid from her grasp.

"WILL YOU TALK TO ME?" Frank was standing next to the chair where she had dozed off.

Mamah started at his voice. She had been dreaming, her brain replaying almost precisely the events of the afternoon she'd spent in Oak Park. Except that in the dream, Catherine Wright passed her on the street, walked behind her like a ghost, rode on the train just across from her.

Mamah stared around the room, then knew she was in Chicago, in the coach house. "When did you come in?"

"Just now."

She flicked her eyes toward a nearby chair, and he pulled it over to sit across from her.

"I won't stay long—I know you came here to be alone. I just wanted to say something to you."

Frank's eyes were watery, drooping. She nodded.

"I've never been a good friend to anybody. I don't know how to be. I'm stunted in that way. I have always felt as if I could take what I wanted because I deserved it. I thought it was my reward." He bent his head and momentarily pressed a thumb and forefinger to his closed eyes. "For the hard work I did, for what I gave to the world. And the world has put good and kind people in my path who have indulged me and propped me up and not allowed me to fall flat on my face when I should have. It's my gift, you see, that causes people to make allowances." He smiled ruefully. "I know that. Contrary to what you may think, my conscience haunts me. There are nights I can't sleep for the pain I have caused." He shook his head. "I'm sorry for all of it. I'm sorry I failed you as a friend. You of all people."

Mamah stared at him impassively.

When she did not respond, he stood up. "I will try to put the shambles of this soul of mine into some kind of decent order. If you never wanted to see me again, I would understand. I cannot tell you how much I regret that I pushed you to this point."

The room was stifling. She could smell the lone grapefruit she had noticed the night before, rotting in a bowl.

She sighed. "Pull me up." When she extended her arm, it felt heavy as lead. "I need some fresh air."

THEY WALKED NORTH along the lake, stepping off the path from time to time to slog through the sand.

"There are things you need to hear, Frank. The truth is, I don't know if you really can change the worst of it. You've worked yourself into quite a corner. We both have.

"Right now I feel as if my world is the size of a nickel. And worth about that much. I've done what you've done—we've cut ourselves off from everyone. Perched ourselves on high ground up there at Taliesin, like moral monarchs. But we know the emperors wear no clothes, don't we?

"I blame myself for plenty. I've been an expert at self-deception. But you . . ."

They had stopped and were facing out toward the east, where sunlight flashed on the lake's waves like neon.

"Look at yourself. As gifted as you are, you're holed up at Taliesin, cursing the architects who once worked for you, behaving like an arrogant ass. How dare you diminish Marion Mahony! I don't care if she married Walter Griffin. Marion was your translator, Frank. She made you comprehensible to people who didn't understand your work. She helped you sell yourself, not to mention the fact that she burped your babies. Why can't you give other people credit? Are you that fragile?"

Mamah waited for him to say something, but he stared straight ahead, blotting his eyes with the heel of his hand. She saw that he could be browbeaten when he was down, but she could not stop herself.

"You've made yourself into a tragic figure in your own mind. You go from feeling persecuted one minute to being God's annointed messenger the next." She kicked the wet sand with the toe of a shoe. "Why do you have to be grandiose? Why do you buy things you can't afford? You don't pay people . . . *little* people! The very first ones who should be paid."

She shook her head in exasperation. "You say you're at a fork in the road. We shall see. I think you've been this way a long time. I know about your father leaving and your mother's coddling and all your blessed relatives' persecution. None of it is an excuse. How many times have you said, 'It's the space inside that's the reality of a structure'? And what you put into that space will shape how you live. For God's sake, Frank. Can't you see that that's true of your own heart?"

They walked for what seemed like miles, but he remained silent, his face downcast. For a moment the swell and release of her fury had felt righteous. In the ten years she'd known him, she had never spoken so brutally to him as she had in the past couple of days. Nor had he ever been so contrite. But she did not enjoy humiliating him, and she felt spent.

"Look," Mamah said when they stopped to turn back. "You're a grown man, and you have to choose what kind of person you're going to be. You can go on living from one financial crisis to the next. You can go on cheating people and making yourself ridiculous with your talk about hewing to a higher standard than the common man. Or you can actually make good on that talk."

At the coach house, they stood in front of the door. "Come back home," he said.

She sat down on a low wall to brush the sand off her shoes. When she looked up, the brown circles under his eyes seemed darker.

"No," she said. "you need time to think about all the things that must be fixed. It is no small change you are commiting yourself to if you want to remain with me."

IN THE DAYS that followed, Mamah walked Chicago's streets, glad for the anonymity they afforded. It was refreshing to be among these open-faced people, going about their lives. She and Frank had become strange in their isolation and self-absorption. She went to the library that week and sat reading poetry. She happened upon some lines in a Wordsworth poem that seemed to sum up Frank Lloyd Wright: "There is a dark / Inscrutable workmanship that reconciles / Discordant elements, makes them cling together / In one society." Frank was his own society, a one-man band of transcendental harmony and discordant cymbals.

She had believed all along that his soul was visible in his work. That he was what he believed, as true to his ideals as any human could be. But she had not seen that there were missing pieces. What dark inscrutable workmanship had left such holes in his conscience? Did Frank lie because he was insecure, because he had never finished a formal education? Did he promote himself as a natural genius because he lacked a university diploma?

It was possible, though unlikely. He had enormous confidence in his gift. She thought of the story Catherine used to tell about when they were newly married. The great Daniel Burnham came to Frank and offered to send him to be schooled in Paris at the École des Beaux-Arts. It was an extraordinary honor to be called out of the crowd in that way by such a powerful and brilliant architect. It would have assured a comfortable life for Frank and Catherine and their children.

"And Frank said no," Catherine would say in mock exasperation when she told the story. Both times Mamah had heard it, the tale had provoked amusement among dinner guests, who enjoyed speculating on how Oak Park would look if Frank had had a classical education.

What courage for a young man, Mamah had thought when she heard the story. What confidence in his own artistic instincts. How often had she heard him say *I'd rather be honestly arrogant than hypocritically humble*? It took a superior attitude not to succumb to the rewards of joining the establishment.

Unfortunately, the attitude had become his persona; he believed it himself now. He had come to mistake his gift for the whole of his character.

The memory of the Daniel Burnham story stubbornly inserted Catherine Wright into her mind. Mamah had no illusions anymore that they could one day sit down and talk. Catherine would go on withholding herself, refusing to compromise, keeping Mamah an "illicit" woman until they were all dust. The price both of them had paid for loving Frank was dear indeed.

ON THE SIXTH DAY, Frank appeared at the door, clutching a bouquet of flowers. "From your garden," he said. His whole body looked contrite.

A strong wind came off Lake Michigan as they walked along the shore. He was the one talking this time.

"A long time ago, you and I promised to keep each other honest. If you come back to Taliesin with me, I can change. I'm going to get rid of the rottenness inside me, Mame. But I can't do it without you. I need you there every day, to tell me the truth."

She held on to her hat in the wind. It felt comforting to be walking next to him. She tried to imagine what their lives would look like if she did go back. Once she had wanted to marry him. Not that a marriage certificate meant anything, but it seemed to be the one item that could change their status so they might have normal lives. It seemed the only solution to their problems. "If Catherine would just let go" had been their mantra for so long. Now Mamah understood Catherine's dilemma better. She wouldn't divorce Frank because she feared he wouldn't pay her child support and alimony. And there was revenge to be sure: By refusing to divorce after twenty years of accommodating him, Catherine was squeezing recompense from Frank for a longstanding emotional debt. But that was only part of it. Catherine held on because she still loved him, and remembered what it was like to be loved by him. Nothing else in the world compared to the incandescent joy Frank brought to his best beloved.

To never have known him or known his love for her—what a loss that would have been.

If Mamah could marry him now, though, she doubted she would. If she went back, she would either have to separate his finances from hers, or completely take over all of them. It would be a trial either way.

The pluck of her father; the faith of her mother. Those were the traits that would be required to get through the rough spots ahead. She hoped she'd inherited enough of both.

"The children are what matters now," she said. "There is some major mending to do, if they will permit it. I can't be spending all my time worrying if you have paid your bills."

"I understand," he said.

Out on the water, a sailboat was struggling toward harbor. It heeled over suddenly in a great gust of wind. She stopped walking to watch the boat until it righted itself.

"Last week," she said, "I went out to Oak Park and I begged Lizzie to forgive me for treating her life as less important than my own. I don't know if she ever will. But I wanted so much for her to see that there is some good in me. I think that's what you want, Frank.

"If you had asked me to forgive you even two days ago, I would have said no. But if I can't believe in your chance to change, how can I believe in my own? How can I ask Lizzie to wipe the slate clean if I can't find it in my heart to forgive you?"

Mamah saw the furrows soften to joy in his face. It was a thing to see. It was genuine. There was so much in Frank Wright that was noble and gallant and good. Maybe she was the world's biggest fool, but she knew she'd go back with him and try to start over. But from here on out, it was a life of vigilance that she was in for.

Still, standing here and gazing at his face, she knew it was love that filled the space inside her. And she couldn't help believing that love, more than anything else, would divine the way to a better place.

CHAPTER 46

John poked around in the living room, inspecting objects that had appeared since the previous summer. The rugs and chairs Frank had bought were long gone; only the Steinway remained from his mad shopping spree. Still, there were plenty of exotic new things to keep the boy interested. He lifted the lid off a brass incense pot and sniffed inside, then trailed his fingers down the long table to a Buddha statue, where he paused to rub its belly. He explored until he found what he said was the best thing in the room: a fox skin flung over the back of a chair.

Martha sat on the edge of the living room window seat, stroking Lucky's big head. The girl's own head was bent down toward his, her soulful, black-fringed eyes locked on his almost-human face. The dog had a raffish air about him, with bushy brows and a beard, and a downturned mouth that almost begged for a pipe to be stuck in it. Mamah knew Lucky for what he was, a beggar who charmed scraps out of the toughest party. And Martha was anything but tough, except to her mother.

The girl kept her coat on, saying she was cold in the room. Her stockinged legs and new black patent-leather boots with pointed toes dangled below the hem of the coat. She was such a beautiful, solemn child. Mamah wanted to embrace her, to devour her. Instead, she picked up a letter from a table and pretended to read it.

Two hours earlier, when Edwin had delivered the children to Spring Green, he'd glanced at them smothering the dog in hugs. "Martha picked out the shoes she's wearing," he'd said, nodding in her direction. He'd shrugged, smiling. "She has a mind of her own when it comes to clothes."

Mamah had laughed. "She likes fancy, it appears."

It had been a welcome exchange—brief, but enough to make her feel as if an ocean had been traversed. She wanted to say more. She wanted to say that Martha was tall, like Edwin's side, and that John had his father's gentle nature. But it would have been too intimate. Talking about John and Martha had once been the greatest pleasure between her and Edwin, but it wasn't hers to have anymore. Something had opened just then on the platform, though. Next time she would venture more.

When Edwin climbed onto the Chicago-bound train, Mamah walked the children over to the dry-goods store. "Let's get you both some overalls and boots," she said. "You're in farm country now."

Martha sulked when her mother pulled heavy brown boots from a rack along the wall. "Those are ugly."

"Just try them on, Martha. Mud and cowpies can ruin your nice shoes pretty fast." The girl grudgingly put her feet into the boots.

"Yours fit, too?" Mamah asked John.

He looked pleased. "Yup."

Outside the store, Mamah had stood still when she heard a familiar throaty trill overhead. Near the street, a round-bellied farmer was pointing at the sky. "The cranes are back," he said.

"THERE'S A SQUIRREL IN THE HOUSE," John said now. He pointed to the woodpile.

Sure enough, a squirrel had gotten in through one of the windows. He stood atop a log, his tiny paws wrapped around the stem of a stalk of wheat he must have pulled from one of Frank's arrangements. The animal was working at the unopened wheat buds as a child might eat a piece of corn. Flakes of chaff snowed onto the wood around him. When Mamah stepped closer, the squirrel froze in midbite.

Martha watched, as still as the squirrel, from across the room. Small animal visits were something Mamah had grown used to, but the squirrel's appearance was clearly alarming to the children. In fact, even the pile of wood where the squirrel was perched must have seemed peculiar to them. Taliesin was part camp, part art gallery. People didn't stack half-cords of wood in their Oak Park living rooms the way Frank did here. If Martha or John looked long enough, they would come upon spiders merrily weaving webs among the split logs, a condition Elinor surely wouldn't tolerate in her house. But neither would she hang a painted silk kimono on the wall.

Mamah opened a door and shooed the squirrel toward it, but the animal hopped across the floor and jumped up on the window seat. Martha leaped up with a screech and fled across the room, setting the dog to barking. At that moment Mamah remembered herself as a girl of nine, a Sarah Bernhardt in training, weeping over stray cats and imagined insults, hieing herself to her room in snits, passing hours reading dime novels.

"If we open all the doors," Mamah said, hurrying to do so, "he'll find his own way out." Martha's shrieks continued until the squirrel made his exit.

Part of the strangeness of this visit was the fact that the children were here out of season. During their long visit last year, they had accustomed themselves to summer playmates and hot weather. It was spring now, and cool. The place was full of new people out in the courtyard. And there was an air of excitement and tension throughout the household.

In the past week, Mamah had questioned her decision to invite the children up over Easter. The Midway Gardens job had turned into something of a nightmare. The owners wanted the place to open June first. Workmen had been excavating and building on the south Chicago site since the beginning of March. And even at this late date, Frank kept changing his mind about the details.

He had brought in Emil Brodelle to do drafting, and the deadline pressure was palpable in the workroom, where Frank sat designing and redesigning. At one point Mamah had walked into the studio just as Frank snatched Emil's latest drawing from his table, crumpled it, and threw it with a "Goddammit!" into the wastebasket. Mamah had stepped out of the room quickly and gone to the kitchen to cook. She was careful to respect Frank's domain. They were both careful about a lot of things now.

Emil was not the only new face at Taliesin. There was also David Lindblom, a young Swedish immigrant who tended the orchard and gardens. And there were Tom Brunker and Billy Weston. Sometimes Billy brought his son, Ernest, over to help in the garden, as he had today. And another face was about to join the crowd: Frank had hired a Japanese cook while they were abroad. But the man was having trouble getting into the country, and in the interim Mamah was once more cooking for a crowd.

If the family at Taliesin kept changing, so did the children. Martha was not the little girl who'd spent last summer on horseback. Mamah could see that she had begun to have a private, interior life. As had John. What a shock it had been when she saw John climb off the train. His hair was parted down the middle, a sure sign that he had begun to take notice of himself in the mirror. A sense of urgency had gripped Mamah. She'd lost so much time with them, and there was much to get done. How to squeeze into these visits the kind of moments that had given her such pleasure as a child? This visit she wanted to invite the neighbor kids over to put on a play or talent show, maybe plan a tree fort they could build this summer. But she dared not force any of it. Each reunion required a slow series of adjustments until they all breathed the same air easily.

"FRANK," MAMAH SAID SOFTLY. He was lost in concentration at his table, his forehead in his palm.

Emil saw her and the children standing at the studio door. "Mr. Wright," he said.

Frank looked up, his eyes glazed.

"Is this a bad time?" Mamah asked.

"Martha! John!" he called out. He stood up, his arms flung wide as he walked to them. When he saw the girl's stiffness, he checked himself, extending his hand to each of them and bowing a little for Martha. "There is never a bad time for these two."

"I thought you might want to show them what you're working on."

"I can tell they're interested." Frank's eyes were teasing.

"Sure." John was all politeness. Martha slumped, her back an arc of disappointment.

"Frank is designing a place in Chicago that I will take you to when it's done. It's a huge building that will have an indoor garden for winter concerts and an outdoor area with a beer garden and a bandshell."

"Like the amusement park in Forest Park?" John asked.

"Well, no roller coasters or rides," she said. "It will be like no place you've ever been. You've heard of the hanging gardens of Babylon, haven't you?"

"Third grade," John said.

"Well, it's going to be a little like the paintings you see of those gardens. It will have lots of levels—"

"Do you still have that horse, Champion?" Martha asked abruptly.

"I do," Frank said.

"Can we go riding?"

"We can."

"When?"

Frank turned toward the window as if he were gauging how much daylight was left.

"The cranes are back," Mamah offered.

"Why didn't you say so? Let's go now."

Emil looked up in disbelief. "Sir, Mueller says they can't go forward with the architect's box unless—"

Frank put on his hat. "You do know Paul Mueller and I built Unity Temple together, don't you, Brodelle?"

"Yes, sir."

"Mueller knows how to wait."

The four of them rode on horseback down the driveway and out along the county road, until Frank turned off onto a small road. They followed it past wooded areas and fields to a boggy, nearly flooded area. Frank found a stand of trees where they tied up their horses.

"It's not a long walk." He searched around the ground and found four straight branches. "Don't fall over in the mud," he said, handing out the staffs. Frank went first through the high wet grass, followed by the children. Mamah brought up the rear, just behind Martha, whose new boots sank an inch or two in the mud with every step. Up ahead, Frank turned around, made a "shhh" gesture with his finger. Soon they stood in a clearing.

Beyond them was a meadow of grass and, here and there, pools of standing water. A dozen gray sandhill cranes, their heads capped in red, stood in the great puddles. Two cranes were just landing, descending from the sky with their wings wide and their long skinny legs hanging down, like parachutists. The cranes in the water threw their red skulls back and called out.

"I used to come to this very place when I was a boy," Frank whispered. "But there aren't as many cranes now. People hunt them. I don't know how they are for eating. Never tasted one."

Mamah passed around the field glasses she'd brought. They took turns watching as the cranes straightened their necks and beaks into spires pointed at the sky.

"Those fellas are probably just arriving from South America," Frank said, gesturing toward the birds that had just landed. "That's what they do. Every year they fly thousands of miles south. They could probably stop in California or Mississippi and wait out the winter, but they don't."

"Why?" Martha said.

"Because it's their nature. They do what feels right to them."

Mamah had the field glasses to her eyes. "I like to think about how they only know what they know."

John looked at her blankly.

"What I mean is, they probably don't care a whit about people. We're ants to them, at best. They don't know anything about governments or cooking or newspapers or religion. What they see is water and fields and sky. They don't have words for them like we do. Yet they *know* them. And they know among themselves all kinds of things that we don't know, things about the wind, and how to find the places along the way that they return to every year. Maybe they have a language we know nothing about. Their experience of this planet is completely different from ours, but it's just as real."

"If we're lucky, we'll see them dance," Frank said.

"They dance?" Martha asked.

"Sometimes. They mate for life, and when it's time to have babies, they do a dance."

The four of them crouched down, waiting. After a while their legs began to ache, and they stood up to go home.

"Look," Mamah said.

In the tall grasses, the cranes had begun a kind of minuet—bowing, jumping, flapping their wings. They paused to throw back their heads and call, then commenced feinting or digging up tufts of grass from the mud.

"There'll be some eggs soon," Frank said.

CHAPTER 47

By May it was clear that there would be no Japanese cook. The chef who had so delighted them in Tokyo was not simply delayed but, according to a brief note he sent in English, not interested in coming to Wisconsin at all. Mamah would have to launch a new search, and the competition for household help was stiff with summer coming on. Within days of the letter from Tokyo, Frank announced that he had found a new prospect. John Vogelsang, the man who ran the restaurant at Midway Gardens, told Frank he had just the solution, a wonderful woman from Barbados named Gertrude.

"Makes all the regular things and brilliant desserts, apparently," Frank said to Mamah one evening. "She's got a husband who would come along. Vogelsang says he's an educated fellow who pitches in, does a variety of things. We could use another chore man, don't you think?"

"Why is Vogelsang willing to give them up?"

"With his connections, he can get good help in Chicago any day. It's a little favor to us, I think. He said he thought these two would like being out in the country."

Mamah wavered. It would be not only one person but two. As usual, there was the uncertainty about money. Frank had gotten a small advance for Midway Gardens. There would be money coming in for the Imperial Hotel, but when, no one knew.

"Why don't you invite them to work for a weekend?" she said. "Let's see how they do."

WHEN GERTRUDE CARLTON arrived from Chicago, she carried a pillowcase full of food. She was young, with smooth brown skin and a gentle, confident manner. Dressed in a white waist and blue serge skirt, she carried a parasol above her Sunday hat.

Mamah showed her around the kitchen and the garden. The young woman stood with her hands on her hips, surveying the vegetable patch, approval flitting across her face. "Peppers," she said.

"Not nearly ripe, though," Mamah said.

"Don't worry, I got some, fresh pick." She bent over and yanked up a handful of chives and parsley.

Back in the kitchen and covered in an apron she'd brought, Gertrude wrapped a bright scarf around her head. Mamah's jaw fell slack at the food she took out of the pillowcase. Guavas. Okra. Limes.

"My land, where did you find those things?"

Gertrude laughed. "Mr. Carlton got friends." Her voice had a sunny, singsong quality. In that moment Mamah saw a girl more than a woman. How old could she be, twenty-two?

When Gertrude's hand brought out jars of red and yellow spices, Mamah sighed wistfully. "Mr. Wright prefers simple food. Fish and chicken. Potatoes."

Gertrude smiled. "Just you wait. I make simple food."

"We have chickens. Do you want to cook a chicken tonight?"

"Tomorrow. Tonight fish from the river. Mr. Carlton will catch some."

"Mr. Wright doesn't like fried things."

"I won't fry, madam."

"Or spices."

Gertrude wore a look of forbearance. "Just a little 'pon the fish, madam."

JULIAN CARLTON SEEMED an odd match for his wife. He was about thirty, small but well built and handsome, with a serious demeanor made more so by his immaculate shirt and tie. His English was clipped and British, unlike his wife's lilting dialect.

In the courtyard outside, Frank was pointing to windows that needed to be washed.

"Let Julian go fish," Mamah called to him. "He's going to catch our main course."

The couple spent that Saturday in a flurry of activity. By two o'clock Julian had caught six fish. Smells of garlic, onions, and curry soon wafted from the kitchen into the living room, where they met the lemon scent of the furniture polish he was spreading over the chairs and table. For the past couple of hours, he had been a blur of motion, polishing silver, pressing linens, climbing up a ladder to clean windows.

At dinnertime Mamah and Frank walked into the living room to find him dressed in a white jacket.

"Madam," he said, nodding slightly. He escorted Mamah, followed by Frank, to the dining table, where he pulled out a chair for her, then one for him. The napkins he had pressed that afternoon were arranged in elaborate folds on the plates. In a matter of moments he was bringing food in to them on a covered silver tray he'd found, carrying it above his shoulder on his palm. When he returned to the kitchen, Mamah shot Frank a worried look.

"This is too much," she said. "This house is too small for formalities."

But when they cut into the fish, it was tender and savory, seasoned in a delicate, unfamiliar way that had to be Caribbean, and when dessert arrived—a simple apple pie but perhaps the best either of them had ever tasted—they looked at each other and grinned.

"Where did Gertrude learn to bake like that?" Mamah asked Julian when he came back to clear the plates.

"I made the dessert tonight, madam."

"When did you have time? And where did you learn to make an apple pie?"

"I was a Pullman porter, madam, before I went to work for the Vogelsangs. I learned how to do whatever needed to be done."

"So that's it," she whispered when Julian was out of earshot. "That explains the formality, the way he carries the tray. My father always said that Pullman porters are better trained than the world's best waiters. That white jacket he's wearing? It's a porter's jacket. They buy their own when they go to work for Pullman."

Her father had been a great admirer of the men who worked the sleeping cars. Julian's formality suddenly seemed familiar and endearing. His bearing was dignified, respectful, but not fawning.

"And I know where the guavas came from. New Orleans. I'll bet he has his porter friends bring food up to Chicago for him."

"Well, the fish couldn't be better," Frank said. "What do you think? Should we hire them?"

"If they'll have us."

WHILE THE CARLTONS cleaned up inside, Mamah and Frank sat out in the garden under the big oak. It was early June, and the mosquitoes had not yet become a menace. Frank was rarely home now. Midway Gardens was to open

June 23, and the place was nowhere near finished. Everyone was in a panic, he told her, from the construction foreman to the orchestra conductor to the investors.

Frank regaled her with stories about life at the construction site, about the sylphlike young woman working as a model for Iannelli, the sculptor, who was creating the mold for the concrete sprites that would decorate the winter garden. He described how she walked every day past the leering union men to the sculptor's shack, her head held high. How the sculptor faced away as she stripped off her clothes, then turned back when she gave the word. How the girl stood with both arms raised over her head for hours on end holding an imaginary sphere, while the artist shaped her round breasts and muscular thighs from his block of wax.

"What a professional," Mamah said admiringly.

"I wish Iannelli were half the pro."

"Why do you say that?"

"Ah, he's bullheaded. I told him precisely how to change the tilt of her head, and he ignored me. He spent an entire week making another model that was no better."

"What did you say to him?"

"Words are useless with him."

Her eyebrows went up when she saw Frank's face flush. "What did you do?"

He shifted in the slatted chair and played with the crease in his pants. "Poked a couple of holes in the damn thing."

The air went out of her chest. She waited. As Frank let go of a few details, the scene began to form in her mind. Frank entering the sculptor's shack alone, raising the cloth covering over the wax model only to discover a new version as wrong as the last. Frank lifting the tip of his cane reflexively and thrusting it into the soft eyes of the figure, then covering up the model for Iannelli to make his own rude discovery.

"I lost my head," he said.

Mamah considered the battle at hand, judging whether to choose it. Frank was under pressure; everyone at the site was short-tempered. She began to speak but held her tongue. She did not belong in this fight.

"I'll start over with him on Monday—apologize," he said.

Mamah relaxed and leaned back in her chair.

The only sound in the evening quiet was the clatter of pans in the kitchen. When the noise ended, she saw the light in the bunk room go on.

"Do you think the Carltons will survive all right?"

"They want the job. Vogelsang says they're churchgoers. I'm sure they'll hook up with a congregation."

"That's just my point. In Chicago, even in Oak Park, there's the Colored Baptist Church. They would find friends there, go out in the evening. But up here I don't know what they'll run into."

"They'll make their way. I'm not worried about it." He ran his hand along her forearm. "What are you going to do now that you'll have some spare time?"

She breathed in contentedly. "It's a luxury to think about."

"Is Ellen out of the doghouse?"

"You mean will I go back to translating for her? Yes, I will."

"And all this business of who she authorized to do what?"

"Oh, I'm not letting her off the hook on that account. And heaven knows, I don't agree with her that women will somehow doom the human race if they go out into the workplace in large numbers. Still, I don't believe anyone else has written as powerfully about personal freedom or reforming the institution of marriage. What can I say? She's not perfect, but I can't forget what she did for me."

"She should be grateful to *you*. Ralph Seymour called the office this week and said sales of *The Woman Movement* have been quite brisk."

"Pardon me while I gloat." Mamah chuckled to herself. "That's good news for Ralph, too. I remember when his head proofreader came to him midway through *Love and Ethics* and said, 'Mr. Seymour, I have been with you twenty years, but I would rather give up my job than finish this book.' Ralph had the courage to publish Ellen when others wouldn't."

"Ralph agrees completely with us. Ellen Key is the new star of the movement in this country. She never would have gotten to such a place if you hadn't translated her."

"Wouldn't it be nice if she would just acknowledge that? We shall see. I have a couple of essays to do still. But I'm nearly finished with the work she authorized. Anyway, I've been thinking about doing something of my own."

Frank's face lit up. "Funny you should mention that. I ran into Arnell Potter at the station when I came in this morning. He's ready to retire. Sell the newspaper. And I was just thinking, why don't we buy it? Why don't you become the new editor of the *Weekly Home News*? You'd be dazzling. I could write a guest editorial every once in a while."

Mamah began to laugh. "You're not serious."

"Don't say no yet. Just consider it."

"Ah, the ironies are rich."

"I know a country paper is small potatoes. But think of the potential. If you wrote your own stories—and you probably would at first—you'd have an official reason to call people up and say, 'May I come out and look at that prize hog everybody's talking about?'"

Mamah smiled at the prospect.

"You think I'm kidding, but I'm not. You'd be brilliant at it. The minute people meet you, they'll love you. Everyone does. And you'd actually care about their damn hogs. I know you. Anyway, it's something that could work for you, especially if you're not going to come to Japan for the whole time."

Mamah had already told him that she would not be going for the duration when the Imperial Hotel work began in earnest. Her mind was made up. Six months had been too long the last time. Frank had not taken the news well, but the fact that he was discussing it meant that the idea was finding some acceptance.

"Look, Mame, if you want your own project, this is a great one. God knows it would change our profile around here. And you don't have to do it Arnell's way. Break some new ground—introduce Ellen Key to the ladies of Iowa County. Get them buzzing about erotic love."

Mamah chuckled again. "Now, there's a notion."

"Sleep on it a couple of nights. That's all I'm saying."

THE NEWSPAPER IDEA kept her wide awake that night.

Mamah played with the editor role, imagining herself reading the wire service messages as they clacked over the telegraph machine. What could be sweeter than to commandeer the enemy's ship? But another idea had taken hold in her mind. She believed she was ready to write her own book.

Freedom of the Personality. She said it out loud. Too stuffy for a title, she thought, when it came into her ears. But that would be the gist of it. The book had to be less philosophical than Ellen's dense prose. Simpler, more direct.

By morning the concept had shaped itself into something new. She woke up knowing she would collect stories of contemporary women, all kinds of women who had struggled against the odds to make authentic lives for themselves.

The idea made Mamah's heart leap. It was too expensive to travel around interviewing. For now she would make up a sheet of questions to mail to those who immediately came to mind. Ellen Key. Charlotte Perkins Gilman. Else Lasker-Schüler. And others who weren't famous at all. If things got better between them, she would ask Lizzie, too.

She wouldn't lie, though. She'd tell about more than the triumphs. She would write about the pitfalls—the way some women mistook sexual freedom for true selfhood. She would write about walls up ahead that were waiting to be hit. The mistakes. The guilt and regret. Not just the chances seized but the chances missed.

The problem with Ellen's books was that they were too philosophical, with few real-life examples. What would she have given back in Berlin to read true stories of other women's journeys toward personal freedom? Everything. If she could collect real accounts from women who'd gotten past their fears and the scorn and gossip to find their own worth in the world, to author their own futures, how powerful that would be.

She would have to tell her own story, too, though she didn't know where to begin. For now she would write in her journal simply to get words on paper. She would imagine Else's face, that's what she would do, and tell it as if her friend were sitting across from her in the café.

Mamah felt an excitement she hadn't experienced since she discovered Ellen's work. Ideas were snapping like sparks inside her head, and she was afraid she might lose them. She ran out of the bedroom to fetch a pen and paper from her office and nearly knocked Julian to the ground, so surprised was she to find him standing quietly in the hallway, straightening a Japanese print.

CHAPTER 48

JUNE 23, 1914

BREAK OUT THE BEADED DRESS.

F.

The telegram arrived the day before her departure for Chicago. She had told Frank she would wear the beaded dress on the twenty-seventh. What he didn't know was that the gown he'd bought her in Italy had long since been "broken out." During the past month, she had put on the slip and gauzy beaded overdress a dozen times, turning in front of her bedroom mirror to assess her backside, then her silhouette, debating whether to wear it to the Midway Gardens opening. In the four years since he'd given it to her, the dress had hung unworn in a series of closets while her body rearranged itself.

Mamah had always hated vanity in middle-aged women. She and Mattie had promised each other they would let age take them gracefully, without the henna and powder. But looking at her reflection now, she hated what she saw. It wasn't the dress, which was loose and forgiving. It was the softer, less-vivid, slightly out-of-date woman who stared back at her. At forty-five, she didn't mind gray hair coming in or the crease between her brows. What she despised was the pull of gravity, because it made her look tired, while inside she felt young, with the crispest clarity of mind she'd known since she was twenty-five.

She tugged off the dress, folded it, and put it in her suitcase. How she looked wasn't the important thing. It would be Frank's night, anyway—a celebration long overdue.

Frank had not been home at all for two weeks, and only intermittently for the month before that. They had missed observing each other's birthdays. In the last days before the opening, he wasn't even returning to his pied-à-terre, sleeping instead on a pile of moving quilts and who knew what at the Gardens. He was working into the wee hours until he couldn't anymore, then rising at six to work again.

During his last visit home, he had paced the floor, spilling out his worries. The developers hadn't been able to raise adequate funds to cover building costs, but, overconfident, they had begun the construction anyway. They'd paid him five thousand dollars but now they were talking about settling the rest of his fee with stock. Poor Mueller, the contractor, had been forced to break the news to his workers on Friday that their wages for the week would be late.

Still, the place was going up, he told her, by God, it was going up. And what a cast of characters was on-site every day—painters, sculptors, master tradesmen, engineers, musicians, chefs. All of them talented, all trying to make their mark. Between the artists and the union reps, the place was crawling with more prima donnas than an opera company reunion. Iannelli was but one. Frank had the creeping fear that he'd made an awful mistake in hiring a couple of well-known Modernist painters to do murals. He'd given them general guidelines and specific colors to use. What he'd seen so far, however, was all wrong.

"The murals are going to fight the architecture," he told her. "I know it already."

"Then stand your ground," Mamah said. "You're worn down, but now is not the time to falter, not on a job this important. This is the first time the public will really experience one of your buildings. It's going to open the eyes of thousands—millions—over time. Why use murals that don't make you happy? You can do them later."

"You're right, of course." Frank squeezed her hand.

She knew he didn't need her advice. It took immense ego to build an enormous structure the likes of which had never been seen before, all the while assuring doubters that it would turn out brilliantly. But it took courage and vision, too. What he needed was her support, and she gave it without condition.

Break out the beaded dress. She laughed out loud. With bricklayers and angry artists to deal with, he was planning each little detail of opening night, down to what Mamah would wear. It was pure Frank, orchestrating every bit of the experience. And in his way, Frank was telling her what they both knew—the opening was a coming-out for them. It would be the unveiling of his first public building in Chicago, and their first public appearance together since the scandal. He wanted the whole thing, including her, to be perfect.

WHEN SHE ARRIVED in Chicago, she left her bags at the coach house and hopped on the El train to the south side. She got off at Fifty-ninth and Jackson Park, the same stop she had exited so many times when she was attending classes at the university. Looking at the young people passing her along the Midway Plaisance, she imagined what a curiosity she must have seemed ten years before, when she was studying the novel with Robert Herrick. She had thought of the students as peers. But these college kids—had she grown hopelessly old, or were they babies even then and she just hadn't noticed?

In the distance, she saw that the two square towers anchoring either end of the long yellow-brick building had risen higher since she was last here. Frank had stacked up more balconies, one on top of another, in a feat of derring-do. He called these towers belvederes, and she could see that the balconies would offer fine views. Above the top floor, a cantilevered roof seemed to float free of the building beneath it.

As she got closer, she saw how complex the surface texture of the building was. How playful. Every plane seemed to be decorated in some pattern, from the yellow-brick-and-mortar base to the concrete-block walls above that were patterned like woven fabric. To announce the carefree atmosphere of the space within, Frank had stationed statues of sprites on either side of the main entrance, their heads bent down. They seemed to wink at Mamah as she passed through the entry.

Inside one belvedere, an artist standing on scaffolding was putting the first brushes of color on the dreaded mural. She could see lines sketched out on the wall above her but could not discern in them the disaster Frank envisioned. She walked on, down a long hallway and into the soaring indoor winter garden, where tiers multiplied into more tiers as her eyes went up and around.

A concrete mixer in the middle of the room made the space rumble. Fumes from wet mortar floated in the afternoon light pouring through the windows. A spry old deliveryman tipped his hat as he whizzed past her with a cartful of flowers and green plants. "Ain't this something?" he called out.

She tried to imagine what the tiers would look like tomorrow night. Diners would be sitting at tables, looking down on the checkerboard dance floor at the center of the room. All the balconies would eventually trail ivy. The place *did* bring to mind the Hanging Gardens of Babylon. Frank had said some people thought it looked like Aztec pyramids.

She saw those things and more—the beer gardens she and Frank had visited in Berlin and Potsdam; the terraces they'd walked in Italy. The statues of women Frank had used to line the sunken gardens brought to mind the rectangular stone pillars topped with carved human heads that she'd seen in Italian gardens. But they reminded her of Japan, too—their angular headdresses like abstract geisha wigs. Frank had fused what he'd experienced and seen into something entirely new: a waking fantasy.

More than anything, what struck Mamah was the absolute joy he had expressed at Midway Gardens. After all its changes, the structure had turned out to be as playful as the sprites at the front door. *This* was a "good times place." It would bring delight to so many people.

Everywhere she looked, she saw him at play. Up at the top of the walls, in a frieze of stained-glass windows, scattered red-glass kites trailed black tails against the sky outside. She imagined Frank holding the strings to each of them, keeping them all afloat at once, his heart as full as any kite flyer's ever was.

"May-mah!" John Vogelsang was flying through the winter garden when he spotted her and bent down to buss her on the cheek. "How are you? Does Frank know you're here?"

"No, I sneaked out here to taste the excitement."

"Don't talk to me about tasting. I have tasted so much today, my tongue hurts."

"Are you ready?"

He shrugged. "If the waiters show up. If the cooks show up. If the people come."

"The people will come," she said.

"Say, how are the Carltons working out?"

"They're wonderful, though I think Gertrude is a little lonely out in the country. She confessed as I left that she wished she were going into the city."

"She can cook, can't she?"

"It's a miracle."

"Have her prepare callalloo. We couldn't get enough of it in our house. She can't get real callalloo in these parts, so she uses spinach." A worried-looking man approached Vogelsang then, and the restaurateur made his apologies to her. "Okra and crab meat," he called as he waved goodbye. "You won't believe it."

Mamah walked out to a balcony overlooking the summer garden. The orchestra was rehearsing in the pavilion, and she listened closely. They were playing Saint-Saëns, and it sounded exquisite. She understood what Frank had done—created a symphony hall with these receding terraces and balconies. Cars might be rumbling down Cottage Grove Avenue, but from where she stood, the music was as clear as if she were in the first balcony of the Berlin Opera House.

She caught sight of him below, going over some drawings with a bearded man, probably Paul Mueller. Out in the vast open-air square, chairs and tables were lined up in perfect rows. The sight of them sent a pleasant shiver of anticipation down her arms. Lord, how long had it been since she'd gone to a party? How she loved them! She thought of the beaded dress and the frightening prospect of people staring at her tomorrow night, eager to get a gander at Frank's "affinity." She turned and hurried out the front door to the train stop.

A HALF HOUR LATER, Mamah sat in a barber's chair in the hair salon at the Palmer House. Once before, when she was staying there during a visit with the children, a sweet woman had trimmed her long hair. But that woman was nowhere in sight. A young man stood before her now, holding the picture she'd seen displayed in the window. She had come to the salon not knowing what she wanted done to her hair, only something miraculous that would make her feel pretty and young again. When she'd seen the picture in the window, she'd stopped in her tracks. The illustration showed a woman with short hair cropped at the jawline. It was Else's haircut.

"It's called the Curtain, madam," the hairdresser said. The man had a solemn demeanor at odds with the name embroidered on his barber coat—Curly. His fiercely wavy hair, which he had chosen to celebrate rather than fight, was clearly the source of his nickname. Parted on the left, his hair rose up and out from the right side of his head in a mass of miniature waves that shaped themselves into a tilted cone, the point of which was a good eight inches from his scalp.

Mamah shifted on the red leather seat of the barber chair. Looking at the man's outlandish hair, she regretted the impulse that had propelled her in here. Damn vanity! She wondered if his haircut had a name, too.

The barber wrapped paper tape around her neck and threw a cape over her. Mamah breathed in and pointed to the picture of the Curtain. "I'll have that," she said.

"But madam, your hair is not straight," he protested.

"Straight enough," she said. "I'll take my chances."

He began chopping her hair off in chunks a foot long, then worked to get the thick mop even. It shocked her to see mounds of dark brown hair piled like hay on the floor. The man had a low stool on wheels and rolled around on the thing, circling her, snipping her hair from underneath. The whole experience seemed bizarre, yet she found herself confiding to the barber about the opening and what she planned to wear.

When he stood up, he took a tapered comb from a jar of alcohol, rinsed and dried it in the sink, then neatened the part down the middle of her head. In the mirror, a woman not unlike Else stared back at her. A smile spread across Mamah's face. The haircut was wonderful—stark, unconventional, and pretty all at once.

"Very European," the hairdresser said, pleased with himself. "Tip your head down."

She obeyed, and the hair fell forward. "You see how the Curtain works? Now lift up your face." The barber beamed. "And there you are," he said triumphantly. "Unveiled."

CHAPTER 49

There were things she wanted to remember from the opening night of Midway Gardens. The music, to be sure. The smells of corsages and wet cement. The feeling everyone seemed to have that they were the lucky ones—to be here at this moment in this magical place.

Some things she would not be able to forget even if she wanted to. The lights in particular. Midway Gardens was a fairyland at night. Inside the winter garden, globes hung like bunched balloons in corners around the dance floor. Outside, poles studded with small white lights soared upward from the tops of walls like glittering needles. Candle flames flickered along the tiered balconies.

Frank called Midway Gardens his "city by the sea." It was not a city, and it was not by the sea. But if one squinted just right, as Mamah did that night without her spectacles, the candlelight on the terraces brought to mind vistas she had seen from the deck of a ship—villages flung across the sides of mountains, their cottage window lamps glowing in the distance.

She would never forget the warmth of people toward her that night. Frank stood by her side, his cheeks high with color, gallantly introducing her to one person after another. Among them was Margaret Anderson, the owner of the *Little Review*.

"Frank showed me a little while ago the Goethe poem you translated." The towering beauty drew on a short cigarette and winked at Frank. "Quite an impressive find."

Mamah laughed. "He's rather proud of it. Carries it in his pocket."

"I'd like to publish 'Hymn to Nature.' We're scheduled up for another six months, but sometime after the first of the year." Her keen gray eyes panned the room as she talked. "What do you think?"

Frank beamed. Mamah summoned some presence. "That would be lovely," she said. As the woman walked away, Mamah whispered excitedly to

Frank, "She publishes Sandburg and Amy Lowell, for God's sake. I can't imagine . . ."

"She knows a comer when she sees one."

He took her hand and walked her into the winter garden. The scene was a blur of color and motion, evening gowns swirling. It had been so long since she had danced with Frank, she'd forgotten how graceful he was on his feet. They waltzed through several songs. "I love the haircut with your dress," he said at one point, burying his nose near her ear. "Have I told you that you are the most beautiful woman in this place?"

Mamah laughed. " 'In Xanadu did Kubla Khan a stately pleasure dome decree . . . ' How does that poem go? 'With walls and towers . . . and gardens bright . . . ' "

"Did you hear me?"

She drew back to look at his face. Earlier, when he was talking to journalists, he'd lifted his chin and literally looked down his nose at them; later, there'd been a wicked glee in his eyes as he shared some inside joke with Ed Waller, one of the partners in the Gardens. Now there was a familiar tenderness on his face.

"Yes," she said. "Thank you."

More than anything, she would remember John Wright that night. He'd been working tirelessly next to his father during the construction of the Gardens. He had to be as exhausted as Frank, but across the room, he looked ebullient as he laughed with his friends. This was his night, too.

She had not seen him since he was a boy of perhaps sixteen. He was a handsome young man, with Catherine's coloring. When he caught her watching him from across the room, he didn't hesitate. He walked immediately to her.

"How are you this evening, Mamah?" He took her hand into both of his.

They stood talking for a few moments. It was warm but small talk, nothing that veered close to the wounds.

John Wright was flaunting his mother's rule by even standing in the same room with Mamah. But he was a man now, his own man, evidently, for she found him gracious and seemingly unruffled by her physical presence two feet away, or by the glances their nearness attracted from others. When he took his leave, his eyes lingered for a moment on hers.

"My father is happy," he said.

Mamah struggled to keep tears from spilling over.

CHAPTER 50

My name is Mamah Borthwick. Mamah is a nickname for Martha, and is pronounced "May-muh." It's a name that puzzles when first encountered. People ask,
"Is that 'Mama,' like 'Mother'?" Most new acquaintances begin, as this one does,
with an explanation.

My parents did not pluck Mamah out of the Bible, nor did they name me after a
beloved aunt. I'm the only Mamah I have ever heard of. I wish there were a great
heroine from history who inspired the choice, but there isn't. It is simply a loving so-
briquet bestowed by my grandmother.

There may be a handful of readers for whom the name will prompt a memory,
though. It's possible that they will recall reading the scandalous headlines about a
woman named Mamah whose affair with a married man was the stuff that "news"
editors dream of. I am that woman, and this book includes my own account of the
events that led to those painful headlines.

I have traveled a harrowing path since the yellow journals put me on their front
pages. Yet in my darkest hour of humiliation, I found hope in the words of a wonderful Swedish philosopher. I have translated her work so that others can benefit from
her wisdom. But I've come to understand that many women throughout my life
have eased my journey. To all of them, I am deeply indebted.

In the following pages you will find the stories of women who are struggling
to live true, to make honest and meaningful lives for themselves despite the fact that,
as a gender, we do not share full voter enfranchisement, equal pay, or the freedom of
personality men take as their right. This book is an attempt to name those struggles.
As a group, too often we talk of the vote when we speak of the Woman Question. But
there are many other aspects to realizing one's selfhood.

Women are storytellers. It is how we bring one another comfort and illumina-
tion. Thus the format of this book. There are those of you who will read my own
account looking for the comeuppances. You will find plenty. I hope you will also recognize the moments of love and grace. If I can cast a little light on someone else's

path, if another woman can take courage for her own struggles from the true stories in this volume, then they will have been worth the telling.

MAMAH LEANED CLOSE to her typewriter to reread the introduction she'd just written for her book. She changed a few words, then stretched her arms and arched her back. *Not so bad for a first swing at it,* she thought.

Outside, Lucky set to barking as horses clip-clopped into the courtyard. The children were back from the Bartons' house. Since their arrival at Taliesin a week earlier, they had been mostly on horseback, riding either to the Porters' or back and forth to the next farm over. Out the window, Mamah could see four children, her own plus Emma Barton and Frankie, Jennie and Andrew's son. When the four of them weren't out riding, they were in the barn hanging around, helping Tom Brunker groom the horses. Tom was a tender mark—a widower, with young children of his own over in Milwaukee. There was another draw for Martha and John in the barn, too: the imminent birth of a foal.

"See that belly?" Tom said when Mamah came into the barn. "She's bagged up good. Her teats has been waxed over for a week."

John pointed to a crusty discharge on her nipples. "The wax keeps the milk in till her baby's ready to suck," he said. He turned to his mother with a look of pride at being the bearer of that information.

The mare nipped from time to time at her distended belly.

"Won't be long now," Tom said, chewing on his pipe.

"Today?" Martha asked. She was crouched down with her bottom resting on the back of her boots, peering through a space in the middle of the gate.

"Could be today."

The children went back to the barn at intervals throughout the morning. They were excited and restless, racing through the house and into the studio, where they were chased out by the draftsmen.

That afternoon Gertrude made sliced-beef sandwiches for all of them. The kitchen was the other room where they'd figured out they were welcome, and they often hung about the cook as she worked.

Listening to Gertrude recite a funny Bajan rhyme, Mamah recalled a conversation she'd had in Italy with Frank about moving to Wisconsin. "How will I survive without art galleries and opera?" she'd asked him wryly.

"We'll bring culture to the farm," he'd promised her, and he had kept his word. There had been plenty of music and poetry at Taliesin. But Mamah thought the Carltons, in their own way, also brought a connection to the bigger world outside Spring Green, and she was pleased that the children were getting a dose of it.

Mamah tagged along with them as they headed down to the river with their poles. She lay back on a flat rock and covered her face with her hat.

The children had developed their own rhythm at the farm this summer. John came in from Waukesha full of good humor after a visit with the Belknaps, though Martha had started off anxious. Mamah thought it was because Lizzie had brought her up from Oak Park and was taut as a spring when they'd arrived. Thankfully, Frank was away. Lizzie commented very little about the house or farm, though Mamah caught her inspecting everything closely.

Mamah longed for the old familiarity she'd shared with her sister, the times when they'd stayed up past midnight talking about so many things—their parents, Jessie, love, life, a woman's ambitions in a man's world. Now Lizzie was cool. She was warm with the children, though. They loved her, and over the days they seemed to soften her. A couple of times when Mamah said, "Do you remember . . . ," Lizzie went back with her into childhood, where they both felt safe.

There was an uneasy peace between them by the time Lizzie left. Mamah was afraid to hope for too much too soon. And she worried about what the future held for her sister. She'd come to realize how much Lizzie's world had been torn apart when she left.

When Mamah married Edwin and brought her sister into the household, Lizzie had reveled in being the quirky auntie living in the basement. That was long over. She had already moved out of her apartment downstairs in deference to the new Mrs. Cheney. A single professional woman like Lizzie could keep her social standing though she was not part of a larger household; old friends would still include her in their dinner parties. And she would always be adored by the children. But Mamah could not deny to herself the obvious: Something irretrievable had been lost to her sister.

WHEN MAMAH AND the children returned from the river a couple of hours later, the commotion around the barn caused all the kids to break into a run. She hurried behind them through the barn door.

"Got a foal!" Tom hollered when they neared the stall.

A colt lay on the straw. The mother horse licked its eyes and nostrils. Tom stood in the corner of the stall. They watched as the foal wobbled to his feet, then found his mother's milk.

"Didn't have to do nothin'," he said. He patted the mare's hindquarter. "Mama took care of everything."

Huddled together with John and Martha at the stall's gate, Mamah savored their closeness. The smell of their heated little bodies, mixed with the odor of hay, was sweet indeed. She watched with them for a good while before going back to the house.

In the kitchen, she was dismayed to find Gertrude crying.

"I think we should leave," Gertrude said, wiping her eyes with her apron. "Things don't go so well."

"Are you homesick?" Mamah asked.

"Yes. In Chicago things are better."

"Are you happy with the work you're doing here?"

"Yes," Gertrude said. "That's not a problem."

"Then why don't you go back to Chicago next weekend? It's not hard. Julian has gone back a couple of times, why shouldn't you?" Mamah put her hand on Gertrude's shoulder. "We think you're doing a wonderful job. And we would love to have you stay."

The woman shrugged. "Thank you, madam."

THAT NIGHT, MAMAH climbed into bed with Martha. John had Lucky under the covers with him in his bed across the room.

"Are you awake, John?" Mamah asked.

"Yes."

"Martha?"

"Uh-huh."

"I wanted to ask you something. Are you sometimes homesick when you're here?"

There was a long silence.

"Uh-huh," Martha said finally.

"I know it must be hard for you to leave your friends every summer to come here."

John's voice came through the darkness. "Don't you ever get homesick for Oak Park?"

The question caught her by surprise. She knew what he was asking. *Don't you ever miss us?*

"There isn't a day goes by that I don't miss you. And some days . . . well, I just wish for things that can't be right now. But I carry both of you around in my heart all the time. It's funny—it's as if I have a little room inside where I can go, and there you are. And that makes me calm as can be."

No one spoke after that. The only sound in the room was the wheezing in and out of the dog's breathing.

CHAPTER 51

"I keep wondering if Else has left." Mamah spoke to Frank from a corner of the dining area, where she was scraping mud from Martha's boots into a wastecan. Else had been on her mind since the Austrian prince's assassination took over the headlines. Mamah scoured the *Dodgeville Chronicle* for the few dribbles of international news the paper might print, but she had to wait until Frank brought home the Chicago papers to catch up with the crisis in Europe. The papers he'd brought Friday night were full of news about women and children crowding Berlin's train stations, trying to leave the country.

"I had meant to write her and ask if I could put her in my book. You know, have her respond to some questions. Now . . ." Mamah brushed the boots, readying them for a coat of oil. "I keep thinking of all those young men who hung around the café, talking about art and philosophy. They've probably all been conscripted by now." She shook her head. "Whenever I think of Else and her son, or Berlin, I find myself praying."

It was Tuesday morning, and Frank was eating a quick breakfast before he left for the train. He was headed back to Midway Gardens to finish it up, and was leaving behind Herb Fritz. Herb had expected a cool country sojourn when he came to work with Emil on the architecture exhibit for San Francisco. But it was unbearably humid in Wisconsin. When Mamah had gone to open her bureau this morning, she'd found the drawers stuck hopelessly shut.

She walked out to see Frank off. "Take the kids to see the threshers," he said, pecking her on the cheek.

"Plan to." She waved as he drove down the driveway and out to the highway through the fields. Men in giant threshing machines were expected momentarily at the homesteads around Taliesin; they were pushing their way across the countryside, farm by farm.

Standing in the garden after he left, she could smell the rosemary she'd planted. A surprising number of flowers were thriving. She was drawn to motion around a bushy feverfew and walked over to have a look. White butterflies orbited crazily around it while a hundred bees dove in and out of the universe inside, collecting pollen. When she took off her spectacles to wipe the sweat from the bridge of her nose, the whole bush appeared to quiver with moving life.

Usually at this time of year, she could barely look at her garden without thinking of work. In the ninety-degree humidity, some stems slumped over. There were asters and coneflowers to deadhead. The peony leaves were turning deep purple and needed to be removed.

"David," she called out when she saw the gardener. "I see some things that are begging to be cut back." She pointed out the decaying foliage.

"I'll get on it." David Lindblom wiped a sleeve over his face. "I need to talk to you about something, Mrs. Borthwick," he said.

"Surely." She sat down on a bench in the shade and motioned to a chair nearby.

"I don't want Julian Carlton helping in the garden anymore," David said. "He's got a bad temper. I can't work with the man."

She frowned. "What does he do?"

"Says he only takes his orders from Mr. Wright. He gets mad when I ask him to do something."

"Did you speak to Mr. Wright about it?"

"I was going to, but I missed him. I guess Emil's had his problems with Carlton, too."

"When you see Julian, will you tell him to come and talk to me?"

"Yes, ma'am."

JULIAN'S FACE WAS covered in tiny beads of sweat when he appeared a few minutes later. He stood stiffly in front of her, as if at attention. He was spotless, as always, but there was something distressing in his demeanor. He seemed terrified.

"They all pick on me. Emil has turned everyone against me. He has the men running to Mr. Wright with lies."

"That's not true," Mamah said. "Mr. Wright has never once mentioned it. But why do you argue with Emil and David?"

"They order me around. Some of them call me George. I am a man. I don't have to take that."

Mamah knew what it meant to a Pullman porter to be called George. It was an insult, though it was used all the time. It said, *You don't have a name.*

"Do I work for them, or do I work for Mr. Wright?"

"You work for Mr. Wright and me, of course. But in the garden, you have to take David's direction. And in the barn, Tom is the boss. You'll have to find a way to make peace. We can't have people getting into arguments all the time. I'll speak to Emil."

A satisfied smile spread across Julian's face. "Very good, madam," he said.

ON THURSDAY AFTERNOON, Mamah went out to the barn with the children to look at the foal. They were crouched down, as usual, in the dark aisle between the rows of stalls, looking through the gate to where the foal was. What sounded like mayhem broke out at the end of the aisle.

"Saddle it!" It was Emil's voice. In the dimness, she saw him standing next to a horse. On the other side of the animal, she could see only Julian's legs.

"I don't work for you, white man." Julian's voice quaked with rage.

"I said saddle it, you black son of a bitch!"

"I'll saddle it," Julian cried out. "I'll send you and your goddamn horse straight to hell."

Mamah held her breath, certain the two men would start punching each other. Martha leaned in to her side, covering her ears. When Julian turned and ran out, Mamah gathered up the children as Emil mounted his horse and rode away.

In the studio later, Mamah found Emil worked into a lather, recounting for Herb what had happened in the barn.

"He's not right in the head," Emil told her. "Blows up at the smallest thing. Threatens people. David has been afraid of him since the day he came."

"I just talked to David not a day ago. He didn't say he was *afraid* of him."

"Before I ever met Carlton, David told me to stay out of his way. Said he was an angry, hotheaded devil. Well"—Emil inhaled deeply—"that he is."

Out in the courtyard, Billy Weston confirmed it. "He's smart and acts polite, but he's got a desperate streak. He can't get along with any of the other men."

Mamah went to her bedroom and sat down at her writing desk to gather her thoughts. It took her only a moment to reach a decision. She would have to let the Carltons go.

The whole situation was a pity. Gertrude was as fine a cook as any Mamah had ever come across, and a lovely person on top of it. Even Julian was an ideal servant. He'd seemed so good-natured before all this. He'd been here only a few weeks, though, hardly long enough to really know a person. There was an angry part of Julian that he obviously hadn't shown the Vogelsangs when he'd worked for them. She had no illusions about changing his personality.

Still, it could not have been easy for Gertrude and Julian to come into a situation with so many personalities to adjust to. Mamah remembered her own first months at Taliesin. What must it be like to be a complete outsider, and a colored man to boot, among these fellows? She chided herself for being so naive as to think a dozen people could live together without repercussions. It was darn near miraculous that there hadn't been trouble before now.

Makeshift as it was, Taliesin was a real community. There were strong ties among the men. To her, they were family. She knew about their fiancées and wives and children, their worries. A few of them had been here during the worst of the scandal. She would never forget how they had stepped forward to protect her and Frank when the posse of vigilantes was supposedly on its way.

If there was cruelty among them, Mamah never saw it, and she thought she saw them pretty clearly for who they were. It had taken time, but the men had enfolded her into their society. They accepted her as the boss when Frank was away. Only yesterday Emil had approached her with a design question, and Billy with a construction decision. She had managed to give both of them direction. She grew more confident by the day about running the farm. "Nice work," Frank had said the few times she'd made decisions in his absence.

Still, she wished he were here now.

After dinner Mamah called Julian into the kitchen, where Gertrude was cleaning dishes.

"I'm not putting all the blame on you for the trouble we've had here, Julian," she said. "Your work, and Gertrude's, has been very good. But you seem to have too many personal differences with the rest of the men. It may look big, but this is really a small place, and when people don't get along, we all feel the strain. I'm sorry, but I think it's best if you and Gertrude go back to Chicago."

Julian's voice trembled as if he were about to cry. "Does Mr. Wright know this?"

"I speak for Mr. Wright," she said. "When you finish the week Saturday night, it will be the end of your stay here. Someone will drive you to Spring Green on Sunday to catch the train."

Gertrude had kept her head down as Mamah spoke. Now she glanced fearfully at Julian. In that one look, Mamah saw a whole relationship. She didn't doubt that Julian bore down hard on Gertrude.

"Very well," he said finally.

Mamah touched Gertrude's arm before turning and leaving the kitchen.

THAT NIGHT SHE COULDN'T fall asleep. She went into the children's bedroom and cuddled next to Martha's damp little body. Mamah had always slept deeply here in the country. Now she heard the hot breeze stir the oak outside the bedroom. The trees roused themselves intermittently to rustle leaves, then fell back into a torpor.

She stayed awake listening to the high, sustained trills of frogs and insects. For a few minutes, she was a girl in a thin cotton nightgown again, splayed out on her bed, trying not to move in the stifling humidity. She took all of the sounds for granted, back then. As a child, she had never bothered to ask what insects made which part of the nighttime racket. The sounds seemed to her now the very essence of her early summers. She thought of the houses on her block when she was a girl. Voices from the dark porches. Families sitting on steps, speaking low, laughing. The certainty of it all.

Mamah stroked wet strands of hair off Martha's forehead. *How charmed a childhood I was given,* she thought. As she began to drift off, it occurred to her that it was time to start French lessons for Martha. She made a mental note to find a tutor in Oak Park for the fall.

FRIDAY PASSED WITHOUT any fights. At lunchtime Julian served the men in the dining room, and there appeared no rancor between them.

Saturday, Gertrude knocked on Mamah's bedroom door at eight in the morning. She wore the same worried look she had two days earlier. "You have a phone call, ma'am," she said.

"The threshermen are here!" Dorothea Barton's voice was girlish on the other end of the line. "Are you coming over?"

"We wouldn't miss it."

"Can you hold off until after lunch? The men want to get everything running."

"Around one o'clock?"

"That's perfect. Now, say, I hope you'll stay on for dinner. We always have a little celebration. Sam plays his fiddle, and people dance. You know how our living room floor kinda dips down in one corner? By the end of the night, we're all bunched up in that spot. Oh, but it's a hoot."

"What can we bring?"

"Yourselves. And we wouldn't turn away one of Gertrude's cakes."

Mamah glanced over at the scowling cook, who was frying bacon. "I can't promise it, but we'll see." After she hung up, she considered speaking to Gertrude, then walked instead into the dining room, where Julian was putting out plates for breakfast.

"Good morning," she said to him.

"Good morning." His aspect had changed from the weepiness of two days before. Julian was her height, and he gazed into her face with an arrogant coolness. He had on the white jacket he always wore to serve, and then she noticed what else. He was wearing a pair of Frank's linen trousers.

Mamah walked outside into the courtyard, trying to calm herself. She circled the house, looking for the men, but could not find any of them. Were they out in the fields helping? She went back inside and called into the kitchen, "The children and I won't be here for breakfast." Then she hurried into the bedroom to change clothes and awaken Martha and John.

In minutes she and the children were out the door with biscuits and bacon Gertrude had wrapped for them in a napkin. Mamah felt better the minute they were away from the house.

"Why is Gertrude angry, Mama?" John asked when they were in the car. The cook had not responded to the boy's morning hello.

"She and Julian are leaving, honey. They haven't worked out. Julian seems to fight with everyone."

"Oh."

"Are you sad to see them leave?" Mamah asked.

"Her, yes. Him, no," John said.

"Where are we going?" Martha asked.

"We aren't invited to the Bartons' until one. So I thought we'd go fishing in a new spot."

They ate breakfast on a sandy stretch along the river, then set to digging for worms. When the children had a supply, Mamah sat down on the blanket near a patch of Queen Anne's lace. She yanked off one of the pods and worked at peeling it open.

It *was* possible Frank had given Julian those pants. Unlikely, though, since they were part of the suit he'd had tailored in Italy. No, it was more likely that Julian had gone into Frank's closet and helped himself. There was an awful sense of violation in that notion. She didn't want to picture Julian creeping around their bedroom while they were out of the house. But she suspected that was what had happened.

Around eleven-thirty, they piled back into the car and left a dusty cloud behind them as they bumped over the rutted road toward Taliesin. Ahead, heat shimmered in waves; red-winged blackbirds started up from cattails as the car approached. When they passed the Bartons' house, the sound of the steam engine was deafening. The smell of the breeze had changed from cow manure to diesel fuel. Why had she found threshing time so captivating last summer? True, it was a time for neighbors to gather and help one another. Now, though, it seemed noisy and dirty. In the field, the engine sent a black plume of smoke snaking up, and spreading out to smudge the sky. She didn't want John or Martha near the thresher—you could lose a limb in a blink. She would have to be on alert all afternoon to keep them at a distance.

When Mamah walked into the house, she sought Julian out. He was setting the table in the worker's temporary dining room near her office. He turned a baleful stare toward her when she spoke.

"Julian, I've thought it over," she said. "I believe it would be fine for you to leave today. We will pay you for the full week. You and Gertrude can pack up after lunch."

"We will finish up properly," he said matter-of-factly. "We plan to go to the church in Milwaukee tomorrow morning, then take the train on to Chicago afterward. We will go to Gertrude's sister."

"I see," she said.

The thought of spending one more night in the same house with Julian frightened her. If she couldn't get rid of him, Frank could.

Mamah walked to the kitchen and found it blessedly empty of Gertrude. She picked up the telephone receiver.

"Selma," she said when the operator finally came on. "I want you to connect me to the telegraph office."

There were clicks on the line, and a man answered.

"Charley, it's Mamah Borthwick out at Taliesin. I need to get a message to Frank immediately. He's at Midway Gardens in Chicago."

"Righty-o. What do you want to say?" he asked.

"Say, 'Come as quickly as you can. You are needed at Taliesin immediately.'"

"All right, Mrs. Borthwick." His voice grew sober. "Is there some way I can help?"

"No, no," said Mamah distractedly. Perhaps she was overstating the situation. She considered rewording it. "Just some strange doings. I have a houseful of men here. We're safe. But wire him right now, will you?"

"Yes, ma'am," he said, and hung up.

Frank would have the telegram by two, she thought, and would be home late that night if he took a train in the afternoon.

Mamah composed herself and walked out to the living room. The workmen were filing into the house now, then down the hall to the room on the west end where they took their lunch. Mamah looked at their expressions. None of them revealed the discomfort she felt inside about Julian. They were joshing one another, as usual.

Suddenly, Julian was standing next to her, ready to seat her. She wanted to get through lunch without another confrontation with the man, then she would go talk to Billy. She'd ask him to take the Carltons into town this afternoon so they would be gone when she returned from the Bartons'. *There are six men out there, counting Ernest and the new draftsman,* she reassured herself again.

"I can seat myself," Mamah said to Julian. She walked through the family dining room and out to the screened porch where the children were already seated. It was their favorite place for meals in the summer. When she joined them, she felt the mildest breeze coming up from the river and over the pond. Mamah wiped her forehead with the napkin before she put it on her lap.

While they waited for their food, she tried to explain threshing to Martha and John. How to make sense of the fan belts and gears and pulleys, the smoke-spewing engines?

"It removes the grain from the stalks," she said. "They belt the threshing machine up to a steam engine—"

She looked up to see Julian, walking through the dark dining room with a tray held high in one hand. In the other, he carried what looked like a bucket. Her stomach tightened. *Now what?* she thought, sliding on her glasses. As he approached the porch, light fell on his face. His eyes, wide open, had the feral look of a shot deer. Something—urine?—soaked the front of his pants. It hit her. She was looking at a madman.

Her heart hammered as she watched him stop, set down the tray, and lift something. In that instant the object came into focus. A shingling ax, blade glinting, waved in the man's hand.

"Run!" Mamah screamed to the children. Outside, she heard a sound like a slamming door. In an instant, flames whooshed in a line around the walls of the porch. She smelled gasoline and knew. Her neck and chest heaved as a wave of strength rose in her body.

"Run!" she screamed. John jumped to his feet. She saw Martha leap up as smoke began to pour through the screens.

Julian hurtled toward them, the unbuttoned white jacket hanging half off. "Whore!" he shouted.

Mamah was on her feet, wedged between the table and chair. "Stop!" Her wail rose through the crackling sound of burning wood.

Julian was upon her. Grabbing her throat. Hands reeking of gasoline. "Whore!" He was screaming, eyes insane. "Whore!"

Mamah grabbed the arm wielding the ax. The top of her body whipped back and forth as she struggled to pull him over. His body was iron, and he shook her off. She fell back into the chair. Gasoline from the bucket splashed over her head.

"Die!" he roared. "Burn!"

Both his hands were on the ax, and he raised it in an arc above his head. John clung to the man's leg, trying to pull him over. Mamah leaped up again, reached out her left arm to shield her son with it. Her right hand rose in the air, and her head tilted back. She saw the blade above her, the honed edge a black line hovering, then blurring, thudding.

Mamah staggered backward and crumpled to the floor. Blood blinded her eyes. In her ears, behind the roar, she heard John's voice crying out for her. She crawled toward it.

CHAPTER 52

"Come on down, John, you can't do both." Frank Lloyd Wright is standing in the tavern room at Midway Gardens, looking up at his second son, who is kneeling on scaffolding. The young man is eating a sandwich with one hand and painting in the circles of the new mural with the other.

"Can you see the lines well enough to tell?" John asks.

"I can tell," Frank says, leaning on the glass-topped cigar stand in the tavern. "This is the right design."

Frank is relieved to have the previous half-finished painting covered over. It had driven him crazy, its Greek-robed figures entirely out of sympathy with the rest of the Gardens, its scale absurdly grand. He has designed the new mural to be circles intersecting circles, like bubbles or balloons floating up into the air. Light. Airy. Abstract. Festive.

Frank is hungry. He needs a bath. They both do. He and John have been sleeping at Midway Gardens on a pile of wood shavings covered by a tarp for a couple of nights.

The money is all gone. Everyone in the place is working on credit. The mural is one of the last things they can complete without more funds. Ed Waller can't understand why Frank would want to paint over a dandy mural by some of the city's finest painters. But Waller has come to understand that he can't move Frank Wright off his toehold the way he can the others. Waller has too much at stake to dwell on a painting, anyway. Creditors are screaming. The boat has to float whether it's done or not.

Opening night of the Gardens reappears in its full glory for the hundredth time in Frank's mind. Sweet vindication. He can see Harriet Monroe's face as her eyes move up the balcony tiers, as she scans the hordes in glittering evening gowns, swaying to the orchestra's music.

"Brilliant" was the word she'd used. "This elevates Chicago architecture to a new level."

Mamah had turned to Frank with a wry smile after the dreaded art critic wandered off. "One less fly to swat," she'd said.

"Telephone, Mr. Wright." A fellow from Waller's office snaps Frank from his reverie.

He looks up at John. "Come down here, son, and eat your lunch properly."

Frank and Waller's assistant walk through the winter garden, then descend the stairs to a basement office.

"Wright here," he says into the receiver.

"Frank," a voice says.

It sounds like his friend Frank Roth in Madison. Why is he calling here?

Frank laughs. "Say, you old coot! How are you?"

His friend hesitates. "Frank," he starts again. "Has anyone called you? There's a fire going over at your house."

"What? What's happening?"

"Something terrible . . ."

"Where is Mamah? Was anybody inside?"

"I don't know. I've only just heard of it from a friend who works at the newspaper. Have you not had a telegram?"

"No! Is it bad?"

"I think it's big."

"I'll be there as fast as I can."

Frank hangs up and calls Mamah. He waits but gets only clicking sounds, not even an operator. He hurls the receiver and runs through the building. When he reaches John, he can barely breathe.

"What is it?" his son calls to him.

Frank grips a table and groans. "Taliesin is burning."

THEY HAIL A TAXI to Union Station and race to Gate 5, the same gate he always goes to when he returns to Spring Green. But it is nearly two P.M.

"It's a local," a porter tells them.

"Ahh," Frank cries out. "Nothing else?"

"No, sir."

Frank knows the train. He has taken the local before and sworn off it. It stops at every damn puddle between Chicago and Madison. It will be ten P.M. by the time they get there.

"There's no choice at this point, Dad," John says grimly.

Frank stares at the throng of people ahead of them. He and John probably won't even be able to get seats together by the time they get on. The people are sluggish as they climb aboard. They carry shopping bags, suitcases, children. A man in the crowd turns his head and looks straight at Frank. It is Edwin Cheney.

Frank walks over to him. Cheney's face is white, his lips almost blue. "Ed," Frank says grimly, grasping his hand. "What do you know?"

"They called me and said there's a big fire. My kids are there."

"I know."

John Wright has pushed his way to the front of the line. He is talking intensely to the conductor up ahead. Heads turn back to look at the two men behind them. John waves to his father and Edwin to come forward. People in line look at them, annoyed, as they push to the front and are pulled up the stairs by the conductor.

Edwin collapses on one seat, Frank on the other. John works at getting their briefcases stowed overhead.

"They would be outside." Edwin's words are half question, half declaration.

"I'm sure of it," Frank replies. "They're probably over at the Bartons' house. It's threshing time." He looks at Edwin. "Even if they were in the house, there are doors all around."

It is another twenty minutes before the train chugs out of the station. It rattles north through Chicago's suburbs as if it is a vacation excursion train. Within an hour, it makes its first stop. Now it will slow and stop, slow and stop, the rest of the way as it takes on and lets off people in the prairie towns of southern Wisconsin.

The compartment is stifling. The men get up in turn to remove their jackets in the cramped space. Across from Frank, Edwin is drenched in sweat, his heavy face a mask of worry. He has spread into a thick older man with a large round head. From time to time, the train jolts and Edwin's knees bump into Frank's.

Somewhere after Beloit, a man taps at the window of the compartment. John cracks the door open.

"*Milwaukee Journal,*" Frank hears him say.

"Go away," John says.

"Wait." Edwin is on his feet. "Ask him what he knows."

John opens the door. The man glances at the faces in the compartment and rests his eyes on Frank. Recognition flashes across his face: This is the man he was assigned to find.

"What do you know?" Frank growls.

"The editor told me the house has been burning for a couple of hours. The Spring Green fire department is over there. And a lot of others are trying to put it out."

"What about the people? Was anybody inside?"

The man appears puzzled. He shifts uncomfortably, from foot to foot. He expected to be the observer, the asker of questions, not the bearer of news.

"Last I heard was two hours ago." He looks at the three faces in the compartment. "There's some dead," he says.

Edwin reaches out and grabs the man's lapels with both hands. "Who? Who is dead?"

Now it is fear on the man's face. "I heard there were three murdered."

"Murdered?" Frank cries out in disbelief. "Someone *set* it?"

The reporter looks around and swallows hard. "The Negro. The servant. Bolted the doors shut all around, they think. Poured gasoline along the perimeter of the wing where they were all having lunch. I guess it went up—" he snaps his fingers—"just like that. When they all came running out the one door he didn't secure, he axed them. Then he got away. They're looking for him."

The man is trying to back out of the compartment. Frank is frantic and has him by the sleeve. "The woman of the house," he says. "Mamah."

The reporter looks horrified and hesitates. "I was told, sir, that she was . . . She has passed."

Frank sways and falls back on the seat.

Edwin lurches forward and grabs his other sleeve. "Her two children are staying up at that house. A boy and a girl . . . they are my children. . . ."

The reporter hangs his head. "They can't find the boy, sir. The girl . . . I guess she's burned pretty bad."

Edwin Cheney cries out and slams his fist into the wall of the compartment. His body shakes with sobs. In the corner, Frank's arms and legs have begun to shiver furiously. John throws his jacket across his father's lap.

HOT AIR BLOWS in the window. Flies swarm around the compartment as the train creeps into the Madison station. Down the platform, in the light of a lamp, Frank sees his two aunts, Nell and Jennie, along with his cousin Richard.

"They've come to pick us up," John says. He helps his father stand.

Passengers in the aisles are not moving yet. The three men stand and wait.

"Extra!" a newsboy on the platform shouts. Edwin pulls coins from his pocket, leans out the window, and buys a *Wisconsin State Journal* from the boy, who strains to hand it up. Edwin unfolds it and holds it up for Frank to read, too. "Negro Maniac Kills Three and Burns Home of Frank Lloyd Wright."

Frank's eyes dart to the list of names in the column below.

> "The Dead: Mrs. Mamah Borthwick, whose head was cleft in twain, plus Two Caretakers. The Wounded: The 9-year-old daughter of Mrs. Borthwick, who was axed in the head and badly burned. The Missing: 12-year-old son of Mrs. Borthwick, possibly kidnapped. Also missing is Julian Carlton, the murderer.

Frank's knees buckle as he comes down the steps onto the platform. His cousin Richard grabs him and shakes him hard. "Brace up," he says, shouting as if Frank cannot hear him. "It's bad out there, as bad as it gets. Get a grip on yourself." Richard leads the men to his car.

"They found my son?" Edwin asks from the backseat of the automobile. He is dazed-looking.

"No," Richard says. "He was in the house, they say. The kidnapping business is all speculation, because Carlton is missing, too."

"Martha, my daughter?"

"I'm deeply sorry, Mr. Cheney." Richard chokes, struggles to keep speaking. "She died this afternoon."

Frank cannot see Edwin Cheney's face. "Who else?" Frank asks after a time, weeping.

"A thirteen-year-old boy. Ernest Weston."

"Billy's son," Frank says numbly. "He was helping in the garden. What about Billy?"

"He's injured but alive."

"And a draftsman," Richard says. "A draftsman died."

"Brodelle? Emil Brodelle?"

"Yes."

On the drive to Taliesin in the darkness, the hills appear as they always do in August, great dark curves beneath a banner of twinkling stars. As the auto approaches the house, the stars disappear in a shroud of smoke. On the ground, hundreds of lanterns flicker. When the car comes around a bend, Frank can see, even in the darkness, that half the house is missing. Smoke clouds waft up from the black scar in the hillside. The auto turns off the highway, and he sees men with rifles and hounds walking down the road, heading away from Taliesin.

Later, he will learn that seven hundred people came to help. Men left their tractors and threshers to rush over to Taliesin. Women ran out of their kitchens with pots and buckets to fight the fire.

The hunt through the cornfields is finished, though Frank does not know this yet. Neighbors and lawmen have already found Julian Carlton hiding in the basement furnace, mute and weak from having drunk muriatic acid. Sheriff Pengally has already saved the madman from a crowd bent on lynching. What Frank sees now are the tired and dirty faces of his neighbors, illuminated by their lanterns, as they walk home to their farms.

In time to come, Frank will try to erase from his mind the things he is about to see at his sister Jennie's house, where the dead and injured have been carried: Mamah's body when he pulls away the sheet—her skull split down the middle, her hair burned away, her blistered flesh hanging from bone; Martha Cheney's lifeless burned body, the sapphire ring the only recognizable thing about her; the hideously injured bodies of Tom Brunker and David Lindblom, still clinging to life but unconscious. Later, he will think of battlegrounds when he remembers Taliesin as he is about to find it. He will struggle to push from his mind the anguish of what Edwin will do tomorrow morning—claw through the smoldering rubble with his bare hands, looking for proof, looking for the bones of his son. By tomorrow noon he will have found them.

. .

CHAPTER 53

Frank awakens confused about where he is. He is lying on his side, curled into a ball on the hill, his ear on the ground thumping with his heartbeat. He smells the green odor of wet grass, feels the blades that were pressed into his skin pull away from his cheek when he sits up. The arm on which his body has rested during the night is numb. He unbends it and shakes it until it tingles.

Consciousness flows into him like the blood pushing into his arm. He sees Jennie's house and knows he has slept the night in the pasture nearby. That thought completes itself before another replaces it.

Mamah is dead.

Frank remembers the night before, lying down briefly in his sister's guest bedroom. Below it, the dining room has become an infirmary where the men injured fighting the fire rest on cots. When he first came into the house last night, he went to Mamah first. Then to Tom and David, who he could see were dying before his eyes. At the cot of each man who had so bravely fought the fire, he knelt down and thanked him for his courage. One neighbor, a man he didn't know, put his hand out and touched Frank's shoulder tenderly, as if in benediction.

In the night the sound of their suffering floated up the staircase to his room and drove him from it. It was not only the moans but the knowledge that in the living room below him, Mamah's body lay on the floor, covered with a sheet. Next to her was Martha, covered as well. When he descended the stairs in the middle of the night, he stood outside the living room, wanting to go in and sit with them. But a terrible fear seized him that if he went into that room, if he saw Mamah again as he had a few hours earlier, he would never again be able to remember her any other way.

As he watches the sun rise, what grieves him is that he failed her. He thinks of the terror she felt. They tell him it was quick, as if that will somehow confine the horror. For the hundredth time, Frank imagines how it might have turned out if he had been there. He sees himself grabbing the legs of Julian Carlton, pulling him over, wresting the ax from his hand as the others run.

The grass's fragrance gives way to the smell of smoke. It's in the air, his clothes, his hair. His throat is full of it. He coughs and coughs, then stands up, certain that if he doesn't put his mind elsewhere, he will smell burned flesh again. He will be retching and useless all day.

People are still asleep in Jennie's house when he goes in the front door. He climbs the stairs to her bathroom and draws only an inch or two of water. There will be others who will need hot water this morning. Sitting in the tub, he feels the weight of it all like a sack of rocks on his chest. His arms and legs are so heavy, he wonders how he will get out of the bathtub. Yet he must dress and go make a coffin for Mamah.

He pictures himself standing up. He says out loud, "Get up," and then he does it. In the bedroom he finds a clean shirt, socks, and underwear laid out for him on the counterpane.

Edwin is sitting at the table in the kitchen, his face ten years older than it was yesterday. Jennie's husband, Andrew, sits quietly with him, along with their son, Frankie, who looks up from his cereal bowl wide-eyed. Jennie was in Madison when the fire broke out. She is asleep now, having worked through the night tending the injured.

Edwin has already announced that he will carry his children back to Oak Park for burial once a casket is built to contain what remains of them.

"We could have a service for Mamah here in the house," Andrew ventures.

"No," Frank says. "I will bury her today."

He does not say aloud in front of Edwin what he thinks, that the idea of an undertaker or a traditional wake strikes him as unholy. He wants no false words from some stranger. There was not a false bone in her body. She would want it simple.

"Frankie and I will go into town and get some wood for the caskets," Andrew says. "What do you want?"

"Pine," Frank says. "Clean white pine."

Edwin nods.

WORKMEN AT THE SITE are still dousing the rubble with water when Frank arrives. The morning sun comes and goes behind clouds.

These men who have laid brick for him, and carried sand from the river to stucco his walls, come forward now to express their sympathy. They, too, are grieving for their close friends who were lost or injured and for her, whom they had come to respect. They were all here yesterday fighting the fire. They're tired and haunted-looking, and they want to make sense of what happened. They stand in a loose circle, their hands in their pockets. One of them says out loud what they are all wondering: How is it possible that one man could overpower seven people, four of them strong men, and burn down a house?

Danny Murphy, a carpenter, talked to Herb Fritz and Billy Weston before the two were carried off to a hospital. He has been trying to put together what pieces he knows. "The men was having lunch in their dining room," he says to the others. "Miz Borthwick and the children was on the porch off the sitting room. Carlton seats and serves everybody like he always does, then he goes to Billy and asks can he clean some carpets. Billy don't suspect nothin'. He says all right." Danny sighs. "That's why the men didn't worry when they smelled the gasoline."

He continues reconstructing what happened. Julian went around the house and locked everything shut, except for a window in the workmen's dining room. Then he went and poured gasoline around the outside walls of the wing where Mamah and her children sat. He lit a match, raced onto the porch, and killed Mamah first with the ax, then John. Martha ran away while he was dousing her mother and brother with gasoline.

Danny is sure it went that way. "He caught up with the little girl. It wasn't just the fire that got her," he says softly, "on account of the three ax marks above her ear. How she lived on for those hours . . ." He shakes his head.

Frank is close to vomiting. He is relieved that Edwin has gone off somewhere.

"Then the bastard comes over to where the men was and sets that wing afire. One after another, they come out that door and window, and he got 'em. It was a shingling ax he had, and Billy said his strength was more'n three men's. Tom Brunker was right ahead of Billy when he finally busted down the door. Julian just stove in Tom's head . . ." He stops here, a whimper wheezing from a deep place. "By luck"—he shakes his head—"by God's luck, Billy stumbled when he come runnin' out, so the devil hit him, but he ain't dead, is the main thing. Outside, he finds David all cut up but on his feet still, and they run together over to the next farm. Then I guess David just . . ." He shakes his head sadly and wipes a tear. "He just fell down. Couldn't go no more."

Another of the workmen picks up the story. He tells with awe how Billy Weston came upon his son, Ernest, dead in the courtyard. "Billy was howling and crying, Herb said. And then you know what he did? He got the hose and fought that fire alone until people came."

There is silence for a while before the men puzzle out loud over Gertrude. She was found yesterday in her best Sunday clothes, walking down the highway. "She told the sheriff that Julian was sleeping with his ax on his pillow for three nights before he snapped. Said she was scared to death of him."

"But why was she dressed like she knew ahead of time what he was going to do?" someone asks. "She could of stopped it all." They're glad she's in jail with Carlton.

They shake their heads and talk of why it happened. Because Mamah fired Julian. Because he thought people picked on him. Frank's mind is troubled by his own questions. He wonders how one man can be transformed over three days from a mild-mannered servant to an assassin. He wonders if the unstable man was set off by some preacher at his church sermonizing about wickedness, about people living in sin. Did he believe, in his madness, that it was a righteous slaughter he was about to carry out as he locked the doors?

"He was insane," Frank says to himself aloud. The men turn to him, surprised by his voice suddenly entered in the conversation.

Danny concurs. "Before he died, David told Billy that the night before, Carlton come into the gardener's shack with a big butcher knife, talkin' crazy."

If only David had told Billy about the knife. If only Gertrude had come forward and told someone about the ax. The men scuff the ashen muck with their boots, working and reworking the possibilities, thinking of the ways by which the thing might have turned out differently.

"What use is it?" Frank mutters.

The men stop then. One asks, "Can we start to cleaning up, Mr. Wright?"

"No," he says. "Don't touch anything. Not yet."

Edwin appears, walking over a hill toward them. When he reaches the house, he asks where the porch was that his son and daughter had been sitting on when the fire started. Frank shows him the area, now just a sunken hole, where small plumes of smoke still rise.

Frank steps away, out of respect, as Edwin begins digging through the rubble.

BY THE EARLY AFTERNOON, Edwin has carried his son's bones back to Jennie's house. When Andrew returns with the wood, the men begin constructing the pine boxes. Frank looks down and sees that he is wearing boots that are not his own. He has no recollection of putting them on. Under his feet, there is still blood on the limestone terrace.

He walks through the rubble, searching. Here and there, small shards of pottery glint in the sun like shells on a beach. He gathers up what is still recognizable, though nothing is in one piece, not even the things that were rescued. His piano was thrown out a door and has no legs. Someone has put it in his studio and propped it up with wood blocks. A few salvaged chairs have landed there, too, and a couple of blackened metal urns from China. Only thirty of the 500 copies of his monograph stored in the basement were saved. All the rest—just gone. Even the children's dog has vanished into thin air—incinerated, he assumes, like everything else.

Frank searches through the afternoon while Danny Murphy hammers in the background. He finds a thumb-size chunk of diary with fragments of words in Mamah's elegant handwriting. . . . *so glad that* . . . He looks for a complete thought and finds only fragments. *I love the idea of it* . . . What idea did she love? What prospect was she contemplating so happily when she wrote those words?

Someone brings him a box, and he fills it with the pieces he finds.

HOURS PASS. Frank is brought food that he does not eat. Uncle Enos appears during the afternoon to tell him it's all right to bury Mamah in the family plot near the Lloyd Jones chapel. Frank looks at old Enos, as wrinkled and hoary as his grandfather was right before his death. He thinks of the generations who made these hills sacred family ground. It is an act of loving generosity for the clannish old man to allow a stranger into the family churchyard.

"Thank you," Frank says.

He watches as Danny and the others finish the two pine boxes, one for her, one for the children. When they are done, he and his son John ride back to Tan-Y-Deri in a truck and stand outside while the men take the small box to the parlor. A car is waiting to ferry Edwin and the remains of his children to Spring Green.

Edwin emerges from the house, dressed in the suit he wore yesterday, his eyes swollen and red. They all wait together silently until the little coffin is loaded into the automobile. Then he turns to Frank and extends his hand. Frank grasps it with both of his. The two men stand together in this way for a long moment. Frank wants to say, *They were wonderful children. I loved them, too.* But such words coming from his mouth would be profane to the other man's ears.

"Goodbye, Frank," Edwin says finally.

"Goodbye, Ed."

They look into each other's eyes once more, and then he is gone.

WHEN THE WORKMEN carry the larger pine box into Jennie's house, Frank and John follow them. Father and son gently lift Mamah's charred and battered body into it.

"Meet me back at the house," Frank tells John.

He returns on foot to Taliesin, sick and shaking, trying to pull himself together. He doesn't want to collapse again in front of his good, brave son. Up ahead, the black hole in the hillside looms like a mirror image of his heart.

Only his studio remains, and the barn. He asks one of his cousins who is in the barn to harness Darby and Joan, then he collects a scythe and walks to Mamah's garden. It stands, incredibly, nearly untouched by the destruction. Some of her roses have just opened.

He sinks to his knees among the flowers and speaks to her in his mind, waiting to hear her voice come back. Her spirit is not here, though, not even in her garden. He sits back on his heels, smelling the fragrance of a half-dozen different plants, trying to find some comfort in it.

After a while he swings the scythe and cuts down the flowers she loved. John opens the pine box so his father can cover her body with hollyhocks, roses, sunflowers, zinnias. Then he closes it, and they load the box onto the wagon, throwing armfuls of phlox and daisies onto the wagon bed.

It is evening by the time they are ready to go to the chapel graveyard. Storm clouds passing overhead land heavy raindrops on Frank and John as they walk beside the spring wagon, leading the sorrels. At the churchyard, two cousins of Frank wait to help him lower the coffin into the fresh-dug earth. The box is surprisingly heavy. The air is filled with their grunts and the sound of rope rubbing against wood. When it is settled at the bottom, father and son toss flowers onto the box until it is covered and the hole is strewn all around with yellow-, blue-, and red-petaled flowers. Then Frank asks everyone to leave him there alone.

Standing by the open grave, he speaks to her. "You stood everything so bravely, my friend." They had spoken so often of their spirits and souls as if they were palpable things. He feels no presence, yet he speaks. "You were such a good woman, Mamah," he says. "The best on earth."

Before darkness falls completely, he pulls from his pocket a handwritten copy of the Goethe poem they translated together. Some of it he knows from memory, and the rest he reads aloud.

> *Nature!*
> *We are encompassed and enveloped by her, powerless to emerge and powerless to penetrate deeper.*
> *Unbidden and unwarned she takes us up in the round of her dance and sweeps us along, until exhausted we fall from her arms.*

Frank reads the long poem to the end, his voice quaking as cool rain meets hot tears on his face.

> *She has placed me here; she will lead me hence—*
> *I confide myself to her.*
> *She may do with me what she will: she will not despise her work.*
> *I speak not of her. No, what is true and what is false, she herself has spoken all.*
> *All the fault is hers; hers is all the glory.*

CHAPTER 54

I n the little bedroom behind the studio, Frank huddles in bed, reliving the past week. On Tuesday both Tom and David died, and on Wednesday Frank buried David in the family plot. Seven dead in all. Only Billy and Fritz have survived.

When he does fall off to sleep, his limbs twitch as he dreams of batting his hands at the mad face of Julian Carlton. He sees Mamah's burned scalp, the few remaining wisps of her thick hair poking from her head like wild grasses. He leaps up in terror, runs outside to lie on the ground, but everything is soaked. Rain has poured down since the night he buried her. On Sunday night, in fact, there was a hailstorm.

Some would take the hail, along with the whole nightmare, as a sign of heaven's reckoning with Mamah Borthwick. He doesn't have to hear "It was God's hand" to know that it is being said. On Monday, when he reads the account of the tragedy in the Sunday *Chicago Tribune*, every line seems pregnant with unwritten words: divine retribution.

In a spurt of rage, he composes a letter to the *Weekly Home News*. The pen's tip nearly slashes the paper as he writes.

To My Neighbors:

To you who have rallied so bravely and well to our assistance—to you who have been invariably kind to us all—I would say something to defend a brave and lovely woman from the pestilential touch of stories made by the press for the man in the street, even now with the loyal fellows lying dead beside her, any one of whom would have given his life to defend her. I cannot bear to leave unsaid things that might brighten memory of her in the mind of anyone. But they must be left unsaid. I am thankful to all who showed her kindness or courtesy, and that means many. No community anywhere could have received the trying circumstances of her life among you in a more high-minded way. I believe at no time has anything been shown her as she moved in your midst but courtesy and sympathy. This she won for herself by her innate dignity and gentleness of character but another—perhaps any other community—would have seen her through the eyes of the press that even now insists upon decorating her death with the fact, first and foremost, that she was once another man's wife, "a wife who left her children."

That must not be forgotten in this man-made world. A wife still is "property." And yet the well-known fact that another bears the name and title she once bore had no significance. The birds of prey were loosed upon her in death as well as in life. . . . But this noble woman had a soul that belonged to her alone—that valued womanhood above wifehood or motherhood. A woman with a capacity for love and life made really by a . . . finer courage, a higher more difficult ideal of the white flame of chastity than was "moral" or expedient and for which she was compelled to crucify all that society holds sacred and essential—in name. . . .

In our life together there has been no thought of secrecy except to protect others from the contaminating stories of newspaper scandal; no pretense of a condition that did not exist. We have lived frankly and sincerely as we believed and we have tried to help others to live their lives according to their ideals.

Neither of us expected to relinquish a potent influence in our children's lives for good—nor have we. Our children have lacked the atmosphere of an ideal love between father and mother—nothing else that could further their development. How many children have more in the conventional home? Mamah's children were with her when she died. They have been with her every summer. She felt that she did more for her children in holding high above them the womanhood of the mother than by sacrificing it to them. And in her life, the tragedy was that it became necessary to choose the one or the other. . . .

Nor did Mamah ever intend to devote her life to theories or doctrines. She loved Ellen Key as everyone does who knows her. Only true love is free love—no other kind is or ever can be free. The "freedom" in which we joined was infinitely more difficult than any conformity with customs could have been. Few will ever venture it. It is not lives lived on this plane that menace the well-being of society. No, they can only serve to ennoble it. . . .

Mamah and I have had our struggles, our differences, our moments of jealous fear for our ideals of each other—they are not lacking in any close human relationship—but they served only to bind us more closely together. We were more than merely happy even when momentarily miserable. . . .

Her soul has entered me and it shall not be lost.

You wives with your certificates for loving—pray that you may love as much or be loved as well as was Mamah Borthwick! You mothers and fathers with daughters—be satisfied if what life you have invested in them works itself out upon as high a plane as it had done in the life of this lovely woman. She was struck down by a tragedy that hangs by the slender thread of reason over the lives of all, a thread which may snap at any time in any home with conse-quences as disastrous. . . .

She is dead. I have buried her in the little chapel burying ground of my peo-ple . . . and while the place where she lived with me is a charred and blackened ruin, the little things of our daily life gone, I shall replace it all little by little as nearly as it may be done. I shall set it all up again for the spirit of the mortals that lived in it and loved it—will live in it still. My home will still be there.

> *Frank Lloyd Wright*
> *Taliesin*
> *August 20, 1914*

When the letter is finished, he is spent. He passes it to one of the workmen to take into Spring Green, then climbs into bed once again.

How he longs to feel the life they had together. Even just a few minutes would be a gift. *My God, how they lived. They were* alive. *Together.* For a fleet-ing moment he can picture the exact green of her eyes. In summer she always wore pale blue dresses, and the green turned her eyes aqua blue.

He remembers a morning a few weeks ago. He had come home from the chaos at Midway Gardens for a one-day respite. "Let's go riding tomorrow," she had said the moment she saw him, sensing how desperately he needed to get away from mortar and cement and the tension of the construction site.

They went out to a strip of prairie the next day with a picnic bag, as al-ways, strapped onto Champion's flank. It was a glorious summer morning, as lovely as he could remember. Even the horses seemed charged by the air. They rode on a trail for a mile or two, then waded through mustard-colored golden-rod and purple asters to a small clearing. Mamah was wearing her old riding breeches. She dismounted and took down her bag of picnic things.

Frank walked the horses a short distance away and tied them to an oak. One of the horses let go a heavy stream of urine, and she called out, "Is that you?" She was teasing, of course, but she knew it could have been him. She found it amusing that he often "marked his spot" out in the woods, like a dog, whenever he was assessing a possible building site.

"Just surveying, dear," he'd called back.

Gertrude had made sandwiches naked of anything but thick slabs of cheese. Frank bit into one and frowned. "She must have been reading the funnies when she made these."

"Ah, but there's dessert," Mamah said. She unwrapped the cookies, delicious-looking things with pecans in them. They ate them all.

"Blue gentian," she said after a while, peering through her horn-rimmed spectacles at a low-growing flower near the edge of the blanket.

"Did you wear your glasses all time when I first fell in love with you?" he asked.

"I don't think so."

He reached over and took them off her. "You know, if you exercised your eyeballs, you wouldn't need the things."

She laughed her trilling giggle that cascaded down to an earthy guffaw. "You are susceptible to some of the silliest ideas, have I told you that?"

"And the boots are certainly a recent development," he said. "I regret to say I bought the damn things. You used to wear the most delicate little leather boots." He unlaced them and pulled them off. "And look at these socks. Where are we, the Crimea?" He removed the thick cotton stockings she wore. He rose on his knees and went behind her back, unbuttoning her loose blouse, then her camisole. Mamah smiled up at him.

"*There* she is," he said, pulling off the dented straw hat. What he saw was dark brown hair shot through with strands of silver. A woman of forty-five sitting nearly naked under the unforgiving sun. And yet, my God, how exquisitely lovely she was!

He stretched her out on the blanket. For a moment he looked up. The sky was almost the color of the gentian, as big and blue as he had ever seen it. The wind raked through the tall grasses, sending up lapping sounds, like waves.

FRANK OPENS HIS EYES. All around his bed, he sees crippled salvage from the fire—a rolled-up carpet reeking of smoke, the two chairs they used for sitting in front of the fireplace, both now missing legs. When he closes his eyes again, the memory is gone. What he does not know is that he will not be able to retrieve her again like that. He will try. He will say to himself, *She loved to joke. She had a wonderful laugh.* But he won't be able to hear it, not for a very long time.

. .

THE NUMBNESS THAT propelled him through Mamah's burial—through the funerals of David and Ernest, through the terrible scenes of mourning when the families of Tom Brunker and Emil Brodelle's fiancée came to get their bodies—has abandoned him. Now there are only two states: pain and, when he manages to sleep, the absence of pain. It is two weeks since he came home to the devastation at Taliesin. When he can't sleep, he rises in the middle of the night to sit outside in the darkness. The memory of the death smell can come at any moment to him, filling his nose, sickening his stomach. His back and neck have broken out in boils. He is thin and listless. Even his heart has begun to beat differently. It leaps up all of a sudden, knocks against his ribs, and then races for minutes at a time. The storm of anger that propelled him to write the letter has shrunk to a rock of sorrow inside his gut.

He asks why: Why such a decent woman who wanted only to do good with her life? Why now, after so much struggle, when the life they coveted—together—was finally upon them?

No answers come. He wonders if there is some cosmic logic to it all, that those who stand tallest are the ones that lightning finds. But he tosses aside the notion. To believe that would be as wrongheaded as to believe it was God's retribution. No, it was the kind of bad luck that life deals out at random. Mamah was in the way of a madman. There is no better explanation.

In the weeks to come, Frank reads that Julian Carlton, too weak to be tried, has died in jail, having revealed nothing of his motives except his anger at Emil. He has starved to death, either from the damage of the acid or from the will to die. Gertrude is found innocent of wrongdoing and is released. For the people of Iowa County whose lives for a few hours that August day were held in a grip of terror, the fears pass. But for Frank, the horror continues.

He allows no one close to him to come near. Anna Wright has visited him time and again, yet he cannot bear the kindness of her or Jennie or his children. He waves his mother away whenever she appears, however stricken her face may be. She has taken to leaving food for him on plates just inside the door, on the floor. Now, if he talks to anyone, it is to the workmen who have come to clear the site. The only relief from the crushing sorrow is work.

There is no hope in trying to communicate with Mamah's spirit. The closest he can come is to ask himself, *What would she have me do?* He doesn't need to hear Mamah's voice inside his head. He has no doubt what her answer would be.

WHEN A KNOCK comes on the door one morning, he expects to see his mother's face. To his surprise, it's Billy Weston. The carpenter stands squarely, his legs apart, his head and one of his arms bandaged. Frank has not seen him since the funeral of his son, Ernest.

"Come in," Frank says.

Billy steps into the studio. He looks around at the room crammed with odd stuff salvaged from the fire. His eyes linger on the battered piano before he speaks. "I heard you're thinking about building again."

"You heard right." Frank shows the carpenter the floor plan laid out on the drafting table. He doesn't have to explain anything to Billy Weston. When he points to the location of a new loggia on the drawing, he doesn't have to say, *This is the place where the worst of it happened.* He doesn't have to explain that he has changed things so he won't be reminded of the murders. Someday, when he stands in that loggia, he will be able to look out and see the Lloyd Jones family chapel and churchyard in the distance. Billy knows that.

"Are you up to building another Taliesin?" Frank asks.

Billy straightens his back and lifts his chin. "A man's got to work."

"What about your arm?"

"Temporary."

"Could you come here every day after all that's happened?"

Billy doesn't answer. The blue eyes grow watery. He looks away and sees the box full of glass shards and paper scraps. He steps over and picks up a chip of pottery. "You going to glue this stuff or what?"

"I'm going to build it into the new house. Maybe mix it into the concrete for the foundation."

"We could do that," Billy says. His eyes return a comprehending gaze. "We could do that."

Frank rolls up the plan. Outside, he unfurls it and holds it open so Billy can see it. The carpenter studies it, then walks beside Frank as they pace out the perimeter.

Loving Frank is a work of fiction based on events relating to the love affair
of the brilliant and controversial architect Frank Lloyd Wright and one of his
clients, Mamah Borthwick Cheney. In 1903, Mamah, along with her husband Edwin Cheney, commissioned Wright to design a house for their family
on East Avenue in Oak Park, Illinois. This book portrays the period from 1907
to 1914, during which the Wright/Cheney affair flourished.

Anyone who lives in Oak Park, as I did for twenty-four years, quickly ab-
sorbs information about Frank Lloyd Wright. The village was a growing suburb of Chicago in 1889 at the time the architect designed a home for his wife,
Catherine, himself, and their family, which eventually grew to six children. In
time, Oak Park was Wright's laboratory during his "prairie period," when he
refined, with each new house he created, his evolving ideas about organic architecture. Today, especially in summer, Oak Park's streets are peopled with
tourists from around the world who come to see the many houses he designed
there and to experience firsthand the architect's legendary spaces. Wright is
Oak Park's most famous citizen (Ernest Hemingway runs a close second), and
his home and studio complex has been restored to its appearance as it was in
1909, the year the architect left town.

I don't remember when I first learned about Mamah Borthwick Cheney,
but I recall vividly a long-ago tour I took of his home and studio, at the end of
which someone asked, "Why did Wright leave in 1909?" While the name of
Mamah Cheney was not included in the answer, the tour guide explained the
awkward truth: The famous architect, who had celebrated in his buildings
the values of family and home, had departed for Europe in 1909 with the wife
of a client, never to reside permanently with his family again. Eventually I
learned that Mamah and Edwin Cheney's house was just a few blocks north
of my own home on East Avenue. I had passed the house many times on my
morning walks, unaware of its history. Upon learning a few facts about

Mamah, I found myself pausing in front of the low-slung brick house, wanting to know more.

Frank Lloyd Wright wrote volumes about architecture during his long life, and also wrote an autobiography. Scholars have documented Wright's life and explored his work in hundreds of publications. Yet very little information has been available about Wright's relationship with Mamah Cheney. The architect's biographers have lamented the lack of any remaining correspondence between the two. In the absence of personal papers belonging to Mamah, I pieced together what details of her life I could find from old newspapers, memoirs by Oak Parkers, census reports, histories of the places she lived, books on women's roles during the early part of the twentieth century, and Wright's brief account of her in his autobiography. How thrilling it was, then, to discover two years into the project the existence of ten letters Mamah wrote to Ellen Key, the Swedish feminist for whom she translated. Here was Mamah's own voice! And while the letters were primarily concerned with the business of translating, in a few sentences here and there Mamah Borthwick Cheney opened her heart and revealed her innermost feelings to the woman she'd chosen to be her mentor. The details provided by the correspondence helped me form a clearer picture of who she was and what her life was like during her affair with Wright.

A historical novelist can approach a subject in many ways. In this case, I chose to hew as close as possible to the historical record, not only because I was writing about real events in the lives of real people, but also because I found the documented parts of their story so compelling. Still, there were great gaps. By overlaying Wright's well-documented life with Mamah's as it played out in her letters and other records; by examining the ideas and events that enlivened the times and places in which they lived; and by integrating what Mamah was translating and Frank was writing, a picture of their characters and experiences over a seven-year period evolved. That framework allowed me a comfortable platform from which to imagine the personal relationship between Mamah and Frank, and to create events and characters, some of whom are based on real people (Mattie Chadbourne Brown, Lizzie Borthwick, Taylor Woolley, and Billy Weston, to name a few) and others who are not.

The excerpts of news articles throughout the book are taken from actual press coverage of the time. On the other hand, all letters in the book are invented, with the exception of an excerpt from one of Mamah's letters to Ellen

Key, written in 1911, and the editorial letter Frank Lloyd Wright wrote in 1914 to the Spring Green *Weekly Home News*.

Mamah Borthwick Cheney was an intellectual, a mother, a feminist, and a translator. In the midst of her tumultuous affair with Wright, she translated from Swedish an essay by Ellen Key titled "The Torpedo Under the Ark—Ibsen and Women." In the essay, Key analyzes the female characters created by Henrik Ibsen, whose 1879 play *A Doll's House* shook the theatrical world when its lead character, Nora, departed her marriage rather than continue to be treated by her husband as a compliant doll. Key notes that the playwright took pleasure in portraying the precise moment when his women characters, feeling confined by their milieu, revolt and struggle for freedom. ("With joy I lay my torpedo under the ark," wrote Ibsen.) Key pointed out that the playwright found it more interesting to explore in his plays the organic, evolving character of the woman rather than the determined, already-defined character of the contemporary male.

"It is the woman who has wholly desired, wholly loved, yes, often wholly sinned," wrote Ellen Key. "Almost invariably it is the woman who breaks out of the cage, or the ark, or the dollhouse. And [Ibsen] believes that she, without the barriers, will find her right road, led by a surer instinct than man. For Ibsen there is no higher moral . . . law than the devotion of the personality to its ideal." In Ibsen's view, Key went on, the proof of a person's greatness is "the power to stand alone; to be able, in every individual case, to make his own choice; in action to write anew his own law, choose his own sacrifices, run his own dangers, win his own freedom, venture his own destruction, choose his own happiness."

I suspect that Mamah Borthwick Cheney reflected deeply as she read that passage in the original Swedish, and surely brought to bear her own life's experience as she translated it into the words above.

Certain books were invaluable to me in the course of researching Frank Lloyd Wright and Mamah Borthwick Cheney. Among these are Anthony Alofsin's *Frank Lloyd Wright—The Lost Years 1910–1922*; Meryl Secrest's *Frank Lloyd Wright*, and Brendan Gill's *Many Masks*, both biographies; Wright's *Autobiography*; and *My Father, Frank Lloyd Wright*, by John Lloyd Wright.

No one wrote more eloquently about his architecture than Frank Lloyd Wright himself. His essays, grouped together in *Frank Lloyd Wright Collected Writings*, edited by Bruce Brooks Pfeiffer, illuminate his work. Other sources include "Taliesin, 1911–1914," *Wright Studies*, Vol. I, edited by Narciso Menocal; *Frank Lloyd Wright and Midway Gardens*, by Paul Kruty; *Wrightscapes*, by Charles E. Aguar and Berdeana Aguar; *Frank Lloyd Wright and Taliesin*, by Frances Nemtin; *Frank Lloyd Wright Remembered*, by Patrick Meehan, editor; *Frank Lloyd Wright and the Art of Japan*, by Julia Meech; *Beyond Architecture: Marion Mahony and Walter Burley Griffin*, edited by Anne Watson. A slender Dover book, *Understanding Frank Lloyd Wright's Architecture*, by Donald Hoffman, explains Wright's work in simple, elegant prose.

A handful of scholars have been in the forefront of seeking to understand Mamah Borthwick Cheney's role in Wright's life. Anne Nissen's 1988 M.I.T. master's thesis, *From the Cheney House to Taliesin: Frank Lloyd Wright and Feminist Mamah Borthwick*, was among the earliest to explore Cheney's influence on Wright's architecture. In a 1995 academic journal called *NORA*, Lena Johannesson, a professor of art history at Linkoping University in Sweden, published an essay titled, "Ellen Key, Mamah Bouton Borthwick and Frank Lloyd Wright." It was this article that alerted me to the location of Mamah's letters in the Ellen Key collection at the Swedish Royal Library in Stockholm.

Family Memories of Four Sisters is a memoir written by Margaret Belknap Allen, who lived next door to the Cheneys and was a playmate of John and Martha Cheney. Her recollections of the children and Mamah were like gold nuggets. Also helpful was *Yesterday*, Jean Guarino's history of Oak Park; and Phyllis Smith's *A Look at Boulder from Settlement to City*. Incredibly moving is the poem "A Summer Day that Changed the World," written by Edna Meudt, a friend of the Cheney children at Taliesin who grew up to be Wisconsin's poet laureate.

Berlin Metropolis: Jews and the New Culture, 1880–1918, by Emily D. Bilski, is a wonderful description of the rise of Modernism in Germany, and introduced me to the poet Else Lasker-Schüler. Sources on feminism in the early twentieth century include Floyd Dell's *Women as World Builders: The Living of Charlotte Perkins Gilman*, an autobiography; and *Feminism in Germany and Scandinavia*, by Katherine Anthony. All of Mamah Borthwick's translations of Ellen Key's work provided a window into the translator as well as the philosopher.

ACKNOWLEDGMENTS

Many people were instrumental in bringing *Loving Frank* to publication. I want to thank Susanna Porter, my editor at Ballantine, my agent, Lisa Bankoff, and the other wonderful people—readers, and sources of information and support—who helped in the making of this book: Elizabeth Austin, Barry Berk, William Drennan, John and Ellen Drew, Kathleen Drew, Heiko Dorenwendt, Dixie Friend Gay, Jane Hamilton, Polly Hawkins, Kathy Horan, Tom Horan, Steve James, Susan Kaplan, Alex Kotlowitz, Bob Kotlowitz, Gretta Moorhead, Karyn Murphy, Leslie Ramirez, Judy Roth, Jim Rutledge, Friedbert Weiman, Bob Willard, and Maria Woltjen.

Librarians became my heroes during the research process for *Loving Frank*. I am grateful for the help of Grace Lewis at Oak Park Public Library, and Wendy Hall at the Carnegie Library in Boulder, and for the assistance of the Frank Lloyd Wright Home & Studio Research Center, the Getty Archive in Los Angeles, the Royal Library of Sweden in Stockholm, and the Oak Park Historical Society. Thanks also to the Ragdale Foundation, where I enjoyed two fruitful writing sojourns as a resident.

Special thanks go to a group of readers whose thoughtful insights were priceless: Elizabeth Berg, Veronica Chapa, Pam Todd, and Michele Weldon; and to my sister, Colleen Berk, for her wisdom, support, and willingness to read numerous manuscript permutations.

Finally, I want to thank my husband, Kevin Horan, for his humor, encouragement, and unwavering faith, and for the love and good cheer of my sons, Ben and Harry, during the writing of this book.

LOVING
FRANK

NANCY HORAN

A READER'S GUIDE

Random House Reader's Circle: How did you become interested in Mamah Borthwick Cheney? Why do you think that it has taken so long for her to begin to emerge from out of the shadow of Frank Lloyd Wright and be seen as an interesting figure in her own right?

Nancy Horan: Anyone who lives in Oak Park, Illinois, as I did for twenty-four years, knows something about Frank Lloyd Wright. His home and studio complex attracts busloads of visitors from around the world, and his prairie houses dot the town. One of those houses belonged to Mamah Borthwick Cheney, the client who became his lover. The house Wright built for her and her husband is on East Avenue, the very street I lived on. When I toured Wright's home and studio several times, I noticed the guides didn't say much about Mamah; understandably, their focus is on his work and family life. What little I learned about her piqued my interest, though. She was a highly educated woman, a wife and mother of young children, a translator. Her affair caused me to wonder: Who was she, and why did she risk so much? A couple of biographies about Wright whetted my appetite. The more I learned about her, the more I felt compelled to tell her remarkable story.

Some scholars and Wright admirers have resisted discussing Mamah's role in his life, convinced that personal details they consider unsavory diminish his architectural achievements. Recently, though, a few scholars have taken a look at Wright's architecture while he was involved with her and have acknowledged Mamah Cheney's role in influencing the direction of his thinking.

RHRC: I understand that you spent seven years writing this novel.

NH: It took that long to complete the book. I should point out that I actually wrote the book twice. The first version, begun in 1999, included four points of view and was not very good. Two years into the project, when I decided to write from Mamah's perspective, the research became more focused. There was limited material. I assumed, from reading Wright bios, that no correspondence of Mamah Borthwick Cheney remained. So I went to original and secondary sources of information, reading newspaper clips from 1900 to 1914 and scholars' works on Wright, as well as his own writings. I visited the places Mamah visited and lived, and read the books she translated. I found an amazing memoir, written by a woman who grew up in the house next door to the Cheneys, in which the author reminisced about Mamah. Material on the Chicago School of Architecture proved captivating reading, as did books on the Modernism movement, which was happening in Europe at roughly the same time. Some primary research also turned up small details that illuminated her life, as well.

I came to see Mamah's time with Frank as a journey marked by a series of dilemmas and choices along the way. In the absence of letters, I made educated guesses about why she chose to do certain things, and the possible emotional consequences of those decisions. Her character began to come alive. Then, in 2001, I learned that ten letters written by Mamah to Ellen Key, the woman whose work she translated, were stored in the Ellen Key Collection in the Royal Library of Sweden in Stockholm. You can imagine my joy when the library sent me copies of the letters. All along I had been creating a character out of the pieces I could find to fit together, even composing letters she might have written. Suddenly, here was her actual voice, her actual handwriting. To my unending relief, I found her personality shining through in those letters. And while the content of her correspondence dealt largely with the business of translating, she included a number of paragraphs about her own life and mental outlook.

RHRC: It sounds as though the writing and research went on simultaneously.

NH: Yes, I researched heavily at the beginning, but continued to do so as I wrote. New discoveries found their way into the book. Last year, for example, a rare book of photographs of Taliesin in 1911 was auctioned on eBay and was purchased by a group of Wright devotees in Wisconsin. When the book went on display at the state capitol, I traveled to Madison to see it. Soon after, the album was in my novel.

RHRC: I'm curious about your title. While loving Frank Lloyd Wright was certainly the catalyst for Mamah to radically change her life, the novel shows that there was a lot more to her personal evolution than that. Why did you choose to stress this particular aspect?

NH: Mamah Cheney undoubtedly would have continued to evolve in interesting ways, but it was the condition of loving Frank that launched her on a path she could never have foreseen. While the novel explores ideas about gender roles and marriage at the turn of the twentieth century, it is fundamentally a very human story about loving someone, and having that experience change your life.

RHRC: The other great influence on Mamah's life was the Swedish feminist Ellen Key, whom you mentioned a moment ago. Key is not a familiar figure to most Americans—what made her such an important figure in Western history, and in Mamah's history?

NH: Ellen Key was a Swedish feminist philosopher whose teachings on free love, the rights of the individual and of children, the social value of motherhood, whether in or outside of marriage, and the need for divorce reform were highly influential in Europe at the turn of the twentieth century. The Women's Movement, or Woman Movement as it was then called, had its own personality there, compared to the movement in the United States. Ellen Key's ideas about the rights of unmarried mothers and their children had particular resonance for women in Germany and Sweden, while in the United States, the Woman Movement had shaped itself more in terms of gaining equal rights to vote, work, and earn as men did.

Ellen Key appeared in Mamah's life at a critical moment. Her impact on Mamah is best expressed by Mamah in one of her letters to the Swedish philosopher: "You have meant more to me than any other influence, but one, in my life. In your writings we have met close together, closer than I have been to almost anyone in the world."

RHRC: That "but one" being Wright himself. But what of the reciprocal influence that Mamah exerted on him?

NH: I believe Mamah had a profound influence on Frank Lloyd Wright. She took a leap of faith with him that changed both of their lives forever. She introduced him to Ellen Key, whose dedication to educating young people may have inspired Wright to devote himself to creating his own school for aspiring architects. And I think it can be argued that Mamah was the love of his life.

RHRC: Your writing is so assured, it's hard to believe *Loving Frank* is your first novel. What kind of work did you do previously, and what was your path to publication?

NH: I came to writing through journalism. I wrote newspaper and magazine pieces on subjects ranging from invasive Asian carp to Oprah's wardrobe to breast cancer, and eventually co-authored a book on garden design. About eight years ago, I took a couple of fiction-writing classes through the University of Chicago and found I loved that form. One of my instructors said to me after an assignment, "You could write a novel, but you haven't found your material yet." As it turned out, my material was right under my nose the whole time I was living in Oak Park. Eventually, the story of Mamah Borthwick Cheney and Frank Lloyd Wright took hold of me and wouldn't let go.

RHRC: Although some aspects of Mamah's story, such as the scandal attached to the notion of a divorce or separation, are very much reflective of their time nearly a century ago, other aspects, especially her struggle to balance personal fulfillment with a fertile and loving connection to the lives around her, seem quite contemporary. Have those things really changed so little for women?

NH: While researching Mamah's story, I was struck repeatedly by how similar the struggles of early twentieth century women were compared to those of women today. Seeking fulfilling work was a relatively newfound possibility for women in those days, though the need to bring money into the household was nothing new. Whatever their motivation—economic necessity or the realization of their personal potential—women were very much concerned about the conflicts inherent in trying to manage both work and motherhood. It was a subject that was widely discussed and publicly debated, and feminist thinkers sought social solutions, such as collective child care or, in the case of Ellen Key, a state subsidy to the mother so she could stay home and take care of her children for a period of time.

Contemporary women have come a long way professionally, and have found ways to adapt. But the struggle hasn't gone away, and the dialogue, I think, tends to be more internalized by women these days.

RHRC: As a writer of historical fiction, how much leeway do you give yourself to invent and improvise? Frank Lloyd Wright himself once said, "The truth is more important than the facts." Do you agree?

NH: I felt strongly bound to stay with the major facts I had regarding the historical outline of this story. Some writers might find that approach stifling, but I found it liberating because it provided a compelling framework from which to work, and pushed me to try to understand the characters' motivations for what they did. Yet not all of the "facts" were reliable. Some of the newspaper information was inconsistent or clearly invented; Frank Lloyd Wright's own account of his relationship with Mamah was sketchy, and comments by people of the day have to be interpreted within the moral context of the times. While I included a number of characters based on real people in the novel, besides Mamah and Frank, I also invented plenty of characters and certainly invented scenes. I took small liberties with matters of chronology, such as placing a speech by Frank Lloyd Wright in 1907 rather than when it was given, in 1909.

The beauty of fiction is that it allows a writer to get at truths of the heart that don't make it into history books or newspapers. In that sense, I agree with Frank Lloyd Wright's quote.

RHRC: It's one thing to set out the facts of the past accurately, but how do you enter with confidence into the inner, emotional life of a historical character? What was the key to unlocking Mamah's inner life?

NH: I entered into Mamah's emotional life by looking at the pressures she faced and choices she made throughout her relationship with Frank Lloyd Wright. I was well on my way to imagining how Mamah felt and behaved during her journey when I found her letters. In them, I discovered a woman whose inner life was not so different from contemporary women. There are emotional experiences of the heart that were universal in 1909 and remain so today. My own understanding about love, motherhood, loss, and the need to find one's personal strengths naturally found their way into Mamah's fictional life.

RHRC: Was it easier for you to find that key for Mamah than for Frank? I would imagine that the wealth of historical documentation of Frank's life, both in his own words and the words of others, might have served to obscure, rather than to reveal, the man behind the legend.

NH: Well, Wright did talk a lot. And write. And expound about architecture and all kinds of other matters. But on the subject of Mamah, his words were spare and profound. I paid attention to them. It's important to keep in mind that I was portraying the forty-year-old Frank Lloyd Wright. Much of the verbiage for which he is famous had yet to be spoken, or written, at the time this book takes place. In *Loving Frank*, he is a complicated person at a critical juncture in his life, and not yet famous in the way he is today. By looking at him through Mamah's eyes, my hope is that readers can see the complexity of the still-developing, younger man, rather than the stereotype of the grandiose, white-haired legend.

RHRC: What would Mamah think of the condition of women in the United States today? Would she be satisfied with the progress since her own day, or would she believe there was still a long way to go?

NH: Mamah would be delighted to see that girls have the opportunity, more than ever before, to "realize their personalities," as she would have put it. She would be astounded by modern women's educational and career choices. I suspect, though, Mamah would be disappointed that the highly evolved culture of love that Ellen Key envisioned for the future has not panned out.

1. Do you think that Mamah Borthwick is right to leave her husband and children in order to pursue her personal growth and the relationship with Frank Lloyd Wright? Is she being selfish to put her own happiness and fulfillment first?

2. Why do you think the author, Nancy Horan, gave her novel the title *Loving Frank?*

3. Do you think that a woman today who made the choices that Mamah makes would receive a more sympathetic or understanding hearing from the media and the general public?

4. If Mamah were alive today, would she be satisfied with the progress women have achieved or would she believe there was still a long way to go?

5. In *Sonnet 116,* Shakespeare writes, "Let me not to the marriage of true minds/Admit impediments. Love is not love/That alters where it alteration finds . . ." How does the relationship of Mamah and Frank bear out the sentiments of Shakespeare's sonnet? What other famous love matches fill the bill?

6. Is Mamah's story relevant to the women of today?

7. Is Frank an admirable figure in this novel? Would it change your opinion of him to know that he married twice more in his life?

8. What about Edwin Cheney, Mamah's husband? Did he behave as you might have expected after learning of the affair between his wife and Wright?

9. Edwin's philosophy of life and love might be summed up in the following words from the novel: "Tell her happiness is just practice. . . . If she only acted happy, she would be happy." (pg. 5) Do you agree or disagree with this philosophy?

10. Carved over Wright's fireplace in his Oak Park home are the words "Life is Truth." What do you think these words mean, and do Frank and Mamah live up to them?

11. Why do you think Nancy Horan chose to give her novel the epigraph from Goethe, "One lives but once in the world."?

12. When Mamah confesses her affair to her friend Mattie, Mattie demands, "What about duty? What about honor?" (pg. 68) Discuss some of the different meanings that characters in the novel attach to these two words.

13. In analyzing the failure of the women's movement to make more progress, Mamah says, "Yet women are part of the problem. We plan dinner parties and make flowers out of crepe paper. Too many of us make small lives for ourselves." (pg. 74) Was this a valid criticism at the time, and is it one today?

14. Why does seeing a performance of the opera *Mefistofele* affect Mamah so strongly?

15. Why is Mamah's friendship with Else Lasker Schuler important in the book?

16. Ellen Key, the Swedish feminist whose work so profoundly influences Mamah, states at one point, "The very legitimate right of a free love can never be acceptable if it is enjoyed at the expense of maternal love." (pg. 235) Do you agree?

17. Another of Ellen Key's beliefs was that motherhood should be recompensed by the state. Do you think an idea like this could ever catch on in America? Why or why not?

18. Is there anything that Frank and Mamah could have done differently after their return to America that would have ameliorated the harsh welcome they received from the press? Have things changed very much in that regard today?

19. What part did racism play in Julian Carlton's crime? Were his actions the product of pure insanity, or was he goaded into violence?

20. How does Frank's architecture parallel his life with Mamah and his philosophy of "living free in nature," expressing the "spirit of place," etc.?

Join the Random House Reader's Circle to enhance your book club or personal reading experience.

Our FREE monthly e-newsletter gives you:

• Sneak-peek excerpts from our newest titles

• Exclusive interviews with your favorite authors

• Special offers and promotions giving you access to advance copies of books, our free "Book Club Companion" quarterly magazine, and much more

• Fun ideas to spice up your book club meetings: creative activities, outings, and discussion topics

• Opportunities to invite an author to your next book club meeting

• Anecdotes and pearls of wisdom from other book group members . . . and the opportunity to share your own!

To sign up, visit our website at
www.randomhousereaderscircle.com

When you see this seal on the outside, there's a great book club read inside.